Robert Banfelder

I0565048

Trace Evidence

A NOVEL

BB
BROADWATER BOOKS
New York

Broadwater Books
141 Riverside Drive
Riverhead, NY 11901

ISBN:978-09859486-0-3

Library of Congress Control Number: 2012954096

To Donna

who knows the meaning of the word sacrifice

Also By Robert Banfelder

No Stranger Than I

The Author
Award Winner
Best Suspense Thriller 2007 ~ NewBookReviews.org

The Teacher
Award Winner
Best Suspense Thriller 2006 ~ NewBookReviews.org

Knots

Acknowledgements

During the course of the unprecedented fifteen-month-long Robert Shulman serial killer trial in Riverhead, New York, I met a myriad of folks who proved invaluable in the development of this fictional account.

My gratitude goes to the Honorable Arthur G. Pitts, who presided over the Shulman trial; Honorable G. Ann Spelman, then serving as Judge Pitts' law secretary; the prosecution team of Georgia A. Tschiember (retired judge) and Assistant District Attorney Patricia Brosco; the defense team of Paul Gianelli and William J. Keahon.

A big thank you goes to my dear friend, Richard Roberts (retired court clerk for Suffolk County), who was my anchor during trial proceedings.

Thanks also to John Collins, ADA, Suffolk County and Steven A. Hovani, Chief, Suffolk County District Attorney's Appeals Bureau.

To Court Officers George Gerle, Glen Hellerman, Robert Rebecci, Mark Roberts, and Denise Zeitler, who made me feel right at home.

My sincere gratitude goes out to Detective Lieutenant John W. Gierasch, Commanding Officer, Homicide Squad, Suffolk County Police Department (retired) for granting me an interview, thus providing me with vital information which lent verisimilitude to the novel.

I never would have received a call from Detective Lieutenant John Gierasch if it had not been for Ron Gibbons putting a bug in John's ear while playing golf. Much appreciated, Ron.

Many thanks to the following Suffolk County Homicide Detectives: Patrick J. Paladino, Robert Vessichelli and Joseph K. White (retired).

A special note of thanks goes to Deputy Commanding Officer, Detective Sergeant Robert M. Edwards, Homicide Squad, Nassau County Police Department (retired). Bob, you set me straight referencing my first novel right on to my present works. I enjoyed our many conversations and especially your continued support.

Forensic science played a major part in Robert Shulman's trial. I am in awe of the field and the folks whose job it is to interpret the evidence: Glen A. Hall, Cellmark Diagnostics; Nicholas Petraco, forensic consultant~detective NYPD Police Laboratory (retired); Frank Tegano, Suffolk County Crime Scene Unit; Charles S. Wagner, forensic serologist; Thomas D. Zaveski, Hair & Fiber Examiner, Trace Evidence Section, Suffolk County Crime Lab.

For inviting me to lecture before students and psychiatrists at Kirby Forensic Psychiatric Center, Wards Island, New York, NY, I am grateful to Dr. Bruce H. David, former clinical director at Kirby. The tour of the men's and women's facilities at Kirby was an enlightening experience.

Many thanks to psychiatrists Alexander Sasha Barday, M.D. and Eric Goldsmith, M.D., called as witnesses during trial.

During my penning of this novel, I approached my optometrist, Dr. Rory Simpson, with a *novel* idea I had involving vision. He told me he had a text that I could use as a reference. Shortly after speaking with Dr. Simpson, he called and invited me to his office to pick up the book, which was tagged with numerous notes and Post-Its, referencing precisely those pages I needed to research. I cannot thank you enough for going that extra mile.

A special thank you, too, goes to Andrew Smith, reporter for *Newsday*, whose coverage of the trial did not miss a beat. Andrew encouraged me, quite wisely, to write my story as fiction.

Also, thank you to Henry S. Ford, former assistant to *Newsday*'s publisher; Victor Chen and Oscar Coral, former *Newsday* reporters; Daniel J. Wise of the *New York Law Journal*.

For giving me a different perspective on the death penalty, I thank both Russell Stetler, Director of Investigation and Mitigation and John M. Youngblood, Deputy Capital Defender, New York Capital Defenders Office.

Thanks to Monica Arboleda-Peña for her assistance with the Spanish language and locations.

Members of Parents of Murdered Children were in the courtroom providing support for the victims' families and friends, specifically, Dennis and Kathy Folk; June M. Ginty, co-leader and member of the Board of Directors; Frank and Madeline Olivieri. My heart goes out to all of you.

~ *Robert Banfelder*

AUTHOR NOTE

Trace Evidence was inspired by Long Island, New York's first death penalty case in nearly a quarter century—the Robert Shulman serial killer trial—1998. On a daily basis, I spent an unprecedented fifteen months following pretrial, jury selection, trial, and penalty–sentencing phase; lectured at Kirby Forensic Psychiatric Center for the criminally insane, Ward's Island, Manhattan [where Shulman had been evaluated]; then interviewed the head of Suffolk County Homicide, Detective Lieutenant John Gierasch, for the finishing fictional touches. Additionally, scores of folks connected to law enforcement and the courts, as cited in my acknowledgements, assisted me so as to build verisimilitude into this account.

On April 6, 1996, Robert Shulman was arrested in Hicksville, Long Island, New York for murdering and dismembering three women. Subsequently, Shulman was linked to the murder of two other women in Westchester, New York. After a lengthy trial, Shulman was convicted and sentenced to die by lethal injection; that is, before the Court of Appeals declared the New York State death penalty unconstitutional. Robert Shulman died in prison on April 13, 2006.

PUBLISHER NOTE

While remaining true to many of the facts referencing the Robert Shulman serial-killer trial in Suffolk County, Long Island, New York, award-winning novelist Robert Banfelder brilliantly weaves his fictional account of murder and mayhem through the fabric of the criminal justice system.

~ Broadwater Books

— Book I —

December 1995

Chapter One

Whereas Howard Mills appeared rangy and round-faced, his half sister, Beth Tracy, stood statuesque, with chiseled high cheek bones and aristocratic features. A classic beauty. Her slender neck bore a semblance to a swan's. Smooth, erect shoulders and a prominent chin followed what her dead eyes failed to see. The young woman's mouth was a marvel, sensuously oval, delivering a pattern of prose to complement her mood and moment, each and every word weighed and crafted quite carefully. Her remarks, at first blush, could appear somewhat evasive if not downright obscure.

Nonetheless, Beth's voice was lovely to listen to. Like an early morning songbird's serenade. Howard loved her dearly.

Young men, in general, did not care to hear the note of deception Beth's words surely carried, allowing themselves to be lulled into a kind of sweet reverie that fueled the need to feed and nurture this seemingly vulnerable rare creature. And for the Walter Mittys of this world, of which there are so many, rose one's high-flown flight of fancy . . . to soar away together as lovebirds and be forever free . . . to ostentatiously display their wounded thorn bird upon the proverbial pedestal for all the world to see. Still, others greedily chose to safeguard their treasured dove most secretly, unwilling to share so much as a single solitary glimpse, but rather to shield, shelter and protect their fragile precious prize at any price—warning and warding off any and all wild and wicked birds of prey whose wingspans overshadowed the foreboding, dense, dark forests of imagination.

Beth Tracy was a seductress.

Men's whimsy was Beth's ultimate weapon.

Women found her magnificent.

1

Howard worshipped her unconditionally.

When Howard Mills brought his prostitutes home from midtown Manhattan or Jamaica Avenue in Queens, he was ultimately bringing them back for Beth. Even during the fifty or so evenings Howard had spent with Darla, he knew she would be Beth's in the end. Howard knew, too, there would come a time he would never see Darla alive again, especially now that Beth felt Howard was growing particularly fond of the young woman.

Beth would travel from her condo in Orient Point, Long Island, to Howard's single room apartment in Hicksville. She would either leave immediately after a murder or stay overnight until the following evening so as not to be seen—bathing in sheer elation—swearing that she could *see* the world in all its glory. What transpired from the time of Beth's arrival to her departure might not be believed had someone actually videotaped the event, followed by a blow-by-blow confession.

Howard recalled Beth's flagrant disappointment the first evening Darla was a no-show, and how his half sister's unfulfilled expectations had escalated into a full-blown fury before his fearful eyes. Howard promised himself that he would not disappoint her ever again.

Beth would become a powerful maelstrom of madness when angry. Never an uncontrolled rage, but rather a calculated vortex of violence, a channel-driven force that could tear the hair from a victim's scalp. Beth would then again breathe easily and smile demurely with cold dead eyes into those that had lost their light forever.

"Tell me how beautiful Darla is. Tell me about her eyes," Beth prodded with a slender finger thrust between her brother's ribs. "Is she really and truly all that beautiful, Howie?"

"Darla is the most beautiful of them all," Howard swore quite truthfully. "The most beautiful of eyes, Beth. Like two shining diamonds. Honest. You'll see—so to speak," he added awkwardly.

"I will, indeed," she said warmly, taking Howard's hands firmly into hers. Beth was truly pleased and excited.

"You will," his voice trailed as he stared blankly about the dimly lit room.

Beth listened to the silence for a moment before speaking.

"Howie boy," she teased, knocking him playfully upon the noggin. "Anybody in there?" she inquired. "Hum? You're so damned transparent, my dear half-wit half brother. It's a wonder I even bother. You know I can see right through you. Yes? Your tone is as distant as that endless stare," she said perceptively. "Now, look here, my dear."

Howard looked. "Beth, Beth, Beth. My precious sister," he lamented, gently removing his hands from hers, crossing the room to a rear window.

Beth followed after him, taking his hands back into her own. "Come. Sit and relax with me. Come on, now," she coaxed.

Howard allowed himself to be led back to the tattered black sofa bed.

"There. Now, tell me. Is she as beautiful as *moi*?" she teased.

"No one in all the world is as beautiful as you, Beth. No one."

"Are you going to be sad when I take her from you?"

"A little, I suppose."

"Sentimental forty-two-year-old fool."

"I'm not sentimental. Maybe mental," he said, forming a sad smile.

"Maybe just completely nuts," she goaded, grabbing his crotch.

Howard laughed. It was rare for him laugh.

Beth sighed, tracing the outline of his mouth with a nitrile glove-covered index finger, firmly squeezing Howard's genitals through his jeans with her other gloved hand. "Jeffrey behaving?" she asked, pointing her chin toward the ceiling to the apartment above.

"I guess."

"I worry about him, Howie, dear. Too quiet."

"He's always quiet. Keeps pretty much to himself."

"Except when he has to help you clean up after me. Then he just won't shut up," she snapped.

"I hate to involve him. He really wants no part of this business."

"But he being a part makes it all the more safer for us. Yes?"

"I suppose. I really need his help getting rid of them. I think he hates me for it."

"You want me to talk to him again?"

"No. The less that's said, I think, the better."

"Okay, Howie, my love," she deferred, gently massaging his privates. "You're not going to start anything with Darla in the car before you get here, are you?" she questioned rather coquettishly.

"Nope."

"Better not."

"I never do."

"I'd know, you know."

"I know."

"You going to have your way with me after I send her into the next world?" she asked archly, putting her head down into Howard's crotch and kneading his erection with her perfect teeth.

"Yes," he said, shivering while stroking the back of Beth's neck. "Oh, yes."

"You like to fuck your baby sister? Hum?" she continued, mouthing her words with a hot breath that sent Howard's mind reeling into ecstasy.

"I love you, Beth," Howard prattled with mounting excitement.

Beth suddenly sat up straight and smiled satisfactorily. "Oh, I know you do, dear Howard. I know it with all my heart."

"I have to pick her up soon," he breathed deeply, taming his lust for Beth and finding his composure.

"When will you be back?"

"Couple hours."

"She have good stuff to cook up for us?"

"Always does. Pure as snow," he offered. "Not like the shit that other broad brought."

"Well, she won't be coming around here anymore. That's for damn sure. How did it go with her? I forgot to ask."

"Good."

"No problems, I take it?"

"No problems. We put her out in Manorville, like some of the others."

"I really liked the way she danced. Some body on that girl; very shapely."

"She was really flying high."

"I think she knew that I was going to clobber her, and she didn't even seem to care."

"I don't think she saw it coming."

"A bowling ball? A bowling ball you see coming, Howie."

"Not with your speed and power, Beth. You swung it as if you were swinging a balloon. It was amazing you didn't wake the landlady."

"Just so long as I didn't wake the dead," she said through a giggle. "Your landlady's eighty-something years old. Pushing ninety would be my guess. Probably thought the house was still settling after all these years," Beth kidded.

"And Mr. Hammond?"

"That old fart upstairs across from Jeffrey? Dead in the head, I'd well imagine."

"I wonder if either of them ever saw you here."

"They're ancient, Howie. And what are they going to see at night? Tell me. Forms coming and going if they even bother to look at all. Downstairs, her drapes are drawn day and night, except when she cleans. Upstairs, his blinds are closed night and day. And he never cleans."

"How in God's name would you know that?"

"At night you hear everything, dear. Things are quiet. That's when she does her cleaning. I hear her sliding open the drapes along the rod. Then she starts the vacuum, tapping the windowpanes with a plastic attachment on the hose. Back and forth and up and down she bangs, taps and brushes. Whoosh, whoosh. Finally, she slides the drapes shut and starts attacking the heavy fabric. Brocade would be my guess. Whoosh, whoosh, whoosh. An even denser sound. Like the machine wants to suck it all in but can't," she teased, driving her head back down into her brother's crotch before sitting up again. "During hot spells, she keeps the windows open, but those drapes remain closed to keep the sun out. Occasionally, you can hear them batting in the breeze. In the colder months, she holds the heat in by drawing the drapes. My point is that her drapes and his blinds are virtually always drawn."

"Christ, Beth, you sound like a detective."

"Just a blind woman trying to level the playing field. Trying to get by in a topsy-turvy world. You learn to use your other senses to an advantage. You'd be amazed at how heightened they become. But you have to work at it, Howie dear. It becomes a study. Like Mr. Hammond and his blinds. If he only knew how transparent he can be. I can read that handyman as if he were the drawing plans for one of those projects he never quite finishes. Like the replacement windows he promised your landlady, Mrs. Cully, he'd put up in Jeffrey's room. How many years now? Three? Four? He keeps those blinds shut throughout the apartment twenty-four hours a day, moving around from window to window, bending the old aluminum slats back and peering out at the world below him for minutes at a time. When I stay over, I hear him traipsing around upstairs, just like Jeffrey does," she confirmed with a smirk.

"Still, I wonder if any of the other neighbors ever saw you come or go."

"Like my world, I come and go in the dark. What they'd see, if they see anything at all, is one of your harlots dropping by or leaving. That's all. And now that your landlady is pretty much wheelchair bound, I don't think you have to worry about her whatsoever. As long as you keep your activities confined to the evening hours, I don't think you have to concern yourself so much. It's those long drives out to Suffolk that worry me though. If you ever got pulled over—"

"I keep it five miles under the speed limit, and Jeffrey and I are constantly checking brake lights, backup lights, and headlights before we head out. I make sure the tires are in good condition and that I have the proper pressure, too."

"And if there were ever a routine inspection? If a cop just pulled you over for the hell of it?"

"I told you."

"Told me what?"

"I'd take care of it."

"How?" Beth both asked and glared.

Howard didn't say anything.

"Well? What would you do if a cop said, 'Step out of your vehicle and open up the trunk, Mr. Mills.' Hum?"

"He wouldn't because—"

Beth backhanded Howard with a force that sent her half brother to the floor. Orbit, Jeffrey's cat, scurried across the floor of the upstairs apartment, then back again.

"But what if he did?" Beth pressed. "What if he said, 'Get out of the car, Howard Mills. I think you've been drinking.' Huh? Or what if he found a vial of crack that Darla or one of the other girls might have dropped? What if he just didn't happen to like your fucking face and planted some stuff? Then what?"

"THEN I'D BLOW HIM AWAY!" Howard bellowed, picking himself up off the floor and standing before his sister.

"And lose your cool and alert the world around you like you just alerted Mrs. Cully in the front part of the house, or her other upstairs tenant, Mr. Hammond?"

"I wouldn't lose my cool," Howard whined, wiping a line of blood from the corner of his mouth before sucking on his bottom lip. "I wouldn't," he insisted.

"Right," Beth smirked. "So, tell your little sister. What would my big brother do if you were ever pulled over?"

"I'd be calm and do everything the officer told me to do."

"Unless?'

"Unless his suspicion was raised."

"And?"

"And he told me to get out of the car."

"Or?"

"Open the trunk."

"At which point?"

"Jeffrey would distract him."

"Go on."

"And I'd squeeze off seven rounds into the officer. And the last one I'd save for myself, placing the barrel up into the roof of my mouth and pull the trigger."

"And Jeffrey?"

"Jeffrey would make the call on the police radio, regardless of whether or not he believed the officer had called in the plate number before coming up to our car. He wouldn't run."

"And his story?"

"That he very reluctantly agreed to help me dispose of only two bodies. That he took no part in the killing or dismemberment of those women."

"And you would do this for me? Protect your baby sister to the very end?"

"I swear it on Mom and Dad's and little Lenny's grave."

Beth rose to her tiptoes and gently kissed her half brother on the forehead. "I don't think that we have anything to worry about concerning Mrs. Cully, or Mr. Hammond, or the neighbors," Beth assured him. "All the old lady wants is her rent money and no trouble. Mr. Hammond is a mixed-up, harmless old man who really doesn't bother anyone. And you do not bother with your neighbors. Just so long as we're careful, this house is a perfect place for what we do, Howie. I just want you and Jeffrey to be careful on the road. That's the dangerous part. All right?"

"All right."

"I know that you're doing this for me," Beth said, staring blindly into Howard's eyes as though she could see the worry on his face.

Howard nodded as if, indeed, she could see.

"Yes?"

"Yes," he answered in a whisper.

"Tell me, so I know you know."

"I know."

"Then tell me," she insisted. "Tell me what we agreed. Let me hear those words."

"To take from them the light that God has forsaken you."

"To *steal* from them the *sight* that God has forsaken me. Say it."

"To steal from them the sight that God has forsaken you."

"And in that moment, I can *see* the entire world before me in all its glory, Howie. I can see our mom and my dad. I can see your father, and dear little Lenny, too. But most clearly, I see the two of us, my dear brother, lover, and confidant . . . finally at peace before an understanding angel, in a place as far away and as green as Iceland."

"In a place as far away and as green as Iceland," Howard recited as if he were surely in a trance.

"For Greenland is actually mostly ice," Beth encouraged enchantingly, motioning him to continue the recitation.

"And things are rarely as they seem," Howard rejoined.

"Yes, Howard. Things are rarely as they seem," she repeated, moving her lips to the corner of his bloody bottom lip, licking away luxuriously with a teasing sultry tongue.

Chapter Two

Jeffrey Mills crossed the orange polyester carpet in his bare feet, cradling Orbit lovingly in his arms. He stepped over to the VCR and popped in a tape, pushed the power button, then adjusted the volume just above a whisper. Putting Orbit down, the man reached for a bottle of beer from a cardboard six-pack on the floor. Grolsch. A premium lager. Nothing but the best for Jeff. From a high, dusty plastic shelf, he removed an expensive Austrian crystal beer boot. Heavy. Manly. Nothing but the finest for this fellow. Jeffrey took the beer and boot over to the couch then settled in, wiggling ten toes at the naked foursome on the screen. He struggled momentarily with the bottle cap before realizing it was not a twist-off.

"Shit." He couldn't recall where he put the opener. "Fuck."

Two males stood straddling their female partners who were on all fours, their large breasts but a foot above a beige carpet. The men were now hunched forward, holding straws in their noses, each of them drawing up a line of white powder off the women's backs. It was Jeff's favorite part of the two-hour porn flick that he had borrowed from Howard.

Where did I put that damn bottle opener? he wondered, getting more agitated by the second. *A twelve-hour shift at the post office in Manhattan, and then that horrible train ride home from John Street, and now I can't even enjoy a good, cool beer.* Yes, cool. The way the man at the beverage store had instructed Jeffrey to drink the lager.

"Piss, shit and corruption."

He tore the wool blanket from his bed; two magazines took flight like startled birds, the bottle opener leading the pair before striking a wall with a ping, followed by two dull thuds. One of the magazines flapped then flipped open on the floor to a full-color shot of a middle-aged, loin-clothed, husky blond male choking a naked, dark-haired teenage girl from behind—the side of the man's forearm driven forcibly across the woman's throat, her mouth agape.

Orbit had darted for cover behind the couch, wanting no part of the pair of erratic bird-like paper objects that had flown noisily across the room, crashing into a wall. A clear window, yes—but never, ever a wall. They were unlike any birds Orbit had ever known in her outdoor world, for the feline was now a sorrowful, full-fledged indoor cat.

Jeffrey reached for the church key, opened the green bottle of brew, slowly poured its amber contents into the tilted glass boot, studied the high, thick white foam head, then finally settled back upon the couch. He hit the rewind button and brought the foursome back to his favorite frame, freezing it before reaching for his own white powder.

It was a good hour before Orbit came out of hiding, cautiously moving toward the magazines that had taken flight earlier, still lying motionless on the floor alongside the wall where they had fallen. Not a peep from either object. Orbit seemed to stretch herself to the full length of an expanded Slinky, slinking furtively closer to the more colorful of the two publications . . . one with its wings spread wide; the other lying flat. Still, not a stir from either . . . not even when she put a paw quickly to the first. Nothing but the smell of paper and print—quite familiar. Unthreatening. The odd winged shape of the fraudulent bird intrigued her. She shot a glance to the flat unmoving entity. Unmoving was good. Sudden pings and thuds, crashes and smashes were not.

Orbit once witnessed a far greater disturbance; hair-raising would have literally described the scene. It happened in the downstairs back room apartment the evening she and her owner had descended the staircase together. Well, not exactly together, for Orbit was not permitted out of the apartment. She was what her keeper called a housecat; therefore, Orbit had not actually followed on Jeffrey's heels that evening but remained at the top of the landing until the downstairs occupant opened wide his door. Curious, indeed. The two men had stood there arguing for a time. Certainly time enough for her to scurry down the steps, making a beeline for and finding concealment behind a dark, dusty black sofa bed. The pair remained oblivious to Orbit's entry.

It was from around the corner of a closet sometime later in the night that Orbit had witnessed the unbelievable. Smashes and crashes. Sudden and instantaneous. Not directed against the wall of the apartment but to the back, sides, top and front of some person's head. Never had Orbit seen such a scary sight with her own two night-vision eyes. And it frightened her. Never in her days or nights as an alley cat prowling the back streets and yards of Hicksville had she ever inflicted such destruction when more than just toying with a bird or mouse. Never, ever!

Jeff had been sleeping on a problem, and now he was somewhat semiconscious. Perhaps there were too many bad dreams, although he had but a faint recollection of any. Perhaps there were too many dead prostitutes whose ghosts would soon summon police to the door. He had been ready for them. Ready for a long time. It was actually remarkable to him that they hadn't come around by now. He even considered alerting the authorities himself. The anonymous phone call to the police. The anonymous tip. But why kill a good thing? And when they finally would arrive, they'd find a bit more than the telltale signs of blood from the many victims murdered in Howard's downstairs, dimly lit apartment. They'd find evidence on the walls. They'd find it on the floor. They'd find it on the ceiling. They'd even find it on a window shade and sash. Subtle. But it was there all right. He made sure of that early on in the game. Not that he had to further the evidence at this point, for the room had become a bloodbath over the course of time. And all the cleaning and rubbing and scrubbing and painting in the world by his older brother wasn't going to make a damn bit of difference when the cops would finally come in with their forensic crew. They'd take apart that apartment. They'd turn it upside down.

In the meantime, certainly, Howard had to do a make-ready so as not to arouse the suspicions of the women of the evening that he'd invite. A single low-watt bulb within the brass hurricane lamp atop a green spindle-legged table was the only light source in the room. If they had to use the bathroom, it was at the top of the stairs right outside Jeff's apartment. Complete with shower.

The three partners in crime had their stories ready. Beth, Jeff and Howard. But Howard was going to take the fall. And how! Howard would finally get his death wish, all right. Beth would move on to other killing fields. And Jeff? Jeff, if he played his cards right, would wind up with a virtual fortune. He had it all figured out. He'd take care of Beth if she'd let him. But first he'd especially see to the single need of his older brother, for Howard surely *needed* to die. After all, what were blood brothers for if not to aid and comfort one another in such time of need?

It wasn't going to be too difficult to lay the blame on his brother and convince the police that Howard alone committed all those murders. The luring of prostitutes back to his single-room sty. The drug parties. The S & M clubs Howard attended sporadically in New York City, with the Hell Fire Club being one of his favorite spots. Jeff was sure that the required application for the slave auction Howard had filled out less than a year ago was certain to be on file. Of course, Jeff had instructed his brother on how to handle himself in the initial interview in order to curry favor from the stately she-wolf in charge who would ultimately decide, from a rather lengthy list of applicants, those who would and would not be permitted to participate in the coveted slave trade extravaganza.

In order for Howard not to thwart any chance of acceptance, Jeff had made him promise not to reveal to the procurer his penchant for postmortem amputations of prostitutes' arms and legs. Jeff made Howard swear before God not to tell her the vicarious high he'd receive from viewing his favorite videotape, *Blood Sucking Freaks*, portraying the torturing of women via antemortem amputations. Instead, Howard would simply tell her that he was into bondage, spanking, cock 'n ball and nipple torture, that he had a foot fetish, was a worshiper of women's bodies, solely—and that he would prove to be the very best bondslave any dominatrix could ever desire. Last but not least, Howard would show her the many scars across the inside of his wrists and forearms, on his legs just above his socks; and then, for the *pièce de résistance*, he'd tear open his shirt and display the half-dozen stab marks across his hairless chest, finally falling prostrate to the floor before her, pleading that she drive her spiked heels firmly into his back. Who could or would ever forget such a performance by way of interview?

The police would certainly key in on Howard. Not that Jeffrey was going to walk away unscathed. He'd hand the cops something on which to hang their hats . . . such as hindering an investigation or admittedly transporting dead bodies without possessing a funeral director's license. *Ha, ha.* Something to make it all fall into place for the fuzz. Misdemeanors at best. Serious misdemeanors to be sure. Perhaps a year or two of jail time at worst, with a reduction for cooperation and good behavior. He'd somehow work things out. Anything to make himself look credible in their eyes. Poor, stupid younger brother, Jeffrey. So naive. So misguided and misled, they'd surely believe. Trying to be loyal to his older, domineering and nuttier-than-a-fruitcake brother.

Jeffrey would be sure to cry hysterically and tell the police that he was truly, truly terrified and only went along for the ride so as to protect his big brother who had begged and pleaded with him to help carry and dispose of the bodies, and how Howard had threatened to kill himself the way that their baby brother, Lenny, had if big brother didn't get his way. Actually, Jeff *had* made Howard beg the last time out, for it was freezing weather, and Jeff really didn't want to go anywhere with the wind chill factor making it feel like twenty below.

Oh, he was a good actor, all right. But if the police were going to play hardball with him, they wouldn't even get to first base. If he had to step up to the plate, he knew how to force in a run. If they really fucked with him, he'd blast the ball out of the park.

"Orbit. Where is my pretty pussycat?" Jeff questioned groggily.

Orbit was disinterested, contemplating climbing a drape, having temporarily forgotten about the horrible removal of her claws.

"Orbit," Jeff repeated anxiously, wiping the catnap away from his eyes.

It was the keeper's tone that made Orbit think twice about her ascent. She remembered well the whoosh of the wooden club he had wielded as she clawed away at the couch one night, with Jeff missing her head by the width of a whisker. He was like a different person that night. The female visitor who Jeff and Howard called Beth would never behave like that. Beth would never ever treat her that way—although Orbit was sure it was a woman who had wielded the wooden club that night in the downstairs dweller's apartment.

Curious.

Jeff stretched, yawned and gradually withdrew himself from the low-volume action of cracking whips, jangling chains and muted screams from she-wolves, reminding himself to hand over the tape for his brother's growing collection of such videos, along with another gem he had procured: *Ilsa: She-Wolf of the S.S.* One more pre-death prelude that filled Howard's head and heart with sure-fire desire. Jeff knew he was a fool for even having such material in his apartment. And he'd damn well better remember to drop off those two magazines lying on the floor where he had thrown them earlier, he told himself angrily.

"Orbit!"

Jeffrey got up and grabbed himself another Grolsch from the six-pack. Except for a small cooler kept in the porch area just outside Howard's room, neither of their apartments had any refrigeration. Jeff could have kept the beer cold downstairs, but he recalled that the beverage store owner in town had told him how to serve the prize lager. Room temperature. At least from late September into May. It all worked out rather nicely, too. Except for the hot summer months, Jeff didn't have to fetch and schlep up and down the stairs every time he wanted a brew. He'd even have a beer before breakfast. Many times it *was* his breakfast. *A fine bottle of brew and a bathroom to piss, shit, and shower in, right across the hall. What more could a man ask for? Nothing but the lap of luxury for this kid.* And next week Mr. Alfold was getting in a few cases of some "really nice stuff" from Belgium, the proprietor had said. A small but ancient brewery dating back several hundred years, would you believe? Hoegaarden, or something like that, Jeff remembered. Jeff was even promised special drinking glasses with the brewery's name inscribed. A free hexagonal-shaped glass with every six-pack purchased. Grolsch from Holland, and next week, Hoegaarden from Belgium. Better than collecting stamps, which is what so many of his fellow workers at the post office rounded up daily on the job, while he was busy soaking up suds and knowledge, rapidly becoming worldly in a different way. Even refined. *What a guy.*

He had to empty his bladder badly, yet lumbered toward the door. *Where the fuck is that cat?* he wondered. "Orbit, you scuzzy fuzzy ball of shit. Want me to find the bat?"

Jeff knew where the bat was all right. Down in brother Howard's room. Or was it? No. Howard threw it out the last time. Or was it the time before? *Shit.* He couldn't keep track anymore, but there were plenty of tools on the old man Hammond's workbench just in case Beth pulled one of her reappearing acts for which she was famous. Jeff didn't mind too much. But most times he'd rather it just be the two of them. *The guys! Yeah!* Their parents had loved it when the boys played together as kids. Howard, Jeff, Ronald, and little Lenny. And then along came Beth by way of a second marriage later in life. Well, their mom and dad and Lenny were now dead. And Howard was soon to follow. Then Jeff would finally be free. And rich! Of course, there was their estranged brother, Ronald, always looked upon as the square one.

Ronald would pose no problem, for he and his family had money and a life of their own to lead. Besides, Jeff was next in line to assume the inheritance should Howard die. It's the way their mother, Sophie, wanted it. But for the moment, Howard held the purse strings—held them for twenty-one years in fact.

Jeff was moving up in the world. Up and out of 42 Willow Lane, after the smoke cleared, that is. He wondered what he'd do with Orbit for the time that he'd be away. First his own arrest, perhaps—then bail. A short stretch after sentencing at worst. Nothing he couldn't handle knowing what was waiting for him at the end of the rainbow. He thought about having the landlady look after Orbit while he was away, as Beth certainly couldn't do it. Do it right, that is. And the old woman was now handicapped, too. Pretty much wheelchair bound. He knew that the cat would somehow get out on either of them. He couldn't chance it, for the cat came in handy every now and then. Orbit really wouldn't be much trouble to anyone responsible because she had been declawed, fixed and given all her shots. She was a good cat but loved to run around in circles since the day he picked her up on Old Country Road. He'd figure something out.

"There you are, my precious little sneak. Practically every time I'm headed out the door you show your puss. Get it? Otherwise, I find you sound asleep."

With a sudden feint followed by a gentle foot sweep, Jeffrey brushed the cat back and away from the door. Stepping out into a dimly lit, shadowy hallway in his bare feet, he locked the door behind him and padded across the carpet to the bathroom.

"Shit."

The bathroom door was locked. It was his neighbor from across the hall, Mr. Hammond. Mr. Fix-it. The old man hardly ever fixed a thing except his own lunch, Jeff sighed. Some handyman. His lunchbox was bigger than his toolbox. Jeffrey figured that the old geezer probably made more money going around charging people for estimates than from actual work performed.

"You in there, Howard?" Jeff hollered, knowing damn well it wasn't Howard. Howard never locked the door. Not even when he showered.

"No, it's not Howard. It's me. And don't you be rushin' me neither. I been rushin' 'round my whole life."

"Nobody's rushing you, Mr. Hammond. Just tell me how long you're going to be."

"You see. That's exactly what I mean. Rushin' me. Everyone's always rushin' me. Now go 'way. Can't even take a dump in peace," the man mumbled.

"Do you have your teeth in, Mr. Hammond?" Jeff questioned with a grin. "I'm having a little trouble understanding you."

It was hard enough to understand the old man when he did have his dentures in his mouth. It was almost impossible to understand him when he had them out, unless you could read lips, gums and body language, Jeffrey considered comically.

"You hear me jus' fine. Now, scat."

Listening to that old fart was a lot like listening to a bad impersonation of Gabby Hayes, Jeff conceived. "You shower yet, cowboy?" Jeff pressed.

"No, I didn't shower yet. And I didn't shave either. And if you leave me the hell alone, maybe I can finish takin' a crap."

"You didn't finish doing your business yet, chief?"

"You wanna come in here and wipe my ass for me maybe?"

"Maybe I can just piss between your legs while you're seated, sport. I really gotta go real bad."

"All right, for cryin' out loud. I get the pitcher."

"You mean the *picture*, grandpa," Jeff enunciated.

"No, *you* mean the *picture*, smart ass. *I* mean a *pitcher* for you to piss in, fairy boy, who wants to urinate between my legs. Now, beat it."

"Yeah, beat this, wise guy," Jeff retorted, grabbing his crotch while giving the old man credit for getting one up on him.

"I'll give a knock on your door when I'm out," Hammond mumbled.

"And turn on that exhaust fan before you leave."

It was a standard joke between them as there was no such fan.

"It's broken," the old coot crowed.

"Well, then fix it," Jeff called over his shoulder, putting his key back in the lock and narrowly opening the door to the apartment, save Orbit should scurry by him.

The old man took the dentures from his mouth before flushing the toilet. "I'm workin' on it," he grumbled with a toothless grin from behind the door.

"Can't understand *or* hear you, now," Jeff said with a hearty laugh, closing then locking the door behind him, scooping up the cat in his arms. "Can we, pussycat? No we can't," he insisted, speaking for the both of them, brushing his nose affectionately against Orbit's.

Orbit couldn't wait to escape from all the love and attention her keeper heaped upon her.

Chapter Three

Beth was sitting on the arm of the tattered black sofa bed in Howard's apartment when she heard the car pull into the narrow driveway. A moment later, he brought Darla to the back of the Levitt-built home. Beth sat waiting crossed-legged, wearing skin-tight navy blue pants, impatiently pumping one leg above the other, listening while Howard dillydallied with his keys at the door.

A moment later, the pair stepped into the dimly lit one-room apartment. Darla caught the stranger's movement as Beth stood.

Darla was startled. "Who's this?" the confused woman demanded.

"My sister," Howard said, blowing his nose into a crumpled tissue pulled from his jeans pocket.

Beth stepped toward the pretty woman. "Hi. I'm Beth," she greeted and smiled, introducing herself while Howard fidgeted for another tissue. "I just dropped by to see how my brother Howie's doing. Doing pretty good from what I can see," Beth said, although she couldn't see a blessed thing.

Darla turned to Howard. "I thought you said *alone*," she whispered nervously, though somewhat relieved that this third party was another female instead of some other john, for she had found herself in some mighty uncomfortable if not downright dangerous situations during her five years on the streets.

"I'm leaving. All right already, bitch?" was Beth's immediate response, as she certainly picked up on Darla's every word, her tone notwithstanding.

"Who the fuck are you callin' a bitch, bitch?" was Darla's extemporaneous retort, although it would have been the young woman's comeback had she thought about it for a month of Sundays. Not that the twenty-year-old prostitute was witless. It was simply the way she handled herself when going up against any opposition whatsoever. Do or die. A fist of fire if need be. A trashy tongue saddled to a stalwart spirit usually spelled the difference between survival and disaster. She had stood at death's doorstep at fifteen and vowed never to cross its threshold. Not without a ferocious fight.

Yes, Beth Tracy would enjoy taking this one down. Beth could almost feel the heat of anger burning in the young girl's defiant eyes.

Beth suddenly turned away, went quietly back to the sofa, put on her coat then roughly grabbed the handbag off a cushion. With a free hand, she blindly ran fingers back and forth alongside a metal cabinet, awkwardly searching in vain for something before bending down and feeling along the floor.

"It's over here," Howard said, moving toward the other side of the brown metal cabinet. "Here." He handed Beth her white cane.

Beth grabbed at it anxiously then headed toward the door, the length of stick marking her measured steps.

"Oh, my God!" Darla exclaimed, bringing a hand to her mouth.

"What?" Howard uttered sharply.

"She's . . . ."

"Blind," he offered indifferently.

"Jesus Christ," Darla said, walking up to the woman and taking Beth by the sleeve of her coat. "Where do you think you're going at this hour?"

"Home."

"Where's home?"

"Orient Point."

"Where the hell is that?"

"Suffolk County. End of the line."

"And how are you going to get there?"

"Cab to the Long Island Railroad. Same way I came."

"Nonsense." She guided Beth back to a corner of the room and sat her on the sofa. "Now, look," Darla said with a sigh.

"I'm looking," Beth remarked, staring up with dead eyes at Darla.

"I mean, listen," she added clumsily.

"I'm listening," Beth rejoined.

"It's starting to drizzle out there and they're threatening snow," Darla lied, shooting a sinister look at Howard. "It will take you hours to get home. Howard can get me a cab and—"

Beth raised her cane for silence, pulling the strap of her pocketbook securely over one shoulder. "I know the two of you want to be alone. I had no business coming without calling. I came here on my own steam, and I can find my own way back."

"We can do this another night," Darla insisted, addressing Howard. "I'll—"

"I have an idea," he interrupted. "Beth, why don't you stay here tonight like Darla says? You can take the sofa or open it up, and Darla and I can sleep here on my bed." He gestured to the box spring and mattress against the other wall. "We're just going to party some, and you really won't be in the way. Really. Whattaya say?"

"What do you mean, party?" Beth asked coyly.

"You know, like we did some years ago when Mom and Dad were out of the house. Smoke a little crack. Shit like that."

"No, I'll just be in the way," Beth said, holding her pocketbook close to her body and getting up off the couch.

"Party with us if you want. Okay, Darla?" Howard coaxed.

Darla studied Howard for a moment then shrugged. "Sure. Why not? If she'd like."

"I haven't done stuff like that since college," Beth fibbed. "Darla. I'm sorry I snapped at you. I've been going through some rough times lately. Trying to get past some things. Maybe a little partying might be just the pick-me-up I need. But I don't want to be a sponge. I've got some cash in my bag, and I insist that I pay my own way. All right?"

Howard looked over at Darla and smiled reassuringly.

Darla smiled back. It was a relaxed smile. She trusted Howard. It was not the first time he had picked her up in Queens and brought her back to his apartment.

Beth and Darla were doubled over in fits of laughter. Howard was on his back in his underwear, pedaling an imaginary bicycle toward the ceiling, heading straight for Jeffrey's apartment above them. Beth crawled to her brother on her hands and knees and pushed him over with one finger. Howard rolled away then returned with a small packet of pure white powder that he carefully tapped out onto Beth's bony naked back while she rocked slowly to and fro on all fours, her full breasts brushing against the blue-gray nylon carpet captured in the gloomy light.

"Don't move or you'll blow fifty bucks," Howard swore.

"Don't blow or you'll fart fifty smackeroonies," Darla blurted out with a sidesplitting belly laugh as she lay curled up in a corner of Howard's mattress. The young woman wore a low-cut blouse, spilling a little rye whiskey down its front. Thinking better of it, she set the shot glass aside.

With the back of a single-edged razor blade, Howard carefully raked the powder on Beth's back into two long, thin lines, from the top of her coccyx up to the cervical bone in her neck. "Here," he said, handing Darla a clear plastic straw.

The young woman came over and straddled Beth. Bending forward from the waist, Darla inserted the straw in one nostril, closing off the other with a fingertip, drawing up half a line in a single breath along Beth's backbone. Inserting the straw within the other nostril of her pretty pixie nose, the prostitute repeated the act. She handed the straw to Howard. Kneeling beside his sister, he followed suit, finishing the entire second line. He flicked the straw away as if it were a cigarette butt and ran his rough hands up Darla's silky, coltish shapely legs. She unbuttoned her blouse, unhooked her bra, and gently clawed his back with long painted nails.

Beth drew a breath and lay flat upon the carpet. Darla moved her hands to Beth's long, dark head of hair and combed her fingers through it, continuing the stroke down to the elastic band of the prostrate woman's bikini briefs. Beth sighed sensuously. Howard turned his sister over and pushed his pelvis against her mouth. Beth darted her tongue then lightly clamped her teeth around the turgid cotton-covered mass, teasing him insanely.

Darla wet a finger in her mouth and put it back beneath Beth's panties, stroking her ever so gently. Beth inserted two nitrile glove-covered fingers filmed with salve between Darla's long legs. Darla lowered her body to greet them, gliding up and down while Beth steadily finger-fucked her. The pair gradually picked up a rhythm: one of them recklessly flirting with a single-minded fantasy; the other, hellbent on solid reality coupled to a soon-to-follow climax.

The two exploded simultaneously. Beth was breathless. Darla lolled her head languidly, feeling positively spent. Poor Howard was just sitting there on his haunches, taking in the scene. But he had learned to hold back for his sister . . . to keep his hard-on handy for the final act. Oh, the titillating expectations of taboo, he tarried. The thrill of reserving the very best for last. Still, he could hardly contain himself, knowing full well that after the final curtain fell, and Beth would return to Orient Point, he would be alone as before. Lonely and remorseful. A mail handler by day. A presumed monster by night. Certainly not every night, but most assuredly, every now and then—positively whenever Beth happened to blow into town.

Howard got up and went over to a dresser, sorting through a jumble of socks, underwear and drug paraphernalia scattered throughout the top drawer: hash pipes and small transparent packets of powders, baking soda and a scratched-up compact mirror, candles and packs of matches, razor blades and rubber tubing, an alcohol lamp and a tarnished silver spoon, hypodermic syringes, along with an assortment of clear glass vials. He picked through and selected a few of the items, tossing a short length of rubber tubing over to Darla.

Darla dropped then picked up the flexible snake-like hose and giggled, winding a yellow coil once around her arm, tying off the section tightly in a single practiced action with her teeth. "Hi*sss*," she sounded and smiled so prettily, stretching her neck and rolling her head around and around in slow motion, closing her eyes in a lingering reverie.

"Gonna fly high, pretty bird," Howard promised, worming his way impatiently to the final resolution. He held up the glass plunger, affixing a needle to it, pushing the tiny, shiny hollow point through the top of the thin red stopper that capped a vial. Next, he drew the clear liquid within the glass chamber, past its calibrated markings before ejecting a tiny stream. Taking Darla's arm, he inserted the needle into a cooperative vein, pushing down upon the glass piston and plunging the drug into the prostitute's system. Withdrawing the needle, he untied her temporary tourniquet.

Beth came up off the carpet and caressed the young woman's features, lovingly cupping Darla's face within the pair of nitrile glove-covered hands as though about to drink from the prostitute's parted lips. Darla opened and closed her eyes and smiled. Beth was already smiling and could see deep into Darla's soul. Darla's blue eyes were vapid and fluttering as Beth kissed them lovingly. Beth's were surely dead.

Howard busied himself before the dresser drawer, stashing the items beneath his socks and underwear. He went out onto the freezing porch and returned with a hammer from Mr. Hammond's workbench located beneath the stairs. Howard went back to Beth, handing her the tool.

Darla's eyes were closed again; she was still smiling and breathing peacefully.

"Let's open up the sofa bed and put her there," Beth said.

"Come," Howard instructed, helping Darla from the floor.

"Come again?" Darla quipped with a chuckle, helping Howard help her into Beth's arms as he sprang the mechanism and unfolded the convertible bed. "Where're we going?"

"Gonna lie down now, little bird." Howard smiled as he and Beth set Darla to rest.

Darla shook her head. "Birds don't fly down," she floundered. "I mean, lie down," she slurred. "They sleep standing up . . . I think."

"Well, you're a wounded bird," Howard explained. "And so we have to lay you down."

"Lay, lay, lay, lay, lay," Darla resounded. "I know what you want," she teased wisely, waving her finger like a tiny wand while smiling sillily.

"Wounded as can be. Like me," he said sadly.

"Not wounded," Darla protested, her speech weakening.

"Maybe not just yet," Howard granted, gently lifting Darla's long legs onto the bed.

Jeffrey's cat suddenly orbited the upstairs apartment several times before it settled down.

"What's 'at?" Darla questioned, staring up at the ceiling.

"Cat," Howard answered.

"Is 'at how I get wounded, by a cat?" she questioned and chortled, drawing her head and limbs into her body like a ball.

Howard tittered, and Beth responded with a powerful blow to the back of Darla's head with the hammer, fracturing her occipital lobe. Darla went limp. The next thundering strike splintered the temporal region along the right side of her skull. Blood poured from the wound. Reversing the tool, Beth straddled Darla's body and blindly went to work on the victim's face, repeatedly gashing and prying up the cold metal claw against a prominent forehead, the bridge of Darla's upturned nose and marble-like cheekbones, inching toward two perfect blue pools, then on down to that trashy, fleshy, flashy mouth . . . back again to those cool-blue liquid-like eyes. Beth saw God in all His glory. She could *see*, not just perceive, but *see* and *feel* the cool blue color in her own mind's eye. So she *knew*. Yes! Absolutely *knew* the hue of the daytime sky high above Jeffrey's apartment and out around Howard's windows and walls, all the way to Orient Point and beyond a blue horizon. Around the whole wide world for that matter. Beth continued, and blood flew freely about the bed and floor. Darla's open blouse was soaked. Even her bra, now up around her neck, was bathed in red. Beth *knew* positively that she could *see* and *feel* the color red. Reaffirmed it in her mind. She knew it with all her heart. Like her prizewinning tomatoes that she grew by the Sound on Orient Point . . . rarely bragging about her produce and end product to a soul. The source of her award-winning sauces . . . which she occasionally couldn't help but tout to Howard and Jeffrey.

Howard went over to the stove to put up a pot of tea. Soon, very soon he'd make love to his sister. His half sister, that is. And he'd be whole again—until she'd leave for home. And then the real work would begin. The dismembering. The cleanup. The removal and disposal of the body. He'd have to ask Jeffrey to help him once again. He hated asking a favor of his younger brother. Then off to work they'd go to their respective postal assignments. Jeffrey to Manhattan. Howard to any one of several branches on Long Island.

Chapter Four

Howard Mills pulled the dark blue Cadillac into the driveway and parked. He stepped from the vehicle and took a slow, deep breath of frigid February air into his lungs. He dreaded the cold months. But the cold had helped conceal the bodies. The cold helped cover up the murders. Of course, Jeffrey helped, too. The younger brother got out and swung the passenger door shut, throwing up the collar of his coat. The cold had truly been their blanket of blessing, enveloping the women from the scent of say a nosy set of nostrils sniffing suspiciously around some industrial lot. Sometimes Howard would pack the torso into a plastic garbage pail. Together they would dump it along the side of some country road out east off the Long Island Expressway. Most times they'd deposit the body in some Dumpster, far enough away from home.

"Dump-de-dump-dump," Jeffrey would sound off then laugh anxiously.

It hadn't been but several weeks since the pair had carried out Darla's dismembered body from Howard's apartment, placing it in the trunk of the 1986 Coupe de Ville. Then off the two had driven, traveling to predetermined destinations. Body parts and all. The limbs were usually disposed of separately: an arm, a leg, perhaps a pair of hands dropped off here and there before depositing the remains in Suffolk

County. Tonight, the woman's body had gone into a convenient, desolate Dumpster. Her corpse left behind to decompose in the peacefully-green, roomy, cold steel box. They had discarded scores of women in that fashion over the years. No muss. No fuss. It was Howard's rental apartment that got to be a mess.

Their most recent harlot hadn't necessarily been the prettiest, but she certainly had the sexiest body to date.

Howard, Beth and Jeff, together, proved a deadly team.

Chapter Five

Officer Dan Fowler and Max were a team, too. The two were not part of the homicide squad, although they were highly trained professionals and often called to a crime scene. Fowler was a police officer for eleven years. Max was with the unit for four-and-a-half. Dan Fowler was born and raised in the United States. Max had been brought over from West Germany for his specialized capabilities. The two worked well together in the field on scores of exercises. Fowler was a competent trainer. "One of the great all-around instructors, ever!" the homicide boys would boast, for they had seen the pair in action and would always come away amazed, especially Detective Michael (Mick) Connolly. Mick could not stop talking about them, deciding Max, hands-down, to be the best of a breed, the very top of his class.

Fowler was continuously training his partner for highly specialized assignments. Max was constantly being evaluated. He was quite intelligent and, without question, the best canine partner and friend that Fowler ever had. He had had two such companions during his early career as a cop. The first was forced into early retirement after six years of loyal service: a hip dysplasia disability that broke Fowler's heart. The next German shepherd was killed in the line of duty after taking a bullet in the side while taking down a gunman in a burned-out building in Wyandanch, bravely holding the perpetrator at bay until backup finally arrived. It was a situation gone sour. A situation Fowler had never quite gotten over. Never really would.

The funeral was of massive proportion. There had been a turnout and outpouring of love and sympathy for the animal, the likes of which police officers in Suffolk County had never seen nor would likely see again. One would have thought the police commissioner himself had succumbed.

Fowler had sworn he would never take on another canine partner, but one day the officer was ordered to the airport. It was there he met Max. A one-year-old pup. A little wet behind the ears. A bit wobbly, too. Probably jet-lagged from the long flight across the Atlantic, yet eagerly waiting to please like any new recruit. All the paperwork was in order. Proof of pedigree as pure as mountain snow. Mother and father? A lineage chaste in Teutonic old-world stock. Fowler had taken Max home to meet part of the family as the officer's two oldest boys were away at college. It was love at first sight for all parties present. The two youngest children were ecstatic. And Max, with a heartfelt throb, communicated in kind. Fowler's wife greeted the newcomer as she would a member of her own family, for in fact Max was, indeed, family, as he would be living with them permanently. Barbara was reminded of the time she had taken in exchange students from Frankfort, ironically not very far away from where Max was born, somewhere along the Main River near Wiesbaden, she recalled.

Barbara Fowler had spoken to Max in High German, and he immediately followed her into the kitchen, suddenly ignoring the rest of the family.

"Your mother speaks his language," Dan had explained to his youngest son and daughter who followed to the threshold with the unmistakable look of dejection on their faces.

"Doesn't he understand English?" his precocious four-year-old wanted to know, looking up at her father with wide and wondrous eyes.

"Not a blessed word," he assured his daughter, smiling down at her lovingly.

"But you speak German, right Daddy?"

"Only a few words, sweetheart," he had freely admitted. "So I guess we'll all have to go to language school. Right, kids?"

"Oh, brother. Give us a break, Dad," Dan Fowler, police officer and father of four, recalled his five-year-old son saying on that late summer afternoon.

Dan's youngest two children never knew their father's former partners, but they were certainly brought up with the stories, and there were pictures on a wall in the den as constant reminders. It wasn't but a few months after Max's arrival that a new portrait was added: a picture of Dan's new partner and the entire family playing ball in the backyard. Of course, Detective Connolly had taken the picture. Who else? For it was Mick who had put the bug in his boss's ear to make the well-placed phone call that eventually resulted in bringing pressure to bear on Dan to head on out to the airport for the express purpose of picking up Max and getting back in the game of doing what Dan did best.

Max was still being evaluated for his temperament, determination and drive. It was all part of procedure. Dan Fowler would cut no corners. For shortcuts might one day mean putting fellow officers' lives at great risk. Dan would go to any length to minimize that danger.

Dan and Max had been through many courses together, training in several key locations throughout the country, one being the FBI Academy in Quantico. There were times that Dan, alone, received instruction and training. Dan, in turn, trained Max. It was an ongoing process. Perpetual. The two never stopped learning. Some officers teased him mercilessly, seeing the relationship as symbiotic. They could say whatever they wanted. Dan and Max got the job done. They left no stone unturned.

Officer Fowler was engaged in an exercise when Detective Mick Connolly pulled up in a sector car alongside a field across from a wooded lot. A light rain had just let up. He got out of the vehicle carefully, for his back had been bothering him. He walked over and waited patiently until the drill was finished.

"Got something important going down tomorrow morning, Dan. How ya doin' there, Max?" Connolly grimaced in pain.

The detective had pulled a muscle in his back while working on his boat, having tried and failed to get things shipshape for the kick-off of the April 1st flounder season. He had tried last year, too, but something always seemed to pop up. This time around it was surveillance that he and the members of Teams One and Two were conducting on both Howard and Jeffrey Mills. At first, efforts had been concentrated on the younger brother, Jeffrey. But as time marched on, energies were shifted to Howard. Howard Mills was now the focus of their investigation. Howard Mills was their prime suspect. Howard W. Mills, mail handler, was their target.

"Trouble with that back of yours again?" Dan asked.

"Pulled a muscle. Fucking boat. Actually, it's that fuckin' bilge. How any human being can work down there is beyond comprehension. You gotta be a midget."

"Then put Masselli down there," Dan suggested jokingly.

Mick laughed. "Put a tool in that man's hand would be like putting a wrench in Max's paw."

Max looked past Mick then walked off several paces.

"What did I do? Hurt his feelings?"

Dan smiled. "Maybe you need a bigger boat."

"Bigger headache."

"What's on for tomorrow?"

"Big," Mick stated with a big smile. "Very big."

"Where we going?"

"Hicksville."

"Got it cleared this time? Last time, I had some explaining to do. This on the up and up?"

"Bear shit in the woods?"

"I know Max does."

"All cleared," the detective said as Max watched Mick remove a fuzzy round object from the large left front pocket of Dan's Windbreaker. "Hey, Max!" Mick called out, carefully drawing back an arm, winding up for the pitch as if the ball were about to travel into Nassau County. Mick hurled his arm forward, throwing out nothing but his back. "Shit!" Mick stiffened, easily shielding the tennis ball in a sizeable palm.

Max's eyes never left the detective's oversized mitt that could pass for a catcher's glove. The two locked on to one another like radar. Mick grimaced and again slowly drew his arm back for all its worth, giving the impression that this time, for real, the fuzzy green tennis ball was about to be hurled into the more distant county of Queens. It was as Mick raised his right leg high and leaned rearward for the delivery that Dan called out a command.

"*Unterdrucken!*"

In an instant, Max took the man off balance; Mick was falling backward then hit the ground. "Shit!"

"*Holen!*" Dan instructed.

The fuzzy ball landed in Max's court and bounced but once before the shepherd secured it squarely in its mouth, carrying the prize over to his partner.

"*Gut*, Max. *Sehr gut*," Dan praised, taking the ball from his partner and tossing it high into the cool April air.

Max ran off and waited under the ball like a fielder while Dan walked over to Mick to lend a helping hand.

"Just in case you're interested, I'm not so *gut*, you hot-dog handler, you. Tomorrow we got a mail handler on our hands," Mick grumbled, shaking off Fowler's grip immediately after being pulled to his feet. "Maybe two of them. Postal workers. *Verstehen*? The Mills brothers. Not a song-and-dance team. Although they'll probably be giving us one after we haul their sorry asses in," he finished explaining, complaining next by way of unintelligible sounds and certain gestures that all was not well with the small of his back, nor was he happy about the fresh soil mark on a suede elbow patch of his freshly dry-cleaned sports jacket.

Max seemed alert to the situation and came over to inspect, dropping the ball at Fowler's feet then nuzzling his nose against Mick's knee.

"Just remember that I helped get you into this country you ungrateful immigrant," Mick barked, looking down at the animal with a degree of feigned disgust. "It's an INS check I'm gonna run on you, you mutt, if you don't watch your step."

Max acknowledged the man's apparent disappointment and nestled his nose firmly against the inside of Mick's leg.

"Yeah, you're dog meat, *hund*," he menaced playfully. "For as me German-Irish mother would always say when the cupboard was completely bare, 'Tis genuine shepherd's pie in lieu of leftovers you'll be havin' tonight, laddie,' Mick yammered away. 'Me lit'l man shall never starve lest they rid this city of cats and dogs.'"

"I thought you said you were brought up in the countryside," the K-9 unit officer disputed playfully, "and that your father hunted deer and that there were always venison steaks on hand."

"Was me uncle that was the *jagermeister*; me father was on the dole."

"I see."

"See nothing. Tomorrow you'll see. Tomorrow we three go a huntin'."

"Where do we meet?"

"Two blocks south of the Hicksville train station. West Marie Street. Look for me and Bailey. Zero five-thirty, sharp. I'll pick you up coffee and a buttered roll. And wear your street clothes."

"Max's target?"

"Trunk of a vehicle."

"Nobody in there now, I take it."

Mick shrugged.

"How long ago we talking?"

"No telling for sure. Maybe a week."

"The nose will know," the dog handler affirmed, staring down at Max proudly. "Last week, Officer Frye buried a rib bone three feet down in that field behind us, and Max had it scented and out in six minutes flat." Fowler looked down at Max. "*Ja?*"

"*Woof*," Max answered up sharply in a single syllable, his brindled coat all clean and shiny from an early morning brushing.

"A real conversationalist you got there," Mick snapped. "How long has he been in this country? And not one word of English. Tell the immigrant I'm neither fluent in dog nor German. Tell him to get on the stick."

No sooner said, Dan Fowler withdrew a heavy stick-like object from the right front pocket of his Windbreaker and sailed the missile some distance through the air, the three of them watching as it spanned the treetops before disappearing into the nearby wooded lot.

Mick could have sworn he heard a splash.

"*Suchen!*" the trainer directed, and Max ran obediently into the timber.

Mick knew he heard another splash much louder than the first.

Less than a minute later, Max, soaked to the bone, was hurrying toward them with the article in his mouth. As Dan was protected with light rain pants and the Windbreaker, Mick took most of the bath as Max shook himself off.

"*Sehr gut*, Maximilian. *Das ist gut*," Dan commended. "*Blick, Herr* Mick," the handler signaled, directing the German shepherd to give over the narrow six-inch plastic tube to the detective.

"'*Blick, Herr* Mick?' What the hell does that mean?" Michael Connolly wanted to know, taking the treasure from Max's mouth.

"Means 'Look, Mr. Mick,'" Fowler translated.

"So what the fuck am I looking at?" the cop inquired, turning the tube over and over in his hands.

"*Geruch.*"

"What?"

"Smell," Dan directed.

Mick held the hollow cylinder an inch or so from his nose and took a good whiff before it hit him. He almost gave up the greasy burger and French fries he had thrown down an hour earlier for lunch.

"Three drops of cadaverine," Fowler clarified, pausing for a mumbled curse and a derogatory comment from Mick. "Fresh from University Hospital over in Stony Brook this morning. Extracted from fingers and toes, they told me," he stated rather stoically, delighting in the taradiddle.

"Bastard," Mick said quietly, dropping the container to the ground. "If Max weren't here to mangle me this minute, I'd put *your* goddamn body in *my* trunk right now and transfer you tonight to Mills' for tomorrow's outing. Prick."

"Tomorrow, zero five-thirty, sharp. Two blocks south of the Hicksville train station. West Marie Street. Street clothes. *Ja?*" Dan said, repeating Mick's instructions to a T, snatching up the tube while chuckling and trotting off with Max for another exercise.

"Paybacks are a bitch, Dan," Mick said decidedly, hands raised level with his shoulders in mock surrender. Disgust flooded the homicide detective's face as he smelled his fingers before filling his nostrils with the fresh nippy spring air.

Actually, the chemical used on the cotton plug inserted within the white plastic tube was Putrescine, the trade name given the synthetic compound. Just as offensive. Just as lasting as the real stuff. Expensive, but easy to come by whenever the hospital claimed they were fresh out of body parts.

The trainer truly found it amusing that his detective friend behaved so squeamishly, recalling the time the two of them poked around a refrigerated compartment where body parts and chemicals were stored within glass jars. But it wasn't he, Dan Fowler, who had initiated the plague of perpetual pranks over the years. Dan never forgot the time some prankster had attached a soaking wet, blood-red raccoon tail to the overhead pull-string at the darkened entranceway to the cadaver locker as it was commonly called—someone knowing full well he had the nine-to-five duty that evening and would be picking up and preparing a new dog for the morning's exercise. He couldn't prove the prankster was Mick, but he *knew*.

Mick's mind was already racing as he headed toward the car, entertaining a plan of action on how to get one-up on the dog handler when the detective knew he should have been concentrating his efforts on the pair of mail handlers. But members of Teams One and Two had him covered for the moment. Full-time surveillance on both brothers had begun a week ago. So back to childish thoughts on how to even the score, realizing that it was Dan's first overt act, ever, of a practical joke. Mick wondered if Dan somehow knew that it was he who had hung the simulated bloody shepherd's tail fashioned from an old raccoon hat and fastened it to the pull-string some years ago. Mick felt badly after the deed was done, for it was the following day that Dan's own dog, Buster, was killed while making a collar in the abandoned building back west. Why did the department have to send those two back there in the dead of night? Mick had questioned privately. But you didn't ask why openly. You just did your job and kept your trap shut. No two ways about it.

As Connolly stepped into his vehicle, he saw a *present* on the seat. He believed he could almost smell it. Max would often jump into Mick's car and sit right beside him, but never ever when Dan was off doing an exercise. Mick studied the mess carefully, poked it with his pen and gave a smile. It wasn't dog shit at all. Just a rubber mass of look-alike. Oh, Dan knew, all right! Mick lifted its edge gingerly, as if the seat might suddenly explode. Beneath the base was a Post-It. Mick removed it and read: You're truly April's fool; had twice. Happy April 1st. Your friend, Max.

But Dan and Max hadn't been out of Mick's sight since the second he stepped from the car, except for Max's run into the woods, pond, and back. Mick turned his head and noticed a familiar car parked nearby. An equally familiar figure stood on the other side of the road. Tall. The man's head was down, knees slightly bent, lining up his shot. He took a practice swing. This was war! It was Dan's other partner. The human one. Riverhead's D.A.R.E. (Drug Abuse Resistance Education) officer, Dennis the Menace. Dan's golfing partner. He was omnipresent. Mick saw him wherever he went. On every fairway and in every field. Wherever the man could swing a club. Mick leaned on the horn and held it there as the D.A.R.E. officer took his swing. The fellow never so much as flinched. Smooth as silk with perfect follow-through. The little white ball sailed straight and true. A mile or more or so it seemed. Dennis drove a few more balls in quick succession.

"FUCKER!" Mick called out.

The D.A.R.E. officer never missed a stroke, picking up his clubs and walking off in the direction of the balls. He never looked back, finally disappearing behind a berm.

Oh, yes. This was definitely war, Mick swore. One day, when the Riverhead police officer least expected it, he'd find a body in his trunk instead of those expensive clubs. *Fowler's body,* he frowned. *Let him explain that one to his chief.* Mick swung his head in the other direction. Fowler and his four-legged follower were gone, too. They'd all pay. He'd pay Fowler's unit commander good money to pour a pint of Bud into Max's personal water bowl and fill the Cremora container with flour the next time Dan pulled morning duty in the cadaver locker. Damn if he wouldn't, the homicide detective mischievously vowed.

Chapter Six

Both Max and Dan were relieving themselves in an empty lot behind a vacant building just south of West Marie Street in Hicksville as Detectives Frank Masselli and Victor Posteraro turned off Newbridge Road. Mick Connolly and John Bailey had arrived several minutes earlier and were sipping hot black coffee and sharing a fried egg sandwich on a seeded roll. Vic pulled alongside, positioning the vehicle so that the two senior detectives could jaw away, face to face. The engines were left running. Frank and Mick sent down their windows simultaneously.

"Do they shower and sleep together, too, Mick?" Frank asked, gesturing toward the pair urinating in the open lot with their backsides toward the foursome. Dan had one hand on his hip. Max had one leg in the air.

"Quite frankly, Frankie, I think they even go to the movies together," Mick remarked.

Frank smiled. "Remarkable mutt."

"Which one are you referring to?"

"The one with the bigger schlong."

"That would definitely be the shorter fella."

"Morning, guys," Vic called past his partner, addressing Mick and John. "Did you bring me coffee, John, like you promised?"

"Plain forgot how you took it, kid. So I didn't bother getting yours," John kidded, reaching in the back seat for the compartmentalized cardboard tray in which sat three large lidded towers of coffee. Two containers were for Vic. Several jelly doughnuts wrapped in waxed sheets were stuffed into other cut-out sections. "Here you go, fellas." John handed over the tray to Mick, who passed it to Frank, who took one container then passed the tray to Vic.

Vic was a happy camper. He had to have his caffeine and sugar fix. Vic, who was generally thought to be pretty even-tempered and levelheaded, could be hell on wheels whenever the team was on the move but hadn't the time to stop for coffee and sweets. You did *not* forget Vic's coffee, or there would be a sorry scene.

Max and Dan were coming toward the cars. "Guys."

"How you doing, Dan? Max?" Frank Masselli asked, greeting the pair cordially.

"Doing good."

"Barbara and the brood?"

"Everybody's fine."

"Hiya, Maxie," a familiar voice called out.

Max recognized John's voice and went around to the far side of the vehicles.

John put down his window and handed Max a small piece of egg sandwich.

Max took it gratefully but received no more.

"Don't give the dog people food," Mick complained. "And close that fucking window; there's a draft."

"Grouch," John growled, sending up the window.

"Remember to bring my coffee?" Dan called over to Mick, noting that it was impossible to maneuver between the two cars.

"Oh, Jesus. I truly forgot," Mick answered, looking up with the same sort of sincerity a nine-year-old might display if suddenly asked if he had completed all his homework.

"Let him have one of mine," Vic insisted, handing over one large container along with a jelly doughnut.

There was an immediate commotion among the other team players. Mick even offered Dan the rest of his. Frank claimed he had two cups before leaving the house, didn't need it, and would probably float through the window had he drunk another.

Affecting a sudden recollection, Dan snapped his fingers, smiled and most graciously waved off all offers, explaining that he had a full thermos and a buttered roll waiting in the van. Max followed his partner back to the vehicle with hope and determination in mind. Max was trained not to be a beggar, but he also knew how to *handle* Dan in certain situations—as well as a few of the other detectives.

"Now, what the hell was that all about?" John wanted to know. "I asked you if I should pick up coffee for him, and you said no."

"I said that? Don't rightly remember," Mick said coolly.

It was the word *rightly* coupled with Mick's composure that clued the detective. "Oh, really?"

"What is that supposed to mean?"

"Oh, I don't know."

"What do you mean, you don't know?"

"I guess it means I don't know."

From the other unmarked sedan, Frank and Vic were busy trying to figure out Dan and Mick's problem.

Dan returned with coffee and a roll. Max followed right alongside. The pair went around to John's side of the car. John sent down the window anew. Mick just shook his head.

"What's the deal here this morning?" Dan inquired, directing his question more to John than Mick.

"You're going to have Maxie do a walk-around, around half a dozen cars as soon as the target leaves for work on the six-fifty," John explained.

"Where's the car?"

Mick gave John a little tap on the leg. John glanced over at his partner then addressed Dan.

"We want to keep this thing fair, Danny," John set forth, "in case you have to testify in court. Don't want to have you fabricating on the stand," he added for lack of not knowing what else to say.

"Wonderful. So, tell me where these six or so cars are at."

"Should never end a sentence with a preposition, Dan," Mick said matter-of-factly.

Dan looked down at Max. "Well, tell you what, fella. We might have to end this walk-around before it ever begins. You see, Max looks a little glassy-eyed to me. Not himself lately."

"Max is fine, and you know it." Mick replied.

"I don't know, Mick. John says you want to keep this thing fair."

"I just saw you two yesterday and—"

"I don't want to have to tell the Court that Max really seemed a bit under the weather at the time," Dan bantered. "Wouldn't want to have to lie under oath, Mick."

"Look at him. He's fine." Mick stretched his neck, unable to see the dog from where he was sitting. "Tell him you're fine, Max."

Max was looking askance at Dan's roll.

"Probably be best if we put this exercise off till next week sometime," the trainer suggested with a straight face.

"Next week! This is not a fucking exercise, Dan. This is for real," Mick barked.

"If he alerts to a particular vehicle, and I happen to think it's gas, Max's that is, I'm going to have to write that down in my report. But not to worry, Mick. I'll be careful not to end my sentences with any prepositions."

"All right. All right, already. Enough!" John Bailey decreed, waving a paper napkin and declaring himself official referee before bringing the flag of truce to his messy mouth and chin. "He'll probably park himself—"

"Who?" Dan questioned.

"Jeffrey Mills. Howard's brother," John answered straightaway. "He'll probably park two or three blocks back thataway," he elaborated, indicating a direction further north on West Marie Street. "Closer spots to the station fill up pretty early. His routine has been to grab a spot along a center island back there."

"From what Mick told me, we're focusing in on the trunk area. Right?" Dan asked of John as if Mick were suddenly invisible.

"Correct," John said.

"Well, here's what Max and I will do."

"Now, wait a second," Mick ordered.

Dan pulled a brown nylon leash from his parka pocket. "When you guys give the word, Max and I will take a leisurely stroll. Of course, somebody has to point out the start and finish lines. When Max and I reach the row of vehicles, I'll put him on a short lead. More so, so he doesn't piss on any hubcaps," he kidded. "I'll start curbside."

"Hope he pisses on your shoes and socks," Mick snapped, letting Dan lay the groundwork, for it sounded pretty good so far.

"I'll lead him around one car at a time," Dan continued. "Start out counterclockwise. If Max alerts anywhere along the line, I'll still keep him moving, finishing up all the vehicles on return—clockwise. See if he gives the same response." He waited for a comment.

"I thought *I* was the lead detective," Mick reminded everyone.

"Mick needs to be put on a short lead, Dan," John joked.

"The shorter the better," Frank broke in, chuckling and wiping powered sugar off a lapel. "Kind of guy you give an inch before he has two feet in his neighbor's yard."

Vic looked up from his coffee and caught Mick giving Frank the evil eye. Vic pondered the remark in those seconds of silence. He had heard rumors that Mick was perhaps a little too chummy with the widow next-door. But as the newest and youngest member of the team, Vic had not been taken into their confidence concerning matters apart from police business. As a fellow detective working cases together, Vic was always consulted—never left out of the loop. The team considered him to be one of the brightest. However, personal business was off-limits to their newest member of the team.

"So. What do you think?" John asked Mick, breaking the silence. "Good game plan?"

"Seems to have covered all the bases," Mick conceded.

"Frank? Vic? Whattaya guys think?" John urged.

"Sounds good," Frank admitted. "It's really Dan and Max's show. Let's just decide where the four of us suits are going to take up positions. Train station area? Two on opposite ends of the platform? Can't have five guys and a dog hanging around that island. Don't want to alert John Q. Public. Vic?"

"Well, suits certainly blend in with the early commuter scene here, but the next train after Mills' isn't for another sixteen minutes. Five guys and a dog milling around for a quarter of an hour is going to create some suspicion. You don't know who these two brothers might know around here. Dan have a hand-held?" Vic asked John, speaking past Frank and Mick.

John reached in front of Mick and plucked a hand-held radio from the glove compartment, passing it through the window to Dan. "He has now," John said. "Channel's set."

"You got one for yourselves, guys?" the handler asked.

Frank reached under his seat and handed a radio to Mick. "We're all set."

"Anything else, Vic?" John asked, noting Vic's concern.

"Yeah. A man and his dog milling around half a dozen vehicles is still going to look suspicious."

"Good point," Mick said.

"Dan's looking for his lost keys!" Frank suggested sagaciously.

Vic shook his head. "Some good Samaritan might want to join the search and then offer Dan and Max a ride someplace. Could create an awkward situation."

"Yeah, especially if some guy asks Dan if his dog bites," John joked.

Frank laughed loudly.

"I don't get it," Mick snapped.

"That's because you rarely go to the movies or watch TV," John explained, unfolding the celebrated comedic scene played by Peter Sellers in *The Pink Panther Strikes Again*. "Inspector Clouseau asks the Swiss innkeeper, '*Does your dog bite?*' whereby the innkeeper answers, '*No.*' Well, the inspector reaches down to pet the mongrel, when suddenly the animal mauls Clouseau's hand. '*I thought you said your dog does not bite,*' complains the angry inspector. The innkeeper replies, '***That is not my dog***,' Frank exploded, delivering the punch line in an exaggerated German accent.

"Max never bit anyone but the perp," Mick said seriously.

"It's a joke, Micky. Christ, lighten up some," John reproached.

Everyone but Mick and Max were guffawing.

"Not funny. Let's get serious here. If not keys, then what?" Mick solicited.

"Any ideas?" John pressed.

"A contact lens," Vic offered.

"A contact lens?" Frank questioned, trying to recover from his fit of laughter.

"No, that's beautiful," Mick thought aloud.

"Nobody wants to get involved with someone looking for a contact lens," Vic expanded, "especially outdoors. It's like looking for a needle in a haystack. They'll beg off and go on about their business. Maybe try and help out for a few minutes at most. Dan can kind of keep his head down as if searching around and between the cars. If someone actually does approach, Dan can simply say he lost a lens in the area when he tripped on the dog's leash."

"Brilliant," John said.

Dan liked it, too, nodding in agreement.

"Oh, by the way. You two guys ever meet?" John questioned.

"Never had the pleasure," Vic said, leaning forward and acknowledging Dan Fowler through windows and around bodies.

"Officer Dan Fowler. Detective Victor Posteraro," John said, making the introductions.

"Heard a lot of good things about you, Dan," Vic said sincerely.

"Fowler's only the handler," Mick said with annoyance. "If you want to meet the real star, meet Max. Max, take that two-legged flunky of yours around and meet the newest member of our team. And you," he said to his partner, "put up that fuckin' window."

Max and Dan walked around the vehicles.

Vic opened up the driver's door, smiled and stepped from the sedan. "Well, I'll ask anyway. Does your dog bite?"

Everyone laughed heartily, including Mick.

"Only the bad guys," Dan assured him. "*Sitzen.*"

Max sat down smartly.

"*Pfote,*" Vic said politely in German, surprising everyone.

Immediately, Max put out his paw, and Vic bent down to take it. The two junior members of the force greeted one another warmly.

"I thought you were of Italian heritage," Mick Connolly questioned Vic.

"German on my mother's side, through and through. But me father 'twas a bastard, so no one *rightly* knew," Victor Posteraro chanted with a brogue, mimicking the senior detective's storytelling antics, for it was Mick, the spinner of tall tales and many accents, who usually entertained the team with his farfetched accounts relating to the case detective's questionable heritage. Vic was gently rubbing his fingertips behind Max's ears.

"Hey, that's pretty good, Vic," Dan Fowler offered appreciatively. "You got that dick down pat. Damn if you don't," the handler swore and grinned.

Max licked Vic's hand as the detective straightened up.

Mick looked among the others. "What the fuck are they saying? Are those two making fun, or what?"

"I don't know, Mick," John shrugged. "You're the lead detective. You figure it out."

"So now you're a comedian like this wiseass college kid," Mick complained to his partner, John.

Vic gestured toward the tracks. "Train's coming," he announced, erasing any trace of brogue from his tongue as well as the smile from his face. It was now serious showtime.

Chapter Seven

Dan Fowler walked Max along Division Street, then headed east to West Marie Street. He didn't have far to go before spotting the first vehicle that Mick had assigned to begin the walk-around. The rear license plate was faded and splattered with mud but readable. It hung on an old Dodge Dakota pickup truck. A rustbucket without even a cap for concealment. More of Mick's shenanigans, Dan figured, observing the six vehicles in question. At curbside, Dan had a little pep talk with Max. Max was primed.

"*Suchen aus!*" Dan commanded. "Seek out. *Gut*, Max. *Finden.*" The two proceeded forward, heading toward the rear of the first vehicle, working in a counterclockwise fashion. Slowly. Carefully. Max moved most methodically, scenting along a rusty rocker panel. The animal's tail was busily wagging to and fro. The shepherd took in every inch of cold metal, his nose operating feverishly. They made their way around the mid-size pickup, rounding the right front fender, working the pitted chrome grill area, then down along the driver's side, finishing up at the rear tailgate. Max was not at all impressed.

Dan led Max over to the rear bumper of the next vehicle; a 1991 Honda Accord EX that recently joined the nation's most endangered species list. Right up there with the Toyota Camry. Barbara had the same Accord. Same year. Even the same color. Thieves loved them, he knew. Information services that report such findings compile their facts from police reports, and Dan had recently learned that the major reason concerning the high rate of stolen vehicles from those two manufacturers was because their respective parts were interchangeable over seven model years to date. That fact, combined with the vehicles' record of longevity and record-breaking sales, put the Camry and Accord at the top of crooks' hit list. Hence, the Crook Lock. A deterrent at best. He made Barbara promise to use it everywhere she drove, even when she visited him at police headquarters. Dan did not broadcast how many vehicles were stolen each year right out of the police department parking lot. It was positively embarrassing.

Max and Dan had just finished with the Accord when a man across the street came out of his house and walked right up to a late model Ford that was being given Max's full attention.

"May I help you?" the man said rather suspiciously, giving the two the once-over.

Dan gave Max a gentle tug, and the dog immediately lost all interest. "I lost my contact lens somewhere along the line of cars," he explained. "I was walking my dog and tripped over his leash earlier. Can't remember the exact spot. Are you pulling out?"

"Yeah, I'm already late for work or I'd give you a hand."

"That's quite all right. Do you mind if I take a quick look before you head out so you don't step on the lens or maybe run it over?"

"No, sure. Go ahead. I knew you were looking for something out here."

"I'll be quick. Won't hold you up. It's just that I don't have another pair. And like a dope, I threw away my glasses. Stupid vanity," Dan babbled, head down, quickly covering the perimeter of the man's vehicle. "*Aufhoren*," he said in a hush, reminding Max that the search for blood and tissue and body fluids was temporarily put on hold.

"I beg your pardon?"

"I was just telling Max to stop. Very antsy this morning."

"Yes, I noticed," the man said while smirking, looking down peevishly at the dog. "I thought he wanted to relieve himself on that car behind you when I was coming out of the house."

"Oh, my wife has the same car. Same color, also. Max, here, probably thought it was hers," Dan explained rather doltishly, not knowing what else to say.

"Huh. Beautiful dog you got there."

"Thank you." *Just don't ask me if he bites*, Dan said to himself.

"And thanks for waiting while I looked. I'm just going to work my way down to the end of the island and call it quits, so don't let me keep you."

"Again, if I had more time, I'd give you a hand."

Dan nodded. "Much appreciated."

The man unlocked his car and slid behind the wheel. Within half a minute, he was gone.

"Shit!" Fowler hoped that the man's Ford was not the car in question.

Max knew when Dan was upset.

The two stepped onto the island behind the other vehicles.

"Damn."

Dan squatted as if to tie a shoe but instead took out the borrowed hand-held. Max stood by patiently.

"Sector Two, this is K-Niner One. Do you copy?"

Vic Posteraro immediately snatched up the hand-held off the seat and pressed the transmit button. "Go ahead, Dan."

"Number three just blew out before we had a good look-see. Copy that?"

"We copy. Not to worry. Run by four through six and get back to us. Over."

"Got it. Over and out."

"Why didn't you ask him about one and two?" Mick called over to Vic rather impatiently.

"Because you told Dan to go through all six vehicles before reporting back for a second pass," Vic answered, unruffled.

"Just checking, kid. See?" Mick said to the others. "College boy pays attention. Little snotty now and then, but he listens. You listenin', John?"

"I'm listening. I always listen. I listen to my wife. I listen to my kids. I listen to the news and weather report. I'm a listener, Mick."

"What about you, Frank? You listen like John and Vic?"

Frank said nothing.

"What I thought," Mick mocked.

The four men sat anxiously. Mick believed they had their man—or men. The brothers grim. He knew it in his heart. His interviews with more than a dozen prostitutes from the Jamaica Avenue area of Queens confirmed it in his mind. Darla, Mick's Melville victim, via her tattoo, had given them their first big break. Probably just her street name. Frank had worked Jane Doe/Medford for well over two years and knew they were finally closing in. And in between those two murders was the body of the young woman who wound up on a conveyor belt at a recycling plant in Brooklyn. Mick maintained that the same person or persons who murdered the Medford and Melville women was also responsible for the woman found in Brooklyn. Same M.O. A bit more gruesome as *all* her limbs had been severed, leaving them with just the torso. But it had the same *signature*, for sure. It was too coincidental to be otherwise: blunt force trauma to the face and head area; the skullcaps of all three women cracked like an eggshell; their noses either fractured or badly broken; the unmistakable telltale sign of saw marks on the bone-ends resulting from amputated limbs. Consequently, Suffolk Homicide had shared most of their information with Brooklyn homicide detectives as well as teams from other jurisdictions.

Mick believed that if there were three connected murders, there were probably more. The problem was that it took four months to gather the intelligence from the time his Melville girl was found to the present. There hadn't been around-the-clock surveillance on Howard or Jeffrey Mills until the week before. Either brother could have had the window of opportunity to kill others and dispose of their bodies. All the evidence thus far was purely circumstantial. They needed something solid. Several prostitutes had pointed Mick in one direction. Collectively, they had located Howard's apartment and blue Cadillac. The next step in the operation pivoted around a dog. Not just any dog, but Max. Max could provide them with probable cause. Homicide was hopeful.

The detectives just couldn't barge in like gangbusters. Of course, they had enough to bring Howard in for questioning, for several of the street girls had identified both his puss and the Coupe de Ville from a series of photo arrays. But then Mick and his team might have tipped their hand prematurely. There were too many unknowns. The trunk of the 1986 Cadillac just might prove to be the bone they needed to secure a warrant. Mick couldn't think of a more befitting retriever of such tidings to bestow upon them than Dan's beloved Maximilian. A million penances and promises Mick made to his Maker if only Max came through as the detective believed he would. Then again, he'd have to renegotiate a deal with The Man upstairs concerning a certain mistress next-door. Maybe take a plea. Maybe plead the fifth. Mick certainly realized that he had a long record of many broken promises. Still, wouldn't God forgive The Mick (affectionately referred to by the brass upstairs) if he built a solid case for the D.A. and netted the fish who was responsible for killing prostitutes and disposing their bodies like household garbage? Surely, God would reserve judgment for such a deserving sinner. Surely, He wouldn't cast Mick down.

If only he knew the politics of the 'other world' like he knew his way around earthly affairs. Mick knew exactly what the Suffolk County prosecutor's agenda was in a nutshell: to apprehend, arrest, prosecute and convict the maniac(s) so as to launch the first death penalty case on Long Island in almost twenty years. It was lovely having the law back on the books, Mick beamed. They needed that Brooklyn victim tied in with the two found in Suffolk in order to meet the burden of three murders within a twenty-four month period so as to fulfill the serial killer requirement. Suffolk Homicide had worked with other jurisdictions in the past; however, they rarely worked as closely as they were working with the lead detective and the Crime Scene Unit boys and girls from Brooklyn.

The Suffolk County District Attorney, Casper Patterson, had chosen Gail Fox to prosecute the case in the event of an arrest and charge. And now that an arrest was foreseeable, if not imminent in the minds of those closest to the case, the pressure that came to bear on all connected, from the top on down, was like nothing that Mick had ever seen in his thirty-three year career in law enforcement.

A simple alert from Max could push their probable cause issue over the top. The police would snatch Howard Mills off a Nassau County street when he would be fair game and a safe distance from his residence on Willow Lane, far enough away from friends and family at a time the suspect would not be missed until maybe the middle of Monday. Homicide had it all laid out. They would deliver Howard to police headquarters in Yaphank and hold him incommunicado. The teams would question him in their 8 x 8 foot Suffolk County cube; for they had the jurisdiction since two of the bodies turned up in Suffolk, thank God. If need be, they'd dry Howard Mills out through lack of food and water. And if that, coupled with selected forms of intimidation and specific themes, didn't loosen a tight-lipped tongue, well, yawns as wide as a canyon (the net result of sleep deprivation over periods of long hours or days, prolonged by constant browbeating in both the figurative and literal sense) usually produced the desired results. Maybe a little catnap now and again so as not to cause a total collapse. A confession would certainly guarantee a suspect more than forty winks. A signed confession in this particular case might even assure Howard W. Mills an eternal rest. And if their boy ever agreed to a videotaped declaration . . . well, maybe that was wishful thinking, for not every serial killer was a ham.

Dan and Max finished working the Mazda, the car in front of the Ford that had pulled out. Nothing. The next car was an older model Cadillac, but still in good shape. Mid eighties. Dan was not a car buff, so he didn't know the year for sure or really care. All he knew was that it was big and blue. A Coupe de Ville, meaning that it was the two-door model, not the four. The four door was for the older generation. *Like me and Barbara*, he entertained. Not that they could even afford the upkeep on such a car, and a gas-guzzler to boot. Not with two kids away at college. Fortunately, he somehow managed to keep up with the payments on her Honda and his Chevy Blazer, the mortgage, college tuition, utilities, and other ordinary household expenses. Dan was making himself depressed, exaggerating a worst-case scenario. This morning he had to pilfer a sawbuck from Barbara's pocketbook for gas money to top off the tank. Good thing he was a cop. At least he'd have half a chance should a judge reprimand him by way of a lecture and let him off with a warning instead of sending him off in cuffs if Barbara noticed and spilled the beans. He was getting giddy. Not paying close enough attention to Max. He pulled the dog back and together they reworked the passenger side of the Cadillac. Just to be certain.

Max made his way around the grillwork, then down along the driver's side. His nose was as busy as a bee pollinating flowers. Sniffing here and there, heading toward the rear of the vehicle. Max paused at the back left bumper, scenting beneath the trunk lid. Suddenly, Max's tail stiffened. It grew big and bushy. The dog stopped dead in its tracks. Max's rib cage expanded as the animal drew terrific breaths. His chest heaved while he whiffed the seam. Nostrils distended. Lips flared up and back. Paws rising then coming to rest upon the surface of the trunk as Dan relaxed the leash. Max looked at Dan with absolute assurance, revealed in the dog's keen brown eyes. If Max could speak the English language, he would almost surely have said, "*Somebody either was or still is in there, partner. I'd bet my bedroll, biscuits and rawhide bone on it, I would.*"

Dan praised his partner. The two had hit pay dirt. Dan's heart was pounding in his chest.

"*Gut*, Max. *Sehr gut hund.*" Then Dan handed Max a fuzzy new, green tennis ball. "You're the very best," he said in English because he didn't know but a dozen German words and phrases. "Micky's gonna hug and squeeze you till he cracks your ribs. So maybe you should bite him before he even begins." Dan was positively punchy.

Dan wondered if Max would really take Mick apart if given the command. Not that it hadn't been warranted in the handler's mind. Not that he hadn't threatened the homicide detective with such destruction at least a hundred times before because he certainly had. But Mick would look down at the shepherd threateningly and swear to confiscate all of the canine's certificates and pedigree papers, forging new ones and declaring Max a mutt if he ever so much as raised a paw against him. '*Just remember that I helped bring you over here, dummkopf,*' Mick would prattle, '*and I could send you back—have you deported in a heartbeat, you Nazi cur.*'

It was Mick's tone that would make the dog tentative. And Max would study Mick like raw meat. But the two were really buddies, and over the years their relationship grew. Outside of family members, a few detectives and other handlers, Dan did not encourage familiarity. Mick was family as far as Dan was concerned. Barbara had her reservations but held her tongue.

Dog handler and trainer Dan Fowler moved his partner and himself perfunctorily through the motions. Simply as a matter of course. Keeping the business aboveboard. They had the target vehicle. They practically had their man. The pair finished up the three remaining vehicles. Dan put his back to the homes nearest him and took out the hand-held.

"K-Niner One to Sector Two. Copy?"

"Copy that." It was Mick's voice at the other end. There was a pause. "Well?"

Dan could hardly contain himself, but he was going to milk this one for all it was worth. And it was worth a lot. "Well, what?"

"Don't fuck with me, Danny boy."

"Profanity over the airwaves is a direct violation of FCC regs," Dan put forth as a mild reminder, grinning from ear to ear.

"Fuck you and the FCC," Mick lambasted. "Tell me what you got."

"Gotta make another pass, Mick. Copy that?"

"He's fuckin' with me," he told the others as if they hadn't heard.

"You wouldn't pick up his coffee or roll. Remember, jerk?" John scolded.

Mick pressed the transmit button. "I want to speak to Max,

Danny." He released the button to receive.

"That's a copy, Mick. I got Max right here. Go ahead. Over."

"That you fella?" Mick asked lovingly.

"*Woof!*" Max answered via a hand command from Dan.

"Do we have an alert, my pussycat?" Mick questioned and fawned ever so sweetly. "Over."

John was practically on the floor, hardly able to contain a fit of laughter. Frank was literally tearing at the ceiling of the sedan in sheer excitement. They knew! Vic remained calm, taking in the antics.

"*Woof!*" Max barked again on command.

"There you have it," Mick tried to say calmly, knowing full well that Dan would never pull a stunt like that if there hadn't been a full alert. "Straight from the doggy's mouth," he proclaimed, punching a serious dent in the padded dash for effect. "Got you, you fucking bastard," he swore up to Howard Mills as if their suspect were actually hovering above the roof of the Plymouth sedan. "Got you!"

"We're gonna take another pass of all the vehicles we just examined," Dan's voice came back. "Clockwise this time. Then we're comin' in. Is that a copy?"

"Affirmative," Mick said happily. "Oh, and I forgive you your playfulness. I'm not going to put you on report."

"Gee, thanks, Micky. You're all heart," Dan announced sarcastically.

"No, not *you*, you . . . when I'm finished with you, you won't be able to get a job as a dogcatcher anywhere on the Island, or the five boroughs," Mick swore. "I was talkin' to your bootlickin', ass kissin' buddy there," the man blasted, but with the biggest of grins.

"Over and out," the handler replied with utmost satisfaction.

Vic smiled and shook his head. "Just imagine if they didn't like one another," he said to no one in particular.

Chapter Eight

Detective Gary York read everything he could pertaining to the new death penalty law. He read all the mainstream and local newspapers. He read news magazines. He'd pop into the Touro College Law Library in Huntington, or the library at John Jay College of Criminal Justice in midtown Manhattan. Of late, he visited the Suffolk County Supreme Court Law Library located on the first floor in the Criminal Courts building in Riverhead, reviewing portions of criminal procedure law as it pertained to felony murder, paying particular attention to the annotated sections published in the Cumulative Pockets Parts found in *McKinney's Session Law News Pamphlets*. He never wrote his name down in the register book as one was supposed to do; he never signed out either.

Around 10 a.m. for the past week, Gary would meet with prosecutor Gail Fox, along with others in her office on the fifth floor of the same building. After their meetings, he'd take the elevator down to the snack bar adjacent to the law library for a second cup of coffee before resuming his research, taxing his brain for hours over a ton of material that would make a first year law student's mind whirl with dizziness. Then he'd disappear into the cool April air.

At home, Detective York would pore over his notes concerning meetings, supplementary reports, and the law. A copy of *Black's Law*

Dictionary lay open on his desk. He would read into the early hours of morning, then get up and go to work. After getting off duty, he would follow the same routine. He was not a frustrated wannabe legal eagle by any stretch of mind, although he knew he could write briefs if prompted; maybe even argue a case before the bench in a pinch if pressed, he'd kid around with the other members of Team Two. Since his fifth birthday, Gary never wanted to be anything other than a detective. Becoming a *homicide* detective was like another layer of icing on that cake. Gary York would not trade places with anyone in any other profession. Not for all the money in the world, not even for a seven-figure income as pulled down by several high-caliber attorneys he knew.

In truth, Detective Gary York especially loathed criminal defense lawyers. He hated the so-called hallowed halls of justice they tainted by their mere presence. He would prostitute himself in a heartbeat for a prosecutor with a justifiable cause, as he had a time or two before. And Gail Fox, as it stood, had a definite mission in mind. Justice was arrived at very simply for the maverick cop. The end result plainly justified the means. He was cool with it. Quite cool, indeed. It was a dangerous tact to take, but it was a wicked world York had reasoned early on in his career in the game of cat and mouse. Convictions would not be as readily forthcoming if the team played strictly by the book. The team was the infrastructure, paradoxically positioned as the seat of power. One who played chess well, and knew the real worth of a pawn, would readily draw the inference. Detective Gary Daniel York was just such a valuable piece. Innovative legal maneuvering was often critical for a conviction and could be compared to the creative accounting practices of a small business wanting only to survive. Too, the game could fast become as complicated as a burgeoning company that greedily, and seemingly through magic, managed to manifest itself into a conglomerate overnight. York was out to win at all cost, come hell or high water, clichés notwithstanding.

Gary put his papers down, reached over, and switched off the night table light. He had practiced the practice enough for today. Tomorrow or maybe the next day would be just another walk in the park. He could walk the walk and talk the talk. He was certain he could convince even the Chief Justice of the United States Supreme Court that he had graduated St. John's Law School in the top ten percent of his class. All he'd have to do is come up with the year. He'd certainly be able to handle a mail handler. Howard Mills would hardly present a problem. Maybe after early retirement, Gary would head for the stage, he entertained jokingly. A run out to Hollywood for a reading. The next Raymond Burr with his own series. "Of course, much better looking and far younger than old Ironsides," Gary affirmed aloud to no one. "Certainly much thinner, too," he added immodestly.

And he was right on all three counts.

The word that would sum up Gary York in a nutshell would be arrogance. He even breathed it as he slept.

Chapter Nine

The following day, a briefing was held in the Suffolk County Crime Lab. Further findings with regard to the Medford and Melville victims were about to be reported. Filing into the meeting room were several detectives from Teams One and Two of the Suffolk County Homicide Squad. Their immediate supervisors as well as other divisional personnel were present, too. Representing the district attorney's office was ADA Gail Fox, flanked by two gentlemen. Heading the group were the assistant medical examiner, Albert Lacara, and a forensic scientist, Peter Danowski. The two remained standing. Everyone else took seats around a long rectangular table. Albert stood by to assist with a slide projector, stacks of 8 x 10 colored glossies of the Medford and Melville victims, blowups of hair and fiber evidence, along with copies of typewritten reports to be distributed at the close of the meeting.

Peter was their hair and fiber expert and about to begin with an update concerning Frank Masselli's December 1994 Medford homicide victim. Peter made sure that his laser pointer was operational by directing the red dot of light upon the projection screen.

Albert was noted for his laconism, Peter for his thorough discourses. Both men were truly professional.

"Gentlemen. Ms. Fox," Peter greeted everyone warmly.

It was the *Ms.* enunciation in Ms. Fox that put Gail's back up immediately.

"We'll begin with the light blue-gray nylon carpet fibers taken from the Jane Doe/Medford, 1994 crime scene, found both on the body as well as items surrounding it. No need to take notes because Albert, here, is going to hand you a most comprehensive, detailed report of our findings at the close of this meeting. So pretend you're a juror listening to testimony. No notes," he insisted, waving a finger in mild rebuke. "No need. Please put away those pads and pens. I need your undivided attention."

Peter was thirty but looked twenty. He was the youngest person in the room, yet commanded the respect of everyone present.

"So. Let's begin. Al, if you'll dim the lights and show us the first slide."

Fourteen seated folks buzzed anxiously among themselves in the moment it took to get business under way. Seconds later, Albert focused in on a single light blue-gray carpet fiber taken from the amputated bone end of Jane Doe/Medford's lower left torso. Everyone in the dimly lit room grew silent, studying the sole thread as though it might reveal the secret to eternal life. Interestingly, the fiber, and others like it, would eventually lend themselves to the definitive connection between a plastic trash container discovered along the side of the road, in which the woman's body was stuffed, and Howard Mills' room at 42 Willow Lane in Hicksville.

Detective Michael Connolly twisted his head sideways in an exaggerated fashion, fixing his eyes on the fine threadlike filament presented on the screen. "Just as I suspected," he announced, breaking the sacred silence. "The thread's upside down and backwards."

The silly remark brought light laughter and smiles from everyone except Gail Fox. She was amused at best, quite conscious of being the only woman present. She felt not the least bit intimidated; she was simply annoyed. Thirty-one convictions to her name versus one acquittal and not one man had escorted her to her seat or pulled her chair out from the table like any gentleman would or should have done. She was not by any stretch of the imagination a prima donna. What she was, was a lady. But Ms. Fox had made the fatal mistake of making precisely that point to her male counterparts during the early part of her career as a prosecutor. Not five minutes had elapsed Gail Fox's sudden declaration when she was forever dubbed The Dragon Lady. She *was* treated like an equal and on an even footing with all the good fellows.

Gail was accorded all the privileges of rank, the rankest of jokes notwithstanding. She experienced the raunchiest behavior by some of the crudest of cops from both the homicide bunch as well as other plainclothes garden-variety types. But to be treated like an asshole buddy rather than a lady lawyer by her office peers was what she resented greatly. It was positively humiliating, yet she refused to be humiliated.

Over the years, she fought fiercely to overcome the brand with which she had been seared. She fought savagely to uphold her dignity. She had fought fairly yet indefatigably in the courtroom, triumphing over her adversaries, winning conviction after conviction after conviction. Still, her male counterparts would do little more than hold a door open for her if she were but steps away from its threshold. Chivalry in the work force for a woman in general under the reign of District Attorney Patterson was as dead as the bodies that the crime lab personnel would carry in shrouds and deposit at the back door of the medical examiner's building. For The Dragon Lady, a simple courtesy from her male associates seemed on permanent holiday. For the first few months, she was naive enough to believe that their treatment of her was a temporary matter.

Then came the sudden rationalization. Jealousy. Everyone knew her early background. A most unhappy homemaker. Rising from the ashes of a bad marriage. No, not bad. Horrendous! The humbling experience of driving a school bus for the first four years following her divorce, just to put food on the table and a roof overhead for her five-year-old and herself. Then a second but, thankfully, successful marriage to a cop, no less. Robbery detective. Was she nuts? But Joseph Fox was a cut above the rest. A man who knew when to leave his drinking buddies and head on home to hit the books, taking the next step for promotion and knocking them dead. Oh, she had checked Joe out so carefully. The man was, indeed, ambitious. A silent partner in a small home remodeling business, which he'd eventually take over after early retirement from the force. Supportive? One hundred percent. Pushing Gail back to college and then on to law school shortly after their marriage. "A three-point-nine cumulative index to remain a homemaker? Not!" was her police husband's decree, practically filling out the paperwork for Gail and pointing her in a single direction. Stony Brook University pre-law studies. "We're a team," he had insisted. "I arrest the bastards, and you're gonna prosecute the scum one day. You'll see."

"But—"

It was but the only word she got in edgewise. *Yeah. Some mouthpiece she'd make*, she reminisced, then went on to become one hell of a prosecutor for the People. Hence, The Dragon Lady.

"You with us, lady?" Peter Danowski asked, drawing her out of her reverie and back into the game.

Gail Fox smiled, and with long, delicate thin fingers, combed back one side of her rust-red hairdo, clearing her mind of days of yore. "I'm with you, Peter."

Mick Connolly still had his head twisted about, staring stupidly at the screen.

Peter aimed and pinpointed the red dot upon Mick's forehead, holding it there before the detective suddenly slumped over in his seat as if shot. A second later, the scientist became all business and redirected everyone's attention back to the screen, underscoring the evidence.

"This, as you already know, is just one of many such fibers we found on and around your Medford/Melville victims. But what is *most significant* about those taken from the vacuuming we did at the postal guard shack slash security trailer where Howard Mills was temporarily assigned after the Melville incident is something that goes a bit beyond being *consistent*, referencing those two young women."

Connolly went from class clown back to being a serious detective as evidenced by assuming an erect posture. Whereas the term *consistent*, although encouraging, didn't really nail anything down forensically speaking—and in a court of law that's how a forensic scientist had to speak, forensically—the phrase *most significant* implied a greater degree of expectation for Mick as well as everyone present in that room, especially when attached to a qualifier such as *a bit beyond consistent*. Peter Danowski was neither prone to minimizing nor maximizing such statements. His opinions were what they were. Peter was handing them hope.

"These Monsanto carpet fibers, in and of themselves, would connect your suspect to a much lesser degree than what we now have here." Once again, the man highlighted the fiber with his laser pointer before moving ahead. "Al."

Albert clicked the remote and put another image on the screen, focusing in on two fibers. One above the other.

"What we have here is a juxtaposition of the questioned light blue-gray nylon carpet fiber taken from Jane Doe/Medford, pictured above the known fiber recovered from the vacuuming of that security shack. Unknown. Known. Gail. Tell me what you see."

"You're always calling on her," Mick pouted, unable to contain the kid within him.

"They look identical," Gail remarked rather encouragingly.

"I was gonna say that," Mick replied.

"As viewed here, all we can say about them is that they're consistent."

"I was gonna say that next," Mick continued. "Consistent."

"Shut up," one of the ADAs sitting to Gail's left said with annoyance.

"Consistent is still better than unconsistent, or is it inconsistent," Mick went on.

"I said, shut up," the man persisted.

Mick leaned over and looked several seats down to his left. "Hey. Office boy. You're not my fuckin' boss. All right?"

"Shut the fuck up, Mick," Detective Lieutenant Theodore Groche ordered.

"*He's* my boss," Mick told the suit seated next to him, giving the ADA on the other side of Gail the finger before finally giving his mouth a rest.

"So where's this middle ground between *a bit beyond consistent* and what you said was *most significant*, Pete?" Lieutenant Groche asked, cutting to the chase.

"Al."

Albert put up slide number three.

"Right here, Theo," Peter indicated, passing the laser dot back and forth through the blowups of the known and questioned fibers. "Note the debris. Note how very worn these fibers are. Of course, these are highly magnified, but the naked eye is not going to discern their uniqueness. Here, however, we can *focus in on*," he punned and paused with a smile, "their strong associative connection. If I'm called as a witness, I can make a good case. As I've already stated, these fibers are consistent with those found in each of the locations where the bodies were recovered."

Everyone at the table either nodded their understanding and approval or spoke positively and excitedly to the person next to them.

"Now, staying with Jane Doe/Medford for the moment, let's see from where we retrieved these fibers." Peter put a large chart upon the table. Albert turned on the lights. "So," Peter continued, "as you can see here, we have the light blue-gray nylon carpet fibers taken from the pubic area; bone fragments, one of which I already addressed; her legs; upper torso area; the large plastic trash bags partially covering the victim; under the left side of her head; on the towel found covering the head; cloth collar around her neck. Oh, and please put aside any lingering doubts one of you guys still have regarding strangulation. That collar was not used in any way as a ligature. Not even a postmortem consideration by the perp. All three victims died as the result of blunt force trauma to the head, period. Albert here doesn't want to get any more phone calls at his home or office in that regard. All right?" Peter's eyes happened to fall on Detective Frank Masselli.

"Sorry, I can't seem to get that through my thick skull," Frank confessed.

"Well, all three practically got it through theirs, Frank," Peter assured him. "Cracked open like an egg—whatever he hit them with."

"How do you know it was a *he*? Have you ever seen Gail in a rage?" Mick goaded.

Everyone laughed but Gail.

"Has anyone ever seen Mick in a cage?" the lady deputy chief of the Suffolk County office's homicide division declared with a grin.

"Is that a threat, *Ms*. Prosecutor? In front of how many of the boys? One, two, three, four, five—"

". . . fibers on the cloth collar," Peter resumed, "also found within the blue plastic trash container into which he or *she* disposed of the victim," the scientist conceded with a smile.

"Maybe he's a he-she," Mick considered aloud.

"And also, on the transport shroud we carried her in on," Peter continued, ignoring Mick's banter. "Next, we've got those same light blue-gray fibers turning up on Mick's Melville girl, Darla. Only this time the body is enveloped within two sleeping bags, along with plastic bags deposited in a Dumpster, tape-lifts from inside and outside the sleeping bags, other plastic bags found around her head and torso, et cetera, et cetera, all revealing the unique condition of those fibers. Once again, well-worn and embedded with debris. And again, *very* significant.

"Now, I know I could bore most of you to tears by listing every single trace element found and their locations on and around the bodies. So I won't do that because it's all in the supplementary reports. What I'll highlight, here, is our most important findings. I believe you'll find this quite interesting."

Once more, Peter had their attention, except for Masselli, who seemed rather preoccupied and a bit perturbed.

"But before we move on to other elements of trace evidence, along with more of Mick's amusements, I'm sure, why don't we take a five-minute break. We have a lot of ground to cover here, and I want everyone as sharp as Albert's scalpel."

Mick cringed. "Why did you have to ruin this moment for me, Pete?"

"Just a reminder, folks, that Mick is the only one here that has never attended one of Albert's autopsies," Peter announced as everyone rose from their seats.

"Albert's autopsies. Got a nice ring to it, guys," Mick went on undaunted. "I hear it's really a first-rate show. Why don't you guys book it and take it on the road. If it bombs, you've already got a built-in excuse."

This time, around the table, they were all smiling or laughing at Mick, not necessarily with him, or so he thought.

"Wait, wait, wait. I've got it!" Mick held up his hands as if he were showcasing a marquee. "*Albert's Autopsies*. A one-man, one-act show. You don't even have to say anything, Al. Just stand there like a mummy over a dummy and do your thing. The final act—the only act—and the curtain falls. They'll get it. They'll love it. You'll confuse the hell out of the critics. They'll give you rave reviews and sing high praises in their fancy-Dan supper clubs. How could they attack that kind of performance? And when you appear on Leno and Letterman, you simply shrug your shoulders or nod or shake your head when asked a question. Audiences will love you, Albert. I think I'll put a bid in early on to be your agent."

Mick was getting his audience back. Half was practically on the floor. The other half was hanging on to one another. Even Gail couldn't quite catch her breath. If it wasn't Mick's diatribe that infected them, it was the expression on Al's face: deadpan.

Albert stood tall and wore his blank expression well, fixing his eyes on Michael Connolly. Mick knew the man could have your organs out and handed back to you in a heartbeat if he ever found you alone and prone. The homicide boys referred to Albert Lacara as Doctor à la Carte, usually seen standing over a gurney, an autopsy table, or some such surface that supported dead bodies. Albert Lacara: a.k.a. Laconic Lacara. A quiet soul. A good listener. A voracious reader. A most religious man. And a good friend to those around the lab.

A five-minute break always translated to a quarter of an hour, but never more. It gave everyone time to step outside into the fresh air and fill their lungs with nicotine, or hole up in the cafeteria and bloat their bellies with caffeine and sugary treats. The incongruity of such habits, especially practiced by such brilliant scientists in proximity to the morgue, never ceased to amaze Gail Fox. She'd often grab a cup of green tea with lemon and try to find a quiet corner off by herself, contemplating her next move. Invariably, someone would invade her space.

"Hi, dollface. Got half a minute for me?"

Gail looked up from her papers. It wasn't Mick, thank God, but just as bad. It was Frank Masselli, the lead detective on the Medford case.

"Quick question," the cop swore.

Gail put on a painted smile, closed and lowered the folder to her side.

"When are you gonna let us move on this guy?" Frank asked flatly.

Gail shook her head. "I don't know. We haven't even finished the meeting. How can I possibly say?"

"Can I be frank?"

"You are Frank."

"Come on, Gail."

"A minute ago it was dollface, and your half a minute's up," she stated evenly, putting the papers back in front of her nose.

"Those fibers are better than consistent. You heard Peter in there. 'Unique. A strong associative connection.'"

"'A *bit* beyond consistent,'" she emphasized.

"But still 'significant.'"

"That's all well and good, Frank."

"So what's your fuckin' problem, lady?"

"At this moment, you are, Frankie."

"Gail, we got probable cause. We don't have to sit through the rest of this bullshit meeting to know we got circumstantial evidence as high as the cheeks of my ass. Mick has statements from at least a half a dozen prostitutes re his Melville girl. One who said she *saw* Darla getting into Mills' car."

"I know that, Frank."

"So let's haul his ass in now before he murders someone else.

All right?"

"Let's go back and finish that meeting, go through the reports, then see what our superiors have to say. Remember them? You have them. I have them. Or did you forget?"

"They listen to you, Gail. You practically run the fuckin' show."

"And who gave you that idea?"

"Mick," Frank said matter-of-factly.

"And how would he come to such a conclusion?"

"You know," he said rather awkwardly.

"No, I don't know," she lied.

"Because he said that you're the original Dragon Lady. But personally, dollface, I think you're a foxy femme fatale," he swore along with a wink and a smile.

"Personally, I'm surprised you can even pronounce it," she declared, wearing a frown.

"You're all charm, Gail,"

"Gail. Frank." It was Albert waving them back to the meeting.

"**S**o, let's review the trace evidence with regard to hair and fiber and foam we found to date—reference the Medford/Melville women," Peter continued. "We have those light blue-gray nylon fibers, we have orange polyester fibers, the cat hairs, and particles of yellow rubber foam. Four articles found on the two women, all consistent with the vacuuming from the security trailer. And now you may add a new element, but restricted to the body of the Melville woman, Darla. Not Jane Doe. That additional article is jute, folks."

"Jute?" one of the ADAs questioned.

"I won't even go there," Mick mumbled under his breath.

"Correct. A strong, coarse, natural fiber found in tropical East Indian plants and used in the manufacturing of burlap, rope, cord and things of that sort. Years ago, carpet companies used it as padding to lay beneath wall-to-wall carpeting. Additionally, some carpet companies used it as backing for their product. Problem was that it would retain moisture. Today, they use foam padding for the floor and synthetic materials for carpet backing. Not jute. But that's what we believe we're dealing with here. We found jute fibers commingled with those light blue-gray nylon fibers on your Melville girl, Mick."

"I'm not sure I follow, Pete," Lieutenant Groche spoke up. "A second ago you said you *believe* that's what we're dealing with. Meaning you're not sure it's jute, or what?"

"Sorry, I was about to explain."

"No, I'm sorry. I just don't want to lose my train of thought. You know. No notes. No questions till the end. Just Mick's constant interruptions," Theo maintained good-humoredly.

"Hey! I was good, boss. No? I didn't even touch that jute business. Besides the fact that I never knew a one of them to have more than a two-inch putz," Mick approximated between a thumb and forefinger. "Wasn't me who invented words and phrases for their form of fornication. Schtupping says it all," Mick demonstrated from his seat, giving two quick pelvic thrusts before collapsing with a sigh. "'There, done!' And that's if the guy's even lucky enough to have a partner for openers. Then off *she* goes all lah-di-dah, telling everyone, and I mean everyone at the office the next morning, her *big* secret in the teeniest of a whisper. 'Last night, Sammy schtupped me.' 'Are you sure?!' every single person in that office booms. 'Are you sure it was a schtup, Sara?!' Why do you think they all ask that same question? Tell me. Anyhow, I can get on any witness stand in the country and swear in good conscience before God that I never used the J word. And now I got this jute crap commingling with my Melville girl. Is nothing ever easy?" Mick ranted in frustration, pressing the palms of his hands together and stretching his arms outward as if communicating unsuccessfully with the Almighty.

Several people in the room bowed their heads in embarrassment or just shook them sadly and slowly from side to side. Others were holding their sides from splitting, somehow able to contain their laughter. A few let it rip.

"What?" Mick questioned innocently, looking all around the room. "Some of my best friends are schmucks."

What Mick got away with was absolutely outrageous. There was no getting around the fact that he was a funny man. Prejudiced or not. Not everyone agreed with the times and places he chose to be a comedian any more than they approved of his maniacal behavior concerning prisoners he questioned in the interrogation room. He could be a most congenial fellow; what would follow might not be to everyone's liking. But Mick knew how to get the job done. He rarely hit or encouraged members of the team to strike a prisoner or even threaten violence. To Mick, a smack or two on the head of a suspect was not the same as hitting. Deception, mistreatment, and other forms of abuse usually proved just as effective as, if not better than, any serious beating. Only once did Mick cross the line and almost kill a man they held in custody. *The Baby Killer* was the name the newspapers had attached to that animal. All antemortem amputations. Mick had broken that case, too. What Mick had wanted to break with his bare hands was the man's neck. It took seven fellow homicide detectives to restrain and pull Mick from the tiny 8 x 8 foot room.

Peter smiled. "May I continue, Mick?"

"Sure. Why not? Go ahead." Conflict was mapping a course along the detective's brow.

"Thank you. As I was about to explain, there is no question that what we found is jute mixed in with the nylon carpet fibers. Question is, why? Why are there no jute fibers found on the Medford girl, yet we find them on the Melville victim, assuming they were killed in Mills' apartment as you guys speculate?"

"You saying they weren't?"

"Shush, Mick," the lieutenant commanded.

"I'm not saying that at all, Mick. I just want to posit a logical explanation here. You going to let me do that?" Peter didn't wait for an answer. "From the amount of blood loss regarding those two bodies, we can assume that the room looks like a slaughterhouse. And if the perp performed the amputations right there on a carpeted floor, regardless of the plastic garbage bags we know were used, cleanup was still going to be a bitch. He obviously tried to contain the bleeding from the head wound of the 1994 Jane Doe/Medford victim. The towel he used certainly indicated that. Same thing with the 1996 Melville woman, Darla. Men's *Fruit Of The Loom* white T-shirt, size 42-44. Looked like it had been dyed red, found around her head.

"A theory we've been batting around is that the blue-gray nylon carpeting was finally ripped up and thrown out. Again, those bodies lost a lot of blood. An awful lot of blood, folks. Whether we're talking about his apartment or someplace else, we believe that both women were killed in the same area. I think the boys and girls from serology are going to have a field day. I don't believe the foam particles came from any carpet padding in case some of you are tossing that around in your minds. I say that because otherwise we'd have to assume that the carpeting was lifted before Jane Doe was murdered; hence, we'd have found jute—if our theory is correct. If I had to speculate at this point, I'd say the foam came from something used to pad an item of furniture. In other words, probably a tattered couch or chair or mattress.

"Now. The orange polyester fibers are interesting in the sense that they're not nearly as worn as the blue nylon fibers, nor do we find any debris. The cat hairs taken from tape-lifts on and around the bodies are consistent with those lifted or vacuumed up in the security trailer. Nothing new on that. Can't really discuss the questioned human or animal hairs until we take exemplars from the two brothers and pussycat. With respect to the types of white powders found on or near all three decedents, along with paint chips, pieces of black and green plastic bags, and saw markings on the bone ends, we have a meeting set up down the hall at ten o'clock. I'll take your questions now."

Mick's hand was high and waving.

"Mick?"

"I hate fuckin' cats. I volunteer to take the exemplars from puss, making sure I get the root."

"Those are not questions," Peter scolded. "Next."

Practically every hand was in the air. Detective John Bailey had two hands going at once.

"Get anywhere with The Dragon Lady out there?" Mick whispered to Frank.

"On the rag," Frank whispered back.

"That's what I thought."

"What are you gonna do after the meetings?"

"Gonna hit a mattress company near where the scumbag lives. You?"

"Gonna shoot 'im the second he steps out of the house to go to work. Save the taxpayers a bundle."

"Really know how to work a lead, don't you?"

"Any more leads, you could put a ring through his nose."

"Hey, I like that."

"Yeah?"

"Yeah."

The two gave each other the high-five. Bailey still had both hands in the air. Questions were being fired at Peter like a Gatling gun. Gail was talking to the two ADAs seated beside her.

"So, maybe I won't shoot 'im. Save him for the interview room. Let you two get acquainted."

Mick nodded his appreciation with a grin. "Soon, Frankie. Soon."

"Can't be soon enough."

"I hear you, good buddy."

Chapter Ten

"Green light," Mick announced excitedly.

"What?"

"Gail just called."

"Jesus Christ." John Bailey kicked back his chair.

"Where's Frank and Vic?"

"Out working a long shot."

"Long shots are over. We're clear to go."

"We got warrants for the house and car?"

"Sort of."

"Sort of? Isn't that like sort of being pregnant?"

"Theo wants us to hold off on them for now," Mick explained.

"I don't get it."

"Gonna wait for our boy to come out of his apartment. Let 'im get a fair distance away so he doesn't alert anyone as we discussed. Then we grab 'im. We get a confession, then we go in with warrants. If we go in with a warrant while he and his brother or one of the other tenants are around, and we come away with nothing, then where are we?"

"Fucked."

"That's why we need to isolate him. Let him tell us what we're going to find and where."

"Then why this business with search warrants? Why did we bother waiting till now? We don't need an arrest warrant either if we're gonna take him off the street. So what's this '*sort of*' shit you're handing me about warrants anyway?"

Mick looked up and down the squad room before leaning over John's desk, taking his partner into his confidence.

"Oh, boy." John saw it coming. "Here we go. What the hell are you gonna lay on me now?"

"Shh. I'm coming to the '*sort of*' part."

"We ain't gonna get no fucking search warrant for the house or his wheels. Right?"

"Gail's got a draft drawn up. Couldn't get a judge to go along just yet."

John Bailey slowly shook his head in sheer frustration, recalling that both his father and his grandfather had wanted him to become a fireman like them. "So we got zip. So what's so hush-hush?"

Mick leaned in even closer, putting his mouth an inch from Bailey's ear. "Anderson and Bokina are going in sometime after we grab him."

John turned his head and eyeballed his partner for a good moment before he spoke. "Going in. You mean a break-in?"

Mick nodded solemnly.

"Didn't I see something like that on television and in the newspapers? I think it was called Watergate."

"Keep your voice down."

"And all the king's men landed behind a stone wall or something."

"You're mixing that up with Humpty Dumpty."

"Oh, that's right. And woke up with egg on their faces in a federal prison."

"Humpty Dumpty was a fairy tale, John."

"Nursery rhyme, Mick. Regardless, Watergate was for real."

"I'm not talking about a bungled burglary at some office building in Washington, D.C. This is a one-room apartment in Hicksville, for cryin' out loud."

"I think it's the *hick* in Hicksville that's clouding your judgment."

"We're not talking forced entry here, John. We're talking

covert."

"We're not talking at all. All I'm doing at this point is listening."

"I thought you were so gung-ho to move on this."

"Yeah, move on Mills, Mick. With the proper paperwork. Not put ourselves into a goddamn slammer."

"Anderson's gonna pick the lock after we pick up Mills. Then he and Bokina are gonna have a look-see."

"With the old lady on the ground floor in the front part of the house?"

"*Old* is the operative word, John. She obviously didn't hear Mills killing those girls."

"We don't even know for sure if he killed them there in his apartment. You as much as said so a moment ago."

"Oh, so maybe you think he bludgeoned and butchered them inside the OTB parlor he frequents?" Mick blasted sarcastically. "Well, Team One's gonna find out for itself, Johnny boy. We've been surveilling the cocksucker night and day."

"Yeah, not even a week."

"Look. We know his routine backwards and forwards, inside and out."

Again, John was shaking his head. "I don't know, Mick. If something goes wrong, we're fucked."

"All right. All right. You make me tell you every fuckin' thing. But not one word to anyone."

"I'm not sure I want to hear this, Micky. You're making me nervous."

"Not to be nervous. Theo's behind us on this one, one hundred and ten percent. There, you made me say it."

John pondered the ceiling. "It's all coming back to me now."

"What is?"

"The things I learned in kindergarten tied in with lessons from working under Theo."

"Say what it is you have to say," Mick snapped impatiently.

"The difference between a nursery rhyme and a fairy tale."

"What about them, booby?"

"'All the king's horses, and all the king's men, couldn't put Humpty Dumpty together again.'"

"We're not talking about Humpty Dumpty, meathead."

"No? What are we talking about then?"

"Team Two," Mick said ceremoniously. "You in or out?"

"Does that mean I don't have to chauffeur you around if I say no?"

"It means that if I have to, I'll put the prisoner in a fuckin' cab by myself."

Deflating right before his partner, Detective John Bailey released the air from his lungs in a single sigh. "Anderson know what he's doing?"

Mick smiled broadly. "Are you shittin' me or what?"

"Whattaya mean?"

"Ever hear about his JD record? Ain't no Mother Goose story, you should know."

"How'd he become a cop?"

"Same as you. Had his record expunged," Mick said with a sly smile.

Several detectives from another squad were passing through the room.

"You pick up Mills yet?" one of them asked abruptly, continuing his march adjacent to the others.

"Waitin' on warrants," Mick half lied.

"Warrants? We'd have busted into that guy's flat by now and had his ass sitting in the interrogation room signing a statement before you guys could change your suits," the man called back without breaking stride.

"Oh, yeah? That's why you numskulls are narcs," Mick called out. "Here, we do everything by the book, pal."

"Right. By the book," John parroted in support of his partner.

The narcotics detective spun smartly around on the soles of his shoes. "You, Mick. They're gonna *throw* the book at you one of these days. Mark my words," the man proclaimed, marching backwards before making an about-face and continuing toward his own squad room situated not sixty feet around the corner from Homicide. "And all those around you, too," he added most solemnly.

"You hear that, Mick? That's an omen," John swore quietly.

"Ain't no fuckin' omen. Come on, now. Don't get spooked on me. You're gonna feel like a million bucks when we get that fucker in the interview room. You'll see."

"Why the hell do you tell me everything? Why didn't you just keep your trap shut and let Anderson do his thing?"

"Because you're my partner," Mick explained. "No secrets between us," he swore, putting an arm around John's shoulder.

John cracked a mindful grin.

"All right?" Mick pressed.

"All right," John agreed.

"Besides which," Mick continued, "if I go down alone, who am I gonna have to play gin rummy with? I don't know from no fuckin' solitaire. Who's gonna teach you that in solitary, pal?" It was a menacing smile that Mick bore, not letting the moment of torment pass for his friend who had just committed to the team—for better or for worse.

"Swell, Mick. Fucking swell."

Chapter Eleven

Team Two was minutes away from an arrest. An arrest that took fourteen months from the time Frank Masselli's Jane Doe was discovered in a trash container along the side of a road in Medford. Fourteen months of intense investigation by scores of detectives from the Suffolk County Homicide Squad. Howard Mills and his brother Jeffrey had been under constant surveillance for the past four days. Howard was now their prime suspect. The game plan was to apprehend Howard away from the house and isolate him at police headquarters in Yaphank, while Jeffrey was at work in Manhattan.

On Holy Saturday, April 6th, 1996, at 1100 hours, Howard came out of the house. A moment later, he was heading south on Willow Lane, riding his bicycle. Detective Connolly alerted the other units to the activity. Howard cut across Grape Lane, making a right onto Petal Lane, pedaling east toward Newbridge Road.

Within seconds, two unmarked cars traveling in opposite directions along Brittle Lane came up on Howard Mills as he made the turn. One vehicle suddenly shot directly behind the suspect. Detective Bailey braked abruptly in front of him and Connolly jumped out.

Howard had almost lost control of the bike but managed to stop without going head over handlebars. Mick straddled the front wheel of the old Schwinn, clamping Howard's hands firmly to the rusty chrome bar while Bailey fumbled in excitement for his cuffs, wresting the man's arms in back of him, snapping on the bracelets.

"In case you're wondering, Howard, I'm the Easter bunny. A day early, but I'm here for you, son," Detective Michael Connolly assured the man.

Detectives Vic Posteraro and Frank Masselli were at Howard's back. Connolly pulled his prisoner roughly off the bike, letting it fall to the ground.

Vic and Frank immediately put the arrestee into the back seat of Connolly's squad car.

Howard looked around dumbfounded.

Chapter Twelve

That evening, Detectives Troy Anderson and Eric Bokina crouched low and moved along the rear fence line of 42 Willow Lane. The night was as dark as black boot polish. The two men followed along the edge of the large backyard. A neighbor's light came on above them then immediately went out. The pair continued cautiously, nearing the corner of the house. Eric Bokina suddenly bumped into something in their path. A bicycle. It was Howard's bike that Vic had brought back to the home earlier that day. The same bike that Detective Michael Connolly had stopped in its tracks moments before placing the suspect under arrest.

The detectives sidestepped the obstacle, inching their way along the rear wall of the two-story structure before reaching the back door.

Eric stood with his back to the entrance while Troy studied the lock with a penlight cupped within his gloved hands. A thin ray of blue light cast the keyhole in an eerie hue.

"What do you think?" Eric whispered.

"Tell you in a second." Troy cut the light and went to work on the top lock with a single tapered steel strip.

"When's the last time you did this?"

Troy pocketed the strip and withdrew another. "High school."

It wasn't sixty seconds after selecting a narrower gauge band that the deadbolt retreated with the sound of a dull click.

"I don't believe it!" Eric said excitedly. "We in?"

"One more." The man lifted the back of his trench coat and went into the right rear pant pocket for his wallet. He withdrew a plastic credit card and inserted it between the door and its frame. The second lock slid back easily. "Now we're in," Troy said smugly, turning the doorknob quietly and stepping inside. "Haven't lost the touch."

"I can see that," Eric said, rather impressed, the detective's right hand on the handle of his holstered weapon as he followed his partner. "I'm just glad there are no alarms. Silent or otherwise."

"Like I said before. Silent we'd know about. Vic had checked for tape and wiring as best he could when he brought the bike back earlier. Didn't think we'd have a problem."

"Problem is he almost killed me where he stuck that damn bike," Eric exaggerated, carefully closing the door behind himself.

"Okay, let's see what we got here. Ready to go to work?"

"Yep." The man raised his fingers and wiggled them into a pair of latex gloves. "Need one of those lights like you got, though."

"Here you go," Troy said, taking another from his pocket. "Keep it low. And keep it pale-blue. Twist the head clockwise, and the neighbors behind us will probably call the cops because clockwise will give you a bright white light. Counterclockwise, to the left, will give you more of a blue hue. *Off* is in the middle where it is now. Try it. Keep it low."

Eric twisted the head of the penlight to the left. A dim beam of blue light narrowed while intensifying in color on the wood floor.

"Okay, hold it there. Don't want to go too bright. Good that the blinds are drawn. Can you see all right like that?"

"Fine."

Troy pulled a copy of a sketch from his pocket. "According to one of Mick's witnesses, Howard's bed should be over there against that wall . . . box spring and mattress on the floor. Here we go. Why don't you start with the sofa bed, which . . . should be near the other wall . . . there," he whispered, illuminating the base of the couch with the beam of soft blue light.

"Right."

Eric crawled over to the suspect's nest, tracing the outline of the twin-sized fabric frame with a beam of blue light. At first he thought it might have been a waterbed, but setting his hand firmly upon the mattress proved otherwise. He felt somewhat strange kneeling there in that dark single-room apartment. It wasn't the fact that he was an intruder or that they were breaking the law; it was a queer feeling that he just couldn't quite nail down.

"Troy."

Troy turned around. "Got something?"

"Aren't these lights also supposed to make blood appear another color or something?"

"Not these. But the lab boys have fluorescents they bring in. Shows up the color of blood as purple. Never used them. Why?"

"I think I'm looking at bloodstains here. Wait a second." Eric raised his light a fraction. "Jesus Christ, Troy. I think I found the source of the foam." Eric ran his light back and forth along the front panel of a black sofa bed. The dark material was badly torn, a section hanging loosely. Large sections of foam padding were visible beneath the fabric. Broken up particles of the stuff were strewn across the bare wood floor.

Troy crawled over and picked up a piece the size of a pea, pinching it flush between a latex-covered thumb and forefinger, relaxing the hold, feeling the spongy rubbery foam forming itself back into shape. "Hold this." Troy put the piece into Eric's hand. "Kneel lower and cup your hands." Troy moved closer to his partner and placed a hand over Eric's pair, forming a globe—the two men seemingly embodied in some sort of secret, sacred pact. With the thumb and forefinger of Troy's free hand, he adjusted the head of the penlight clockwise until its beam went from blue to *off* to a focused pure white light that revealed the true color of the piece of evidence in hand.

"Yellow foam rubber," Eric declared, peering down into their unearthly sphere. "It's a start." He deposited the piece along with several others into a small Manila envelope taken from his coat pocket.

"Where do you think you saw blood, partner?" Troy asked, closing his light and trying to remain calm.

"I think we're kneeling on the spot," Eric answered, passing the blue beam along the floor. "Move back a foot."

The two of them drew back.

"Right there." Eric bathed the stains in blue. "Could be bloodstains. Right?"

"Tell you what," Troy said excitedly.

"What?"

"Let's work together as a team."

"Team Two, brother."

"I'll work the white light. You do the blue. Form a cup with your hands. We'll cover the floor along the sofa bed and work our way around."

"Gotcha."

"Let's see what we have here."

Eric cupped his hands over the stain in a half-moon manner, and Troy turned on the light, illuminating the spot. A rust-red starburst blot, roughly the size and shape and color of a copper penny, loomed up at them, highlighted in the softened beam.

"Sure as hell could be blood," Troy acknowledged, turning off the light again and reaching inside a jacket pocket for a kit, its dimensions consistent with a box of wooden kitchen matches.

"Whattaya got there?" Eric questioned, directing the light.

"Q-Tips and a vial of Luminal."

"Really?"

"Mick's got a forensic buddy standing by so we don't involve the lab just yet."

From a vial, Troy lightly dampened the head of a cotton swab with the chemical then ran its tip through the stain. The two detectives watched the tip of the white swab turn blue. "We got blood, partner. We'll have Mick hand this over to his forensics guy for confirmation."

Eric nodded excitedly.

The two men worked together on their hands and knees for the better part of an hour, taking notes but no further blood samples so as not to contaminate the scene. They moved around the room in a clockwise fashion. Eric pointed to the remnants of what appeared to be a light blue-gray floor covering tucked beneath sections of molding where wall-to-wall carpeting had been crudely cut and removed. He dug out a small chunk of the material with his penknife and put it into another tiny envelope. Troy called Eric's attention to the stains along the baseboard heating.

Keeping to the lower quarter of the room, the duo observed what they believed to be additional bloodstains on the balusters supporting a green-legged table and chair; the base of a dresser; a metal clothes closet and cabinet; box spring and mattress; cotton sheets; wood paneling and floor—then back to where they began at the tattered sofa bed. For the time being, the detectives had gathered enough evidence and scribbled sufficient information to convince themselves that they were, indeed, dealing with either the killer of prostitutes, whose lair they believed they had entered, or a person who merely decided to use his own apartment as a slaughterhouse to butcher a side of beef.

The two were getting up off their hands and knees when they heard something.

Eric immediately had his Glock out, its muzzle pointed toward the ceiling.

Troy fanned a portion of the room with his revolver, the latex-gloved fingers of his left hand gripping his right wrist for balance and support.

"What the hell was that?"

"Shh."

Suddenly, there came a strange sound above them. Running in one direction. No, circular. It didn't stop. Around and around the overhead the sound traveled. Eric followed it with the business end of his weapon until he was dizzy. Troy put away his weapon and laughed quietly.

"The other brother's cat."

"Cat? Sounds like a plane circling."

Just as suddenly as the commotion had started, it suddenly stopped.

The two steadied their nerves and became giddy with excitement.

"I'd say we have probable cause," Eric ruled, holstering his piece.

"I say we had that before we ever broke in."

"I'd say we have every right to be here."

"I wish we could sell that notion to a judge."

"We'd have search warrants for this fucking house."

"In our hot little hands."

"And another warrant for the car."

"Instead of a lot of worry."

"And Gail would have a Grand Jury warrant for Howard Mills' *official* arrest in a heartbeat."

"I'd say we did good."

"Better than good, partner."

"But we still need that confession."

"I'd say you're absolutely right."

"So, it's not a perfect world."

"I say we beat feet."

"Got everything?"

"Good to go."

Troy and Eric stepped out into the chilly April air and closed the door behind them. The bottom lock clicked into place. Troy then withdrew the tool from his pocket, returning to the top lock and securing it for good measure.

"What more proof could anyone want in there?" Eric bleated.

"Positive proof of hopefully human blood," Troy answered up, deeply inhaling the cool night air.

"At least we're giving Mick and his standby guy something to work with."

"Let's pray that we're giving them gold."

Chapter Thirteen

Warren and Harding, Suffolk County homicide detectives from Team One, sat at a small folding table a foot away from where their suspect stood in the 8 x 8 foot interrogation room at police headquarters in Yaphank. Just outside and above the door to the space hung a large plaque scribed in Old English letters that read, 𝕿𝖍𝖔𝖚 𝕾𝖍𝖆𝖑𝖙 𝕹𝖔𝖙 𝕶𝖎𝖑𝖑.

Howard Mills was completely naked, both legs fettered to a three-foot length of chain running through a steel ring held in place by a metal plate bolted to the floor. Attached to the other end of the chain was a set of manacles that Howard wore behind his back. Warren and Harding, nicknamed The Presidents, got up from their seats and stepped over to the prisoner. Team Two would be working the first block of questioning shortly. Detective Michael Connolly would be running the show. But in the meantime, Warren and Harding were handling the preliminaries. Warren stepped back from their suspect. Harding circled Howard like the figure zero. Howard was scared. Soon he would be terrified.

Warren read from a Rights Card. Harding pushed two of three chairs beneath the table then unshackled Howard's hands. Warren withdrew a pen from his shirt pocket and told the prisoner to initial the card. Howard hesitated. Harding swooped up one of the chairs and went after him, but Warren put his bulk between the two.

"He'll initial it," Warren assured his partner. "Right, Howie?"

Howard was trembling and quickly nodded his head.

"Atta boy," the detective said calmly.

Except for the doorway, there was no apparent opening in the cube-like chamber. No visible window. No rear exit. No trap door nor any avenue of escape had Houdini himself been in the room and contemplated such a feat.

A baldheaded detective standing in the hallway on the other side of the room peered in through a one-way aperture.

Howard was initialing the card. The prisoner was cooperating. A moment later, Harding snapped the manacles back in place, telling Howard that he didn't like his handwriting. The shackled suspect was told to stand quietly, not to sit or lie down but to stand there until someone else arrived.

There was no clock on the wall or anywhere in the room. Howard had no idea how long he had been standing, still naked, cuffed and shackled to the floor. He had worked the night shift, putting in a few hours overtime before returning home to his apartment. He had not slept, deciding to ride his bicycle to the bagel shop for coffee just before the cops closed in on him. He had known that they were onto him. An article that had appeared in *The New York Post* following Darla's death stated that the police were looking for a middle-aged white male seen driving a blue Cadillac. Darla was last seen getting into his car before calling out to her girlfriend that she was going to a motel and that she'd be back in an hour.

"Yeah, right," her friend had said.

And it *was* the last time she had seen Darla.

Yes. It must have been that bitch friend of hers, Howard thought. She seemed so spacey on the street. Oblivious. *Why did Darla have to jump into the car at that moment?* he stewed. He had been cruising up and down the strip when Darla spotted him. Popped out of a doorway, and before he knew it, she was inside the car. He wanted to catch Darla alone. They'd been together some fifty times, and not *once* had she been seen getting into his car, he was sure.

The two would smoke marijuana on the way to his apartment in Hicksville. They'd do crack cocaine in his room. Of all the nights Beth had to come over. He tried to keep Darla out of her claws. He really did. But he also knew that their meeting was inevitable. Beth was becoming more and more insistent. More angry as time went by. Why did he ever tell her about Darla? Why didn't he just keep her for himself? Sex was certainly not the issue with any of the girls he'd brought home. He'd merely cuddle up with them. Fondle them. Once in a blue moon, Darla would perform oral sex. She was special. He liked her a lot. Or at least he thought he did. The simple truth was that he was a very, very lonely man, and Darla seemed to enjoy his company.

Howard loved the moments he shared with prostitutes. In fact, he felt much like one himself. Hadn't he prostituted himself for more than twenty years as a mail handler for the post office? Hadn't he kissed his bosses' asses all along the line? He knew that he was so much smarter than them. Smarter than most of his fellow employees, too. And they knew it. Some resented him when he was made shop steward; he was strict, but more than fair. He knew that many considered him cheap. That bothered him a lot. If they only knew the money he threw around on drugs and women. At one point, Howard had kept copious records of all his women in a little black book he carried. How much they charged. Their street names. A brief description. How much he paid for drugs, and so forth. No longer. One time, he even showed the book to Jeff. The one book he did not show anyone was his bankbook. Actually, Howard had several bank accounts—with a balance that would turn all of them green with envy. Those were the only monies authorities would soon discover, he believed. Liquid and long-term. He had also made wise investments. Other assets were hidden in another hemisphere.

"Cheap Jew, that Howard," one of his fellow employees had once commented when Howard's back was turned, unaware of his presence.

"Yeah, just like his asshole brother, Jeffrey," another employee remarked. "I hear the two of them eat canned goods and compete for the lowest utility bill," the other added, dropping a pair of canvas mailbags onto a tailgate.

Just what Howard would like to do to the two of them. Drop the pair onto a tailgate and can them for good, he had contemplated.

But Howard was nonconfrontational, unlike Beth who was combatant. Beth would have pulverized them on the spot. Beth, his blind half sister, would have sent them to their Maker.

Howard wished he could muster but a thimbleful of the strength, confidence and courage that Beth bore and wore like a badge. But the fact remained that he was and probably always would be a coward.

Howard the coward. He wondered if he truly would have had the nerve to pull the trigger had a cop ever pulled him over in the Cadillac with a body in the trunk as Beth had made him promise he would do. Now, he would never know. For they had nabbed him pedaling his silly-ass bike. How apropos, he shivered, stripped naked and standing there in his silent shackled state. Had it been Beth, she would have, in a blind rage, wrapped the handlebars around the detective's ears and driven him into the ground. Surely, she would have.

Howard was still standing when Detectives Connolly and Bailey stepped into the room.

"What the fuck is this?" Michael Connolly blared, turning around to his partner then back to Howard Mills.

Bailey shrugged. "Don't know, Mick."

The lead detective ran the fingers of his right hand through his thinning light brown hair. "Get those bracelets off of him."

"Gotta go drum up the keys," Bailey said.

"And come back with his fuckin' clothes."

Bailey left the room and closed the door behind him.

"How long you been standing there?"

Howard stood there staring off into space.

"Sit down," the homicide detective said.

It was more of an invitation than an order, and Howard sank clumsily to the floor.

The detective pulled a chair away from the wall and straddled the seat backwards, similar to the way he bestrode the front wheel of Howard's bicycle at the time of the arrest.

"Smoke?" the detective asked, tapping the front of his shirt pocket against a fresh pack.

Howard shook his head.

"Probably a good thing. We light up together in here, we'd probably both asphyxiate," he affirmed. "So listen. We'll get you out of that jailhouse jewelry and your clothes back on. Then we'll have a little talk. Okay?"

Howard shook his head.

"What? You wanna keep that jewelry on? Hang around in your birthday suit? Need some more time alone to think?"

Howard shook his head again. He was crying.

"I think you're the kind of man who can think better standing on your feet. Get up."

"I want to make a phone call," Howard whined.

"All lines are busy now. I'll let you know when one becomes available. Stand up!" Connolly ordered.

"I want to call a lawyer," Howard bawled loudly.

"A lawyer?" the lead detective questioned and laughed.

"I have rights," his prisoner insisted.

"But Detectives Warren and Harding told someone that you waived them away in here."

"One of them was going to hit me with a chair," Howard tried to explain.

"I told you to get up," the cop barked. "I'm not gonna tell you again."

"I am an American citizen. I pay my taxes. I have a right to make one phone call. I have the right to an attorney," Howard Mills declared, struggling to his feet.

"Funny," Connolly said coolly. "And I thought you were a serial killer. By the way, your taxes are due this month. I wonder if you'll be free to file them. But I'm sure you could ask for an extension. Anyhow, as far as your rights are concerned, you lost them when you entered this room. Remember? You waived them all away." Mick smiled, tapping the front of his shirt pocket before removing the initialed Rights Card from behind the pack of cigarettes, waving the little document defiantly through the air as he exited the room, closing the door behind him with a clang of finality.

Chapter Fourteen

"How much longer you gonna let him sweat, Mick?" John Bailey asked his partner.

"Look," Connolly said. "He went from begging us to kill him on the ride out here to hollering for a fucking lawyer. Personally, I liked him better when he was pleading with us to put a bullet in his brain."

"Once again, how much longer you gonna let him stew?" John repeated.

Mick smiled. "Well, laddie. 'Tis like me Scottish-Irish mother use' to say when I was just a tyke standin' thar in her kitchen. 'Till the meat falls off the bones if it's to be a good stew worth servin', Micky, me sweet lad.'"

"He's been in the pot for a good many hours now," John reminded Mick, "after being up half the night working. Besides, your mother was Puerto Rican and cooked everything in lard you told me when I came aboard," he cited the storyteller.

"That a fact? Well, that was 'fore me father took her under wing and taught her the proper tongue and the more civilized way of preparin' meat," Mick insisted.

"Your father never cooked a day in his life and ate whatever she put in front of him. You forget the stories you tell—you've got so damn many of them."

"That a fact?"

"Yep."

"Well, let me tell you something, Mr. Recall," Mick declared, giving up the brogue. "You start remembering those case files like you remember my upbringing, and you just might make First Grade. *Verstehen*?"

John clicked his heels together, gave a Nazi salute, and smartly did an about-face, heading toward his desk.

Detective Posteraro came up behind Mick.

Mick looked up. "What say, Vic?"

Victor Posteraro stood six-foot three. "Mick."

"What's up?"

"Lieutenant wants to know just that."

"Is this a fuckin' conspiracy, or what?" Mick demanded. "Tell me it's not, college boy."

"You've had him in there for hours."

"Don't you guys know anything about stew?"

Vic smiled and shook his head. "What do you want me to tell Theo?"

"That a stew pot's gotta simmer."

"I think he thinks the stew's ready."

"You do?"

Vic nodded.

Mick thought for a moment. "All right. Tell him we're going back in. JOHN!"

Detective John Bailey did another about-face and looked back across the squad room.

"We're going in," Michael Connolly ordered.

"Glad we had that little chat, Mick, and that you're finally coming to your senses," Bailey rejoiced, shooting a glance at Vic. "See, Mick does listen to me from time to time."

"You fuckin' guys. All of you. You don't know how to let things sit," Mick went off. "Meat's got to sit in its own juice. Mr. Mills has got to—ah, what's the use of talking anymore. Let's see if he's ready to do just that. Ready, John?"

It was an inane question. John as well as everyone on the team had been ready for many, many months, dating back to John's Jane Doe/Medford case from December 1994. John was on Mick's heels. The pair headed for the interrogation room. The claustrophobic concrete cage. Other members of Teams One and Two were champing at the bit. They all wanted a piece of Howard W. Mills.

Chapter Fifteen

The prisoner's feet and hands were still shackled; however, he was fully clothed and seated at the table along a wall. Bailey sat across from him, prepared to take notes. Mick Connolly stuck an 8 x 10 colored glossy of his Melville victim's dismembered naked body beneath Howard Mills' nose.

"Full name," Connolly commanded in a firm tone.

"Howard Willis Mills," Howard responded immediately, shifting nervously in his seat.

The two detectives looked at one another. Bailey cracked a smile. Connolly cracked his knuckles atop the suspect's head.

"Not *your* name, stupid," the lead detective whispered. "HER NAME, ASSHOLE!" he bellowed, shaking the photograph before Howard like a windblown leaf caught in a violent storm.

"Darla," the prisoner trembled, his bleary eyes jumping from the picture to the angry eyes of his keeper.

"Darla, what?"

"I don't know, honest. Wait. Like Vasso or something. I only heard it once. I didn't pay attention. They don't use real names."

"Who doesn't?"

"The prostitutes. They're all street names. Darla's first name is the only one I know for sure," he swore, staring back down at the mutilated postmortem figure, depicting his handiwork, wishing to God he had cut out her tattoo at the time he took her hands.

Connolly spoke, but Howard did not hear him. Their prisoner viewed the familiar tattoo with its bantam red heart and Cupid's arrow piercing the indelible design on the victim's upper right arm—the name Darla printed in the banner beneath it. Howard's own heart was pounding furiously, wishing he could pass an arrow through it in the very next second. Instead, it was a blow to the side of the head he received, knocking him clear off his seat.

"I asked you what you used to kill her, Howard."

"I didn't kill anyone. I swear to God."

"Where did you pick her up?" Connolly continued, trying a different tact.

"Queens Boulevard."

"Where on Queens Boulevard?"

"Around 212th Street."

"Get up."

Howard struggled to lift himself off the floor. His hands secured in back of him. His feet fighting with the links of half-inch chain. Finally, he stood.

"Sit back down in that chair."

Howard sat.

"What'd you do after you picked her up?"

"Smoked marijuana."

"Where?"

"In the car."

"Where'd you go after that?"

"Back to my place."

"Hicksville?"

Howard nodded. "We'd always go back to my place. We'd feel safer that way."

"You'd always go back to your place?"

"Yes, sir. With Darla."

"How many times were you with Darla at your place?"

"Around fifty."

"Fifty?"

"Yes, sir."

"And what did you do there?"

"Drugs."

"More drugs?"

Howard nodded.

"Was that a yes?"

"Yes."

"Have sex with her?"

"It wasn't like that."

"No?"

"No."

"You never had sex with her?"

"Sometimes."

"Fifty times?"

"Oral sex, once or twice."

"You've been with this girl fifty times and she gave you a blow job once or twice?"

Howard didn't answer.

"You have intercourse with her?"

Howard shook his head.

"How much she charge you?"

"Fifty."

Connolly shook his head slowly. "So what did you do with this girl if you didn't fuck her and she only gave you head once or twice?"

"I told you. We'd do drugs."

"Where?"

"On the bed."

"With your clothes on?"

"We'd be naked."

Detective Connolly slapped Howard on the knee as though he were a member of the good ol' boy's club. "Ah, I knew you had it in you, Howard. So, tell us. How did this business come about? Hum?" He flagged the photo in front of Howard's face. "Finally figure out that twenty-five hundred dollars for two pecks on your pecker was a ripoff, Howie? Not to mention what you shelled out for drugs and gas."

"I told you. I didn't kill anyone."

The two seasoned detectives stared skeptically at one another. Connolly gradually returned his attention back to Mills. Bailey looked down at his notes.

"So, did you take her back to Queens that night or in the morning?" Connolly inquired.

Howard sat there as still as a statue, as though he had suddenly turned to stone. There was no fidgeting. No shifting around in his seat.

"Or did you drive her out to Melville and put her in a

Dumpster?"

Howard Mills didn't move a muscle. Didn't blink an eye.

"Let me lay it out for you, Howie. Let me tell you what we've got." Connolly pulled out a chair and sat. The detective enumerated on his fingers. "Human hair. Fibers. Blood. Tissue. Animal hair. And that's for openers. You told us in the car on the way out here that Jeffrey has a cat. Forensic boys and girls are going through your apartment as we speak," he lied. "Tell me what else they're going to find. Are they going to have a fucking field day, Howie? So. Once again. Did you drive Darla out to Melville and put her body in the Dumpster?"

"I want to see a lawyer," the prisoner cringed as though another blow would be forthcoming, as if in a nanosecond he would be sailing off his seat again.

Detective Michael Connolly merely shook his head

"Please," the mail handler begged and began to sob anew.

"Oh! By the way. Let me tell you what else we've got. The trunk. The trunk of your vehicle. 1986 Cadillac, Coupe de Ville. Actually, registered to Jeffrey. You see—"

"The car belongs to me, not Jeffrey," Howard interrupted.

Connolly felt that he had struck a nerve but continued the dialogue, keeping in mind to work Jeffrey into the colloquy. "Anyhow, we set up surveillance by the train station along West Marie Street. Jeffrey left the Caddy there and went to work in Manhattan. Boys from the canine unit brought in a cadaver dog. Those dogs can pick up the scent of shit off roof shingles of a high-rise and find their way to the fucking top, God bless them," the cop continued with a smile. "Guess how the pooch we brought in reacted to the trunk of the car."

Howard Mills sat staring Mick Connolly dead in the eyes. It was a pleading sort of stare, paradoxically mixed with a modicum of defiance. Somehow Howard was mustering that thimbleful of strength, confidence and courage. Certainly not a wellspring of daring derived from Beth's wrath, which he had witnessed through the years. But the resolve was real. Personal. And his.

"Leave my brother out of this," Howard warned.

"Then, for a third time. Did you drive Darla out to Melville? Not as any sort of seated passenger, but rather prostrate in your trunk."

Mills said nothing, ready for the unexpected, expecting to be beat about the head for starters. How he wished Beth could be by his side. He wondered if he'd ever see her again. He wondered if she really and truly knew how much he loved her. She would when this was over.

He'd protect her. And he'd protect his young brother, Jeffrey, too.

"All right. You're on your bed doing drugs and whatever else you do. You're both high as a kite. Jeffrey comes down and does her. Where do we go from there?"

"Jeffrey doesn't do drugs or anybody. He's not like me. He minds his own business. Goes to work every day."

"Jeffrey's in a room down the hall from us," Connolly fibbed. "We haven't spoken to him yet. But what do you think he's going to tell us when we ask him these same questions?"

Howard looked toward the door, wondering where down the hall Jeffrey might be.

"Think you two got your stories straight?" Connolly probed. "Or do you think he'll spook? Know what my guess would be?"

"Jeffrey will tell the truth," Howard offered emphatically.

"So why can't we hear it from you?"

Howard was still staring at the door.

"Look. Let's talk openly and honestly about these girls. They're prostitutes. Right? They make their living on the street. Correct? They rip their johns off. We know Darla sure as hell ripped you off. You sure as hell just told us that. Fifty dollars times fifty tricks. Only *her* trick was a drug trip to the corner with more of your money. Yes? How many times did you hand those girls money for a buy, and they never returned? Huh? Maybe not Darla. Seems the two of you had a good rapport."

"That's right. So why would I kill her?"

"Well, I've been thinking a lot about that, Howie. And I'll tell you what I come up with. A bad batch of some shit that made you crazy. You went into a rage. And you killed her. Didn't mean to. But you did. Couldn't very well carry her out to the car without someone seeing you, and you didn't want her ID'd if she was ever found, so you cut off her hands and put her into a sleeping bag, waited till it was dark, then drove out to Melville and stuck her in a Dumpster."

"I told you in the car. I haven't seen Darla in over six months," Howard declared, holding back a yawn.

"And I have an eyewitness who last saw Darla getting into your car in Jamaica four months ago. *Last* is the operative word, Howard, because she hadn't been seen until the discovery of her body. Got another witness who's been to one of your soirees. That was her word. A Haitian girl using that expression for one of your S and M get-togethers. Tells me you were snorting a line of coke off her naked backside that you'd beaten black-and-blue with a hairbrush. Not that she didn't let you, mind you. She told me she was into that sort of thing and got your engine goin' good. Described your apartment, its contents, and work area where the handyman, Mr. Hammond, keeps his tools. How am I doing, Howie? We know more about you than you probably know about yourself. Wanna challenge that? Want me to head into a conversation I had with your psychiatrist in Texas? How about the shrink from Hempstead Hospital?"

Howard's eyes were ablaze.

"What's the matter, Howie? You don't believe all that privileged communication bullshit between a doctor and his patient, do you?" Connolly shook his head disgustedly. "More of your hard earned money down the drain. But let's get back to the prostitutes," Connolly expounded, continuing the dialogue with the first of the team's psychological themes. "They get people hooked on drugs. They spread diseases. In the long run, they, too, kill people. Tit for tat? I suppose Darla wasn't the one meant to die. If you told me that right now, I'd believe you. But you and I both know that there were others, Howie. We have a Jane Doe found in Medford. Found in a garbage pail along the side of a road. Got a similar case concerning a young woman who turned up at a recycling plant in Brooklyn. Paperwork found around her body tells us that she came from an area here on Long Island. Found some postal forms among those papers, too.

"Now, are you going to continue to sit there and tell me that this is all coincidence? Or should we move into the area of trace evidence, adding to a growing list of fibers and hair and other items I mentioned before? Like plastic from the bags you wrapped the victims in before you sawed through them, Howie. I could go on and on. They're taking apart your apartment as we speak," he lied again.

Howard said nothing.

"So. Where did we leave off? The two of you were on your bed doing drugs. But there's a big gap between your bed in Hicksville and that Dumpster in Melville. Care to build a bridge?"

Howard Mills stared at the ceiling. Little by little, he lowered his eyes to the floor. "I blanked out," he said.

"Did what?"

"I blanked out," Howard repeated.

Detective Bailey raised his eyes up from his notes.

Detective Connolly furrowed his brow. "You blanked out?"

Howard nodded. "It's like you said. We're doing drugs.

92

Watching TV from the bed. Last thing I remember."

"Where was Darla when you woke up?"

"On the floor."

"On the floor where?"

"Next to the bed." Howard took in the stark white concrete walls surrounding him. "She's covered with blood."

"She dead?"

"Just lying there."

"Lying there dead," Connolly said, moving Howard along with his confession. "What did you hit her with?"

Howard looked at the detective vacantly. "I never hurt anybody. I swear to God. I'm being framed. I can't explain it."

"You killed Darla, and you cut her up," Connolly stated in an exasperated tone. "You didn't mean to, but you did. Then you put her body in the trunk."

Howard was shaking his head. "My life is over. I'll lose my job. I've been with the post office for twenty years. I tried to commit suicide since I was thirteen. Just take a gun and shoot me. Please. Let me die." Howard was on the verge of tears again. He was exhausted. Thirsty. Hungry. He had to go to the bathroom.

"Look at me, Howard," Connolly said with feigned compassion that a seasoned drama coach would have had trouble detecting. "You're not a child. You're a man." The detective placed a hand on the man's shoulder. Howard flinched. "Just relax and listen very carefully to me, Howard," the cop continued in a calming manner. "I want you to get this business off your chest. I want to help you lift this heavy weight off your shoulders," he went on, gently squeezing Mills' shoulder. Howard stiffened. Connolly put his round-featured cherub-like face an inch away from Howard's, rocking the captured shoulder with the gentleness of a mother lulling her infant in a cradle. "Tell us the truth, and it will feel like my removing these heavy chains from your body," Detective Connolly vowed, withdrawing a key from his sports jacket and standing Howard up, unlocking and removing the fetters from the prisoner's ankles, the manacles from his wrists. "Sit down."

The scene was drawing to a close. Detective Michael Connolly had been handed the distinct honor of coming onto center stage for the opening matinee. It was a fine performance, given the point in time: Act I, Scene 2; the real McCoy, cop as well as father confessor, segueing consummately from the Prostitute Theme to the team's Heavy-Duty Burden Theme. But not every captive was an audience easily taken in.

And Howard Mills proved no exception.

"I couldn't kill anyone," Howard stated and sniffled, sitting back down and shifting his teary eyes to the note taker seated at the table.

Detective Bailey was busy roughing out the script. It reflected very little of the lies they believed that Mills had told till then, editing the big and small ones that the lead detective was setting forth.

Connolly set the stainless steel hardware on the table and settled back in his chair. "I can help you with that lawyer you want," he offered calmly. "Not just any lawyer, but a lawyer who can save you from your fate. Get you into a hospital where they can help you."

Howard had all to do to hold back the smile that was forming on his face. Now, it was *help* the detective wanted to offer in exchange for his confession. Didn't they know by now that he really and truly wanted to die? Hadn't they seen the stab marks on his chest above his heart when the first two detectives made him take off all his clothes then photographed him? Hadn't they observed the slashes on his wrists? And if the police really had conversations with his doctors in Texas and here in New York, surely the detectives knew that he had tried to take his life since he was thirteen: sitting with the car running in the closed garage; ingesting handfuls of pills; self-inflicted wounds. He even tried to cut his own hands off the evening after he had put Darla in the Dumpster. But he knew he could never kill anyone. Not even himself. That was the irony of it. Killing took courage. Beth would commit murder in a heartbeat. Beth lived for the moment.

"You cut her up, Howard," Connolly pushed.

It took a good moment for Howard to carefully think things through. He gave the detective a questionable nod of the head.

"Yes?" the cop exhorted.

"Yes," Howard answered with another nod.

Detective Connolly nodded, too—somewhat satisfactorily.

Bailey raised his pen then lowered his head.

"Put her in the trunk of your car and disposed of her body in a Dumpster in Melville?"

"Yes," Howard Mills said flatly.

"Hit her with a hammer on your bed?" Connolly coaxed.

"Not even with a hairbrush," the postal employee said solemnly.

"How about a bat?" the cop pressed unrelentingly.

"I have to go to the bathroom, bad," Howard swore.

Detective Michael Connolly rose and declared an intermission.

Down the corridor from the interrogation room, Mick Connolly spoke with his lieutenant.

"He's on the verge of confessing," Mick assured the man. "But we may have to bring Gary in later."

"What do you have, Mick?" Theo questioned.

"Got Darla in his room, dismembered, in the trunk of the car out to Melville, and into the Dumpster."

"But can't remember killing her, huh?" the lieutenant said with a sour grin.

"Blanked out."

"*Blanked* out?"

"Yeah, that's a new one. Kind of creative, don't you think?"

"Probably shooting blanks," the lieutenant quipped and laughed.

"Don't laugh. He gets off on cuttin' 'em up. Can't say he fucks 'em and leaves 'em. Lays them out with drugs and liquor then clobbers them, me thinks."

"So the semen they found in the Brooklyn girl probably wouldn't match Mills' anyway?"

"He's not a lover boy. Still a shame it came back degraded."

The lieutenant shook his head in disappointment. "I need that confession and fast, Mick. Can't move officially on that house or car until we get it. We don't have a hell of a lot of time left before the younger brother becomes suspicious and steps into the picture."

"We could pick him up in Manhattan and detain him."

"Yes, but there's that other brother out there. Ronald. If the family's somehow alerted and they get a lawyer out here, we're dead. You saw the records referencing those bank accounts of Howard's. Man can buy talent. That's why I had to move you along on this."

"I got the picture, Theo. But you know I like to work with zombies on the nod," he needn't have explained.

"He's been up a long time, Mick?"

Mick nodded. "I got 'im nappin' on the floor. He crawled under the fuckin' table."

"Napping?"

"Catnap. Fifteen minutes. A nice jolt to the body when Vic and Frank go in."

"Need that statement, Mick," the lieutenant said again.

"We'll get it. John's putting together a first draft now. You got a judge standing by?"

"Hefferman."

"He's good."

"He can only do so much, Micky."

Whenever the lieutenant called him Micky, he knew that Theo was practically out of rope. The lieutenant would owe him one. The top gun wouldn't forget. The man was truly a prince. Pull this one off, and it was the same as having a promotion in the bag. Mick also knew that when the smoke cleared, they'd all be rewarded, for Howard Mills was going down. They'd need those three homicides in order for the prosecution to seek the death penalty. Two counts would mean life in prison without the possibility of parole if convicted. Three murders within a twenty-four month period would mean they had a serial killer on their hands in Suffolk County, other jurisdictions notwithstanding. Death penalty qualified. The heat was coming from the district attorney's office. District Attorney Patterson wanted blood. Howard's.

The lid was supposedly on securely concerning two additional Westchester murders, but somehow information was being leaked to the press. Mick knew that some of those disclosures were intentional and had originated from Theo's own office. Mick loved the intrigue. The politics. The homicide detective secretly hoped that one day he might be the puppeteer pulling all those strings.

Chapter Sixteen

The military clock on the wall marked time quietly as the second hand swept its face. The next pair of detectives from Team Two marched down the hallway and entered the interrogation room. Howard Mills was lying under the table when Victor Posteraro and Frank Masselli each pulled up a chair and took a seat. Howard Mills immediately woke up, wiping the sleep from his eyes. He was directed to take a seat.

"Little nap?" Detective Posteraro questioned with a bright smile.

Howard studied the pair, the two who had put him into the back seat of the sedan when Detective Connolly made the arrest.

Victor Posteraro was very tall, young, and good-looking. Gentlemanlike. Nothing what Howard imagined a homicide detective to look like. He wondered if the man thought that *he*, Howard W. Mills, looked like a murderer. A stoneface killer. Ted Bundy didn't look like a killer. Clean-cut and smooth-shaven was he. When Howard shaved, pockmarked from smallpox at an early age, he felt as if he were running a razor across the surface of the moon. *Craterface*, his schoolmates would call him. Post puberty left him with a countenance that his college classmates commonly described as features hewn from a hardwood board, compliments of a hatchet. His rough complexion exaggerated a kind of deprecating defiance, exacerbated by a deliberate

97

craning of the head and shoulders when he turned to speak, as if suffering from a stiff neck.

At forty-two he was balding. Not too badly. Just around the crown. The manager from the Hair Replacement Center in Westbury had joked that Howard should leave it alone, that he had a permanent yarmulke just for the baring. But the man didn't think it was so funny when Mills thrice returned the hairpiece to the store, claiming customer dissatisfaction after having contracted and received their two thousand dollar, top-of-the-line bonding system procedure; a process gone asunder. Twice the company made good on their warranty. The third time, however, the manager recommended a removable hairpiece that would snap on to Howard's head with stainless steel grommets attached to his surrounding hair. Actually, there had been nothing wrong with the first product or procedure. The fault was to be found in the fact that one of the prostitutes had ripped a chunk of replacement hair out of the plastic netting glued to his scalp after Beth had violently struck but failed to incapacitate her victim with the initial blow.

"Want something to drink?" the shorter of the two detectives asked.

Oh, they were both being so very nice to him now, he beamed inwardly. Perhaps he had given them too much too soon. He craned his shoulders and tilted his head toward the little man but said nothing. He knew in an instant that he had irritated the midget. *Well, good,* Howard reflected.

"How about some won ton soup?" the taller, more talkative of the two suggested.

"Can I see my brother?" Howard asked evenly.

"Not right now," Posteraro answered. "Maybe in a little while."

"I want to make a phone call. I want to let someone know I'm here."

"By the way. I'm Detective Posteraro, and this is Detective Masselli." Vic put out his hand.

Howard Mills looked at the hand before taking it. It was the first time in a long time anyone had extended such a greeting.

The midget, too, put out his hand. But for one instinctive reason or another not worth entertaining, Howard let it hang there in the balance before the cop withdrew it.

"I'm entitled to a phone call," Howard insisted.

"That you are, but why don't you hear me out first, Howard? You don't mind if I call you Howard, do you?"

"Detective Connolly called me worse," Howard volunteered.

"Well, Detective Connolly has his moods and moments, I suppose," Posteraro said with no surprise. "I certainly can't make excuses for him, nor do I intend to try. As I'm sure you know, he's the lead detective on the Melville case. Detective Masselli is the lead detective on an open case of an unidentified woman found in Medford. That's why we're here. We would like to talk to you about that."

Detective Masselli opened up his notepad and removed a writing instrument from his pocket. He sat poised with pen in hand.

"How come he's taking notes if he's the honcho?"

"Because he's a better note taker," Posteraro patiently explained, giving Frank a wink and Howard a smile.

"And because you're better at asking the questions?" Howard questioned through a yawn.

"The point is, Howard, *I* am the one asking the questions."

"Can I have my glasses?" Howard asked, trying to push Posteraro's buttons with another question. He really didn't need them for reading or viewing the photograph of Darla he'd been shown earlier.

"Why, are you ready to sign a statement?" Victor Posteraro pushed back, studying the suspect carefully.

"Saying what? That I found the women on the floor when I woke up?" he tested, having given the second set of detectives a little bit more with which to work.

Vic and Frank exchanged hastened glances.

"Women?" Posteraro pressed.

Howard shrugged.

"Like in more than one?" the detective pumped.

Howard's eyes seemed to search the room from floor to ceiling for the answer. "It's happened before," he responded after a moment.

"In your room?"

"Yes."

"Where in your room?"

"Floor. Beside the bed."

"Are they dead?"

"Dead to the world."

"One? Or do you mean more than one at a time?"

"Just one at a time."

It was with a nonchalance given the word '*just*' that got to the detective. "What did you use, Howard? Hammer? Hatchet? Claw hammer? Anything on or near the bed?"

Howard shook his head, lowering his eyes to the floor.

"Tell me how it happened, Howard."

"I never hurt any of them. I cared about them. I cared about them all." Howard began to weep and whine. He didn't quite know what suddenly brought it on. "I never hurt any of them," he repeated.

"Tell me everything you remember, Howard." There was a sadness to the detective's voice. A note of genuine concern. "Can you tell me anything about Detective Masselli's Medford case? The woman found along the side of a road." Vic Posteraro avoided negative words like *amputated* and *trash container*, in which the victim was discovered.

Howard nodded, wiping his nose on the sleeve of his wrinkled plaid shirt.

"Did you cut her like the Melville girl, Darla?"

"Yes."

"What did you use to cut her?"

"A knife."

"What else?"

"A hacksaw."

"To cut through the bone." It wasn't a question. It was a given.

"I don't want you to hate me," Howard uttered through a sob.

"I don't hate you, Howard. I truly want to help you if you let me." Victor Posteraro sounded so sincere. More like a clergyman than a cop.

"I could get the death penalty for this," Howard Mills said in wonderment—as if the statement hung somewhere between the poles of a rhetorical and actual question.

It was a dangerous area, Vic knew. But it was out there. It couldn't be danced around. Not without losing the ground that the detective had gained. Howard's remark required Vic to leap way ahead of Team Two's intended Blackout Theme. The detective could always backtrack if he could only manage to stay on his feet without stumbling.

"Yes, you could," Posteraro said solemnly.

Howard noticed Detective Masselli dart a look of disapproval at his partner. *Was this the game of good cop bad cop?* Howard wondered. *Or was this the way the subordinate detective played it, hitting straight from the shoulder?*

"I guess you guys think I did something really bad."

"We believe you did. But we're getting ahead of ourselves here, Howard. Let's back up some."

"All right."

The detective took a breath. "Did you saw her legs off?"

"Just one."

"Which one?"

"The right one, I think."

"Why did you do that, Howard?"

"So she would fit into the container better," he answered matter-of-factly.

"What kind of container?"

"Blue."

"What kind of blue container?"

"Like a lawn and leaf container. Big."

"Where did you get it?"

"T.S.S. store. I think they're Kmart now."

"And the hacksaw?"

"Home Depot."

"Which one?"

"Patchogue."

"And you don't remember anything about the murders?"

Howard shook his head.

"You're on the bed with this girl. You're smoking crack?"

"Yes, and watching TV," Howard amplified.

"And then what?"

"I blank out."

"You mean you black out."

"Yes."

"What's the last thing that you remember before blacking out?"

"David Letterman."

Frank Masselli unsuccessfully tried to suppress a laugh. Vic ignored it and went on with the interrogation.

"And what's the first thing you see when you wake up?"

Howard was silent for an uncomfortable moment.

"Regis Philbin and Kathie Lee Gifford," Masselli managed through an uncontrollable guffaw.

Detective Posteraro was on his feet in a hot second, ushering his partner to the entrance. Less than a dozen words were spoken between them when Victor took the notepad and pen from Frank, opened the door and gently moved the lead detective out into the hallway before returning to the table.

"Clown," was the only excuse that Victor Posteraro could offer for the inexcusable behavior of his senior partner.

Howard was exhausted. He wanted to crawl back under the table and go to sleep. He had told them all that he really wanted them to know for the moment.

"Maybe it's better that we're alone now, Howard. Maybe you can find it easier to tell me."

"Tell you what?"

"How you killed them. Maybe even the reason why."

Howard laughed lightly. He felt that in another minute the detective would be witnessing a slip into unconsciousness. Might even believe the story he was handing them of his blank-outs. Howard closed his eyes and smiled. His lids were heavy. It felt so good shutting down. If he could only have an hour, he'd be fine.

"Howard."

They just wouldn't leave him alone.

"Howard!"

Howard squinted, becoming half alert.

"Are you listening to me, Howard?"

"I'm listening to you, but you're not listening to me."

"Meaning?"

"Meaning, I didn't kill anyone, anytime, nohow."

"You black out."

Howard nodded, his chin coming to rest upon his chest.

"After the drugs, you said," Posteraro added.

"Now, you're listening."

"On your bed."

"Yes."

"You'd pick the women up and drive them to your apartment in Hicksville. After doing drugs, they'd wind up dead. On the floor beside your bed."

"You're a poet."

The detective kept his cool. "How many bodies are we talking about?"

Howard shrugged.

"Two? Three? Maybe five?" the detective questioned.

"Uh-huh."

"Did anybody help you?"

"I'm not saying another word until I see a lawyer."

Detective Posteraro put down the pen.

Chapter Seventeen

At police headquarters in Yaphank, members from four Suffolk County homicide teams were standing in Detective Lieutenant Theodore Groche's office. The Suffolk County Homicide Unit was brimming with more warm bodies than pounds of flesh found at a meat processing plant. Homicide divisions from Westchester, Brooklyn, New York City and Nassau were well-represented, but it was clear that Suffolk County was running the show. It was their ballpark, their investigation. Additionally, two, two hundred-plus-pound detectives from a distant jurisdiction stood in a corner of the room closest to the doorway. It was your *Show of Shows*.

Howard Mills was back under the table in the interrogation room. Fast asleep. He lay there on his side; the rolled up olive-green military jacket that he was arrested in served as a pillow for his head. It was 1630 hours. Even in his sleep there was no escape. Soon he would be theirs again.

Toward the end of a dream that Howard would not be able to clearly recall, he was nevertheless back with Beth again. The two of them were walking hand in hand through a sunny field of chest-high golden wheat. As they moved together into the backdrop of the movie in his mind, both he and Beth were being elevated through a thin cloud covering. A human chain of hands and arms clinging to one another pulled the pair upward, passing the two from one familiar face to another. The first image was that of his youngest brother, Lenny, who handed them over to his father, who in turn remanded the pair to Howard's mother, who reacquainted the couple with the remains of their victims, starting with a sixteen-year-old Colombian girl from Hauppauge, dating back to 1978.

Howard awoke and fought furiously with several detectives, one of whom put their prisoner back in leg irons and manacles, forcing his arms behind his back while others held him down like a huge and slippery fish. It took a good two minutes for Howard Mills to recognize his surroundings and finally calm down. The 8 x 8 foot interrogation room was a grateful welcome-back-to-reality check compared to the hellish-haven he had just encountered, its visions quickly fading from his mind.

Howard was back in his seat, breathing heavily. Mick gave Mills a box on the ear with an open hand and would have roundhoused the mail handler had the detective been able to find the space to deliver such a blow. Vic and Frank moved Mick and the rest of the boys out of room. Frank closed the door and stepped back inside.

When Howard was settled and breathing evenly, Vic began.

"Were you in that kind of a rage when you were with those women, Howard?" Posteraro asked quietly, taking the same seat he had taken earlier.

Detective Masselli did likewise, opening up the notepad then searching through his pockets for a pen.

"It's over there in the corner," Howard gestured, glancing at the detective's watch as the man turned his head.

Masselli got up and went over to the corner, sweeping the pen off the floor in a single exaggerated movement before returning to his seat.

"Get good and angry with these girls?" Detective Posteraro prodded.

Howard Mills said nothing, wondering if Jeffrey had remembered to remove the handgun from either the glove compartment or under the front seat of the Cadillac. The two of them only brought the weapon whenever they carted off a body for disposal. It was Jeffrey's responsibility to hide the .45 caliber behind the wall in the porch area while Howard tidied up the trunk with cleaning chemicals and a thorough vacuuming. He wondered if the police had found the pistol. A Colt MK IV/Series 80 Commander (Lightweight), with an aluminum receiver in lieu of steel. He pictured the police tearing up the house.

Howard felt badly for the landlady. He had secretly hoped that the police might turn their attention to the upstairs handyman if and when they ever developed a lead that directed them to Willow Lane via some sort of careless discarding of the instruments of death, for most of the tools belonged to that crazy old fool, Howard simpered. God how he disliked the man. If Beth used the old man's hammer or hatchet on a victim, Howard would replace it immediately. If she used a crowbar, he'd run out and buy a brand new tool. Maybe even a better one. Who in their right mind would ever register a complaint for doing that?

"Howard," Vic spoke quietly.

But no, Howard obsessed. He had to be seen by a friend of Darla's as she was climbing into the front seat of the Cadillac. Whenever he picked up a prostitute, he tried to be careful and made sure she was alone. Especially if he knew he wouldn't be bringing the woman back to her neighborhood. And what prostitute would dare point a finger at the sanctity of his apartment all the way out in Nassau County? Or even recall the route? *Who was she?* Was she the girl he had picked up one windy, wintry Sunday evening when the snow was piled as high as her backside as she paraded back and forth along the empty boulevard? He had cruised along Francis Lewis Boulevard at least a half a dozen times before he picked her up and brought her home to Hicksville, feeling so sorry for her, being out there all alone in the freezing cold. She really wasn't much to look at, but she was very, very funny. That and the fact that she had no problem whatsoever getting drugs. *Was that the one who ratted me out?* Howard wondered.

"Earth to Howard," Detective Posteraro said to no avail.

She and Howard had almost gotten killed by a tractor trailer as he was driving her back to Queens late that evening, the two of them laughing away like loons. *Yes. She had been out to the house three or four times before. Cunt! Wasn't the relationship between a hooker and her john not as sacred, private and as privileged as the bond between a psychiatrist and a patient? A cleric and his confessor? How about a lawyer and his client?*

"You asleep in there, Howard?" the detective asked patiently, gently shaking the prisoner's shoulder then playfully pulling his chain.

Oh, Howard was wide awake, now, and ready for the inquisition. "I'm awake," he answered. He was so much smarter than all of them—once he knew the score, he swore.

"Good, because we have a lot of ground to cover. Why don't you tell me how long you've been seeing prostitutes and using drugs?"

"I started in the late seventies."

"Twenty years ago."

Howard nodded

"Long time drug habit, Howard."

"I'm not a junky, if that's what you're getting at."

"Then what would you call yourself?"

"A recreational user."

"Really?" The detective smiled. "Wouldn't call yourself an addict?"

"I could stop anytime."

"Could you have stopped what happened on those nights in question, with the girls? I guess the question is, could you stop the bogeyman?"

Not if my life depended on it, Howard was tempted to tell the detective. But it had nothing at all to do with murder or blackouts or the drugs that Posteraro was addressing. For the drug that Howard's mind and body craved was his intoxicating half sister, Beth. He simply had no choice in the matter except to abide by her prescription of life and death. Beth and death, and there was no other way around it. He kept wondering if he would ever see her again. Would she somehow find her way to him in *his* moment of darkness?

"Howard."

"Yes."

"No one is buying into this blackout business. Maybe once or twice. But you don't wake up time after time with a body lying on the floor next to the bed and not know what happened. You have to admit it doesn't make any sense. Help us help you, Howard. Please."

"Can't help you there."

"Can't or won't?"

"I wake up, they're there."

"You're in a rage. You kill them. Morning comes and—"

Howard was shaking his head violently.

"All right then. You black out. Your mind doesn't *want* to recall the details because they're so horrible. Is that a fair and accurate description?"

"I don't know. I'm not a mind doctor. Detective Connolly said he went to my shrinks. What do they think?"

"I really don't know what conversations Detective Connolly had with any doctors concerning you," Posteraro fibbed.

Time was running out for Team Two. They needed Howard's murder confession. Regardless of the fact that Howard had waived his rights, whether under duress or not, Howard's lawyer-hopeful had to be thwarted from entering the picture at all cost. A competent criminal defense attorney could and would put up impenetrable walls. The clock was ticking away quickly for the team.

All the players knew by now that this was not your run-of-the-mill murder case. Nor was it just another postal worker 'gone postal,' like the route David Berkowitz had plotted for himself during the early to mid-seventies, delivering destruction and sending a message of fear into the hearts of thousands throughout New York's five boroughs and beyond, encouraging a rash of wannabes who wished to follow suit. This was, perhaps, the biggest case to hit New York. No, not hardly your run-of-the-mill mass murderer but a serial killer who was still miles away from a stone-cold confession, Posteraro believed—unlike Connolly, who felt their captive was on the brink of spilling his guts. *What would it take to shake Howard?* Vic wondered. *What would it take to rattle those chains?*

Vic was vacillating.

Why would Howard Mills hold back his true confession if, indeed, he truly wanted to die? Vic asked himself. *Why would he prolong the agony? Because maybe Howard really didn't want to die*, he reasoned. No. He had seen a Howard or two in his ten-year career as a cop. And this bird wanted to put both feet in a coffin and pull the cover down tight. He was sure of it. Mills had all the makings and markings of a suicide waiting to happen. What or who was holding him back? What kind of game was he playing? Was there a game? Or was he simply nuts? *Absolutely not*, Vic told himself, although there was always some asshole civilian who'd be ready to argue that they *all* had to be nuts to commit any number of horrific deeds like Howard had. There were those who were indeed crazy and belonged in a mental institution, granted. And there were those who were crazy like a fox. Then there was Howard Mills who fell into neither category for the moment. Vic couldn't pigeonhole the bastard, and it was driving him mad.

"The mind is a fascinating study, Howard," the detective continued. "I'm not a doctor, but I know what drugs can do. I've been a cop for ten years. A detective for five of those years. Two years in

Homicide. Yet, I'm the new kid on the block. Most of the detectives here have twenty under their belts. Truth is I've seen it all. Fact is they've just seen more of it. Like Detective Masselli, here. Right, Frank?"

"Right," Masselli answered without picking up his head.

"So what do you think of Howard's story?" Vic asked. "Buy his blackout line?" He turned his attention to Frank.

"Full of shit if you ask me."

"I am asking you. So tell me what you think."

"Told you. Fucker's lying through his teeth, and if the lieutenant would let me have my way, they'd be scattered throughout this fuckin' room."

"Then I guess it's a good thing the lieutenant's been in a good frame of mind," Vic rejoined, the two of them having their own conversation as if Howard weren't even there. "But what I'm asking you is why?"

"Why what?"

"Why you think Mr. Mills is lying about the blackouts."

"His fuckin' brother have blackouts?"

Vic shifted in his seat, facing back to Howard. "Jeffrey have blackouts?"

"I don't know. I don't think so."

"Jeffrey know you have blackouts?" Frank Masselli asked.

Howard hesitated.

"Well, does he?" Masselli snapped.

"I don't think so."

"Fuckin' A he don't. Know why?" Masselli didn't wait for a response. "Because you *don't* fuckin' black out, fuckhead. That's just your excuse to get around tellin' the truth. We're talkin' blunt force trauma to the head and face." Masselli reached for his case folder from the corner of the table. "Here. Take a good look, fuckface." The detective's voice was rising. "She's been beaten so bad, her face is unrecognizable." He slid the color enlargement past Vic and parked it beneath Howard's gaze. "A mother couldn't recognize that face, if you could even call it a face. Know what we did, motherfucker? Went you one better. Had the M.E. cut the head off and send it south so an anthropologist could do a rendering with clay and crap. But no luck. So she remains unidentified. We got flyers goin' around Port Authority where you picked the Jane Doe up. Still, no one came forth to claim her body either. And how about the one who turned up on that conveyor belt in Brooklyn? Your handiwork, Howard. Your signature's all over it. Only this one you took down to her torso. Boys from that jurisdiction as well as others are pacing the floor with their open case files, right outside that door," he blasted and pointed. "Just waiting to get their hands on you. And guess what? We won't be in this room with them. We won't hear a fuckin' thing if they get a little out of hand. We got one guy out there who just got off a double shift and drove all the way out from Yonkers, just to meet *you*. He said he's goin' home with somethin', even if it's a piece of your hide. Strange lookin' dude, Howard. Two hundred fifty pounds. I'm surprised what they'll let on the force these days.

"No, you remember damn well, Howard. You remember it all too well. Just look at that Kodak moment and tell me that you don't. I double dare you," he declared with sheer anger and frustration boiling through his veins. "Just look at it!"

"What we're trying to get across to you here, Howard," Detective Posteraro tabled, "is that Detective Masselli and I are not in the minority. Every detective out there connected with these cases believes you killed those women."

"You can all believe anything you like."

"Say what?" Masselli snarled, lifting his frame several inches off his seat.

"All right!" Posteraro interceded, extending his arm like a railing between the two.

Howard was getting ballsy now. Just like Beth. She'd bust his balls, but he'd never say a word. She'd abuse him verbally and physically, and he'd just stand there and take it. And then she'd lace into him even more for being such a wuss. She loved calling him that.

"The only one I may have killed is Lenny," Howard commented, shifting uncomfortably in the metal chair.

"Your youngest brother," Vic said knowingly.

"The one who committed suicide," Masselli added for clarification had there been any doubt.

"Am I under investigation for that?"

"Not if you didn't assist him, you're not," was Posteraro's quick reply.

"But I was the first one to find the body. Isn't the first one to find the body always a suspect?"

The two detectives saw the diversion for what it was. A stall tactic.

"Let's get back on track. Shall we?" Vic Posteraro insisted.

"Twenty years ago, and I still feel responsible," Howard Mills remarked.

"Whole fuckin' family's probably nuts," Detective Frank Masselli said under his breath but still loud enough for Howard to hear. "Yeah, like I really give a flyin' fuck what he thinks," he said to his partner, reading Vic's thoughts coupled to the disappointment sketched across a sullen face.

Their prisoner clenched his teeth in anger and stared the foulmouthed detective down. Howard was about to say something to the seated midget but thought better of it. He was in no position to say or do anything to help his situation at the moment. Piss them off and he'd only make things worse. It was going to be a long haul. He knew that. Others wanted to speak to him. It couldn't go on forever. Or could it? His wrists and shoulders were killing him. He had been standing or sitting with his arms handcuffed in back of him through most of the day. Beth had said it wouldn't be easy if he were ever nailed. She had told him *what* and *what not* to say in the event of an arrest. She had made him promise. The *what not* was most important. The *what not* would ultimately confound their case against him. He and Beth were smarter than them all. It was Jeffrey's well-being that Howard worried about.

"Got a little problem there, Mills?" Masselli asked, grinning malevolently.

"Enough, Frank," Victor Posteraro again intervened.

Howard relaxed his jaw muscles after realizing they were clamped shut like a vise. It wasn't anger that he harbored anymore. It was a pure defiance. He sat up straight in his seat, ready to continue the round.

Posteraro tried coming at Howard another way. "Did you ever fight with these girls when they tried to rip you off? Ever smack any of them around?"

"Never. Detective Connolly asked me the same question. I never hit anyone. A couple of them hit me, though. I never fight back. I'm weak. People take advantage of me. I'm a nice person."

"You seem to be, Howard. Maybe you really are. And maybe there's another *you* who comes out later on. Maybe drug induced. Got any thoughts about that?"

"Detective Connolly asked me that, too."

"And?"

"And nothing."

"Nothing?"

"No."

"Don't think there could be another you?" Vic pressed.

"'*Oh, there'll nev-er ev-er be a-noth-er you,*' Howie," Frank Masselli sang aloud quite pleasantly, wearing his widest and most winsome grin.

This time, Vic ignored his partner, for it was as if Howard hadn't even heard his tormentor, hadn't even raised a brow. Mr. Mills, their prisoner, appeared lost in time and space. It seemed as though he were staring through a window in the wall. Only there wasn't any window, except for the concealed one-way viewing slit adjacent to the door. No clock was present in the room either, except for the watches worn by the detectives, the time so noted on Masselli's watch earlier when Howard masterfully distracted the two by calling attention to Masselli's pen in the corner on the floor. There was only one problem with that ruse. Howard had no idea whether it was a.m. or p.m. as the overhead light was always left on in the room. He'd try and remember to keep his eye on the door when they'd leave in order to determine if it was night or day.

"Howard?"

Howard brought his eyes to bear on Detective Posteraro.

"Medford girl had a gash on one leg. Know how that got there?"

"I slipped."

"What do you mean you slipped?"

"I went to get a knife. When I returned, I slipped in the blood. Put a cut in her leg. Didn't mean to."

"What happened next?"

"I panicked."

"Go on."

"Scrambling."

"You mean on the floor?"

"Yes. Blood all over the place. Cold when I touched her."

"What did you do?"

"Had to get her out of there."

"How?"

"I must have carried her out."

"I mean before that. What did you do before you carried her out?"

"I don't remember."

"Let me help you out there," Masselli said, standing up quickly and forming a fist by his side.

"Sit down!" Vic demanded, shooting an order at his senior partner.

"Needs his memory jarred a bit, is all. Things are too fuckin' tight in there. Let me loosen things up a bit for him."

"I said, sit down," Vic repeated.

Howard was crying softly. It was not out of any sense of fear of the detective or over the slightest bit of guilt or remorse for the victims. It was over the fact that he might never ever be with Beth again. That thought, more than anything, aside from Jeffrey's well-being, took its hold on Howard.

"Before you carried her out, Howard," Posteraro continued, picking up where he left off.

"I put a plastic bag over her face so I didn't have to look at her," he blubbered. "I couldn't look at any of them."

"And then?"

"Then I cut her leg off."

"With a hacksaw, you said. And later on you got that blue plastic garbage pail from T.S.S. and put her in."

The tears and mucus were pouring down Howard's face.

"Yes?"

"Yes."

Victor Posteraro reached into his jacket pocket and withdrew a clean white handkerchief. Leaning toward Howard, the detective opened the cotton cloth then wiped and covered the prisoner's nose for him.

"Blow."

Howard blew.

"Again."

Howard blew again. Hard.

Frank Masselli looked on in disbelief but said nothing.

"Thank you," Howard said sincerely.

"You're welcome."

Masselli slowly shook his head.

Vic folded the handkerchief and put it near the corner of the table across from them.

"You took her hands, too."

Howard shook his head. "Arms. Took the hands from Darla."

Posteraro nodded.

Detective Masselli smiled satisfactorily to himself. Howard

hadn't clarified that point earlier regarding Mick Connolly's Melville girl. In two short laps of the tongue, their prime suspect had just corroborated what the police already knew. Unfortunately, Howard wasn't giving them anything that they *didn't* know or suspect. In a court of law, competent defense attorneys would make them look like mokes. What they needed from Howard, in addition to a signed statement admitting that he had killed the girls, was information that they didn't have that would hang the bastard high—ideally, the location of one of the instruments of death with Howie boy's *signature* on it. Then again, the lieutenant forever accused Frank of wanting to lead a charmed life. *What's easy in this world, Frank?* the lieutenant would eternally ask. And Frank would always answer up, *Retirement, boss*.

But Masselli had to hand it to his junior partner. Vic was making headway. Clean-cut, snotnosed college boy with a degree in education and a minor in psychology. He wondered if the curriculum covered ass wiping as well.

"Where did you put the limbs?" Posteraro persisted.

"Separate bag."

"Plastic?"

"Uh-huh."

"Same as the others you used?"

"Uh-huh."

The two uh-huhs back to back bothered the detective. Posteraro was getting into an area that Howard had avoided with Connolly and Bailey earlier—both in the car on the way to headquarters and in the initial interview. Howard was no dope. He wasn't an Einstein, but he wasn't a dumbbell either.

"What did you do with this plastic bag with the limbs?"

"Threw it away."

"Away where?"

"Different places. All over. I can't remember."

"But you remember dumping the blue container along the side of the road in Medford. You remember disposing of Darla in the Dumpster in Melville, don't you?"

"What I remember is driving east on the L.I.E. and looking for something open. What I remember is reading an article in the *Post* about Darla's body being found," he said with an edge to his voice. "And I really want to call a lawyer, now!"

The New York Post, Posteraro reminded himself, realizing the round was almost over, just as surely as if a referee had directed the two opponents to their neutral corners.

"Yes. It's my favorite newspaper," Howard snapped.

"How about the *National Enquirer* or *Screw Magazine*?" Masselli concluded. He just couldn't help himself. He couldn't leave it alone. "I'll bet you're a regular subscriber."

"I'm not going to help you with your taxes," Howard said out of left field to Masselli, the look of total gratification written across the mail handler's face.

"So, now we're slipping into our cuckoo bird role, I see," Masselli said, getting up. "Bulletin, shithead. I've got an accountant for that, though I must admit he looks a lot like you, which does concern me some." Frank closed the notepad, stuck the pen in his pocket and headed toward the door. "Oh, and don't forget your snot-rag, Vic. Fucker might find a way to hang himself."

Chapter Eighteen

Pairs of detectives from other jurisdictions were placed at one end of the squad room, anxiously awaiting their shot at Howard Mills. Theo had instructed maintenance to accommodate the group with old desks taken out of storage, keeping the group clustered in a corner, well away from the interrogation room. They'd have their shot in due time.

Detective Gary York made sure his gun, shield and handcuffs were secured in his locker located just outside the squad room. He straightened his sixty-dollar silk tie and studded diamond clip, looked down and inspected the pair of highly polished Italian leather Loafers, admired the crease in his trousers that could cut butter, squared his shoulders within the custom-tailored suit jacket, draped a light mohair overcoat over his left arm, and with his right hand, reached down for the expensive, luxurious leather briefcase standing alongside a chair.

"Ready, counselor?"

"Do I get to keep any retainer I secure in there?" Gary remarked with a confident grin and sparkling blue eyes.

"Just retain what we went over this afternoon and make Theo proud," Mick said, needn't having to remind the detective.

"How about this *borrowed* briefcase and appropriated coat?"

"Let's go, you thieving scoundrel."

Mick Connolly walked ahead while Gary strutted behind him like a peacock.

Mick opened the door to the interrogation room, and York waltzed in, right up to the table next to Howard Mills. Gary set the coat and briefcase down abruptly, displaying his *best bored-as-all-hell* and *I-really-don't-have-to-be-here* look.

"Mr. Mills, I presume."

Howard looked up.

"The cuffs come off," York said flatly.

"No can do, counselor."

"It's Detective Connolly. Is it not?"

"It is."

"Well, Detective Connolly. I don't shake hands with suspects wearing bracelets unless they happen to be female and under thirty. You go tell your sergeant I said the cuffs come off. If he says no, then I want you to go to your lieutenant. I've got about an hour and a quarter before I have to catch a plane." York looked up with impatience. "Time's-a-wasting, Detective."

Mick mumbled something and headed for the door.

"So, Howard. I'm Gary York. How long have they had you in custody?" he asked, continuing to stand over Howard.

Howard Mills was studying the man's eyes. "Not exactly sure."

"About me or the time?"

Howard cracked a smile.

"Shave before they picked you up?"

"That morning. They arrested me around eleven o'clock."

"Probably forty-eight hours from the looks of you. They told me twenty-four."

"They're lying. I know I've been here a lot longer."

"Tell them anything?"

"Like what?"

"Like you killed anybody. Admit to anything?"

"I swear to God, I didn't kill anybody."

"You tell them that?"

"Yes, sir."

"Sign anything?"

"They made me initial a card in several places. Said I waived my rights. One of them tried to hit me with a chair."

"Miranda warning."

"I guess."

"Sign anything else?"

"No, sir. Just for my property they took. Money, keys and stuff."

"You sure?"

"I'm sure."

"Make sure you don't. Understand?"

Mick was coming back into the room.

"Understand?" York repeated.

Howard nodded.

"Your funeral," Mick said to the impostor, going up to Howard and removing the cuffs. "I suppose you want to be alone with your client."

"He's not my client. We're merely getting acquainted is all," Gary said, shaking Howard's hand. "And, yes. I do want to be alone with him."

"As I said, it's your funeral. We know he's killed at least five prostitutes."

"Do I look like a prostitute to you, Detective?" Gary snapped.

"I wouldn't touch that with a ten-foot pole, counselor," Mick countered.

"If you truly had anything on him, Detective, your lieutenant wouldn't have asked me here. So you got dick."

"Oh, we got plenty. Blood. Fibers. Hair. And that's just for openers, counselor."

"So then why *am* I here if your case is so solid?"

"To talk some sense to him. We're the enemy in his eyes."

York laughed. "Got that right."

"You can save his life and maybe get him the help he needs. And believe-you-me, this boy needs a lot of help."

"And why so generous, Detective?"

"Comes right down to something you'll understand perfectly, counselor. Money."

York smirked. "Everything usually does. Go on, I'm listening."

"Without his confession, we've got a long and expensive trial ahead of us at taxpayers' dollars. D.A.'s going for the death penalty on this one. First case on Long Island in twenty-one years. Howard, here, has the honor. Serial killer qualified. It's a forensics case, pure and simple. Trace evidence. Lots of expert witnesses to call. Forensic scientists in their specialized fields such as blood, hair, and fiber; chemists, tool mark experts, medical examiner. Not to mention the regular chaff and wheat. Lots of overtime went and will continue with this case: detectives, prosecutors, defense attorneys, et cetera." Mick paused and looked down at Howard. "Gonna get real expensive. Tell 'im, York. Two counselors at your table on a capital crime, Howard. With those guys and dolls eating up lots and lots of time. And let's not forget our court clerks and officers, court reporters, judge and law secretary. We're talking several million dollars for openers. It'll go better than a couple of years, I'd bet. What with pretrial, jury selection, trial, post verdict arguments, penalty phase and so forth, Howard, here, is going to be sitting in a cell for at least two years before he ever gets to see a judge and jury. And until those people finally decide his fate, either death by lethal injection or life in prison without the possibility of parole, or if Howard is really lucky, and the jury can't agree, well the judge has the choice of giving him fifty to life. So, let's see. Best case scenario. He's forty-two, add fifty—if he's lucky to live that long, well, he'd be ninety-two. Did I leave anything out?"

"How about an acquittal?" York mocked. "Not in your vocabulary?"

"Fat chance of that happening, counselor."

"Who's the prosecutor?"

"Gail Fox."

"Good record."

"It's not a question of talent, York. We're holding all the cards."

"May be a house of cards," the make-believe attorney warned.

"We'll see. But we're willing to deal. You do your magic with the judge. You're in bed with most of them anyways from what I hear."

"Only the female breed," York bragged.

"Stick this psycho in a hospital for a decade versus an eternal rest and we're both ahead of the game. Might even work out some kind of deal for his brother."

Howard was watching the show as though it were a soap opera.

"What about his brother?"

"His brother, Jeffrey, helped him dispose of some of the bodies. I don't want to get into that area at this point." Mick let the bogus proposition hang there a moment before he continued. "You'd be doing the county and your client a great service."

"I'm not taking on charity cases at the moment, Detective. I have a full client list and a plane to catch. I came here because your lieutenant said this might prove lucrative. Ostensibly, I don't see how. Personally, I don't think Mr. Mills has two nickels to rub together. No offense, Howard, but I'm one of those lawyers who's a prosecutor's worst nightmare. I'm pure talent, and I don't come cheap. I see here that the powers that be are more interested in saving the county a bundle than they are in helping you and me." York picked up the briefcase and coat. "I gave you some free advice a moment ago, Howard. I hope you take it."

Howard's heavy dark eyes were darting back and forth between the detective and the pretender.

Mick picked up the slack. "Howard, why don't you tell this money-hungry mako just how many shekels you have lying around here and there, and not to be taken in by your Fayva sneakers and dime-store jeans. Whattaya have to lose but your life? Or better yet, why don't I tell him? You look so preoccupied. It's not nearly what he commands for a fee, but it will whet his appetite. Maybe he'll weigh the rest in terms of free publicity."

York sighed. But he wasn't wearing his bored expression any longer. "This is usually the point in the conversation where I hear about a prospective client's rich auntie and the pending inheritance."

From a jacket pocket, Mick took out a folded sheet of paper, opened it then began reading: "Three hundred thirty-seven thousand nine hundred dollars in liquid assets: Astoria Federal, Greenpoint Savings Bank, Greater New York Savings Bank. Some savings bonds thrown in there somewhere . . . and . . . oh, yeah, IRAs. You Irish, Howard?" Connolly joked. "One hundred eighty-six thousand five hundred dollars in tax deferred assets, for a total of five hundred twenty-four thousand four hundred dollars. Additionally, Howard's co-owner of a house in Long Beach. Well over half a mil all told. Not bad for a mail handler."

Howard Mills was getting green around the gills, and York, thespian for a one-night performance, turned green with envy.

"Well," York said, certainly seeming surprised. "I haven't heard a peep out of Howard. We'd have to consult and discuss some arrangement." York consulted his watch. "And quite frankly, I don't have the time right now."

Howard seemed crestfallen. Suddenly, a tear or two traced the prisoner's cheek. York took Howard's hand in farewell. Howard did not want to let it go.

"Sir?"

"Yes, Howard?"

"Please let me talk to you before you go. Alone. Please. Five minutes. No more. I can pay."

Gary York studied Howard Mills for a moment before he spoke. "Look. Tell you what. No sense even getting into this unless I know exactly what's going on. Can you appreciate that?"

"Yes, sir."

York turned and looked at Mick. "Detective Connolly. With all due respect, take a hike."

Without saying a word, Mick Connolly walked from the room and closed the door but did not lock it, leaving the prisoner and impostor alone.

"Okay, the first thing we do is move this table and chairs against that wall," York instructed. "Stand up."

Unsteadily, Howard got to his feet.

"Help me out here," York said.

Howard look confused but helped the man move the table and two chairs against the far wall. York took the mohair coat off the table and draped it neatly over another chair in back of him, setting it out of the way. He snapped open the briefcase and took out a yellow legal pad and a black Mont Blanc fountain pen.

"Sit down, Howard."

Howard sat, and York joined him, the two of them facing the wall.

"See that wall to the left of the door behind you?"

Howard looked over his shoulder and nodded.

"One-way peephole. They think everybody's stupid." Without turning around, York flipped the bird to whoever might be watching. "They have a woman around here who can read lips. Sits right outside that door. Lips you could die for. Read that anyway you want, Howard. She knows exactly what a client tells his attorney. One fellow thought he was talking to his mouthpiece in confidence. Police now knew exactly where to find the murder weapon, and they did. Fingerprints and all. Afterward, the cops laughed and told the man that his own lawyer had sold him out. Told him exactly what the two discussed. The man fired his lawyer, and the state put the defendant away for life. True story. That conversation took place right inside this room."

"I was thinking that maybe they bug this place."

"You're a smart man, Howard, because as a backup they do indeed."

The thought of such an invasion of privacy was unsettling to Howard. Its confirmation was quite another matter.

"So why are we sitting like this if they can hear everything we say anyway?"

"Well, for one thing, if we whisper," and York was now whispering, "we make things a lot more difficult for them. But if we communicate in writing," and York was pointing to the pad, "we protect ourselves." York's heart was pounding in his chest.

"We going to do this now?"

"If you want."

"But I thought you had a plane to catch," Howard Mills said warily.

"I do. But then we'd have to hold this over for a week. Maybe you want some time to think about it." York started to get out of his seat.

"No, wait!" Howard veritably took the man by a sleeve.

York looked down indignantly. "Howard, these are two thousand dollar threads."

Howard immediately let go. "I'm sorry."

"Look. There'll always be another plane, a train, hopefully another life. If you want to do this now, we'll do it. All right?"

"You'll rep-repr—" Howard couldn't think straight.

"Represent you?"

Howard nodded.

"If you wish, and if we can come to a monetary agreement."

"What about mini cameras?" Howard asked, pointing to the overhead. "Hidden in the ceiling."

"Got that covered, Howard," York assured him, lifting the first few sheets of paper from the legal pad and holding them at a forty-five degree angle, shielding from view whatever would be written on the clean lined page before them. "For example, Howard." York took the fancy pen and jotted down a figure. "I'll want fifty percent of this up front and, of course, power of attorney."

Howard plucked the pen from York's hand and scrawled his first demand: *Keep my brother Jeffrey out of this*, it read.

York, tough as he was, was moved by the man's first concern. He nodded in the affirmative.

Howard nodded back.

"When's the last time you had something to eat?"

"Before I left the house."

"Are you kidding me?"

Howard moved his head from side to side.

"Did they offer you anything?"

"Won ton soup."

York looked furious. "Did they offer you anything to drink?"

Again, Howard shook his head. "Oh, yeah, a cup of water."

York got up from the chair and marched over to the door. He threw it open. Detectives Connolly and Bailey were standing several feet away.

"READ MY LIPS!" York bellowed. "You get my client a decent meal, and I mean immediately. Are we clear?" York didn't wait for a reply. He slammed the door and did an about-face, marching back toward Howard. "You excuse me for another moment?"

"Sure." Howard was smiling.

York took a Nokia cell phone out of the briefcase and raised its antenna. From several steps away, he tapped in a series of numbers. Howard was staring at the ceiling. Thinking.

"Wanda? Gary. Listen. Cancel my flight and reschedule me for sometime after midnight. I'm going to need a few hours here. I know. Tell him I'm sorry. Tell him I'll make it up to him. *I know.* Listen. Tell him I'll knock ten grand off his bill." There was a brief pause. "Well, then tell him to take a flying fuck. No, everything's fine. Love you, too, Wanda. Just don't tell that to my wife. Bye."

Not two minutes later, Detective Vic Posteraro came in and took Howard's food order.

After some Chinese food, a beverage, a trip to the bathroom, and a heart-to-heart, Howard had something he hadn't had an hour ago. Hope. A feeling stronger than his faith in God, at present. And although his thoughts and desires were nothing more tangible than the hole in York's buttered bagel, he clung to them tenaciously. The promise of help and a hospital in exchange for two hundred fifty thousand dollars somehow seemed a bargain. And why not? He wasn't only bargaining for a new lease on life, he was bargaining for Beth's and Jeffrey's well-being. The thought of dying painlessly on some slab in some upstate prison from a lethal, legal overdose didn't faze him in the least. But the idea of having to hang around waiting, God knows how long, for the state to arrange it was devastating to him. He knew he was a sick puppy. He had known it for more than thirty years. York had promised him the help he needed in exchange for dollars and the truth. The dollars were the easy part. The truth? Howard knew he couldn't tell York everything. Beth had made him promise. Still, he'd tell him more than he had told the police, he decided.

"So, we ready to rock-and-roll here, Howard?"

"Yes, sir."

"No lies. The truth. Agreed?"

"Agreed," for York had said nothing about omissions of truth.

"First, what you told me over lunch—the story that you had given the police about blacking out then waking up and finding the bodies. It's a tough pill to swallow, Howard. You're not talking to them now. You're talking to your lawyer. Remember. Don't answer aloud in here. Write your complete answers down as we discussed. I'll ask my questions aloud. Doesn't matter what they hear me ask you. It's your written answers that we'll protect. These papers leave here with me." York raised the first few pages and indicated near the top line where he wanted Howard to record his answers. "Now, had you blacked out or 'blanked out' from taking drugs, as you told the detectives you had, after taking the prostitutes to bed?"

No, I do not black out, Howard confessed by writing the answer with the borrowed Mont Blanc pen.

"Did you alone sever the limbs from the three victims that Suffolk homicide detectives have outlined in their discussions with you earlier?"

Yes. I alone severed their limbs or hands.

"Did you do so before or after the girls were dead?"

I did that after they were dead.

"Did you alone dispose of their bodies?"

No.

"Once again, I need your complete answer, Howard, so that neither the judge nor the doctors, who are going to help me help you, can accuse me of writing in the questions *after* your responses. For example: If I ask you, 'Howard, do you like chocolate?' and you write down, *Yes*, then later on I write in, 'Do you feel remorse?' and you've already written down, *Yes*, I could be accused of manipulating your answers. Do you understand why we're doing things this way?"

Howard nodded and wrote, *No, I alone did not dispose of their bodies.*

"Who aided you in disposing of their bodies?"

My brother Jeffrey.

"Your brother Jeffrey, what?" York asked patiently.

"Sorry." *My brother Jeffrey aided me in disposing of their bodies,* Howard scribed.

York's heart raced as he formed the next question. He recited it quickly and couldn't even hear his own words.

"Did you kill the woman known as Jane Doe/Medford?"

No. I did not kill Jane Doe, Medford.

"Did you kill the woman whose torso was found in Brooklyn?"

No. I did not kill the woman found in Brooklyn.

"Did you kill the woman whose body was found in a Dumpster in Melville?"

No. I did not kill the woman found in Melville.

"Is there another person or entity inside of you who could have committed the murders?"

No. There is no other person or thing inside me who committed any murders.

York posited the next question calmly and carefully. "Did your brother Jeffrey kill one or more of the victims in question?"

No. Jeffrey did not kill anyone.

Gary York prayed that the disappointment behind the mask he wore was not somehow seeping through. He carefully formulated the last question in his head before asking it. It was the detective's last shot before going to Team Two's plan two.

"Do you know or think you know who killed one or all three of the women in question?"

Howard deliberately put the pen down upon the table.

"I see," York said, allowing the top pages to fall along with his spirits. "You're either protecting somebody outside the scope of the questions put forth to you, or you're lying to your lawyer. So. I'm going to ask you another question. Just one. You don't have to write it down. Don't even have to answer it for that matter because I think you know where we have to go from here. Now. Which question concerning the two remaining possibilities shall I ask you? Does the answer to one necessarily cancel out the other? Let's see. Shall I ask you whether you're lying? Or should I ask you if you're protecting someone other than yourself? In which case, you could still be lying. Huh? Good thing the burden of proof is on the prosecution and why I chose to take up defending clients, because I don't give a good crap if the defendant is lying, just so long as the prosecution can't prove it," he continued, gradually raising his pitch. "And I can't know if the prosecution can prove it or not unless I know whether or not my client is telling *me* the truth. Are you with me on this, Howard? Or am I talking to a blank wall?"

Howard was actually trembling.

Oh, Gary—the bogus lawyer—was good.

"I haven't lied to you, Mr. York."

Mr. York. Gary was still commanding Howard's respect.

"Good, Howard. Glad to hear it. Because now I know what question to ask. Are you protecting some—"

"Yes," Howard almost shouted.

"Part b of the same question. Someone other than yourself?"

"Yes."

Gary York lowered his voice a notch. "All right."

"I can't tell you who," Howard insisted and sobbed. "I promised —" He almost slipped and used Beth's name. "I know I'm sick in the head. I don't know what snaps in the brain. But I never killed anyone. I can't and won't tell you who did. But I didn't lie to you. And I never broke a promise to anyone in my forty-two years on this planet. And never will. And that's the God's honest truth."

"Even if it means your life?"

Howard laughed through his tears.

"What's so funny?"

"No one believes me. But I'm not afraid to die."

"But you're afraid of the prolonged wait. Yes, Howard?"

Howard nodded. "I'm so very tired. I wish I could die right here and now."

"Howard. Look at me. No. I mean right into my eyes. Hold them there." Team Two's plan two was about to be given wings. "You've never seen me argue in court. Right? I dazzle a jury, Howard. I show them, not tell them, Howard, but show them that black is white, and they swear to themselves that they can see just how bright. Know how I do that, Howard? I blindside them. You want a trial? I'll get you a trial. And guess what? I'll even get you acquitted. How's that? And they know it." He shot his thumb over his shoulder toward the door. "But here's the rub. You'll rot in a cell in Riverhead Jail for at least two years like Detective Connolly said. Another year before it's in the hands of a jury is three. And when Suffolk is finished with you, you will start all over again in Westchester for the women who disappeared in Yonkers. And I understand there are homicide detectives from other jurisdictions waiting down the end of the hall. Now. You want to take the rap for what someone else may or may not have done, that's your decision. I know you're a betting man. Love OTB. Looked over your file quickly during the break. I'll tell you what Connolly and that crew are betting on by them bringing me in here. They're betting I tell you to take ten years in a private hospital, not a state institution, Howard, but a private facility, and get you the help you need rather than rot in a cell for three years for starters. Because even if you walk, you'll walk right into the open arms of Westchester authorities who will be standing at the gate. You'll walk several hundred feet. No more. And I'll be standing right next to them to claim the balance of your half a million bucks for round two. Got the picture?"

York figured that if the right one didn't get him, then the left one would.

Howard wiped a tear or two away. "What do I have to do?"

York had figured correctly. "Well, for openers, wipe your nose." He handed Howard his handkerchief.

"Thanks." Howard blew his nose.

"You give them the statements they want. The two victims found in Suffolk. The one in Brooklyn. I'll be right here by your side. You'll say and write everything through me. When all is said and done, you'll be out of here tonight. They'll lodge you in the Fifth Precinct in Patchogue. I'll make sure you're brought before a judge in Central Islip. I'll fly out tonight and be back by morning. See you in court at nine a.m. From there you'll be sent to Riverhead. It'll take a couple of days to get everything before the doctor that I have in mind, along with a judge who might sit on it for a week. I'll do what I can to move things along quickly. Have you inside a private hospital within two weeks, max. I'm going to have to fight like hell to get a reduced sentence for your brother, though. He's not going to just walk away from this. Tell you that right now. I know this prosecutor, and she'll have her claws out after she sees what I'm going to do for you."

"I just don't want them going after Jeffrey for any murders."

"How can they? Not with your confession."

Howard yawned again. "Sorry."

"You know what, Howard? To streamline this procedure, I'll take down your statements myself. Otherwise they'll have you up through the wee hours of morning. In other words, I'll draft the documents for Medford and Melville for them. They'll want to write it out themselves, but at least they'll have a draft to work from. They may want to add some details I'm not aware of. But that's fine as long as you say they're accurate. Anything you find fault with, you have them correct. If you have to change anything, you'll initial that change. You don't sign anything until I see it and give you the okay. Okay?"

"I understand."

"The boys from Brooklyn are a different story. They'll want to start from scratch. But that's all right, too. It's better they don't know you have a lawyer. But I'll make sure I see that document before you sign it. Same with pictures of the crime scene. They'll ask you to identify and initial where you disposed of the bodies. Again, that's fine as long as it's accurate. Don't get careless and admit to putting a body where you didn't put one. Your confession to killing these three women is going to be limited to the bodies you dismembered and disposed of. Not some other unrelated homicide that the boys from Brooklyn want to close the books on.

"Also, there are detectives from other jurisdictions as I mentioned. Nassau and Westchester, that I know of. Cooperate with them as best you can. Then just sit tight and wait for me. You want to do this now? Or do you want to sleep a bit? I think I can get them to cut you a little slack once I tell them that you're cooperating. What do you think?"

"I want to get this over and done with."

"You sure?"

"I'm sure."

"Okay then."

"Sir, may I ask you something?"

"Gary."

"I *can't* call you that."

"Try it. Go ahead. You're going to be paying me a quarter million. I'm working for *you*, Howard. You can ask me anything you like."

Howard smiled. "Can I have visitors at the hospital where I'm going?"

"You can even have conjugal visits. How's that?"

"I'm not sure I understand."

"Means you can screw your brains out if she wants to visit you and stay the night."

Howard's face dropped. "Who's she?" he asked rather apprehensively.

"Whomever," York answered, noting the tension in Howard's face and voice.

"Don't you have to be married?"

"Howard. I'm surprised at you. This is the twentieth century. Are you going to stand on ceremony?"

Howard took his forefinger out from under the collar of his shirt and relaxed. "You mean it?"

"Mr. Mills. I mean everything I say. Now, you sure you're up to this?"

Howard nodded warmly. He liked Gary. He felt like a half a million bucks even though he was practically down a quarter of that in ready cash. It didn't matter. No one would get their hands on his other assets. Few in the family knew about his fortune. Beth and Jeff knew. Beth, he could trust. Jeff, he could not. Howard loved his brother dearly but wouldn't trust him when it came to money. But Beth was different. Besides, she had serious money of her own, inherited from their mother. However, Howard was left the bulk of the estate, secreted in offshore accounts and large holdings in Central and South America. He never touched a penny of that money. Jeff was bad with money, and Howard would always wind up loaning his young brother both small then larger amounts of cash. As it stood, Jeffrey was into Howard for eighteen grand. He had tried to teach his brother how to manage money, but Jeffrey would go through it like water. Just like the beer he drank, he'd simply piss it away. No matter what Howard tried, he could not curtail Jeffrey's poor spending habits. They had had a big argument, and Howard finally drew the proverbial line in the sand. Not one penny more until the entire debt was paid.

"Can I ask you another question, Gary?"

"Shoot."

"Will they really be able to help me at this hospital?"

"Big time. These doctors are some of the best in the country. Not quacks."

Howard was floating. If he could get the help he needed. If he could become whole again like when they were kids. Before his father died. Before the abuse began. He'd take Beth and Jeffrey far, far away. Perhaps to an island somewhere in another country. He'd even buy that island if he had to. He probably could after the smoke cleared, for there was a virtual fortune waiting for him in the wings. What was on record was chump change. Imagine. If he could truly be cured.

"Now, I have a question for you," York put forth.

"Shoot," Howard said playfully, drawing a gun-finger off his hip.

York smiled. "Just between you and me, how many are we talking about here?"

"What do you mean?"

"You know. This person you're protecting. How many women,

Howard? Three? Five? Ten? Tell me. It doesn't matter at this point."

Howard picked up York's pen and put it to the page and place where he left off: *Maybe 100. Maybe more.*

York took his eyes from the page and studied Howard.

"Doesn't change anything, does it?"

"Not a thing," Detective Gary York responded. "Not a blessed thing."

Chapter Nineteen

The caravan had been en route for approximately thirty minutes. Homicide detectives from Team Two, personnel from the Suffolk County Crime Lab Unit, members of the Identification Section, including those from Transport, all converged and set up their mobile Command Post trailer in back of the Catholic high school on Newbridge Road in Hicksville, county of Nassau. All unmarked vehicles were used for the operation, with the procession arriving at precisely 2100 hours.

Thirty minutes later, with search warrants for Howard and Jeffrey Mills' apartments at 42 Willow Lane, two unmarked cars proceeded to the address located two blocks away from the school and church. Detectives Victor Posteraro, Troy Anderson and Frank Masselli parked in front of the house. They got out and went around to the rear entrance of the home. Detectives Michael Connolly, Eric Bokina and John Bailey pulled up. John cut the engine and the trio waited in the car.

No one responded to the downstairs back door knocking and announcement. No one was expected to answer. In less than half the time it took Anderson to break into the apartment earlier, the detective had the door open. Masselli went in low and fast. Posteraro backed him up. A second later, Anderson shined a beam of light on the hurricane lamp sitting on the table. Masselli moved over to it and turned on the switch. With gun in hand, he opened up the metal clothes closet—the only place in the one-room apartment where someone could possibly hide. The dimly lit space was cast in eerie shadows. Troy Anderson put away his penlight and pulled out a hand-held radio.

"Unit One, respond."

"Yeah, Troy."

"We're secure in back, but we need lights in here, big time."

"Copy that. John, radio it in so they're ready."

"Affirmative, Mick." John grabbed the microphone and called in the request.

"Troy, when you're secured upstairs as well, I want you to call on the front apartment; try not to give the old lady a heart attack. I'll have the Command Post move our people in at that time."

"Copy that. Unit Two standing by."

"Standing by." Mick put the radio on the seat between him and John. "Almost showtime, but we got a dark stage. Hope they don't have to run to Home Depot at the last minute for lighting," he half joked.

"Lab Unit and Transport's got all that stuff at the ready, Mick. So just relax," John said.

"Oh, they do, do they? Last time we went on one of these outings they forgot the can of gasoline to run the jackhammer. Recall that scene? We all wound up taking turns breaking our backs busting up slabs of concrete with a sledgehammer. *That* tool they remembered."

"It wasn't the gas they forgot. It was the generator for the pneumatic drill," John replied.

"Oh, a little thing like that."

"You're both wrong, gentlemen," Eric Bokina interjected from the back seat. "It was the tank of compressed gas they forgot to bring along."

The pair turned around and looked at Eric oddly.

Mick made a face. "Well, whatever the hell it was, we'll probably be waitin' around on somethin' while they're runnin' up and down the aisles at Home Depot. You'll see," he swore.

"Home Depot is closed at this hour," Eric mentioned.

"I thought they were open twenty-four hours. No?" John questioned.

"You're probably thinking of Pathmark," Eric added.

"What're you? A fuckin' know-it-all?" Mick remarked.

"Troy says he's always like this," Frank funned. He turned to Eric. "Mick's getting jittery is all. You know how he feels about dead bodies. Afraid he might find one or two in there. Mick just breaks these cases for us. Doesn't like to handle the merchandise."

"Well, he's not going to find one in Howard's apartment," Eric assured them. "Troy and I crawled all over that room on our hands and knees."

"Maybe you guys missed one hanging in the shower," John toyed.

"Ain't no shower or tub or sink either. Not even a stove or oven," Eric told them.

"If there was one, I'd stick your ass on it or in it as soon as we got in there," Mick threatened. "This guy thinks he knows every fucking thing," he addressed his partner. "Another Vic, we got here."

"But there is a cat in Jeffrey's upstairs apartment," Eric persisted. "I can't say the last time it's been fed."

"See, he doesn't know everything," John chuckled.

"Troy and I did hear it running around up there. Probably hungry."

"Good, because I hate fuckin' cats. What's takin' them so long? They've only got the handyman and the old lady, for cryin' out loud. Jeffrey Mills is a no-show."

"Maybe Gary sprung Howard, and he beat us back here," John teased. "Got the landlady's front door barricaded with a pile of bodies," he tormented. "At least a hundred from what I heard."

"I think that lawyer act really went to Gary's head," Eric snickered. "Did you see the look on his face when he came out of that room? He actually handed me his card with Detective crossed out and Attorney-at-Law written in."

All three men were laughing hysterically. Mick was guffawing the loudest, trying to get his words out and over the explosive roar.

"In one hand he's holding Howard's signed confession; in the other he's waving a power of attorney and promissory note for a quarter of a million bucks."

"Did you see the look on his face when Theo ripped it up?" John Bailey howled.

"I thought Gary was going to turn in his gun and badge right then and there," Eric hooted.

"Would have, too, had he had them on him."

"And what does the only legitimate defense attorney in the whole damn building at the time scream out as he's tear-assin' down the hall toward Gary and the lieutenant, in search of his coat, briefcase and thieving client?"

"'*There's* my mohair coat and briefcase!'"

"And Gail Fox convinces Sidney Schatz that his own filching client made off with them earlier but was stopped and questioned by Gary at the exit to the parking lot."

"Then after Schatz leaves in a huff, Gary accuses Gail of trying to upstage him."

Gary's performance was, of course, the Academy Award Winner, and nobody was going to take that away from him. He was to be handed the Oscar. Gail had been nominated on the spot for best supporting actress in a dramatic series, laughed it off graciously, then went on about her business. She would be a busy queen bee for quite some time to come.

These stories were among the many that would be told a thousand times over—limited to themselves and family—conveyed in private booths and rooms at any and all of their favorite watering holes: pubs, bars, taverns and saloons across Long Island and the five boroughs; family picnics, weddings, christenings, confirmations, and funerals.

The most recent story, and a favorite on their hit parade, was one where the Nassau County homicide boys got Sidney Schatz's teenage client to confess to the murder of his stepfather by having a bogus call transferred to the interrogation room as though it were from the attending physician at the hospital where the old man had expired. A deathbed confession was supposedly obtained whereby the father named the son as his murderer. The lad immediately confessed then later recanted. At trial, Schatz's defense had been that Marvin Tolliver, having rushed to his father's aid to check for vital signs upon discovery of the body, was the last person the dying man had seen and, consequently, the son believed that his father believed Marvin was the one responsible for his death. "Imagine how *distraught* my client was at that point," Schatz had told the jury. "How *vulnerable*. They had him doubting himself. At that point, my client would have confessed to the assassination of John F. Kennedy!" The defense attorney's closing argument did not fly, and Marvin Tolliver was found guilty of first degree murder for killing his stepparents.

Detective Gary D. York's *coup de grâce* was a sure contender. It would rank right up there with the best and brightest of ploys. Odds would be set as to the outcome just as soon as all the evidence was in. You could make book on it.

After the three detectives caught their breath and settled back down, Mick went back to worrying. "Call again and see if they brought those lights with them."

"What difference is it going to make now? Huh? Eric just said Home Depot's closed."

"Yeah, but Pathmark's open."

"What good is that? They ain't got the lighting we need."

"Yeah, but what if they brought the lights but forgot the fucking bulbs?" Eric said with a straight face.

Static came across the radio. Mick turned down the squelch.

"...opy?"

"Troy? Come on back to me. You're breaking up, buddy."

"Yeah, we're all secure upstairs and down. You guys ready?"

"Ready as rats. We're on our way. You got the handyman and the landlady out of there?"

"Affirmative. Tough old birds. Both of them. Didn't want to let us in. Hammond called headquarters to check us out."

Mick smiled. "Catch you inside."

"Don't forget the lights. Can't see squat."

"Not to worry. Over."

"Oh, right. Standing by."

Personnel from the Identification Section were busy at work preserving the crime scene, photographing and videotaping the surrounding area of 42 Willow Lane before moving into both the downstairs and upstairs apartments of the two brothers.

For the walk-through, one-hundred-ten-pound Detective Denise Harper carried a fifty-pound video camera atop her shoulder like a bazooka. The woman's male counterpart guided her along lest she should trip and fall and break her neck. He pointed out requisite close-up shots or specific angles with which to work the cumbersome apparatus within the confined space.

Members of the Crime Scene Unit started out by gathering and collecting evidence right behind the pair but were left in the dust, for there was dirt and grime and clutter everywhere. A pile of dirty laundry took up an entire corner of the room. A series of halogen lamps fixed within yellow enameled steel frames or mounted on aluminum tripods bathed the entire room in a surreal brightness. Traces of blood could now be seen everywhere: on the ceiling panels, walls, a single shade, drapes and floor; specks of blood the size of a pinpoint; spots the size of a dime to a nickel; even a blot the size of a silver dollar. Along the back of a metal clothes closet hung something that appeared to be dried human tissue. In addition to the evidence of foul play that Anderson and Bokina had discovered earlier, a crusty white powder was found at the base and in the grooves of one of the wood-paneled walls as well as on the blood-stained mattress, sheets and box spring.

"Cleaning agent," Denise said solemnly, sweeping the baseboard with her video camera.

With a cotton swab, another woman was kneeling in the corner taking a sample of blood from the floor.

"Been there, done that," Eric Bokina whispered giddily, nudging his partner and indicating the woman to his right.

"You mean Cynthia or the sample?" Anderson replied.

"Like to sample some of that."

"Why don't you say it a little louder?"

Cynthia looked over her shoulder and smiled. "Looks as though Batman and Robin paid a surprise visit sometime earlier," she said quietly, turning back around and studying a blood spot with a narrow streak running through it.

"Oh, shit," Eric barely breathed as he and Troy stepped gingerly into another area.

Peter Danowski was off in the far corner of the room taking a tape-lift while his assistant was busy with a miniature crowbar, extruding a piece of carpeting with jute backing from beneath a long strip of molding.

Howard Mills' apartment teemed with teams of men and two women. Like busy ants, they went back and forth and around one another without seeming to get in each other's way, recording on paper and into microphones the blood and gore and other evidence surrounding them: a narrow three-quarter-inch gash in the hardwood floor, apparently made by a chopping implement such as a hatchet; blood specks along the baseboard heating covers, across the top of a green spindle-legged table, a single wooden chair, a hurricane lamp, even the handle of a white ceramic coffee cup, the sides of a dresser and the face of its drawers, a TV/VCR stand. Indications of attempted cover-up, cutting up and concealment were found at the bottom of a metal cabinet: two types of carpet cleaners, a large box of baking soda, a small can of gold-leaf paint found covering certain sections of the sofa bed's wooden framework, construction-weight disposable plastic bags ostensibly consistent with those used to dispose of the victims' bodies. In the bottom dresser drawer was a flattened cardboard box displaying a picture and printed matter pertaining to a Master Mechanic brand miter box. The carnage was evident wherever anyone cared to look.

Eventually, teams of detectives and forensic scientists noted but refrained from taking further samples, citing the massive mountain of evidence before and all around them. Instead, a collective decision was made that the entire apartment would be dismantled and shipped to the crime lab. A major undertaking and somewhat reminiscent of the excavation, dismantling and reconstruction of an underground prison discovered beneath the home of a forty-three-year-old Bay Shore contractor who had kidnapped and concealed a ten-year-old girl a number of years ago.

For the time being, most of the smaller articles were handled in a particular fashion; that is, catalogued, categorized, then bagged or wrapped or placed in Manila envelopes before being put in the van.

The teams worked together through most of the night. A flatbed trailer arrived that morning.

The police now had what they needed, including a signed confession. Howard Mills was going down for the murders of at least three prostitutes. The evidence was, indeed, overwhelming. It was now high time to bring Jeffrey Mills in for questioning. He could summon the best lawyers in the country for all they cared. Homicide had the warrants for the 1986 Cadillac Coupe de Ville and Jeffrey's arrest.

Chapter Twenty

As there were no longer any holding cells with bunks, cots or shower facilities to accommodate a prisoner, coupled to the fact that the boys from Homicide as well as personnel from the ID section had finally finished with Howard Mills, the man was in the process of being transferred. Detective Sergeant Cary Carter had made sure that there were enough pics and prints and photocopies for the detectives who had traveled from other jurisdictions. After everyone present was satisfied, and the media notified while eagerly standing by, Detectives Mick Connolly and John Bailey led Howard Mills out a side door of the building and down the infamous ramp known as The Walk of Shame. The circus was back in town. A crowd of people from the press and radio and television stations were asking questions and thrusting microphones in Howard's face. Mills remained mute. Throngs of spectators were standing just outside the barricaded boundary line. It was 9 p.m., Monday night.

With eyes cast downward, Howard was being escorted toward a waiting vehicle, surrounded by several plainclothes detectives. Just before the group reached the car, an aggressive WCBS radio staff reporter jostled aside a Channel 12 News correspondent, inadvertently clipping Mick's right ear with a microphone.

"Do you have anything to say to the victims' families?" the brash young man practically shouted close to Connolly's other ear, the mike held directly in front of Howard's face.

"I'm sorry," Howard whimpered with tears streaming down his ashen face.

John Bailey gently pushed Howard's head down as Mick put him into the back seat of the sedan then climbed in beside the prisoner. John went around to the other side and slid in, sandwiching Howard between them. The car sped away, heading toward the Fifth Precinct in Patchogue where Mills would be held for arraignment before being brought to district court in Central Islip.

"Do you believe that guy screaming in my ear like that?" Mick complained, poking and twisting a pinky into his ear. "Almost took my other fuckin' ear off with his microphone. I thought he was questioning *me*, for Christ's sake. Well-nigh answered the little prick. That would've been real cute. Where do they find these people, John?"

John Bailey was laughing and shaking his head. "I don't know, Mick. I really and truly don't."

The following afternoon, Howard Mills stood in handcuffs at his arraignment hearing before The Honorable Arthur R. Roberts. It was 1:00 p.m. The court reporter was having trouble feeding paper into her machine.

"Off the record," the judge motioned then addressed Howard Mills. "Mr. Mills."

"Good afternoon, Your Honor." The perfect gentleman.

"Good afternoon, Mr. Mills. There seems to be some confusion, sir. I'm getting mixed signals. Are you being represented here by counsel, or do you wish the court to appoint an attorney for you?"

Howard glanced nervously over his shoulder. "Yes, sir."

"Yes sir, what?"

"Yes, sir—Your Honor."

Judge Roberts smiled. "Mr. Mills. Is your attorney present in this courtroom?"

Howard turned around and scanned the back of the room. "No, sir."

A court officer stepped up behind Howard and faced him forward.

"Your Honor, if I may," Assistant District Attorney Gail Fox intervened.

"May you what?"

"Explain that Mr. Mills—"

"Are you representing Mr. Mills?" the judge frowned.

Gail Fox's face flushed. "Judge—"

"Didn't think so."

"Sir, I thought my attorney . . . he was supposed—supposed to be here," Howard stammered anxiously.

Gail was shaking her head. "Judge, if I could be heard— "

Judge Roberts raised his hand like a stop sign and directed his attention back to the defendant. "Mr. Mills. If you do not have an attorney present and wish to call one, or in the event that you cannot afford an attorney, the court will appoint one for you. Do you understand that?"

"Yes, sir. I have a lawyer. Mr. Gary D. York, of York and York, out of Boston. He was supposed to fly out last night and be back here sometime early this morning. But I guess he's not back yet."

Gail Fox spoke up once again. "Please, Your Honor. If I may—"

"No, you may not. I see that we either have a simple misunderstanding or something more along the lines of a conflict here, and I prefer that we be on the record. Are we almost ready, Mary?"

"Yes, Judge. Just another second," the court reporter promised. "There."

"All right. Go ahead, Ms. Fox."

"Thank you, Your Honor. As I was about to say, first off, the defendant is trying to pull a stunt here by telling this Court that he has a lawyer. He was told several times this morning, and as recently as an hour ago, to contact one; and as far as I know, he has refused to do so. Secondly, the only Gary D. York that we know of is a detective with the Suffolk County Homicide Squad in Yaphank, who handled the prisoner activity log while the defendant was in custody, and who briefly interviewed Mr. Mills for purposes of obtaining pedigree information with regard to his medical history. Thirdly, Judge, this man standing before you is most assuredly not of indigent status, as he has over three-hundred thirty thousand dollars in liquid assets and, therefore, does not qualify for any public assistance, which should he be appointed such, would be a fraud perpetrated on the taxpayers of this county."

Judge Roberts stared at ADA Fox for several seconds before he spoke. "May I see you at the bench, please?"

"Sir, I do have—" Mills managed to get out of his mouth before he was interrupted.

"Mr. Mills. You will have ample opportunity to speak to me through your attorney just as soon as we find you one. Now, what I was going to propose was that we assign an ad interim attorney to represent Mr. Mills, and move these proceedings right along. But in light of what I'm hearing here, I think we'll break for lunch. I may put this over until tomorrow morning. In the meantime—Matthew—I want you to locate two phone directories for Mr. Mills. Both the Nassau and Suffolk Yellow Pages. Mr. Mills, I'd like you to start hunting for a lawyer immediately. Understood?" There was no time for Howard to reply. "You may take him out, Matt. But I want him back by two o'clock."

"Yes, Judge," the senior court officer spoke up smartly, leading a very unhappy and confused prisoner out a side door of the courtroom.

"And I'll speak to Ms. Fox off the record for a moment, Mary. Just hang tight."

"Yes, Judge."

Judge Roberts and ADA Fox had a brief conference at the bench, with Gail doing most of the talking.

A moment later, the judge nodded in the affirmative. "Court will recess until two o'clock," he announced before standing and heading to his chambers.

Chapter Twenty-One

Detectives Eric Bokina and Troy Anderson of the Suffolk County Homicide Squad paid an unannounced visit to Beth Tracy in Orient Point. Neither of them was impressed with the supposed security. Beth's condominium overlooked Long Island Sound. The two men stood at the threshold of her apartment for a good minute before the young woman answered the door in a firm but civil voice.

"Yes? Who is it, please?"

"Suffolk County Homicide. We'd like to ask you a few questions concerning Howard Mills, ma'am," Bokina stated.

Beth turned the deadbolt then opened the door ajar against the short length of chain set squarely in its track. "Identification, please," she declared matter-of-factly.

Bokina smiled in mild amusement and reached inside his trench coat for the leather fold to which the detective's shield was pinned.

"Hold it in the door," Beth ordered, her fingers summoning the ID toward her. "The badge, Detective. I want to see your badge."

Both detectives knew that Beth Tracy was totally blind from birth. Bokina extended his shield partway through the door.

After running the tips of her long fingers over the embossed numbers, Beth cupped her hand around the badge. "Your number, Detective."

"I beg your pardon?"

"Your badge number," she clarified. "You don't want me to think that you picked this up in some novelty store, do you, Detective?"

"Three-Zero-One, ma'am," Bokina responded on the verge of a laugh.

"And the taller one standing next to you wearing Old Spice aftershave?"

Bokina grinned. "You want to check his badge, too?" Eric asked politely, eating this woman up alive.

"No," she said flatly. "I want you to tell him where he might purchase that Bay Rum cologne you have on so that he might better hide the hint of garlic from the meal the two of you had at Carlos' around the corner before coming here," she offered with absolute amusement, closing the door to the apartment before sliding the chain off its track, reopening the door widely with a warm welcome. "Please do come in."

The two homicide detectives entered the spacious studio apartment and absorbed the pleasant aroma coming from the large open kitchen.

"Excuse me for just a moment," Beth said, closing but not locking the door before stepping past them, heading toward the stove.

"Tomato sauce?" Bokina asked.

"The very same sauce you had at Carlos'," Beth replied with a satisfactory smile lost on the two detectives as she stood with her back to them. "Although Carlos would never call it sauce, but gravy." Grabbing an oven mitt, she lifted the lid off a huge stainless steel pot, stirring its contents with a long wooden spoon.

"Smells delicious," Bokina said sincerely, coming up behind her.

Detective Anderson walked over to a bookcase and observed a number of Braille books stacked along the shelves.

Beth removed the spoon and put it down upon an oval plate set in the center of the stove between the burners, replaced but tilted the lid of the pot back a fraction, then removed her oven mitt.

Bokina observed the array of cooking utensils: slotted metal and wooden spoons, small spatula, and a pair of scissors. Cooking in a pan, above a low flame, were links of sausages.

"I make the sauce exclusively for that cozy little restaurant the two of you enjoyed. Oh, I hope I'm not taking it for granted that you did enjoy," she added apologetically.

"No, no. Not at all," Anderson said, coming into the conversation. "We were just saying what a find that restaurant truly is. I haven't had such a fine Italian meal like that since I can remember," he swore. "And the two of us raved about the sauce—excuse me, gravy—and sausage. Honestly."

"Well, that's really nice to hear. It's an Old World recipe that my great-grandfather handed down through generations. The secret is in the variety and combination of tomatoes I use. Not to mention a blend of seasonings. I put up over two hundred quarts myself last season. From garden to freezer to Carlos'."

"Impressive," Bokina offered.

"Come, come. Let's go inside," she coaxed, shutting off the flame below the sausages.

"I would think an operation like this would be done in a commercial kitchen," Anderson commented.

"Normally, it would be," Beth agreed. "But I guess the owner feels that I need something to do other than just sit around reading books," she elaborated, gesturing to the bookcase where she knew Anderson had been snooping moments ago. "It kind of works out nicely for both of us," Beth continued. "I won't give out the recipe, for which he offered to pay me handsomely, plus other perks," she said in a rather furtive tone. "Instead, he pays me a handsome per quart price, charges his customers accordingly, outdoes his competition, and everybody is happy."

"Does he provide you with the meat?" Bokina asked.

"Yes, he does, Detective. This is actually a modest operation. I truly wouldn't wish to take on much more. As it is, last season I put up a hundred quarts over what I did the year before. If Carlos' business continues to grow at the rate it has, we'll have to talk about hiring some people to help me out there." Beth gestured toward the expansive gardens beyond the large bay window at the back of the apartment that overlooked the Sound. "Anyhow, you didn't come here to talk about my gravy or fine restaurants in the area. But I thank you for showing an interest and letting me go on."

"Not at all. We came to ask you some questions about your brother, Howard," Anderson repeated.

"Half brother," Beth corrected.

"Half brother," Anderson conceded.

"I heard Howard on the news last night say that he was sorry after a reporter had asked him if he had anything to say to the families.

He's a sorry shit, Detectives, I'm sorry to say."

"Have you had any contact with Howard recently?" Anderson questioned.

"No," Beth said matter-of-factly, shaking her dark head simultaneously.

"No visits? Phone calls?"

"I haven't spoken to Howard, Jeffrey, or Ronald in many years. And as you may or may not know, Lenny, the youngest, committed suicide some twenty years ago. I haven't seen any of them since we were children. When Mom died, so did the family. All ties were abruptly untied for one reason or another. Up until that time, Mom had kept the family together as I suppose moms are meant to do."

"No cards or correspondence from anyone in the family around the holidays?" Bokina inquired.

"No, and if I had, I wouldn't waste the postage on Howard or any of them, Detective. Received nothing. Wrote nothing." Beth took a seat on the couch and crossed her shapely legs. "Why don't you gentlemen sit down, and I'll pour you an after-dinner drink. I might even join you. I know that neither of you had anything stronger than a glass of wine at Carlos'. Otherwise, I'd detect it on your breath."

Bokina looked at Anderson, and Anderson shook his head. "No, we have a good ride ahead of us. But thanks just the same."

"And you have no further questions for me? I must say I am surprised. Actually, a little disappointed, too. I wish I could have been helpful, even in some small way," she said most convincingly, frowning somewhat plaintively.

"No need to feel that way at all. No contact since you were children puts an end to it right there. Not every interview leads to a successful outcome. Lots of dead ends along the way, I can assure you. But I do have an unrelated question out of sheer curiosity, Miss Tracy."

"Beth. Please call me Beth," she said, dropping the wall of formality. "Now, let me see if I can guess your question. Why is it that I have a TV when a radio would make more sense? Am I right?" she questioned and smiled broadly.

"Actually, I half expected to find you with a seeing-eye dog," Anderson said, looking around the apartment as though one might suddenly appear on cue.

"A guide dog," Beth remarked.

"Yes."

"Well, I guess if I went places often, I might need a dog like that. But I pretty much confine myself to a several block area at most. Carlos' for an occasional dinner. The market. Walks along the beach. And, of course, my gardens out back where I spend a good deal of time between June and September."

"I see," Anderson said.

"And I don't, Detective," Beth replied pleasantly.

"I'm sorry. I didn't mean—" Anderson paused uncomfortably.

Beth laughed lightly. "Don't let me make you feel uneasy, Detective Anderson. No negative transference, please. When you leave here, I'd like for you and Detective Bokina to feel uplifted in the knowledge that I do, indeed, *see* more than most folks. Sure, euphemistically speaking, my situation may be referred to as either sight-challenged or sight-impaired, but although I've never seen, say, one of my tomatoes, let alone the color red, I can and do perceive it in all its God-given splendor. During early summer evenings, I can hold one in my hands and feel the warmth that the sunshine has bestowed upon it throughout the day. Then in late fall, before the first frost firms the fruit and kills, I remember that I was there for the early gathering— all shapes and sizes . . . round and oval, big and small—then finally, harvesting the cool ripe fruit before the rot takes hold." Beth uncrossed her lovely legs and rose. "Sorry, I do get carried away."

The two detectives got up, looking at one another and then at Beth. She stood tall and certainly beautiful before them. A fairy-tale princess. A poet. A rare bird. A rare find, like Carlos' restaurant. A caged ripe wonder. Forbidden fruit. Their minds were reeling.

"Well, I think we've taken up enough of your time," Detective Anderson said evenly.

"Not at all, Detective. I'll be planting around the end of May, so if you're ever in the area, gentlemen, don't hesitate to call. I'll give you my private number." Beth tore off a small sheet of paper from a pad lying on an end table beside a white leather couch. "A single woman living alone in an apartment can't be too careful," she explained, jotting down the number. Beth extended a hand, holding out the paper.

"Believe me, we know. So just be sure to lock the door behind us," Anderson instructed, taking the paper from between her fingers, brushing hers with his.

"Good evening, ma'am," Bokina said, heading toward the door.

"Good night," Beth said brightly.

"Good night," Anderson said congenially.

"Night, gentlemen."

"Ah, one last thing," Eric said.

"Yes, Detective?"

"Why *do* you have a TV instead of a radio?"

"Soaps."

"Excuse me?"

"Soap operas. Radio today just doesn't capture the essence of sheer drama."

"Ah," Eric said with a degree of satisfaction.

"But I do have a radio in the bedroom for a gardening hotline that I enjoy. Best of both worlds," she said, smiling, closing and securing the door behind them.

Chapter Twenty-Two

Detective Gary York sat up in bed before dropping a pile of journals and reports to the floor—materials referencing the new death penalty law that had tapped the last bit of concentration from a weary brain. He reached over and switched off the nightstand light. Gary was exhausted. Yet, a lingering thought kept running through his mind—a thought concerning Howard W. Mills' confession. A thought Gary could not put to rest. A thought that he had wrestled with while trying to watch the late night news. The distraction hadn't worked. He hadn't been able to drop the notion like the pile of papers.

Gary York had been a policeman too many years not to know when something was truly wrong. Too many years on the street as a beat cop. Too many psych classes at college and, eventually, training courses at the FBI Academy. Too many years as a detective in narcotics. Then, at long last, the last fourteen years at *home* in Homicide, where he knew he doubtlessly belonged. He had the God-awful feeling that Howard Mills had somehow told him the truth after all. The whole truth. Yet, all the evidence pointed to Howard. Admittedly, some of the trace evidence pointed to his brother, Jeffrey, too. Easily explainable by the fact that the orange polyester carpet fibers and cat hairs could and would be transferable between two cities, let alone two apartments situated no more than sixty feet away from one another. Jeffrey upstairs. Howard downstairs. Still, something didn't jive. *Christ!* It would be so easy just to look the other way, Gary battered about. Or to at least roll over and lose himself in sleep till morning. But he couldn't. Not yet. Only complete and *total* exhaustion would put his mind to rest for a few hours. He was on the brink but would not surrender until unconsciousness finally claimed him.

Howard Mills' arrest and signed confession were a feather in Team Two's cap, and the D.A.'s office would be tickled pink with it in the end, especially if Gail Fox came away with a conviction, which everyone believed to be a given in light of the extraordinary amount of evidence. So why on God's good green earth couldn't Gary make things fit? Why? *Leave it alone*, a voice inside him had said, for he and Connolly were practically heroes. Of course, the other teams, too, had participated in the grandiose event, having gathered important information here and there over the course of many months. Both he and Mick were kind of like authors sharing the by-line of an award-winning news story. A most conniving story that would hopefully, God forbid, never find its way into print. A story that would have to remain behind the closed doors of fellow detectives, family and close friends. Just as reporters sought the truth, so did law enforcement. And no matter what laws were or weren't on the books, Homicide used *any* and *all* means possible to obtain exactly that, which did not exclude threatening, tormenting, scheming, starving, or promising a suspect the moon. In rare instances, the pursuit of truth included hitting and/or beating a prisoner. There was a simple allegiance among the teams. There was a pact. The end justifies the means. Period. And any liberal thinker who thought otherwise was a damn fool. The danger? The preconceived notion of guilt. But Howard Mills was guilty! But of what? Murder? Or solely, postmortem amputation as he had said.

Arresting the wrong man or woman for murder did not sit well with Gary, although there were noted exceptions to that rule, as when the Frenchman from Staten Island, who had beaten, sodomized, then severed the heads of his victims, added insult to injury by beating the rap. The next victim the police found was the work of a copycat murderer. Not Frenchie, although they hauled his ass in anyhow. Homicide as well as the district attorney knew the score. This time out, a jury convicted Frenchie. *C'est la vie.* Not that Homicide ever stopped hunting for the real copycat killer.

If it wasn't Howard who had killed Darla and those other

women, then who was it? Howard had stated emphatically and convincingly that his brother, Jeffrey, was not involved. Again, Gary had asked himself, then who? One of the other detectives from Team Three had checked out a friend of Howard's who lived in the upstairs apartment before Jeffrey moved in. Another postal worker, by God! The man hadn't lasted very long in that apartment or at his job. Maybe it was the glue, Gary considered jokingly. He recalled David Berkowitz, The Son of Sam. Another employee gone postal. *Had* to be the glue, he thought giddily. The prior upstairs tenant at 42 Willow Lane was a drifter. A thorough investigation concerning Howard's friend ended up as another dead end. Nuts, but no killer. And then there was the brothers' middle brother, Ronald. Clean as they come. Clean as the steel deck on a naval vessel just before inspection. Counselor at a correctional facility in Nassau County. Helping to save others. Probably had to save himself in early childhood. Troy and Eric's visit to the half sister in Orient hadn't shed any light on the situation either. Beth Tracy. Tall. Attractive. Intelligent. Ambitious. And totally blind from birth as revealed through a thorough background check.

Gary York was reminded of the phrase, *There are none so blind as those who will not see*, as he hung and stirred in limbo somewhere between semiconsciousness and sleep. What wasn't he seeing? Tonight, like many sleepless nights, he hadn't bothered counting bodies in order to fall asleep . . . for there was a single wolf somewhere out there in sheep's clothing, he now believed. Why was he doing this to himself? What could he have possibly missed? Was he himself blindsided by all the evidence? The thought haunted him as he drifted back and forth and in and out of consciousness.

No doubt Howard Mills was nuts. But that wasn't for Gary to decide. Many a nut out there functioned in society. Maybe because half the world was bonkers. Howard somehow managed to function for over forty years. The question was could Howard Mills possibly be telling the truth? Crazy or crazy like a fox? Wasn't that part of the equation, too?

Gary had slept for no more than forty minutes before he suddenly awoke. It was two o'clock in the morning. Without turning on the light, he rolled over and reached for the phone. On his old black rotary, he dialed Mick's home number—by Braille. The phone rang six times before Mick's wife answered.

"Hello?" It was a sweet and sleepy greeting.

"See, you got men calling you at all hours."

"Only you, Gary. Everything all right?"

"Just ducky."

"Nobody shot?" she chaffed and yawned, knowing from his tone that their world was temporarily safe and well for the moment.

"Mick accounted for?" was his answer and question rolled into one.

"Too tired to turn and tell, but I do feel the lump of a big lug next to me," she said, giving her husband a shove.

"Put him on and go back to sleep."

"Try. Bye." Sheila handed her husband the phone.

"Yeah—Mick," Mick said, rubbing one eye and peering at the radio alarm clock.

"No, I'm Gary. You're Mick."

"It's two a.m."

"What did he come in with?" Gary asked, ignoring Mick's nasty, raspy timbre.

"He, who?"

"You sound like a sick donkey. Howard Mills. Who do you think?"

"I think I'm an ass for talking to you at this hour."

"*Now* you sound a little more like you."

"What the fuck are you doing, Gary?"

"*Now* I'm *positive* it's you."

"Don't try and humor me. I've got a meeting in a few hours. I got to bed after twelve."

"Remember when we used to get by on four hours after partying most of the night? We're getting old, Mick."

"No, your calling me in the middle of the night at home is what's getting old."

"How about when you and the sergeant called me in on the eve of Easter to work the prisoner activity log, then rehearse and play nursemaid to my prospective *client*. How many hours are we talking about?"

Mick was smiling. "Your fault you're single," he grumbled.

"Just tell me what he had on him, and you can go back to bed."

Mick rubbed his other eye. "His house and car keys on one ring, eyeglasses, about two-hundred twenty some-odd dollars in his wallet, railroad stub, credit cards along with a membership card to that Manhattan S & M club, some loose change, a plastic lens case, an old rent receipt found stuck in his jacket pocket . . . let's see . . . tissues, stick of gum, wrappers and some crap like that. That's about it. You'd have to check with Artie for the list. Lots of luck."

"Nothing out of the ordinary?"

"Nope. John checked, and everything checked out. Oh, just one lens in the lens case. Probably lost the other."

"Contact lens?"

"Yeah, boys might find the other in one of his dresser drawers. We got a ton of shit to sift through. It's gonna take some time. Where's all this leading, Gary?"

"I don't know, Mick. I really don't."

"You're not gonna piss on our parade. Are you, laddie? Drum up some questionable shit?"

"Not at all, Mick."

"Statements are ironclad, Gary, tied in with all that evidence. And we're only getting started."

"I know."

"Then what gives? What's on your mind with Mills? And why couldn't this wait till morning?"

"'*Tis* morning, Mick, and a fine one at that because I'm off today. And furthermore, ya know I can't discuss me client with ye, Paddy." Gary hung up and laughed hilariously into his pillow.

Mick glared at the receiver before slamming it onto its cradle.

"Now go to sleep," Sheila ordered.

"Oh, right," Mick muttered, swinging his legs out from beneath the covers and feeling for his slippers with his bare feet. "I'm gonna take a shine to that boy with me father's shillelagh, so help me I am," he swore, loping toward the bathroom in a single moccasin.

"I guess you're forgetting that I'm the only person alive who knows that you were orphaned at birth, Micky dear," Sheila reminded him through another yawn, stretching her arms then hands against the headboard.

"If alive is the way you like it," he called back.

"Don't worry, my pussycat. Your secret is safe with me."

"I hate pussycats," he called back louder than the last announcement.

"That's okay, too, tiger. They don't much like you either. Coffee?"

"I can't hear you."

"*Do·do·do·do do·do. Do·do·do do·do,*" she perked loudly.

"Only if you're having some."

"Right," she said softly, laughing lightly. "Right."

Gary covered his lingering grin and chin with a cupped hand, pondering what Mick had said about Howard Mills having a single contact lens in its case. Howard hadn't needed glasses or contacts when writing or reading over his statement. Presumably just for distance. Like when driving—driving the women to their graves. Gary read into everything. It drove some of his colleagues mad.

Was Howard truly protecting someone? Why did he keep insisting that he didn't kill anyone, even after having confessed to postmortem amputation? Gary kept asking himself that question again and again. Howard had told Mick and John during the interrogation that he wanted people to like him. Maybe it was as simple as that. He didn't want people to think badly of him. Under the influence of drugs, he probably became a different person. A monster. He became enraged. End of story. Yes? No? It was the way in which Howard had said and written things down that was driving Gary mad. So convincingly. Well, sure. If Howard wanted to believe that himself, fine. One thing Gary felt he absolutely knew for certain was that Howard Mills was not afraid to die—like pulling down a dark shade, only Howard couldn't pull the cord himself.

Chapter Twenty-Three

Artie 'No Neck' came to the front of the property cage and pushed the register log toward Detective York. The old man's rather bulbous, bald head sat on a pair of broad shoulders much like the conning tower of a submarine.

"Got to sign for them, Gary." The sixty-five-year-old fellow set the Manila envelope containing Howard Mills' personal effects down on the counter.

Gary turned the register around and signed. He picked up the envelope and started to open it.

"I gotta do that for you, Gary. Sorry. Them's the rules."

"I like rules, Artie."

"That's good because then we're gonna get along just fine," the old-timer scowled. "Only wish more people around here would follow them."

"Amen to that."

Artie emptied the contents of the envelope onto the counter.

"Can I see that lens case open for a second?"

"Hold your horses."

Artie opened the case then reached for an inventory list to make a check mark next to *one (1) white plastic lens case; one (1) green contact lens: right jacket pocket.* He was about to hand the item over for inspection when Gary put a hand on Artie's wrist and pointed down at the lens.

"What?" the old man snapped.

"Anybody dust?" Gary let go of the property clerk's hand.

Artie 'No Neck' looked down at the contact lens then up over his right shoulder, turning completely around while scanning the entire cage before facing front. He shook his head. "Nope. Nobody dusted a damn thing in here in a decade. Kind of like McSorley's in the city. Oh, you mean for prints," Artie kibitzed.

Gary smiled. "I want to take this lens and case with me, Artie."

"Be my guest, but you gotta first fill out a form."

"Gotcha."

"And it don't leave this room until the lieutenant okays it."

"Lieutenant took the morning off and went trout fishing."

Artie shrugged. "Then Sergeant Carter will have to sign for it."

"Can I have a close peek inside? Or do I need a form?" He was still smiling.

"Suit yourself."

"Got some latex gloves back there, Artie?"

Artie looked perturbed. "Let me ask you something, Detective. Do you know the difference between the property locker and the evidence vault? You're asking me for gloves, yet you guys had your mitts all over this stuff. And you know damn well this wasn't dusted 'cause it'd be a mess and wouldn't be in here anyway if it was. Guess where it would be?"

"In evidence in the evidence vault."

"Bingo!"

Gary's smiling eyes locked on to Artie's petulant stare. "Let me ask *you* something."

Artie didn't blink.

"Want to help me work this case?"

"I thought you guys just did that," the keeper of the cage said indifferently, reaching down behind the counter and coming up with a pair of latex gloves, which he handed over.

Gary put them on. "I think there's more to this than meets the eye," he punned, staring down at the odd dark green lens.

Artie leaned across the counter. "You think someone else is involved?"

"That's what I want to find out."

"My wife thinks the younger brother, Jeffrey, is more involved,"

Artie confided, dropping his voice to a whisper.

"Your wife or you?"

Artie smiled. "Little bit of both, I guess."

"So, you want to help me with this?"

"Hum. Let me guess how." Artie looked toward the ceiling as if searching for a clue. "You want me to give you the lens case and lens, but you don't want Sergeant Carter or anyone else to know about it because they're gonna turn gun-shy because a bird in their hand is worth two in the bush. But you want the other dirty bird, too. Do I have it straight?"

"Along with all your marbles, Artie."

Artie was shaking his head. "Tell you what the problem with that is."

"Tell me."

"If *you're* interested in this here lens case, then somebody else might be interested, too. And what am I supposed to do if that person comes around lookin'? Huh? Anybody else aware you're taking a look?"

"I asked Mick what you inventoried," Gary admitted.

"See what I mean?"

"Sure do. So, I'll tell you what."

Artie looked at Gary skeptically. "What?"

"I'll fill out the form, and you hold on to it along with the case."

"But you want the lens because probably nobody put their mitts on it. Just looked at it like you're doing now."

"If nobody inquires before I get back, shit-can my request. I'll have the lens back to you in a few hours. Long before Theo returns with a fish story but no fish, and even before Carter ever has his late morning cup of coffee."

"And if somebody does come lookin' for it and the lens ain't in there?"

"You tell them it was in there when Gary looked last but that the jerk dropped it behind the counter and it probably rolled underneath one of those dusty bins behind you."

"A few hours, you say?"

"Promise."

Artie stroked his chin deliberately. "What's so all-fired interesting about that lens anyhow?"

"It's green."

"I can see that, Sherlock."

"Howard Mills' eyes are brown."

"May be his brother's. Brothers are always borrowing one another's clothes. Maybe Jeff left them in his jacket. Howard grabbed the coat. No real mystery there."

"His brother's eyes are blue. So regardless of whose jacket it is, why would either of them be carrying around a green contact lens? And where's the other lens?"

"Maybe he wanted to change his appearance. Maybe he lost the other one. You know how easy that is to do," Artie said with a knowing smile, referring to Dan Fowler's walk-around, the dog handler ostensibly searching for a contact lens before Max's alert to Mills' Cadillac.

"Change his appearance to what, Artie? Look how dark this lens is," Gary remarked, holding the edges of the tiny optic between his glove-covered thumb and forefinger, raising the contact lens toward the overhead light.

"Isn't there another brother?"

"No contact, and no pun intended. Besides, Ronald's eyes are brown like Howard's."

"Well, maybe one of them can't take the sun. Hurts his eyes."

"From the looks of this lens, I'd say it would block out the noonday sun if its owner were in Death Valley."

"Maybe his eyes are diseased or something—like his mind."

"If it's Howard's, I can understand why he didn't ask for them for writing or reading over his statements."

"He does have eyeglasses," Artie said, noting the list and its contents.

"I wonder if this lens is prescription or what?"

"I'd look along the lines of someone trying to change their appearance like I said."

"Some kind of a disguise you think?"

"As good a guess as any. Seems as though you can rule out one brother trying to look like the other. Because apart from Howard's poor complexion, and the color of his brother's eyes from what you said, they look a lot alike. Same height. Practically the same build."

"You're right."

Artie 'No Neck' picked up a form and pushed it toward Gary. "You got till after lunch to do what you gotta do, Detective."

He handed Gary a smaller Manila envelope into which the detective deposited the lens.

"I heard you were a helluva dick in your day, Artie."

Artie thought for a second. "Don't exactly know how to take that."

"I'm talking about a first-rate cop."

"Most of the stuff I learned from reading Dick Tracy. That's a fact, Gary. Imitated him, too, as a kid. Couldn't wait for the Sunday funny papers. Later, I fulfilled that dream. Never did get one of those two-way wrist radios though," he added with a smile. "Yeah, Dick Tracy was my hero."

Beth Tracy suddenly popped back into York's brain. He'd have to pay her a visit, too, real soon.

Chapter Twenty-Four

Detective Gary York drove from his home in East Patchogue out to Orient Point. It was his second day off in four months since Mick's Melville victim, Darla, was discovered. It had been a grueling twenty-eight months since the Mills madness began with Frank Masselli's Jane Doe/Medford victim. Twenty-eight intensive months with very little rest for the four teams. Lead after lead leading nowhere. All dead ends. Their big break came when Mick interviewed a prostitute who had last seen Darla getting into a dark blue Cadillac driven by a john who frequented the Jamaica Avenue area in Queens. Further investigation turned up two hookers who had been to the suspect's apartment somewhere in Nassau County, but after repeated attempts made by Mick, driving the girls through several neighborhoods, they failed to find the residence.

Several days later, another street girl who had been to Howard's home on more than one occasion had led Mick to Howard Mills' residence.

That's his car in the driveway, and that's the house, she had said with certainty. *Downstairs back apartment.*

From that day forward, surveillance on the two brothers had begun. The problem, however, was manpower. The fact that Mills' apartment was in Nassau, not Suffolk County, didn't help the situation.

To compound matters, the teams had been investigating the homicide of a female Riverhead High School student, knifed by a schoolmate ninety-six times. *Talk about overkill*, Gary entertained.

Today, Gary York felt as though he was back to square one on the Hicksville case. The Mills madness wouldn't let go.

It was Eric Bokina's preliminary report in addition to the conversation Gary York had with Troy Anderson concerning Beth Tracy that piqued York's curiosity with regard to the woman's dark, dead green eyes. Further inquiry reconfirmed the fact that she had been blind from birth. Eric had run a National Crime Investigation Center (NCIC), File 15 check on Beth Tracy. Negative. No drug arrest. No priors of any sort. Nothing. *Not even a jaywalking violation*, Eric had related with amusement. Both Eric and Troy had found the woman remarkable. Charming. Attractive. Intelligent. And well-adjusted in spite of her handicap. The fact that she had never attended any kind of school for the blind, or sought the aid of a guide dog to help herself get around more easily made Gary all the more curious—even though the assigned detectives had explained that the woman was very much self-reliant and kept within proximity to her home.

The Seeing-Eye organization in Morristown, New Jersey had been quite helpful in answering many of York's inquiries with respect to the difficulties and adaptations experienced by the blind. But after speaking to the director and throwing out hypothetical questions, Gary was getting more and more discouraged with his suppositions. However, his interview with an optometrist in Patchogue had offered him a glimmer of hope in that the detective wasn't necessarily heading down a blind alley, so to speak. Still, in the game of guesswork and legwork, it wouldn't be the first or last time that Gary D. York would be wrong. His theory was unlikely to pan out, he had admitted to himself. Yet, he had to satisfy his nagging curiosity.

Besides, he was enjoying the ride out East so that it shouldn't be a total loss. He loved the North Fork's rural roads that ran along sod farms, nurseries, vegetable fields, and shoreline. Sound Avenue was a slice of heaven to him. It was a shame that it was too early in the season for the local vegetable stands to open, but he had heard that Briermere Farm now operated year-round. And that meant fresh baked goodies, all homemade on the premises, supposedly. Cookies to covet. Breads and pastries to behold. Cream pies to die for. God's sinful gift to the locals as well as visitors from near and far. It was one of three of Gary's vices: speed, women and sweets. Amazing he wasn't a roly-poly. High metabolism. Fast-paced lifestyle.

Gary had the Audi up to ninety on a fifty-mile-an-hour stretch of road before letting up on the accelerator, having caught up to the car in front of him. Too dangerous to pass. Thank God there were no cattle farms or crossings. There were certainly deer, but he figured that they were bedded down for the day. It was 8 a.m. His ex hated when he got behind the wheel. He hated his ex toward the end of their relationship and drove her nuts. He didn't miss marriage as he was married to his work. A more honest reason was that he was having too much fun whenever he found the time to play around. But for the past twenty-eight months, it had been the Mills case that literally took up every waking moment. Gary's new girlfriend had been put on hold; that is, if she was still waiting in the wings.

Beth's condo was on the Point; literally at the water's edge. Next stop east, Portugal or Spain—if you cared or dared. The Long Island Sound was alive with four-foot waves crashing against the shoreline. Gary drove his sports car into the gated community of condominiums, then parked. Spring was indeed everywhere. The local nurseries knew how to push the season by forcing bulbs. Tulips, hyacinths and lilies in large octagonal cedar pots fastened with brass straps flaunted their glorious pinks, whites, yellows and purples. He entered the lobby and was stopped by a surly doorman who had just finished signing for a FedEx package.

"Business, sir?" the tall blue-uniformed effeminate snipped snootily from a pair of tight thin lips.

Gary just loved these types. "Police business." He flashed his badge. "Beth Tracy. Unit three. I'll find my way."

The attendant looked down his Roman nose at Gary, unimpressed with his credentials or efficiency. "I'm sorry, sir, but Ms. Tracy is away on holiday."

Gary was caught off guard. "Holiday?"

"Holiday," the man repeated pompously, covering a birthmark with a fingertip to the right side of his face.

"Holiday, where?"

"You'll have to make your inquiry at the front desk."

"Do you know how long Ms. Tracy will be gone?"

"You may pick up the phone at that counter over there," the doorman indicated with a limp wrist, pointing out the direction with a skinny forefinger and pinkie that never quite left the area between chest and chin nor more than an inch away from a set of shiny brass buttons.

Gary wanted to put his own forefinger and pinkie in the fag's sleepy blue eyes. The creep had pedophile written all over him. Instead, the detective elected to use the doorman as a doormat. Gary made sure no one else was around. The FedEx truck was already heading out the iron gates.

"Come 'ere, Ellis," Gary ordered, although the attendant was standing no more than a foot away.

"I beg your pardon?" the man replied, glancing down at his own nametag as Detective Gary York grabbed it along with a hunk of blue material to which it was attached.

The two were standing toe-to-toe, seeing eye to eye.

"I'm really not a phone person, Ellis. And I don't have time to screw around. When did she leave here? Where did she go? And when is she expected back?"

Ellis started to protest.

"Hold back on me and you'll find yourself at headquarters in Yaphank standing in a lineup in your bikini underwear. Got a dozen little boys coming in this evening with their parents from Greenport and Southold who told their moms and dads that a tall man—I believe they said who had a brown mark on the side of his face—touched their private parts and exposed himself," Gary prevaricated, inventing the story on the spot. "You won't be out of there before two a.m. the earliest, unless you're identified, in which case you can be your own doorman in a private cell. How's that?"

The doorman's dreamy blue eyes were now wide awake and on red alert. "Ms. Tracy had somebody come by last night and pick up some of her things. Never saw him before."

"What things?" Gary released his grip.

"Couple of suitcases. Garment bag and a hat box."

"Did he say where she might be going?"

"No, sir."

"When she might be back?"

"I didn't ask. But from the few things he took out of here, I'd say it couldn't be for too long. Besides, she always plants her tomatoes sometime before the end of May."

"What did this person look like?"

"Tall. Medium build. Dark complexion."

"Black?"

"I meant well-tanned. White. Nicely dressed. I really didn't pay much attention."

"Of course not. What color eyes?"

"Brown."

"Approximate weight?"

"One eighty, give or take a few pounds. I didn't pick him up," Ellis joked nervously.

"Because he wasn't six or seven. How old?"

"Early forties."

"Anything else you care to share?" Gary leered.

Ellis shook his head.

"And when they open the carousel in Greenport later this season, you'd be well-advised to keep your hands in your pockets, Mr. Ellis Guzman, and your pecker in your pants."

Ellis Guzman was getting his confidence back as a maintenance man was heading toward them from down the hall. "You have me figured all wrong, Mr. Policeman. I have a twenty-three-year-old lover, and we're very happy together, and have been for quite some time."

Gary smiled. "Well then, I'm very happy for you, Ellis. I just hope you've given me the straight skinny."

"I have."

"We'll see. Toodles." Gary waved and winked good-bye.

Chapter Twenty-Five

It was 3:45 a.m. A cold April night on the city sidewalks of Manhattan's Upper East Side.

The inside of the Hell, Fire & Brimstone Club was garishly furnished in glass, mirrors, brass, red velvet floral patterned wallpaper and plush gray carpeting. Fit male and female tattooed bodies paraded around in sleeveless blue spandex bodysuits, red latex leotards, gold and green bikini briefs, black, brown or gray skimpy leather outfits—accessorized with matching collars, whips and crops in hand. There were several private rooms and lounges; a couple of cubicles and a large stage. Detective Gary York well-imagined that the slave trade auction he heard tell of took place on the raised platform straight ahead of him. He sat in one of the glass cubicles with the manager, Ms. Rebecca Farnsworth, a beautiful, well-endowed woman in her early thirties. Gary had finished up discussing Howard Mills, who had been a member of the club. He handed her an old photograph of Beth Tracy. Rebecca studied the photo for a good ten seconds before shaking a healthy head of long jet-black hair.

"No, I don't believe so, Detective."

"You sure? Perhaps a likeness at least? It's not a recent photo darlin'."

Ms. Farnsworth shook her head again. "Certainly doesn't come around here. I can tell you that much."

Gary's hope sank. "Yet, you were studying her like I'm studying your cleavage," he remarked for effect.

Rebecca looked up without expression. "Then, like my cleavage, there's something familiar but nothing really particular about it. Sorry." She handed back the photograph.

"Maybe you've seen her around another club."

"No. I don't hang out at other clubs."

"Ms. Farnsworth. I'd say that you hang out wherever you go," Gary bantered outrageously, refusing to take his eyes off her ample breasts.

The woman smiled blandly. "A one-track mind, Detective. Maybe you'll visit us again soon or become a member here yourself."

"My member's here with you now, Rebecca Farnsworth."

If Rebecca had an activated recording device, Gary would be in big trouble. But he couldn't help flirting with her. Besides, he felt he was in hell and on fire and didn't really care.

"You *are* a bad boy. If you weren't on duty, I might give you a spanking."

"Well, I'll tell you what. I've declared myself officially off duty the moment you handed me back this picture," he rationalized, trying to cover his tracks in case she found him out of line and wanted to make a stink. "How about I buy you a drink?"

"Buy me a drink? Everything's closed or closing, including the club in ten minutes."

"Coffee," he shrugged indifferently. "Gotta find something open."

Rebecca Farnsworth studied Detective Gary York for a good moment as she had the photograph of Beth Tracy. "I really don't think I'm your cup of tea, Detective York."

"Maybe yes, and maybe no. So why don't we leave here together in a few minutes and sit down someplace and see." Gary had his Audi in mind.

Rebecca knew in that instant that she didn't like this cop. "I really can't."

"I thought you said you close up shop in a few minutes."

"I do."

"Well?"

"Well, when I get out of here, I have things to attend to."

"At four a.m.?"

She smiled. "Wash. Iron. Cook and clean."

"You?"

"Yes, me."

"I would think . . . well, that a person like you would have someone else do those chores."

"Really?" she said with some surprise.

"Rebecca," he replied informally. "You don't mind if I call you Rebecca."

Rebecca ignored the liberty he took, knowing for certain that she wouldn't make hay with this bumpkin if he were the only male around for miles and she were the farmer's daughter.

"In a word, Detective, just one word, tell me what you make of this place."

"I'm not sure I know what you're getting at."

"What do you think this place is all about?"

Gary York looked beyond the glass cubicle into the studio and lounge area, then back at Rebecca, running his eyes appreciatively over the approximate five-foot-seven inch, one-hundred-ten pound bundle of beauty seated in her chartreuse bodysuit. "Hum."

"What do you think we sell here?" she elaborated, helping him along. "One word."

"Sex," he answered smugly.

Rebecca shook her head. "Common answer but incorrect."

"No?"

"No."

Gary hated games and semantics and was another reason why he loathed criminal defense attorneys. He was beginning to dislike Rebecca, in the bargain.

"Then what?"

"Illusion."

"Illusion?"

"Yes."

"Is sex illusion?"

"We don't sell sex here."

"I'd be hard-pressed to see it any other way."

"Then you see what you want to see, not what necessarily is. Very poor outlook for a detective, I well imagine."

He was liking Rebecca less and less. "So I guess I'm living an illusion."

"Delusion would be my guess."

"Look. I'm not Vice. I'm not here to bust this place. I'm not even here to judge. You asked me what I thought this place was all about, and I told you. You see it one way. I see it another. I know what goes on behind those closed doors. Bunch of freaks—"

"People acting out their fantasies is all."

"Weirdoes fucking and flogging one another would be more to the point. Don't you think, Ms. Farnsworth?"

Rebecca was amused at the detective's switch from the familiar back to the formal address. She shook her head of shoulder-length hair and crossed her shapely legs. "People come here who either want to dominate or be dominated. Sex is really a secondary concern," she explained.

York grinned. "Oh, really?"

"Of course, what they do when they leave here is their own business. But the role of control or its relinquishing is the draw and why people gravitate to a club like ours. That's the motivating factor, Detective York. Here they get to feel one another out."

"Not up? And is that why your members run around half naked out there?" he questioned with a sweeping hand gesture.

"I'm not denying that they want to attract and be attracted. What I'm saying is that sex is not the underlying issue. This is not a whorehouse, Detective."

"How about a warehouse of perversion?"

"That's a rather silly and irresponsible remark."

"Well, then let me go for broke and tell you what I really think. But before I do, help me try and gain a clearer understanding. People come here looking for what exactly? Give it to me in a nutshell. What are these freaks really looking for?"

"An outlet for free expression."

Gary York laughed. "I think Howard Mills practiced free expression at home. What did he come looking for here? I think he came to feed on ideas that grew far beyond any fantasy. I think that if he had an isolated country home, he'd have graduated from cutting up the dead to cutting up the living where no neighbors could hear a victim's scream. Where do you imagine he picked up the seeds of such ideas considering what he did to those women? Places such as this, I'd wager. If you granted me the full tour behind the scenes, I wouldn't be surprised to find a torture chamber or two with some very interesting tools and equipment. Maybe even a dungeon filled with brimstone that the fire inspector hasn't listed in the basement. By the way. When was the last time you had an inspection?"

Rebecca Farnsworth smirked. "Don't make threats and take your frustrations out on me, Detective. And let me tell you something further. You don't come walking in here and think you're going to lay this at our doorstep. You want a clear picture, a better understanding? I'll give you one. But you have to open your eyes and your mind, Detective. You've got to look past the nose on your face. Look at the tremendous amount of violence we see on TV and in movie theaters every day. But not everyone runs out and imitates what they view. Gratuitous violence in the form of entertainment in this country is big business. Violence with a story line behind it becomes big box office. Violence is not a cottage industry for your information. A great deal of what we see is fantasy, meant purely to entertain. But if you had your way, you'd probably want to lock up all the writers, producers, investors, actors, and maybe even the movie theater manager. Here, in this club, we do not intentionally feed sick minds who want to kill people and dismember them. And keep in mind that our customers don't come in here wearing signs pasted to their foreheads."

"Why is it that I have the distinct feeling that if they did, you'd turn them around? The signs, that is. Not the people."

Rebecca's face flushed. "I've tried to explain things to you, but I don't think you want to make the effort to try and understand what we do here. I don't think a person with a closed mind can fathom the role of S & M."

"Oh, I believe I have a pretty good understanding, all right. I don't think a person has to dig too deep. I think S & M pretty much sums it up succinctly. Don't you? Sadomasochism spells it out quite nicely: sexual gratification achieved either through the inflicting or receiving of pain, *madam*. And I use the word in its politest of terms unless, of course, I've struck a cord which offends, in which case I offer my sincerest apologies," Gary offered most insincerely. "Your establishment, Ms. Farnsworth, and others like it, is perversion personified. Nothing redeeming about it. Pain is pain. Nothing pleasurable about it."

"From your perspective."

"How about from yours?"

"A moment ago you wanted to buy me a drink, which probably meant in your mind that you were twelve ounces away from taking me to bed. Suppose I told you that I don't get off in your quote unquote *normal* way. Suppose I told you that I need something more than a missionary fuck or a few acrobatic positions. Suppose I told you that I needed my pretty ass whaled. And I don't mean a mild-mannered spanking with a hairbrush but a full-blown thrashing with a barber's strap. Think you'd oblige me?"

"Is that a proposition?"

"Answer the question, Detective York."

"Do I have to draw blood?"

"Not a drop, Detective. But there damn well better be welts and bruises."

"You're a sick puppy, Ms. Rebecca Farnsworth."

Rebecca smiled and satisfactorily noted York's most solemn and ceremonial tone, finally abandoning all familiarity and the taking of liberties. She loved degrading such men as him. She'd be free of this self-serving narcissist in less than a minute flat.

"You'd be a bit reluctant in the beginning, Detective Gary York. But after you saw how much I crave and truly need it, after you learned what a bad girl I can really be and in dire need of much punishment, you'd come around . . . probably on a regular basis to administer my fate, *I'd wager*."

York was shaking his head. "You're putting me on. Right?"

She assured him that she was not.

"So let me get this straight. You're the passive party in this role you assume."

"Submissive," she corrected.

"But I thought you were the head dominatrix here, Rebecca. Oh, excuse me, Ms. Manager. Or is that just between the hours of eight p.m. and four a.m.?"

"You see, things aren't always as they seem," Rebecca said, void of any expression.

"Let me ask you this. What if you wound up with someone like Howard Mills, who wanted to do you bodily harm? Hum? Then what? Tell me."

"Well, if you were a Manhattan-based detective, maybe you'd get the call."

Gary studied her for a moment before he spoke. "Sounds to me like you need the help of a good psychiatrist and not some punishment you feel you deserve."

"Still, you'd like to take me to bed to find out for certain. Am I wrong? Tell me if I'm wrong."

Gary shook his head sadly as he crashed before her very pretty eyes.

Detective York was disappointed that the photograph of Mills' half sister hadn't turned up anything solid, frustrated over the fact that Beth Tracy had apparently vanished without a trace, bewildered by the fact that this woman, Ms. Farnsworth, that he had wanted so badly just minutes earlier was decidedly playing some kind of head game with him. A turnon to a turnoff in less than fifteen minutes flat. York was disappointed, frustrated and bewildered. Maybe even beguiled.

Traveling back east across the 59th Street Bridge, Gary York gradually put all thoughts of Rebecca Farnsworth aside, replacing them with notions concerning the whereabouts of Beth Tracy.

Chapter Twenty-Six

Detective Gary York was summoned to the rear of the squad room and ushered into Detective Lieutenant Theodore Groche's office. The lieutenant's paneled walls were filled with plaques, diplomas, citations, marksmanship trophies and trophy trout. Pictures of his wife and children, parents, past and present politicians, along with the patriarchs of law enforcement dating back to the days of Hoover, bordered the top cop's showcase of pride and professionalism.

Theo sat leaning back in his chair, his tie knotted but loose, like an inverted noose around his neck. He seemed to be perpetually pondering the answer to a question or the possible solution to a problem.

Promoting teamwork and tenacity were the cornerstones of the lieutenant's success. As commander of the homicide squad, Theo was their beloved God. Fair yet ferocious if need be. Any maverick found out of the loop and off grazing in private pastures—after a single warning had been issued—was gone from the team for good. All information and leads were to be shared among the troops. No one worked solo unless it was cleared.

Gary sat across from the lieutenant. It seemed as if Theo were addressing the ceiling and the walls, for he made little eye contact with the detective.

"I heard you felt you had some unfinished business concerning Beth Tracy," the boss stated coldly.

"On my own time, Lieutenant," was Gary's only defense, wondering if it was the fag from Orient Point or the bitch from the Manhattan club who had blown the whistle on him.

"Your time *is* my time when we have pressing cases, Detective. And you know what we're up against with this Riverhead High School student stabbing. I want your energies focused on *that* particular matter. Not some long shot now that things are pretty much squared away with Howard Mills. The D.A. has the case, and he's kissing our sweet asses as we speak. Right now we're the apple of his eye. I'd like to keep it that way. Understand?"

"Yes, sir."

Theo swiveled five degrees and fixed his eyes on the photograph of his father standing in full uniform. "I'm sure you can find a loose end or play out one of your hunches right there in Riverhead. Just don't visit Howard Mills while you're in the neighborhood. Besides, I don't think he's so wild about you anymore. Just wild," Theo assured him.

"I hear you loud and clear, Lieutenant."

"Glad to hear that." Theo faced forward, setting his eyes directly on the detective. "But tell me what intrigues you about Ms. Tracy, besides the fact that she wears a skirt."

"Her eyes."

"She's blind, Gary. So what about them?"

"They're green."

"So are my wife's. Do I need to worry?"

"Mills came in with a lens case with one dark green contact in it."

"Go on."

"Howard's eyes are brown. Jeffrey's are blue."

"Are you going to finish with a rhyme?"

Gary smiled uncomfortably. "I just found it odd is all."

"So, because their half sister has green eyes that are of no use to her, you make the leap from Hicksville out to Orient Point when you should be working the Keisha Topping/Shantay Moore case in Riverhead. Maybe I'm blind, but frankly I don't get it. Can you help me out?"

It was that fucking fag, Gary figured. But he kept his trap shut. He was already feeling foolish.

Theo answered for him. "You reckoned Beth Tracy might shed some light on this," he quipped. "But if you read Eric and Troy's reports, which I'm sure you did, you'd know there's been no communication with her family since they were children. Howard Mills probably wanted to look more cosmopolitan, debonair. Who the hell knows? Didn't he go to that hair club for men? Maybe he thought the appearance of a full head of hair and dark green eyes would make him winsome. Ought to pass along that thought to Artie. He might even see the world as bright and gay again," Theo joked and grinned. Gary watched the lieutenant's smile fade. "Mick told me you were fixated on that missing lens; he went to see Artie." The lieutenant opened the middle draw of his desk and took out the property requisition form that Gary had filled out earlier. "So. What do you want me to do about this?"

Gary lowered his head. "Trash it. I'm busy on the Topping/Moore case, Lieutenant," he caved. "Black is beautiful."

"Glad we had this little talk, Gary." Theo ripped the form along its length and deposited it in the wastebasket at the corner of his desk. "Oh, and I want you to know that I greatly appreciate the way you handled the interview with Mr. Mills. That was a piece of work I won't forget. That's what I call a team effort. You gave it a hundred and ten percent and came away with the desired result. Enough to hang his ass good. Brilliant. Nothing less. Don't undermine what you did in there. So that there is no misunderstanding, I want you to stay away from Ellis Guzman out in Orient Point, as well as Ms. Rebecca Farnsworth in Manhattan," Theo instructed.

Gary shook his head sadly. "She call you, too?"

"Actually, neither of them made the call. It was Mr. Guzman's attorney who made the first call. The second call came from Ms. Farnsworth's live-in. Fancy Park Avenue address."

Again, Gary shook his head. "I'm sorry, Lieutenant."

"No need for you to be sorry this time out. I understand you, Gary. More than you might appreciate. But I need you on the Topping/Moore case. I want you looking under rocks in Riverhead. Not out in Orient Point, or Manhattan, or Hicksville."

Gary nodded in agreement. "Either of them file a complaint?"

"Negative. They just read me the riot act. I promised them you're on report and won't be bothering them again. So, you report to Riverhead," he quipped. "And let's see some first-rate detective work," Theo added. "Any questions?"

"Her live-in. Male or female?"

"Have a good morning, Detective."

— Book II —

March 6, 1998

Chapter Twenty-Seven

Since Howard Mills' arrest, nearly two years had dragged by for practically everyone concerned with the serial killer case. The time had moved at a snail's pace for Howard Mills and his victims' families.

Author and lecturer Robert Redler walked into Judge Steven C. Best's courtroom on the second floor of the criminal courts building in Riverhead for the morning calendar. Redler had recently been the victim of a boat burning that occurred at the Riverhead Moose Lodge while he was off interviewing a Calverton, Long Island teenager in South Carolina. The young man was being held for the better part of three months on a murder charge that had not yet been formalized with either an arraignment or indictment. The fifty-five-year-old writer occasionally freelanced articles concerning the criminal justice system. On his return from Conway, South Carolina, Redler had asked the Suffolk County district attorney's office to keep him informed of the arsonist's court appearance, for the detectives out of Riverhead PD had nailed the firebug. The state had charged the pyromaniac with countless crimes, having set fires to cars, boats, garages and homes.

March 6th was a Friday, and Redler was scheduled to meet a court clerk friend for lunch. The man was working Judge Best's Part and had filled the writer in on what was happening with the Howard Mills matter, well into its second week of pretrial examination.

Continuing his testimony, Detective Michael Connolly, the first witness for the prosecution, was holding up fairly well, giving an account of the alleged serial killer's handiwork. Gail Fox, the lead prosecutor, had Connolly on direct-examination.

Defense attorney Christopher Profeta had gotten a piece of the detective on voir dire. For the past week, the ball was mostly in Profeta's associate's corner, as Nicholas Dunn served up question after question to Connolly on cross-examination.

Fox's second-seated co-counselor, Elizabeth Presant, was busy jotting notes or buzzing away in the lead prosecutor's ear.

Redler watched the doubles action with fascination. It was the boys against the girls. Having written three psychological thrillers to date, the novelist knew where he would find fodder for his fourth.

A colorful and bellicose Nicholas Dunn completed still another day's cross-examination of Detective Michael Connolly, berating the cop for failing to audio and videotape alleged conversations between police and their prisoner, vilifying Team Two for writing in the purported questions asked of Howard Mills *after* the fact. Dunn dramatically denounced Connolly, accusing him and other members of the homicide squad of employing Machiavellian methods, using tactics such as threats, coercion, physical abuse, starvation and sleep deprivation for a period of thirty-one hours in an 8 x 8 foot windowless void, euphemistically referred to as the interview room. Dunn made clear from the onset that Connolly knew full well that Howard had just finished putting in a ten-hour work shift before his arrest, holding their suspect incommunicado for nearly sixty hours before arraignment.

But the unconscionable act of Detective York allegedly misrepresenting himself as a lawyer, and what supposedly transpired, would become the thrust of Dunn's arguments both at pretrial and trial examinations.

It had been a good show thus far for Howard Mills' shekels. Half a million dollars accumulated through twenty years of hard work, lots of overtime and smart investments, found its way into the pockets of Mills' defense attorneys, Nicholas Dunn and Christopher Profeta, two top-notch, high-profile legal eagles. The best that money could buy in Suffolk County.

The prosecutor, of course, had denied such barbarism on the part of the police, painting quite a different scene. The crime scene. Gail Fox pointed an accusatory finger at whom she firmly believed the deceitful and treacherous party truly was. Howard W. Mills. Serial killer of prostitutes. She painted with a broad brush: a description of Howard

Mills' filthy downstairs apartment, spattered with over two thousand bloodstains covering walls, floor, ceiling tiles, furniture and more. Gail Fox referred to the defendant's room as a slaughterhouse.

At the moment, the hearing had Robert Redler wondering if the police had arrested the actual butcher or a scapegoat. Several things didn't fit. Other findings fit too neatly. However, there was no doubt in anyone's mind that the murders of three women, for which Howard Mills was charged, all took place in the defendant's apartment. No question whatsoever. Victim number one: found in a trash container along the side of a road in Medford, referred to as Jane Doe/Medford. Victim number two: identified as Danielle Louise Clarke, discovered by a sorter working a conveyor belt at a recycling plant in Brooklyn. Victim number three: Claudia Rose Stetson, street name, Darla Vasco, encountered in a Dumpster by an employee at a sheet-metal plant in Melville.

A mountain of trace evidence would bare those facts during jury trial when forensic scientists from the Suffolk Crime Laboratory, as well as CellMark Diagnostics, a prestigious and private laboratory located in Germantown, Maryland, would be summoned forth to take the stand for the prosecution. However, the prosecution would be barred from raising the issue in front of a jury concerning Mills' connection to two additional alleged murders of women found in Westchester County.

Still ahead for everyone were weeks if not months of pretrial testimony: law enforcement witnesses to be called by the prosecution and challenged by the defense. Then it would be Dunn's and Profeta's turn to call forth their witnesses. Jury selection would follow. After that, a trial by jury. Many officials believed that it was going to be an exceptionally long trial, predicated on the new New York State Death Penalty Law—the first such trial in nearly a quarter of a century.

Teamwork and commitment would be the watchwords for both the prosecution and defense.

The name of the game?

To win at all cost.

Chapter Twenty-Eight

Howard Mills entered the courtroom in handcuffs that were immediately removed during each and every appearance before pretrial hearings got under way. At trial, the practice would be continued prior to a jury being brought into the courtroom so as to give the appearance that the accused serial killer was a free man who had simply ventured in off the streets and convivially found his place between his two defense attorneys seated at a table several feet to the rear of the prosecution—as they sat today. The charade would be preserved so as not to prejudice the case. Innocent until proven guilty. *Riiight*, thought a rather jaded Robert Redler.

Although Gail Fox had already exhibited several gruesome photographs during pretrial, particular pictures that a jury would not see, depicting the brutal, bloody bludgeoning and postmortem amputations of the three women for which Howard Mills was accused of murdering and butchering, pointing an incriminating finger at the defendant who appeared daily in virtually the same shirt and sweater outfit, looking like Mr. Rogers, the prosecutor nevertheless brandished at break time an array even more horrific than those projected on a screen, viewed before stunned reporters and spectators seated in the audience. Redler's court clerk friend had informed the writer that there were other outstanding pictures even more horrifying than law enforcement officers had ever seen. Judge Best was very selective in what he would and would not allow into evidence regarding those photos. If it were left to Gail Fox's discretion, she would have held up the 8 x 11 colored glossies, one at a time, high above her head while squeezing a sponge saturated with the blood from a side of beef for the full effect.

The prosecution was warming up.

Even during the early stage of pretrial examination, Robert Redler was positive that every person living on Long Island knew that Howard Mills had been sitting in a Riverhead jail cell by his lonesome for a dog's age, awaiting trial. Unless the Island's residents were residing under a rock, they had to know that fact by now. The story was the story of the decade among law enforcement personnel as well as the talk of the town; that is, every town in Suffolk and Nassau Counties—touching ordinary and extraordinary folks alike. The story was on the news nightly and in the daily papers. It was in black and white and in living color. It was bigger than the Amy Fisher/Joey Buttafuoco story. It was larger than life.

Yet, down the road, every juror would be instructed by the judge not to read, watch, or listen to any accounts regarding Howard Mills' case. *Riiight*. Nor to discuss the matter with anyone whatsoever, whosoever might broach the subject. *Of course not*. Not even among themselves until such time that the matter was handed down for deliberation. *Absolutely*. There were just a few problems surrounding such virtuous requests to be so ordered by the Court in months to follow. Namely, most people had pretty good memories when it came to crime stories. Additionally, Judge Steven C. Best would be instructing human beings, not programmable machines, compounded by the fact that the men and women of the jury were not to be sequestered until such time as they began deliberations, which would make the Court's instructions all the more difficult if not impossible to follow.

Oh, there were problems with the system, Robert Redler knew. Little problems like keeping up appearances and creating the inane illusion that Howard Mills was free to come and go. Middle-sized problems such as the Court's wishing to believe that men and women of the jury, with mouths and tongues and the God-given gift of gab, would somehow turn a conversation around from what was foremost on their minds and in their hearts to discussing little more than the weather, until such time when they would be finally permitted to air and weigh their views about a diseased mind and whether or not the body attached to it should be put to death or warehoused in a prison for the rest of Howard's natural life. *Naturally.* Not to mention the big problem of jurors closing their ears to any and all monologues sure to be delivered by coworkers, family members and friends. Diatribes such as, "Hang the bastard, high, Dad." Or "Howard Mills has got to be sick to have done something like that, Auntie. Personally, I'd put the puke away for life without the possibility of parole. But of course it's your decision and yours alone. I wouldn't want to influence you in any way whatsoever." And how about, "He really belongs in a mental hospital, boss; although I understand that's not going to be an option if you find him guilty." Finally, "When are we going to get a decent meal around here, Mom?"

And then there were the far greater problems that Robert Redler grappled with, lost sleep over, and which tormented his very soul. The problems concerning truth. Part of the truth lay somewhere between the tables of the defense and prosecution. The whole truth was rarely seen or told in open courts, he knew. Redler would keep his mouth shut and his eyes and ears open. During testimony, he would read between the lines, not take them at face value. He would make no judgments on Howard Mills' guilt or innocence until *all* the evidence was in. As a spectator/freelance reporter listening to the pretrial hearings, he was and would be privy to a great deal more than what a jury would hear or see. He already knew certain things that its members might not learn until the completion of trial. Information that would be withheld from them in the name of justice and fair play. Knowledge that might taint a jury from the onset. Color or cloud their thinking. Prejudice the entire case.

One of the soundest and sanest solutions to saving a failing criminal justice system in Redler's opinion was for the courts to convert to a system of law that brought professional jurors into play in order to weigh *all* the facts. For nothing should be held back from any fact finder if he or she were to arrive at the truth, the whole truth, and nothing but the truth, so help them, God.

Of course, there were dissenters who believed that a jury of one's peers was the only fair way to decide another's fate.

It wasn't a perfect world, and Redler was not naive to think that there weren't inherent problems in either approach, for he knew prejudices prevailed regarding both systems; that is, lay jurors versus professional jurors. Robert simply believed that justice would be better served with the employment of professional personnel.

Chapter Twenty-Nine

Pretrial examination continued into the third week of March. Nicholas Dunn was still on cross-examination of Detective Michael Connolly. Things were heating up.

Redler's court clerk friend, Richard Towards, addressed the Court: "All rise! This is a continued hearing in the matter of the People versus Howard Willis Mills. All parties are present."

"Morning, ladies and gentlemen."

"Morning, Judge," Ms. Fox said mechanically without looking up from her records.

"Please be seated," the clerk instructed.

Howard was brought into the courtroom from a side door near the railing that separated the spectators from the players. He was unhandcuffed from behind by a dark-haired female court officer, then seated.

"Both sides ready to proceed?" Judge Best questioned perfunctorily.

"Yes, Your Honor," Dunn responded.

"Yes," Christopher Profeta echoed.

"People are ready," Gail Fox said. "Ms. Presant is just going to run upstairs to get some paperwork, but we can move this along for the few minutes she'll be gone."

"All right. Then let's bring the witness in."

Detective Connolly entered from the rear of the courtroom, passed through the railing and into the well, then took the witness stand adjacent to the judge. Mick settled in, prepared to continue doing battle.

"Good morning, Detective," Judge Best began ceremoniously.

"Good morning, Your Honor."

"Good morning, Detective," the court clerk offered formally. "I remind you, sir, you're still under oath."

"Yes, sir."

Judge Best looked down at Dunn. "Mr. Dunn, you may inquire."

"Thank you, Judge. Good morning, Detective."

"Morning."

"Detective, we left off on Friday with my asking you about one of the prostitutes who says she last saw Darla Vasco, who we now know to be Claudia Rose Stetson, getting into a blue Cadillac on Jamaica Avenue. Do you recall my getting into that area before we broke for the weekend?"

"Certainly. Angie Travers."

"Well, did you . . . withdrawn. Detective. When an individual from Homicide calls in for a record check to secure a File 15, I believe that's what you call it, isn't there a record of that request logged somewhere?"

"The Communications Bureau may keep something. I'm not really sure."

"I see. Detective. Would I be safe in assuming that you never asked Angie Travers, Jennifer Dowling, Florence Majors, Tina Bower or, for that matter, *any* of the prostitutes who provided you with information concerning Mr. Mills as to whether or not they'd ever been convicted of a crime? Am I correct on that point, Detective Connolly?"

"Regarding an arrest?"

"I said a conviction. We'll get to arrests later."

"Yes, sir."

"Yes, to the fact that you never asked any of the prostitutes if they had been convicted of a crime?"

"Correct."

"Did you specifically *ask* Angie Travers whether or not Darla had a boyfriend?"

"She never said anything about having a boyfriend."

"No, no, no, Detective Connolly. That's not my question. My question is did you ask Angie Travers whether or not Darla had a boyfriend?"

"I don't think I did."

"Did you ask or learn from any of the girls who knew Darla whether or not she had a boyfriend?"

"No, sir."

"The same question with regard to a pimp. Did she have one?"

"Did she have a pimp?"

"Yeah, Detective. Did Darla have a pimp?"

"Not that I'm aware of."

"As you sit here now, Detective, you're telling this Court that you never asked or learned whether or not Darla had a boyfriend or a pimp?"

"Yes."

"Yes, you asked or learned the answer to that? Or no, you never made the inquiry?"

"No."

"So the answer to my question is that you never asked or learned from anyone whether or not Darla had a boyfriend or a pimp. Am I correct, Detective? Please answer yes or no."

"You're correct."

"Close enough," Dunn mocked. "Thank you."

"You're welcome."

"Now, Ms. Travers told you that she saw Darla get into a vehicle on the evening of December 8th, 1995."

"Objection," Gail Fox said, depositing her pen between the pages of her notes before standing.

"Grounds for the objection, Ms. Fox?" Judge Best inquired.

"Your Honor. It goes to the weight of Ms. Travers' signed statement in that she saw her friend Darla getting into a 'big, dark blue, light-colored interior Cadillac Coupe de Ville,' not simply a quote unquote *vehicle* as Mr. Dunn would like to veer away from—"

"Just as *you* would like to stray from the cockamamie description Ms. Travers gave the detective that fits my client like a circus tent," Dunn interrupted, turning around to face reporters and spectators.

"All right," Judge Best interjected

"—but rather a very specific vehicle, Your Honor," Fox persisted.

"All right, I said," the judge reiterated.

"A vehicle that's registered to my client's brother, Jeffrey Mills.

Not my client."

"Both of you; that's enough."

"—because of your client's DWI. That's the only reason it's registered in Jeffrey Mills' name."

"That's quite enough, I said! And I'm not going to repeat myself again," Judge Best promised with a beet-red face filled with anger and disappointment over the behavior of the two attorneys.

"I'm sorry, Your Honor," Ms. Fox apologized.

"I lost it, Judge. It won't happen again," Dunn seconded. "I apologize, but want—" The attorney momentarily lost his thought.

Dunn's co-counsel rose to the occasion, his left hand on Howard's shoulder. "Your Honor, with all due respect, I'd like to—"

"Sit down, Mr. Profeta. The rules have been set from the onset and are, therefore, written in stone. One counselor from the defense and one from the prosecution speaks at a time. If you have something to say, Mr. Profeta, say it through Mr. Dunn, or hold your tongue."

Christopher Profeta sank sullenly to his seat.

"Now. With regard to your objection, Ms. Fox. You do remember that you raised one?"

"I withdraw it, Your Honor."

Nicholas Dunn turned around to his *audience* again and grinned.

Judge Best scowled. "The objection is withdrawn. All testimony from that point is stricken from the record. You may continue, Mr. Dunn."

"Thank you, Your Honor. Now, Detective. With all your years of background, training and experience, thirty-three years or more I believe you indicated, did you at any point *ask* Angie Travers or any of the other girls if they had done drugs?"

"No, sir."

"Did you *learn* from any of the girls whether or not they had done drugs?"

"No, sir."

"Did you ask Angie Travers or any of the girls you interviewed whether or not Claudia Rose Stetson, a.k.a. Darla Vasco, did drugs?"

"Objection, Judge. Whether Darla did drugs or not has no relevance to anything in this case."

"Sustained."

"I'd like to be heard, Your Honor," Profeta said, rising from his chair as he spoke. He was a short man, but what the attorney lacked in stature, he more than made up for in terms of intellect. Nicholas Dunn was the showman. Tall and charismatic. Christopher Profeta was the technician. One man complemented the other.

"Mr. Profeta?"

"There is no question here in that this issue certainly goes to the reliability regarding statements made to the witness by Ms. Travers after Darla got into the car, Your Honor, as it puts into question whether or not any statements made by her or, in fact, any party, are credible."

"The objection was sustained, counselor."

Profeta sat down dejected, and Dunn continued his cross-examination.

"Detective, am I correct that at no time from the date of December 8th of 1995, when you were interviewing Angie Travers, and up until the arrest of my client on April the 6th of 1996, did you question Ms. Travers as to whether or not she had used drugs on the date she claims she last saw Darla?"

"Objection. Asked and answered."

"Overruled. You may answer, Detective."

"May I have the question again please? Sorry," Connolly said more to the judge than the attorney.

"Can I have the question read back, Judge?" Dunn asked.

"Please read the question back," Judge Best instructed the court reporter.

The court reporter lifted the narrow length of paper that draped her machine and read: "'Detective, am I correct that at no time from the date of December 8th of 1995, when you were interviewing Angie Travers, and up until the arrest of my client on April the 6th of 1996, did you question Ms. Travers as to whether or not she had used drugs on the date she claims she last saw Darla?'"

"That's correct."

"All right. Now, were you aware, Detective Connolly, that on July the 2nd of 1993, Angie Travers was arrested for a Class B felony; specifically, the criminal sale of a controlled substance in the third degree?"

"Judge, I have to object since we're dealing with—and the law is very specific—an arrest, which is no proof of any wrongdoing."

"The objection's overruled. You can answer it."

"Were you aware of that, Detective?" Dunn snapped.

"With regard to that specific arrest, I was not aware."

"Were you not at all interested in ascertaining that kind of information from her?"

"I was more interested in the accuracy and the truthfulness of her information than I was her history."

"Well, wouldn't knowledge of Ms. Travers' history help you in determining whether or not she was a reliable source and deserving of trust?"

Mick was getting mad. "Sir, in my thirty-three years of background, experience and training in dealing with informants and others with priors, you learn to read an individual. You don't ignore or cancel out their information simply because they have an arrest record."

"But you've suggested that you don't even care to know about their rap sheet. Is that not so, Detective?"

"Objection to what Mr. Dunn believes the detective suggested."

"Sustained."

"Did you not factor in your *reading* of Ms. Travers, the fact that she has a twelve-foot-long rap sheet, Detective?"

"Objection."

"Sustained."

Elizabeth Presant entered the courtroom carrying a stack of records with both arms and took her place at the prosecution's table next to Gail Fox.

Dunn stepped forward. "Detective Connolly. In your reading or take of Ms. Travers, as well as the other prostitutes you interviewed, were you aware at that time of what they did for a living?"

"Yes, sir."

"And what made you aware?"

"Appearance. Their actions. Drift of their conversation. Things of that nature."

"So, you do occasionally open your eyes and ears, Detective?"

"Objection. Argumentative."

"Sustained."

"Ever *ask* Ms. Travers or any of the girls you interviewed what they did for a living?"

"It was obvious to me what they did for a living. I didn't have to ask. I just got through testifying that through their actions, appearance, and what they said and how they said it made it crystal-clear how they made their living, sir."

Dunn shook his head impatiently. "Judge, I move to strike all that as unresponsive. My question to him was crystal-clear. So clear and to the point that I don't need to have it read back because it's still in my head as I'm sure it's in the detective's. But in case it's not, I'll repeat it after the Court instructs the witness to please answer my questions and not to hedge. Please, Your Honor."

Judge Best nodded in the affirmative. "Motion to strike is granted. The last answer is stricken from the record. Detective, if you could listen carefully to the question and answer it."

"Yes, sir."

"Mr. Dunn, you may ask the question again."

"Thank you, Your Honor. Now, once again, Detective. Did you ever *ask* Ms. Travers or any of the girls that you interviewed what they did for a living?"

"No."

"All right. Detective Connolly. Do you know if any of the other detectives working the case with you did a record check on Angie Travers, Jennifer Dowling, Florence Majors, Tina Bower, or any of the other girls that provided you with information from the time of questioning them and up until the arrest of Mr. Mills on April the 6th, 1996?"

"They might have. If they did, I'm not aware of it."

"Might that be, Detective, because none of those girls mentioned had given you or the other homicide cops their right name, date of birth, or social security number? Isn't that the reason, Detective? Isn't it?"

"Objection, Your Honor."

"All right, I'll withdraw it and state my position, Judge; that being that it is preposterous for this detective not to have run a record check on these girls to help him determine the reliability of their information. I submit, Judge, that would be common sense. And that's what we're supposed to be dealing with in this courtroom. I further submit that if he chose not to run a check through NYSIS, that there were other detectives either working the case directly or indirectly who ran a check on these gals and came up empty because they hid their true identity from the police. That's why I'm pushing this issue, Your Honor."

"Objection is withdrawn," Judge Best noted for the record. "So why don't you ask the witness if he knows of *any* attempt made by law enforcement to verify the names, dates of birth, and social security numbers of those he interviewed?"

"I was leading up to that point, Judge. But I thank the Court for its suggestion and indulgence," Nicholas Dunn condescended with a smile.

"Move it along, counselor."

"Sure. Detective, did any police officer or detective connected either directly or indirectly with this case, insofar as it concerned those girls you interviewed, namely, Angie Travers, Jennifer Dowling, Florence Majors, and Tina Bower, make any inquiry to verify their criminal history?"

"Initially, attempts were made."

"The answer's yes; is it not, Detective?"

"Correct."

"By whom, Detective Connolly?"

"Members of the One-O-Three."

"The Hundred and Third Precinct in Queens?"

"Yes."

"And initially came up with zip because the names the girls had given them were bogus names. Isn't that so?"

"I'm not exactly sure if they were all bogus names or not."

"You're not?"

"No."

"Well then, can you tell this Court what you are sure of with respect to their names? Can you do that, Detective?"

"I can tell you that there was a mistake in the spelling in at least two of their last names."

"Mistakes, you mean. Plural. Two or more. Correct?"

"Yes," Connolly reluctantly admitted.

"And whose mistakes might that be? The mistakes of the police officers and/or detectives of the One Hundred and Third Precinct taking pedigree information at the time? Or the mistakes of the prostitutes who were providing answers to those questions?"

"As best I recollect, officers from the One-O-Three ran some of those names in the computer with regard to priors. I don't remember whose were whose. But what I can tell you is that the officers are familiar with the young ladies in reference to their activities along Jamaica Avenue, their arrests for loitering, convictions and so forth."

"And you were not?"

"Objection, Judge," Gail Fox blew, shooting to her feet as if the seat of her chair had suddenly caught fire. "This detective has already testified to what the focus of his investigation was. Now, we can rehash this area over and over again until the cows come home. And quite frankly, Your Honor, we have. Mr. Dunn is beating a dead horse. The questions that he is asking the witness have been asked and answered many times. I remind the Court that he's had Detective Connolly on the stand now for three weeks, and we're moving through this same territory at a snail's pace. If the Court allows this, Mr. Dunn will nitpick as he has through every name and ask the same repetitive questions concerning every single witness that Detective Connolly questioned who gave sworn statements."

"Judge, with all due respect—"

Gail Fox swung around to face the attorney. "I'm not done!"

"Of course, you're not, Ms. Fox. I'm Dunn. You're the prosecutor who wants to kill my client. We're the attorneys for the defense. We're trying to save his life."

"Stop, counselor," Judge Best admonished.

Nicholas Dunn stopped.

"Your Honor, as I was about to say," Fox continued. "A sworn statement is a sworn statement and is what gives credibility and reliability to this issue. Whether their names are Angie Travers or Angie Dickenson, Jennifer Dowling or Jennifer Flowers, Tina Bower or Tina Turner, they have voluntarily given this detective information concerning a friend of theirs who was murdered. They have no reason to lie. That's the crux of the matter here, Your Honor. These witnesses are attesting to the last time they saw their friend alive, or who Darla was last seen getting into the Cadillac with, or the route they took out to the defendant's apartment in Hicksville, along with a detailed description of that apartment."

"Is Ms. Fox or the detective testifying here, Judge?" Profeta balked, rising slowly to his feet. "I mean this is totally inappropriate. We are at an egregious disadvantage in that we do not have the witnesses here to cross-examine and are therefore left to extrapolate information from hearsay evidence. We did not create this untenable situation. The Court permitted it, and we are stuck with it; therefore, we have every right to probe into the caverns as well as the crevices of this detective's mind to ascertain the facts." Christopher Profeta sat back down.

Judge Best stared down at the counselor as if he were studying a bug. "Ms. Fox's point is well-noted, and although I have given the defense considerable latitude in this area, I feel it's time to move on. Prosecution's objection is sustained. Counselor, you may inquire."

Ms. Fox sat down smugly, total satisfaction sketched across her face.

Unruffled, Nicholas Dunn continued. "Thank you, Judge.

Detective. Do you have in your notes the description that Angie Travers had given you of the man who was sitting behind the wheel of the Cadillac on the night she claims she last saw Darla entering that vehicle?" Dunn was beaming brightly.

"Yes, sir."

"Would you tell the Court the height, weight, hair color and complexion of this individual Ms. Travers had given you?"

Mick was boring a hole through the center of Nicholas' forehead, his eyes filled with hatred.

"From your notes, Detective. I want you to be accurate here."

Mick looked down at his notes. "This is an approximate description given, of course. As to his height and weight."

"Of course, Detective. I'm not suggesting that your drug addict of a witness had a yardstick or a scale with her at the time, or that she'd even be able to read them if she had."

"Objection, Your Honor!" Gail Fox practically shouted, slamming her hand down hard on the two-foot stack of records between her and her co-counsel.

Judge Best's face was bright red. "I'll see the attorneys at sidebar," he said as calmly as he could, stepping down from his seat and heading to a segregated corner left of the bench.

Reporters, spectators and a sketch artist who had just arrived studied the scene intently, fixing their eyes on the group convened in the corner: the judge, his law secretary, a retired judge (a mentor, friend, and advisor to Best), the four attorneys, and the poor court reporter whose job it was to separate the wheat from the chaff as at least five of the seven parties standing in a huddle were talking past one another at the same time. A moment later, no one was speaking but the judge.

From twenty feet away, Howard Mills sat at the defense table busily highlighting sections of his notes with several colored marking pens.

Chapter Thirty

Detective Connolly had been mercilessly grilled on the stand for a total of thirty-one days before Nicholas Dunn finally finished up with the first witness for the prosecution. It was unprecedented. Thirty-one days for the thirty-one hours Howard Mills had spent in that 8 x 8 foot claustrophobic space was how Robert Redler interpreted the act.

Tit for tat.

Dunn was done with Connolly for the time being.

Two more homicide detectives took the stand in addition to police officer Dan Fowler from the K-9 Unit. Other detectives and police officers were sure to follow. Redler's one regret was that he had not met the dog handler's partner, Max, for the animal proved amazing in its abilities.

Apart from Redler's fiction writing, as well as having been an investigative reporter for a local newspaper, *Towers News*, back in Queens, Robert freelanced articles regarding a failing criminal justice system. Taking advantage of the timing, he wrote an article on the necessity of audio and videotaping suspects' statements, citing the Howard Mills case as a classic example. For here, homicide detectives had in their midst a suspect who they believed to be responsible for at least five serial murders, yet did nothing to secrete a recording device in their car, on their person, or in the 8 x 8 foot interrogation room.

Instead, Mills' incriminating statements were supposedly penned by him voluntarily in response to a series of alleged questions unrecorded by the police at that point in time. Not until the penultimate hour had the detectives bothered to write down their purported inquiries based on what they believed they had asked Mills almost two years earlier.

Another fact which piqued Redler's curiosity was that the information obtained from Mills was information already known to the detectives. Nothing new was ascertained.

Robert Redler's article appeared in the Viewpoint column of *The Southampton Press*.

THE SOUTHAMPTON PRESS / APRIL 23, 1998
The Hampton Chronicle-News
Viewpoint   *On the Record*

by Robert Redler

Howard Mills is seated between his two defense attorneys, Nicholas Dunn and Christopher Profeta, immediately before hearings get under way in Suffolk County Criminal Court in Riverhead, New York. Mr. Mills is the alleged serial killer of five prostitutes; he is accused of murdering and dismembering three of those victims.

Mr. Mills' counselors claim that the Suffolk County homicide detectives fabricated the defendant's oral and written statements and coerced the signed confessions. Central to that theme is the fact that the police wrote in their questions in response to Mills' answers a year and nine months after taking the alleged declarations.

Homicide Detectives Michael Connolly, John Bailey, and Victor Posteraro, three witnesses for the prosecution to date, swear under oath that their questions and the suspect's answers to those questions were set forth by themselves as well as other detectives and were responded to freely by Howard Mills.

Maybe yes, and maybe no—or maybe true in part. Yet, thirty some-odd days thus far to probe this conceivable but *not* necessarily so dispute at taxpayers' dollars is criminal in itself.

And who are the criminals? Are they the defense team, nitpicking as time is ticking away? The three homicide detectives? The district attorney's office, pairing Gail Fox and Elizabeth Presant, objecting firmly to the defense's allegations of police prevarication? The judge, Judge Steven C. Best, fact-finder, timekeeper, and referee?

No. None of those listed above. The criminal here is the system itself. The system is in disrepair.

We have to point an accusatory finger at our legislators. We have to pull them from the clouds and set them steadily on their feet to see the sour soup that's simmering on the stove. As the cauldron is huge and the problems within it many, we must focus on one ingredient at a time. Let's address the problem posited in the first paragraph. Let's take the first step:

Statements and confessions taken from suspects must be audiotaped and videotaped. This is not the panacea. This is not the cure-all. It is merely the first step. The process, of course, will have to be examined, reexamined, refined and updated. Will it tie the hands of the police? Corrupt police, for sure. But will it hamper honest investigators truly in search of truth? It will not. Will it limit the number of convictions police across the country currently obtain? For sure. Why? Because not several but many convictions are obtained by illegal means. Chicanery is legal. Coercion is not. You can trick a suspect. You cannot commit or threaten violence or promise pie in the sky.

Video and audiotaping statements and confessions would help a failing system.

Videotaping and audiotaping statements and confessions of suspects would clearly limit the number of problems inherent in a failing criminal justice system. That, I believe, is self-evident. Sure it will create new problems—for both sides—for those parties interested in winning an acquittal or a conviction at all costs.

Mr. Mills' counselors claim that the Suffolk County homicide detectives fabricated the defendant's oral and written statements.

As always, the role between defense and prosecution is of an adversarial nature—a contest, if you will. Somewhere in the middle lies the truth. If a picture is worth a thousand words, an audiovisual ought to be worth a million. Surely it would. Surely its time has come, its need evident in that at least 2,000 law enforcement agencies across the face of the nation have begun to adopt the practice.

If Howard Mills is the monster that the prosecution says he is, it would be catastrophic for the defense to find a proverbial loophole that could result in an acquittal (even though Westchester County has indicted the man). Conversely, if Howard Mills is innocent of all charges, it would be tragic for the defendant to suffer because a jury bought the prosecutors' claims, attached to the detectives' sworn testimonies.

Each side is out to win whether they are right or wrong. The truth? Obscured in time and memorialized in the minds of at least half a dozen homicide detectives who had Howard Mills in an approximate 8 x 8 foot interview room on the nights of April 6th and 7th, 1996. An audiovisual would have shed light on the truth and helped jurors better deliberate and determine the defendant's guilt or innocence.

Tell your New York State legislators that you want lights, cameras, and action—now!

Robert Redler is an award-winning novelist of psychological thrillers. Additionally, he writes about our criminal justice system.

Redler's articles had helped get an innocent young man out of prison in the early nineties: a Bayside, Queens, New York man accused of the attempted rape of a high-ranking, retired police officer's daughter. Redler's extensive editorials coupled with the eventual release of Richard Tchilinguirian, brought the writer personal praise from Barry Slotnick and Mark Baker, two high-profile Manhattan attorneys who handled the matter after the young man's sentencing—pro bono. Redler had gone on to update the story, writing about a Queens detective who had made the arrest, pointing a suspicious finger at the cop for the purported murder of his mistress. Earlier posturing with the Queen's district attorney's office had brought the wrath of vengeful prosecutors down around the writer's ears. Having spent eighteen hours in a detention cell, another eighteen on Rikers Island, and thousands of dollars in legal expenses because of trumped-up charges, not to mention twenty-two court appearances, Robert Redler felt he had a mission: reporting on the injustices of the criminal justice system whenever and wherever he found them. He never had far to look or very long to wait.

Chapter Thirty-One

Jeffrey Mills was out on bail and still employed at the Manhattan post office on John Street. Howard Mills had generally worked in the Hicksville office, sometimes driving out to the mid-Island branch, either sorting mail or working security in the guard shack across the road. Both brothers' official title was Mail Handler. Howard had worked for the postal service for twenty years. He had been a shop steward for a short period.

Upon interviewing a friend and coworker of Howard's in the hallway just outside the courtroom, Robert Redler had learned that Howard was not especially well-liked by the majority of the employees; however, the man felt that Howard had been a good shop steward, fair but tough and demanding of his men. During testimony, Detective Connolly had expressed that in his questioning of Howard, the prisoner had been quite proud of his position as a shop steward for the union. Redler had seen this middle-aged friend and coworker of Howard's in the courtroom several times over the course of months, learning that the fellow had used his vacation time to come and visit the defendant. Furthermore, the man and his family had entertained Howard on more than one occasion, mentioning, too, that he had been to Howard's apartment at 42 Willow Lane in Hicksville, and had never seen the room the way that the detectives had described it; that is, filthy and disorderly. Certainly not covered with blood.

Additionally, Redler had questioned Howard's friend concerning a missing contact lens that Dunn later brought out during his cross-examination of homicide Detective Gary York—the last witness for the state during pretrial examination. Howard's friend told Redler that he knew nothing about any contact lenses. The defense attorney's purpose in raising the point was that his client may have needed them in order to read and understand statements York had prepared for Howard's signature. The alleged confession. York quickly denounced Dunn's notion as nonsense, explaining that the lens was a far cry from Howard's prescription and that the defendant only needed and wore eyeglasses for night-vision driving.

Nice try, Dunn, York had said to himself, having further elaborated on the fact that the single lens held in the property room at headquarters was a nonprescriptive, dark green light-collecting lens that would neither impair nor enhance vision in any manner whatsoever. Detective Gary York had gone on to adamantly deny misrepresenting himself as a lawyer when Dunn raised the issue. York snickered and called the allegation the most ridiculous and laughable accusation he had ever heard during all his years in law enforcement, citing that it was either the delusion of the defendant or the invention of his defense attorneys.

Dunn later promised himself and co-counsel that Gary-boy would find it less than amusing when he got the detective on the stand before a jury—either as a hostile witness of their own calling, or as a witness for the prosecution. It made no nevermind. The two defense attorneys had a surprise that they were saving for this cavalier abomination of a cop.

Another interesting fact was brought out on cross-examination of Detective Frank Masselli, relating to a work-order issued by the Guardian Cable Company that had repaired Howard Mills' video box one evening, supposedly following the victims' murders. The point being that if the room had been blood spattered with over two-thousand stains, it should have been noticed by the repairman. Masselli had explained that on entering Howard Mills' apartment, with the only light source coming from a single lamp situated on a table in the center of the room, everything would and did appear normal. It was only when the Crime Scene Unit had set up their own lighting did they note the horror of what Gail Fox continually referred to as a slaughterhouse. But would

Howard Mills have chanced to call in a repairman who might have shed some light of his own on such a scene had the room been in the condition authorities said it was? It was a question that troubled Redler. He was certain the defense would call the repairman as a witness. He was sure the man's testimony would be illuminating.

Jeffrey Mills was on a short leash. Ronald Mills, the youngest living brother, had made several appearances during pretrial hearings but was not up to any sort of dialogue with Robert Redler. Redler thought he heard someone in the back of the courtroom say that Jeffrey Mills had made a brief appearance but then vanished before the writer had a chance to confirm. Redler had asked *Newsday*'s staff writer, David Culver, who attended pretrial daily, if he had seen Jeffrey or knew what he looked like. David said that aside from the man's complexion, he had heard that Jeffrey was a dead ringer for his brother, Howard, but had not noticed anyone who remotely resembled the defendant in the courtroom earlier.

On the witness stand, Detective Connolly had described Howard Mills as being "slightly taller and a bit heavier in the face than Jeffrey." An interesting comment when tied to the hearsay evidence of one prostitute in particular whom Connolly had interviewed and who later told him of a dark blue Cadillac seen in her area along Jamaica Avenue in Queens, giving the detective a rather detailed description of the man stepping from the vehicle; a description befitting either brother. It was made clear that at least two of the women had been to Howard's apartment in the past, having provided the police with their second big break. The first had been Darla's naked body, revealing her street name via the prostitute's tattoo.

It was Detective Connolly's damaging hearsay evidence of those witnesses' sworn statements given during pretrial examination and the possibility that Judge Best might allow the prosecution to present them during jury trial that greatly concerned Christopher Profeta and Nicholas Dunn. There were many material issues that troubled the two attorneys, but Connolly's testimony of what several prostitutes had told him was of paramount importance. Would or would not the women be called by Gail Fox? It was what the defense team referred to as the prosecution's prospective ambush, for Profeta and Dunn couldn't very well cross-examine witnesses who they could not locate—or that Gail Fox and her second-seated associate, Elizabeth Presant, might produce in the penultimate hour. The two men felt that the prosecution would probably prefer their fair-haired, blue-eyed, middle-aged detective sitting on the stand presenting testimony before a jury rather than discreditable 'working girls.' The latter of whom Dunn and Profeta hoped to make mincemeat of in short order should the *girls* be summoned to the hot seat. But one never really knew for sure, for game plans changed like the weather, and some witnesses could and would surprise you.

While hearsay evidence was not the norm in such a criminal proceeding, neither was it unheard of, which surprised Redler. Not looking to be cut off at the pass by the prosecution, the defense team had made many applications, objections, and asked for innumerable sidebars concerning other problems that could complicate their case. The contest between adversaries was well along the way. That was the system as Redler saw it. A spitting contest between counselors—or in a capital case, two sets of counselors. The ultimate presentment of truth? Obscured somewhere between the poles of prosecution and defense. That was our adversarial system in a nutshell. Robert Redler would make it his business to somehow uncover the absolute truth.

In wrapping up pretrial examination, Dunn and Profeta had called two of their own witnesses: the upstairs tenant, Mr. Hammond, who occupied the apartment across from Jeffrey Mills; next, the landlady, Mrs. Cully, who lived downstairs in the front part of the house. Not surprisingly, neither of those elderly folks had heard nor seen a single thing that would implicate Howard Mills, or anyone else for that matter, in any murder. Neither of the two elderly people had ever seen a woman enter or leave the home at 42 Willow Lane. Mrs. Cully was positive on that point. Mr. Hammond said that if he had, he had surely forgotten. Again, some witnesses could and would surprise you, be it your own or the prosecution's. Both Dunn and Profeta immediately entertained that fact after hearing Mr. Hammond's last remark.

It was nearing the end of May. Pretrial had lasted three long months. Judge Steven Best had ruled that the arrest of Howard W. Mills, almost two years earlier, was proper and that the oral and written statements he made to the police could (and certainly would) be used against him at trial. Jury selection was scheduled for the middle of June.

Chapter Thirty-Two

Ilona Alfold had a serious crush on the young man who would patronize their family's beverage store once a week. Months had gone by, but she had not seen hide nor hair of him. Ilona was depressed. The sheltered eighteen-year-old Hungarian girl had been too shy to let her feelings be known. She promised herself that if and when he came by again, she would make an effort to let him know that she was interested in his welfare, for she truly was. She cared. She was deeply concerned about him. She was actually worried sick.

Another month had passed when Ilona suddenly looked up and saw Jeffrey Mills heading toward the store on foot. Before Howard's arrest, Jeff had always driven up in the Cadillac, but she figured she knew what had happened to that car: impounded by the police as a matter of course. Ilona also believed why she hadn't seen him for a spell, suspecting that Jeff may have spent some time in jail for his role in having helped his brother, Howard, although she could find nothing in the newspapers to support her suspicion. Ilona quickly finished sweeping the walkway in front of the building before making a beeline through the door. She hurried over to a wall mirror advertising Budweiser beer, pushed her hair behind her ears, bared her teeth, removed a particle of potato chip with a pinkie nail before running her tongue across the top and bottom row for a once-over, then matted her lips. The slightly overweight, pretty-featured college freshman said a silent prayer that her father would remain where he was in the back room taking inventory, or more likely in the bathroom with his copy of *Penthouse*.

"Hi, Jeffrey," she said the second he stepped through the door.

"Hi, Ilona," Jeff rejoined, staring down at the floor.

Ilona glanced anxiously over her shoulder then back again and smiled. "I'm sorry to hear the news about your brother."

Jeff stopped in his tracks not five feet from the counter, eyes still cast down. "Thank you, Ilona."

"I mean that, Jeffrey. If there is anything I can do . . . ."

Jeff shook his head and took the last few steps up to the counter.

"My mother was asking about you," she said nervously, expecting her father to come out from the back room at any second.

Jeff nodded his head up and down with seemingly great difficulty. "I appreciate that, Ilona."

Ilona loved the way he said her name, pronouncing the *I* with a long e, the Hungarian way. She felt the urge to reach out and hold him. The two were standing a foot apart. Ilona stuck the tips of her fingers in the front pockets of her jeans, hoping her father would have a mild stroke or remain seated in the john in a state of constipation, just so long as he stayed where he was. She asked God in that instant to forgive her transgressions and to give her five minutes alone with this childlike man.

"How's Orbit?"

Ilona had never seen the cat, but she certainly heard tell. It was the only thing Jeffrey ever talked about without feeling uncomfortable. Jeffrey was like a different person when he talked about his pet. And after he'd leave, she'd laugh and have to remind herself that she was jealous of a cat. Jeffrey was the sweetest, shyest man that she had ever known. Ilona stood literally less than a foot away from falling in love. If she could only muster up the courage to suggest a date or even a cup of coffee sometime, for Ilona knew that he'd certainly never make the overture himself, not even if Orbit's life depended on it, she'd be willing to wager. The irony being that she was just as shy as he. But what Ilona had read in the papers of late was forcing her to reach out. That and the fact that she didn't know when she might see him again.

"Orbit's fine now."

"What do you mean, now?"

"She wasn't eating while she was staying at my brother

Ronald's house in Hempstead. She looked so skinny when I got back. Had to fatten her up," he elaborated, not taking his eyes off the counter.

Three statements in a row, Ilona smiled. Usually, she couldn't get him to say more than a single simple sentence. But ask Jeffrey a question about Orbit, and he could go on and on about that cat.

"You could have let her stay here if we knew you needed cat sitting," she said with a sincere smile, confirming her suspicions that Jeffrey had spent some time in jail.

Jeff shrugged.

"Mother and I would have been glad to watch her. Honest."

"Thank you, Ilona."

Ilona shot a glance over her left shoulder. "Yesterday we got a shipment in of one of your favorites."

Jeff nodded approvingly.

"Well, don't you want to know which one?" she teased with laughing and batting bright blue eyes. Ilona was turning bold.

"Sure," he answered, catching a glimpse of her fluttering eyelids.

"Pilsner."

"I like that one a lot."

"Six-pack?"

"That would be very nice, Ilona."

Ilona stepped around him and yanked open one of the cartons stacked in the corner, removing a six-pack of premium, pale Czech lager, then returned to the counter. If her father weren't around, she'd have given him a case for free and put the money in the register out of her own pocket. Maybe that would break the ice. Maybe that would give him a hint.

"Jeffrey?"

Jeff looked up.

"Do you need anything?" Ilona asked self-consciously.

"No, the Pilsner's fine, Ilona," Jeff responded, fumbling in his pocket for a crumpled ten-dollar bill.

"No, silly. I didn't mean anything from the store." Ilona swallowed. "I meant like maybe a hand around your apartment. Help you tidy up or something. Maybe fix you dinner up there some evening," she said nervously, not believing she had gotten out the words.

"How do you know I live in an apartment, Ilona?"

It was Ilona's turn to stare down at the counter. "You know. The newspapers."

"Papers said that?"

"Uh-huh. That and that they might be picking a jury soon for Howard."

Jeff nodded. "Guess you pretty much know everything then," he said, putting the crinkled sawbuck down upon the counter alongside the six-pack. Jeff flattened out the wrinkles of the bill with the tips of shaky fingers.

"I know that what you did you did to help your brother."

Jeff nodded uncomfortably.

"That's not a crime, Jeffrey."

"I'm afraid it is, Ilona."

"I mean, I guess what I'm saying is that I know you're not a criminal. Not in *my* eyes. I know that what you did you did to protect Howard. You had no part in it except to help him afterward. I know that. Even the papers say so because he begged you for help. You're his brother."

Jeff nodded anew.

Ilona stole a final look toward the back room. "So how about my coming over and making you a little something to eat sometime? I'm a pretty good cook," she assured him. "And we can talk some more."

Jeff shook his head. "I don't have the facilities up there for you to cook, Ilona."

It was the saddest look on a face that she had ever seen. "How about a hot plate? I could make something ahead of time and heat it up when I get there."

"I don't have anything like that, Ilona. Besides, the landlady wants me out of there real soon. She's been asking me to leave since the day they came for Howard. Now she's *telling* me to go. I've already started packing."

"That sucks."

Jeff nodded.

"Where are you going to go?"

Jeff shrugged. "Been looking around. Maybe Manhattan. I'm not sure."

Ilona nodded anxiously. The pair stood in silence for a good ten seconds before she could think things through.

"Say, I have a great idea!" she beamed. "Why don't we go out for Chinese down the block. My treat. I mean if you want to. Doesn't have to be tonight. Whenever you say."

Jeff was still staring down at the counter as Ilona's father stepped out of the storage room.

"Mr. Mills," the proprietor said somewhat coolly.

"Good morning, Mr. Alfold," Jeff said politely.

Janos Alfold had always called Jeffrey by his first name. It was apparent by the owner's greeting and tone that he was aware of Jeffrey Mills' plight and certainly did not approve of or appreciate his situation whatsoever.

"Ilona, I need you to finish taking inventory. I'll take care of things out here," he stated, stepping behind the counter and picking up the money. "Just the six-pack of Pilsner?" he asked, directing his question to Jeff.

"Yes, sir," Jeff answered.

"*Now*, Ilona," Janos repeated.

"Yes, father," Ilona said obediently, moving quickly from the counter to the back room.

Janos Alfold rang up the sale on the register, handing Jeff his change.

"Thank you, Mr. Alfold," Jeff said as civilly as he could.

"You're welcome, Mr. Mills." Janos put the six-pack into a paper bag. "I want you to know that you've been a good customer, and I enjoyed our chats. But to be quite blunt, your coming here now is bad for business. So I'm telling you as nicely as I know how to take your business elsewhere as of this moment."

Jeff nodded his head in compliance. "I understand completely, Mr. Alfold," Jeff replied quietly, turning around and heading for the front door, cradling the package in his arms as he would Orbit.

Ilona stood crying behind the set of double doors leading to the back room storage area, wishing her father were dead. She would not ask for God's forgiveness afterward for her terrible thoughts.

Chapter Thirty-Three

Through his attorneys, Howard Mills requested a photograph that the prosecution held: a snapshot that the detectives from Team Two had removed from a dresser drawer in his room at 42 Willow Lane. A picture of himself and his three brothers. Size and age order. The Mills brothers. Howard, Jeffrey, Ronald and Lenny. Lenny was long dead. There was no photo of their half sister, Beth Tracy. Howard's thoughts were with Lenny. Howard fell back in time.

Lenny, the youngest of the Mills boys, had come to Howard in an emotional upheaval some twenty years earlier, Howard reflected so sorrowfully.

I'm depressed, Howie. I'm so very, very sad, Lenny declared one cold December evening so many years ago that it seemed as though the event took place in another lifetime. *I can't go on like this much longer*, the boy had whined, despondent over the suicide of their father.

So why don't you go kill yourself? was Howard's flip response.

And so Lenny did exactly that on the last evening of Hanukkah. It was bitter cold when Howard awoke to discover his brother's body alongside the bed. It had also been a freezing cold day in December when the three remaining brothers learned of their mother's death . . . eons ago, or so it seemed, Howard ruminated, calculating his mother's age at the time of her death. She, however, had died of natural causes.

Blood cancer would have claimed their father within a year had he not taken his own life. Howard had wished, no, prayed for a natural death for himself as long as he could remember, attempting suicide several times before . . . before finally realizing he was truly a coward.

Even one of the homicide detectives had called him a coward but for entirely different reasons, for they actually believed that he had killed those women. They actually believed that he was capable of such acts.

"Fine. Maybe now I'll get my death wish—no, prayer answered," he whispered to no one in particular within earshot of his solitary cell. "Maybe soon I'll see Mom and Dad and you, Lenny, and finally get to tell you how terribly sorry I am to have said such a horrible, horrible thing that night—that when I told you to go kill yourself, I was really and truly wishing it was me who could take my own life.

"I told the police that Jeffrey only helped me dispose of two bodies, Lenny. Jeffrey, Beth and I had talked about this beforehand, in case of an arrest, which was inevitable, I guess. I told them how he helped me, so reluctantly, that he was not a part of any killing. I knew they were ready to tear through the house as soon as they had their warrants. I knew that they'd be satisfied with arresting me for the murders. Trace evidence, Lenny. I also knew that they'd figure out that I had to have had some help in dumping the bodies. I endured the detectives' wrath for well over forty hours, I figure, before I finished signing all their statements, before I *confessed* to the murders as my impostor lawyer said I must. They tricked me, Lenny."

Howard Mills paced in his cell like a trapped animal, knowing full well how the state felt about him. Not only the state of New York, but probably the whole country as well, from one end to the other, for he knew that the Melville victim's father, Jack Stetson, had flown in from California to claim his daughter's body and, at some point in time, to attend the trial in Riverhead. The attorneys had told Howard that.

Claudia Rose Stetson: street name, Darla Vasco. Beautiful Darla. The name tattooed on her upper right arm. He had cut off her hands. How he wished he had also cut out the identifying tattoo. It had been their downfall. Time had been their enemy. Beth had beaten her brutally on his bed that cold December evening. Beth had bludgeoned those women to death on either the sofa bed near the window or the mattress and box spring situated against a wall in a corner of the room. He had practically handed the Suffolk County Homicide Squad their case on a silver platter to be delivered to the district attorney's office for their lavish feast. Beth had killed them. He was just the handler. Had been for most of his life. Mail handler and body handler. He loved touching the dead. Howard the coward.

But he would protect his half sister at all cost. He would not send Beth off to her death like he had sent Lenny. He alone would take the hard fall. *That took some courage. No?* Howard considered. Jeffrey had already done a pittance of jail time for his role, which the police and judge believed was limited to helping dispose of two bodies, period. A deal had been cut in exchange for Jeffrey's cooperation, and the matter was kept quiet by both the prosecution and the press. Beth would remain in the clear, unscathed by the teams of detectives who had investigated the case. Beth had the perfect alibi. Beth was totally blind. And if Howard's defense team, comprised of two brilliant attorneys, Nicholas Dunn of Islandia, and Christopher Profeta of Hauppauge, happened to pull off a miracle and somehow save his sorry ass, so be it. Several hundred thousand dollars paid up-front to his two legitimate attorneys offered Howard hope. He had things figured out to a good degree. The mountain of evidence against him was overwhelming, but he had told his defense team that he was innocent of murder from the get-go. And maybe, just maybe, the truth would set him free someday.

Howard really didn't know whether or not his attorneys believed his story, but they had and would continue to put on quite a show on his behalf, gradually pointing an accusatory finger to Jeffrey's upstairs one-bedroom apartment, telling their client that they had no other way to go, but not to worry, that a deal had, indeed, been cut behind closed doors and that Jeffrey Mills was out of the woods: time served coupled with good behavior, followed by community service. Jeffrey was free. Howard firmly believed that he had the best attorneys in the world. There was no question in anyone's mind that he had bought and paid for pure talent.

Three months of pretrial examination. Jury selection was scheduled for mid-June. The defense team had been working indefatigably for nearly two years since the day of Howard's arrest. Talk of a definitive trial date was still premature; however, the scuttlebutt was that it would take place closer to the end of the year. Then the real contest would begin. Nicholas Dunn and Christopher Profeta would endeavor to save Howard's life. No insanity plea was in the works. An acquittal was his only hope. A long shot. He had placed that kind of bet at OTB before and won. Gail Fox and her co-counselor, Elizabeth Presant, would try their case and try to kill him, he certainly knew. Business as usual. The burden was supposedly on the state's shoulder. But as time marched on, Howard came to realize that the onus weighed quite heavily on the defense's shoulders, too, to try and prove him innocent. Like a wanted poster, the price on Howard's head was high, and the noose around his neck was getting tighter. Nevertheless, the prosecution's victory would prove Pyrrhic, for the defendant's death would be, in essence, a state-assisted suicide. Howard had to laugh. His prayer finally answered. The state's utter defeat, however, meaning acquittal, would simply put him back at square one because Westchester County would be waiting in the wings.

There was no hope of any hospital like the police had said.

Howard was forever angry at the police. He called them kidnappers. The homicide detectives' horrendous actions backdropped against the defense team's true support had given him the courage and determination to go on. It was the fork in the road that Howard would be most concerned about should he have to travel down that course. For to rot away in some prison for the rest of his natural life in lieu of the death penalty, or to sit for a decade waiting out appeals was totally unacceptable. But for now he was not to think about such things. He was to remain focused and assist his attorneys in the process of selecting a jury. A tedious but important task. His counselors had made no pledges or guarantees concerning the outcome of the trial, other than the promise to do their very best. And after all the lies, deceit and promises the homicide detectives had heaped upon him, his lawyers' directness was at the very least refreshing.

Chapter Thirty-Four

Robert Redler had been researching the Mills family, which eventually led to Beth Tracy. Redler became fascinated with certain information he discovered and began digging deeper into Beth's past, figuring that books in Braille the woman might have borrowed from a library could offer insight into a most peculiar family. If eyes were truly windows to the soul, and Beth's were surely dark, then books were perhaps Redler's best bet for the moment because he firmly believed that a person's interest in a particular subject was a road map to an individual's being and behavior.

The nearest libraries to Beth Tracy's residence in Orient Point were the Floyd Memorial Library in Greenport and the Southold Free Library. Redler had used the lame excuse of wishing to keep tabs on an old girlfriend to see if Beth was seeking the help she needed. But both librarians, because of strict confidentiality laws, would not give Redler the information he sought concerning Braille books Beth Tracy may have borrowed. Having nothing to lose at that point, he pushed the envelope, requesting that the librarians cross-reference Beth's name through the Interlibrary Borrowing System. The librarians had smiled, shook their heads and suggested that he try the American Federation for the Blind in downtown Manhattan, which housed and maintained the M.C. Migel Memorial Library, the premier source of Braille books and publications relating to the field of blindness and vision impairment.

"A few years back, that library had been a lending library," the Southold librarian had elaborated. "But no longer. Therefore, you might have a shot at securing the information you're after. Why? Since the Foundation is no longer a lending library, one is neither going to find books on Bomb Making 101, nor would a precocious nine-year-old girl be able to borrow *The Joy of Sex*, having a mother worrying about a daughter's newfound predilection. And if I may be so bold, I'd try and be a bit more creative in your reason for securing that information, sir."

"Yes, ma'am." Redler thanked the woman profusely.

Arriving at the American Foundation for the Blind, 11 Penn Plaza in Manhattan, Redler found himself inside the M.C. Migel Memorial Library. He stood pensively before the librarian's reference desk, listening and learning from the woman that the facility had been moved from 15 West 16th Street to its present location three years earlier.

"Even today," Estie Schier went on, "with thirty-five thousand some-odd books on hand, our library is still not automated, forgoing the utilization of bar codes and such. Seeing as we are no longer a lending institution, but more or less view ourselves as an archive, securing, as a researcher, the information you request should not pose too much of a problem."

Robert Redler had told the woman that he was doing an esoteric study, putting together a statistical report referencing texts on blindness and general interest in the field, wishing to go back several years. Redler would at some point employ a ruse whereby he would politely ask the librarian if he could possibly see record cards dating back to the mid-eighties, explaining that it would expedite matters considerably if he could sit and work from the older filed record cards rather than stand and laboriously pull book after book in order to copy information from the pocket envelopes. The record cards would undoubtedly note the names and addresses of its patrons who had borrowed such books.

Finally settling himself in at a corner table, Redler initially went to work recording the stamped 3 x 6 inch Due Date book-pocket envelopes glued to the inside back covers. After an hour or so, he asked Estie Schier if he might peruse the record cards themselves. At first, the woman was a bit hesitant to unearth the old record cards, but then understood the time-saving factor.

Casually complimenting the woman on her blouse and pin, then her hair and shoes earlier hadn't hurt either. Redler also promised that he'd credit Estie with helping him with his research and twice asked and double-checked the spelling of her full name, confirming her title as assistant librarian, noting her many years of employment, too. He told her he would sit at a nearby table and personally return everything the moment he was through. He hoped the record cards were still on hand and hadn't been discarded during the library's move.

Ten minutes later, Estie Schier returned from the basement with the first of several batches comprising over ten years worth of dusty, dirty buff-colored alphabetized record cards. Resettling himself at a table near Estie, Redler went back to work.

There was no card for Beth Tracy. However, Robert Redler uncovered something most curious. Jeffrey Mills, not Beth Tracy, had been a borrower. Not of Braille books, but of print books and publications referencing low vision impairment as indicated on two record cards. The first text was titled *Understanding Low Vision*. The cards had Jeffrey Mills' name and old Manhattan address typed in— momentarily blindsiding Redler's thinking. Seven titles of texts for openers, not on blindness per se, but focusing on low vision impairment in particular. Their titles loomed up at him. There was a lengthy list of periodicals, too, which explained why Mills' file cards were full.

Jeffrey Mills' eyesight was in no way impaired insofar as Redler knew, having later confirmed that fact through several surreptitious inquiries at the Manhattan post office on John Street where Mills was still employed. Mills' half sister, Beth Tracy, was totally blind and had been since birth. So why was Jeffrey Mills interested in books and publications dealing specifically with low vision issues as opposed to literature dealing with blindness in general? The discovery of those particular texts and periodicals borrowed under the name of Jeffrey Mills made no sense to Robert Redler. He pondered the question repeatedly, perusing the lengthy list of materials loaned to the Manhattan postal worker over a period of more than a decade.

Estie Schier located the first five hundred fifty-five page text for the *researcher* before helping him round up the other six. Redler fixated on the pocket card and book envelope.

HV5568   Jose, Randall Y., ed.   c.5
J772   Understanding Low
                 Vision.

(1983)

Mr. Jeffrey T. Mills had withdrawn the book on 12/19/86.

"Why did you begin there, with Mr. Mills?" Ms. Schier wanted to know, glancing over Redler's shoulder when setting down the six additional books he requested.

"Middle of the alphabet," Redler answered, which wasn't an answer at all but an accurate accounting.

"I see."

"Do you know him?"

Estie Schier shook her head.

Creating a time line, Redler made a list of seven books in the order Jeffrey Mills had borrowed them—books pertaining to low vision impairment, inclusive of optics.

Basic optical concepts; *Lenses, prisms and mirrors*; *Normal and abnormal vision*; *The human eye.* Southbridge, Mass.: American Optical Corp., 1976. Series of four programmed self-instruction courses.

Sloan, L. L. *Reading aids for the partially sighted,* Baltimore: Williams and Wilkins Co., 1977.

Faye, E. E. *Clinical low vision.* Boston: Little, Brown & Co., 1976.

Faye, E. E., & Hood, C. M. *Low vision.* Springfield, Ill.: Charles C. Thomas, 1975.

Mehr, E. B., & Freid, A. N. *Low vision care.* Chicago: Professional Press, 1975.

Barraga, N. C., & Morris, J. E. *Program to develop efficiency in visual functioning*: *Source book on low vision.* Louisville, Ky.: American Printing House for the Blind, 1980.

Jose, R. T. *Understanding Low Vision.* American Foundation for the Blind. New York, 1983.

When Redler finished recording the list of books, he perused the multitude of periodicals with which Jeffrey Mills had concerned himself, assuming that the man's interest followed selected articles related to low vision. Redler worked right through lunch and spent a good part of the day reading and recording information from the *American Journal of Optometry & Physiological Optics, Canadian Journal of Ophthalmology, American Journal of Ophthalmology, Optical Journal and review of Optometry, Journal of the American Optometric Association, Journal of Visual Impairment & Blindness, Survey of Ophthalmology, Optometric Monthly, Archives of Ophthalmology, Journal of the Optical Society of America*, and finally, a stack of conference papers from the *Workshop on low vision mobility: Final report of a workshop at Western Michigan University*, November 3-5, 1975.

Although the conference papers primarily dealt with evaluations of visual functioning and visual training with and without the benefit of optical aids, what Redler found particularly curious was the bracketed, starred, and underlined sections highlighting the evaluations of distance vision and the psychological aspects of low vision, all marked in red pen.

Redler had been at it for hours, and his eyes were practically falling out of his head. He pushed the papers, periodicals, magazines and journals aside then ran through a series of pages in the beginning of the first text that the librarian had brought him. Under a section entitled Retrolental Fibroplasia, abridged thereafter as RLF, he read the bracketed portion: [Severe myopia (nearsightedness) is common among persons with retrolental fibroplasia. It may be significantly improved by the use of a contact lens.]

The two sentences were bracketed in red ink. Any borrower, of course, could have been guilty of marking up that page as well as the pages perused in the periodicals. It didn't mean that Jeffrey Mills was necessarily the culprit. But the next book that Redler had scanned, only this time more carefully, pointed more than a suspicious finger at Mills. The text, *Basic optical concepts; Lenses, prisms, and mirrors; Normal and abnormal vision; The human eye*, obviously concerned someone altogether interested in the section on lenses as evidenced by the bracketed, starred and underlined sections in ostensibly the same red ink. That textbook had only one borrower, indicated by the Due Date pocket envelope which corresponded with Jeffrey T. Mills' pocket ID card. Not proof positive, but certainly more than circumstantial, at least in Redler's mind's eye.

Robert Redler had been at it since 9 a.m. It was 3 p.m. He was tired. His eyes were burning, yet he refused to stop. He had two hours left before the library would close.

Estie Schier had noticed hours earlier that the man was doing more reading than recording, but she went on about her business, figuring he was taking himself away from the rather dry and often torturous task of logging statistics to immersing himself in the more intellectual matter of the material at hand. The import of which she could well understand. Estie related to his intensity. She contemplated his furrowed brow. It was as though he were having difficulty following a mystery novel with remarkable twists and turns, she mused. So intense and complex was this man who had asked her for help. Probably a low-paid research assistant for some recondite magazine. Nothing mainstream, Estie imagined. He didn't volunteer the information, and she didn't ask.

This researcher, she thought, certainly seemed earnest and sincere. He hadn't told her she was something she was not: cute, pretty, attractive, charming or anything of the sort. Instead, he had complimented her on her blouse, Bergdorf's, $120; her pin, Cartier's, $500; her shoes, Etienne Aigner, $150; her hair, her own, *thank God!* Estie entertained good-humoredly. Long and lovely. One of God's token gifts for making her so ugly. Hair with which she tried to hide her homely features. Her ears, too. Her entire countenance? "Plain," Estie's mother would often tell her young child, until one day Estie thumbed through an unabridged dictionary and comprehended its definition as it was meant to be applied, noting entry number **7.** not beautiful; physically unattractive; homely.

"Plain," her mother had insisted.

"That's not true!" Estie railed.

Estie was never quite certain why her mother had struck her in that instant, but she had. Rather hard, in fact, as Estie recalled. What Estie remembered distinctly was that she was only eight at the time. What she remembered vividly was that her mother was quite beautiful —even lying in her coffin a year later at the age of twenty-six—the last time Estie would ever see her.

Robert Redler could not further narrow Jeffrey Mills' area of interest regarding RLF. All Redler realized was that the man seemed fascinated with the subject of eyes. Not blind eyes, but rather eyes that could see, however faintly. Shapes. Shadows. Light and dark adaptations. Depth and space perception. Was Jeffrey somehow holding out unwarranted hope for his half sister, Beth? Surely, Jeffrey had to know that she would never see again. Hospital records had confirmed it. Blind from birth. No hope of any sort was on the horizon. What was Jeffrey Mills' concern?

Rather than dwell or speculate any further on what Mills' interest might possibly mean, Redler tried a different approach. He simply noted the gist of the material, for he was too tired to draw any inferences or come to any conclusions. Maybe he would see the light when he got home that night. Maybe he would have to return the following day after reminding himself that the M.C. Migel Memorial Library was no longer lending books. '*Never a borrower nor a lender be*,' popped sillily into his head. He was getting punchy, jotting down in sum and substance the gist from the bracketed, starred and underlined text. Grist for the mill.

He began noting and numbering from *Understanding Low Vision*.

Section I The eye and Functional Vision. Retrolental Fibroplasia. 1) person looks normal 2) almost no vision 3) difficult to diagnose by general doctors and public 4) specialist can spot it easily

Section II Assessment of Low Vision. Minimum Assessment Sequence: The Optometrist's Viewpoint. 1) assessment items may give insight to behavior and motions common to blind people

Comprehensive Preliminary Assessments of Low Vision. Observations of Functional Vision. 1) near-vision clues 2) distance-vision clues

Assessment of Children. 1) good overview of blind people—outlook—problems 2) general behavior and appearance 3) special classes

Section III Clinical Services. Treatment Options. 1) pictures of aids

a} telescopic glasses b} microscopic glasses c} contact lenses

Redler noted the excessive bracketing, starring and underscoring in Section III, reference subsection c} contact lenses.

Section IV Training and Instructional Services. Distance Training Techniques. Unfamiliar areas. 1) behavior; Congested areas.

Training Programs for Individuals with Restricted Fields. Types of Scanning

1) gives idea of eye and head movements a} erratic scanning
b} head scanning

c} shoe gazing

Section V   Assessment of Multiple Handicapped People.
Observing The Child's Behavior. 1) general behavior and actions a}
movement patterns b} sensory responses c} postural responses

Role Model for an Orientation and Mobility Instructor and a
Teacher of the Visually Handicapped. Functional O & M Evaluation. 1)
general actions and behavior

a} fixation b} head position c} use of color

Under the section on color, Redler could not help but again
notice the heavy pressure the person had put upon the ballpoint pen,
practically tearing through the page with red bracketing, starring and
forcible underscoring.

That evening, Redler reviewed his notes and made a few phone calls.
The first was placed to Texas, to one of Mills' aunts. Eleven o'clock
was 10 p.m. Central Standard Time in Dallas. Still a decent hour to say,
'Howdy, ma'am.' Redler's brief introduction was immediately followed
by the woman screaming, hollering then hanging up on him. He never
got the chance to tell the woman how shrewish she sounded, wailing
away in his ear like a banshee. He didn't have blouses or pins or hair or
shoes to pick up on. As a matter of fact, he pictured the woman
barefooted in a large and dirty housedress, suffering from a case of the
screaming-meemies. Redler figured one reporter too many had dialed
her listed number. *Newsday*'s David Z. Culver, to be sure.

In the morning, Redler called a good friend and contact in
Melbourne, Florida, who cheerfully made a series of phone calls,
starting with the courthouse in Broward County where the brothers'
mother's—Sophie Mills—divorce decree had been filed. From there,
the retired eighty-three-year-old private investigator dialed up one of
Mills' distant relatives in California, who spun a wild tale which led
back to a private hospital in Jersey City where Beth Tracy was
prematurely born. Blind from birth. Diagnosed with a rare eye disease:
RLF—retrolental fibroplasia. Severe and accelerated.

What Redler's contact began to sort out was the controversy
over oxygen therapy administered while Beth had lain in an incubator
for well over a six-week period. The hospital had insisted they were not
at fault. Beth Tracy's family and a high-powered lawyer saw it

altogether differently, claiming the oxygen level in the incubator was not properly monitored. They cried cover-up. The battle centered on a male nurse whose license was in question. It never got to court. The upshot was that the hospital wound up paying out several million dollars to Sophie Mills-Tracy, who immediately set up a hidden trust for her eldest son, Howard, telling her new husband that she alone had carried baby Beth for six months, earned the money, and would do what she damn well pleased with the funds, threatening to give it all away to an orphanage or an animal hospital if he bothered her again. Sophie's name was on everything. Solely. She ruled the roost. Howard W. Mills would one day be a multimillionaire. And that was that.

Apart from Beth's inheritance, no one else in the family saw a nickel. Not one red cent. The remainder of the estate was to go to Howard on the day he turned twenty-one. Howard was now forty-four. He never touched a dime of that money. Beth was left a nice inheritance when Sophie died, which her daughter parlayed into a comfortable interest-bearing account. Jeffrey, however, was always broke and forever hounded Howard for cash.

"Where's the family money?" Jeffrey would demand.

"There is no money. Mother gave it all away to an orphanage," Howard delighted in telling and tormenting his younger charge.

"I know better. What's the money doing, Howard?"

And Howard would always wink and smile. "Doing real well, Jeffrey. Growing like Beth's tomatoes. Spreading like their vines. So don't worry yourself none. One day you'll see the fruits of Mom's labor." Howard loved that line. He loved Beth. He loved his irresponsible brother, Jeffrey, too.

"So, how did I do, Rob?" Redler's octogenarian Floridian contact wanted to know upon relaying that and other relevant information concerning the Mills-Tracy family fortune.

"You're worth your seasons in greenbacks, old-timer," the writer answered wisely.

"Then eighty-three smackers you'll wire me this afternoon. When you comin' down for fish and folly?"

"What's running?"

"Right now? Wild and crazy women . . . right along my dock."

"You'll never make it to a hundred, Emiel."

"Oh, I'll get a hundred out of you yet. You'll see."

"Listen. Thanks."

"Yeah. Tell the Empire State, for me, that it needs a new ump." Emiel G. hung up laughing.

Chapter Thirty-Five

It was early Saturday morning, and Ilona Alfold was holding down the fort. She had just opened up the beverage store and left the front door wide open for air. It was warm inside.

"Hi, Ilona."

"Jeffrey!" the teenager beamed, turning around from behind the counter in sheer surprise. "What are you doing here?"

"Do you want me to go?" Jeff was gazing down at his sneakers.

"Of course not, silly. I just didn't . . . didn't—"

"Didn't think I'd ever come back?"

"I hoped you would, but I didn't know. No. Not after what my father said to you."

"I'm not afraid of your father, Ilona."

Ilona smiled prettily, stepping around from behind the counter. "I didn't say you were. Let me look at you," she said, gently lifting his chin with the tips of three fingers.

Jeff let his head be raised and stared into her bright blue eyes, bluer than his own.

"I'm glad you came back, Jeffrey."

"Even though your father told me not to?"

Ilona took her hand back and covered her mouth, about to cry. She nodded her answer, reached out and touched his cheek.

Jeff watched the tears roll down her face.

"Ilona?"

Ilona folded her lips and clamped them in place behind her teeth.

"Are you afraid of your father?"

Ilona shook her head but then quickly nodded.

"Does he say bad things to you?"

"Sometimes," she sighed, having freed her lips and sending out a single sibilant sound.

"Does he ever hit you?"

"Sometimes, when I don't do what I'm told. Not often. Why?"

"You're too old, Ilona." Jeff erased away the statement with a wave of his hand and shook his head before her pretty face. "I didn't mean *old*," he said and swallowed hard. "I mean, too old for him to hit you."

"I know what you mean," she assured him, laughing away her tears. "But I do live under his roof, you have to understand."

"I know that you couldn't do anything wrong that would make anybody hit you unless that person was very mean."

Apart from a story or two about his cat, it was the longest sentence she ever heard him utter in a single breath, and she remained speechless for a moment. It was the nicest thing a man or boy had ever said to her, and she wanted to hold him tightly, right there in the store. He had a man's body and a boyish way about him. When she first met him, she thought he was slow. She soon learned that he was very, very shy. And so was she. So here they were talking about personal things. Ilona wondered if he still remembered her offer of Chinese food at the restaurant down the block. She didn't want to seem too pushy. Maybe he would bring it up.

"Ilona?"

She smiled.

"Did I say something wrong?" He was staring down at his sneakers again.

"Nope. Not at all, Jeffrey Mills."

"I'm glad." Jeff raised his eyes to the counter.

"How's jury selection going for Howard?" she asked, not really knowing whether she should have brought up the subject. Not knowing what else to say at the moment.

"Very slow. Howard thinks he's going to trial near the end of October. First it was supposed to be mid-June. Who the heck knows?"

Ilona nodded, staring up at the ceiling for something to say. "Say, what do you think about those pink elephants I just finished painting up there before you came by?"

Jeff lifted his eyes to the ceiling then laughed. He laughed loudly, and it both startled and delighted her.

"Made you look," she said before laughing, too.

"You did, indeed," he agreed.

He was looking into her eyes. She tried not to look away but became embarrassed, back to staring up blankly at the stark white stippled ceiling.

"Did you notice my spit-shined shoes, Ilona?"

Ilona immediately shut her eyes tightly and kept her head directed toward the ceiling. She giggled quietly, refusing to fall for his ruse. "You're not wearing shoes. You're wearing sneakers, Jeffrey Mills. White and blue," she declared.

"No, I'm not," he insisted, quietly stepping on the heel of one sneaker, removing it. Then the other.

"Liar, liar, pants on fire," she insisted, her eyes still sealed tightly.

"Customer's coming," he whispered.

"Won't fall for that either," she said defiantly, folding her arms across her chest.

"I'm serious. Look."

"Not in a million years."

A slender middle-aged woman in a sleeveless blue V-neck top and matching skirt started through the open door.

Jeff put a finger to his lips. The woman froze, taking in the scene.

"What if I told you that this customer was a woman as beautiful as you?"

Ilona's face turned crimson, but she held her head high and proud, afraid to open her eyes for fear that what she had just heard was but a dream. She felt as though her face were on fire.

"Well?" Jeff insisted. "What would you do?"

"What would I do?" Ilona played along. "I'd tell you to go wait on her and hurry back to me when you're done."

"All right, then," Jeff said, stepping silently in stocking feet past Ilona and over to the smiling woman. "If you'll just step over here quietly, pretty woman, and point out what you want so that we do not wake my sleeping princess, I'll be more than happy to help you," he

220

suggested, taking the woman's hand in his and guiding her past Ilona.

The woman was along for the ride, never having experienced such antics, in a beverage store no less. She could feel the electricity between the couple. *Too old for the teenager,* she thought. *Probably just a good friend having fun.* He seemed nice. She pointed to a big bag of potato chips and a six-pack of seltzer as they traveled partway down the aisle together.

Ilona was standing with her back to them, listening to a single set of footsteps, like the sound of high heels marching away. She peeked down quickly and saw his sneakers out of the corner of one eye, immediately closing it and giggling again, never realizing he had the devil in him, believing he was somehow making those shoe sounds himself and continuing their game.

Jeff removed a carton of seltzer from a refrigerated compartment and grabbed the chips on their return.

"Six-pack of seltzer and large chips. Will there be anything else, ma'am?" he asked, bringing a finger to his lips anew as a reminder.

The woman smiled again and shook her head.

"No? All right then." Jeff set the items on the counter and stepped behind the register. "Let's see what we have here. Seltzer on sale for a dollar ninety-nine, times eight-and-a-quarter percent, plus deposit." Jeff was actually ringing up a sale. "Large chips at a dollar ninety-nine; no tax on food items, comes to four dollars and forty-four cents. Out of ten."

Ilona didn't dare open her eyes to break the playful trance, for there was more at stake here than a game. There was this moment of trust, for he was actually in the register. *Was this a test?* she wondered.

"There you go." Jeff handed the woman her change, took a paper bag from the shelf behind the counter, snapped it open sharply, then placed the items within. "May I help you carry this to the door, ma'am?"

The woman put her money away, shook her head and took her package from the man's hands, turning and heading for the door.

"Please come back again soon," he said politely. "Hopefully, when my sleeping princess has her mind on business instead of her Prince Charming."

Ilona was laughing hysterically. He could have robbed her blind and she would not have cared one bit. She wanted to give away the store today. She wanted to surrender her maidenhood to this man who was twice her age. But all she hoped for was a single kiss. If her father had ever walked in on them at that moment, he'd have half killed her, she knew. Ilona knew, also, that he wouldn't be home until late Sunday night. Jeffrey knew that, too.

The woman customer stopped at the threshold and faced about, realizing that the couple was more than friends, for Jeff took Ilona in his arms and kissed her cool, damp, closed eyes.

"Maybe you should hold on to him," the older woman allowed herself, changing her notion of their age difference—touched by the tender scene.

Ilona gave a start, opened her eyes, and stood staring at the woman holding her package just inside the doorway. "Oh, my God!" she exclaimed.

"I let a man like that slip away from me a long time ago," the stranger added. "I'm not an unhappy woman, nor am I complete."

Jeff stepped back from Ilona, then smiled and waved at the pretty woman before she disappeared out the door, up the walkway and around the corner.

Ilona stooped down for the pair of sneakers on the floor beside her. Jeff knew what was coming and headed for cover, running down the isle in his stocking feet. One sneaker flew by his right ear. The other caught him in the center of his back.

"You horrible person, you," she hollered in a fit of frustration mixed with uncontrollable laughter. "How could you?"

Ilona chased after him, in and out and up and down and back and forth between the aisles before Jeff slowed his pace, allowing his pretty princess to catch up to him on their third trip around the store, swinging around abruptly and sweeping her up in his arms as she came in for the kill. He kissed her hard and hot and passionately, pushing her gently against a wall.

Chapter Thirty-Six

Detective Gary York was standing in the hallway just outside Judge Steven Best's courtroom, waiting to testify for the prosecution at Howard Mills' lengthy jury trial, now well into its fourth month. Gail Fox summoned York as her thirty-first witness, presumably her final round. Once again, Nicholas Dunn and Christopher Profeta noted the irony referencing that particular number. The prosecution, in having called York, made it all the more fitting for what the defense had in store for this hubristic servant of the People.

Howard Mills sat at the defense table. Exasperated.

"Both sides ready to proceed?" Judge Best asked for perhaps the thousandth time since the early days of pretrial examination.

"Yes, if I may just call the detective down, Judge," Fox answered. "I wasn't quite sure how long we would be."

"He's right outside the door," one of the court officers announced, stepping through a set of double doors.

"All right, then. Are both sides ready?"

"People are ready, Your Honor."

"Yes, Judge," Profeta answered quietly.

"Bring our jury in, please," Best ordered politely.

"Jury entering," said another court officer.

Twelve jurors and ten alternates filed back into the courtroom after having returned from their lunch break. They took their seats.

"Case on trial, People vs. Howard Willis Mills. The jury is present with twenty-two jurors seated in the box. Do counsel waive roll call?" a male court clerk spoke up loud and clear.

The man was unfamiliar to Robert Redler, as court officers and clerks were, as a rule, routinely rotated every twelve weeks. Redler's court-clerk friend was either in another Part in the building, or the court complex in Central Islip.

"Yes," Dunn answered anxiously.

"People waive," Fox said.

"Jury, defendant and counsel are all present," the clerk announced formally.

"Good afternoon, ladies and gentlemen," Judge Best addressed and nodded to the jury. "You may call your next witness," he said to the prosecutor.

"The People call Detective Gary Daniel York," Gail Fox announced quite pleasantly.

The doors opened at the back of the courtroom, and Detective York came ambling through. He wore his attitude as proudly as his badge and strutted up to the witness stand, turned about and remained standing in an Armani suit. He glared down at Dunn, Profeta and the defendant.

"Raise your right hand," the clerk instructed. "Do you swear that the testimony you are about to give is the truth, the whole truth, and nothing but the truth, so help you God?"

"I do." York hadn't taken his eyes off the trio.

"Please be seated."

Gary York sat back and crossed a leg, allowing an Italian designer shoe to dangle from the tip of his toes, rhythmically rocking the Loafer to and fro then up and down. No one except the clerk and the court reporter could see the subtle antic.

"Please state and spell your name, and give us your shield and command."

The detective took his eyes off the three men seated at the defense table and set them on the attractive female court reporter. The woman looked up uncomfortably.

"Detective Gary Daniel York. Y-O-R-K; shield number Two-Three-Five. Suffolk County Homicide Squad."

The woman had the distinct feeling that the witness wanted to give her his home address and phone number, too.

"Thank you," the clerk finished, noting the unsavory behavior so unbecoming a cop.

"Welcome," Gary answered, failing to take his eyes off the woman.

"Good afternoon, Detective," Judge Best greeted; no hint of aberration in his tone or stare.

York casually turned his head ninety degrees clockwise to face the judge. "Good afternoon."

"Counselor, you may inquire."

"Thank you, Judge." The prosecutor began her direct-examination of the witness, hopefully drawing to the completion of trial, praying that this dandy but very competent detective wouldn't call her Gail during testimony as he had done upstairs—constantly and even after several warnings . . . her monitions somehow giving way to his beguiling charm. She knew he was dangerous. She pretty much knew but didn't want to *really* know how, exactly, he had solidified their case. There were rumors. *He could make his goddamn goo-goo eyes at whomever he wanted*, she told herself, *just so long as he seduced this jury in total*. In truth, he was as smooth and as cold as ice. As deadly as the defendant, she believed. "Good afternoon, Detective."

"Good afternoon, Gail."

Asshole. "Detective, how long have you been a Suffolk County police officer?"

"Twenty-four years."

"And what is your present assignment?"

"Homicide squad."

"And what is your rank there?"

"Detective."

"And how long have you been a detective?"

"Fourteen years."

"And in the homicide squad, do you have a particular team that you work with?"

"Yes."

"And what is that team?"

"Team Two."

"Sorry, but I didn't hear that," Nicholas Dunn interrupted.

"If you can just tap on the microphone and see if it's on," Judge Best suggested.

"It's on, Judge," the court officer said as York simultaneously flicked the tip of his middle finger off the tip of his thumb, striking the side of the microphone so sharply that it caused an alternate juror to flinch.

"Sorry," Gary York said coolly, his middle finger held in mid-air for a fraction of a second but long enough for Dunn to note that the gesture was directed at and especially meant for him.

Two sets of eyes locked on one another like radar.

"And what team is that?" Gail repeated.

"Team Two."

Gary held up two digits before the defense, palm inward, his middle finger slightly out further than his forefinger in case Nicholas Dunn hadn't caught the affront the first time around. Dunn reconfirmed which of the two fingers singled him out. *Glad to have you back, Gary-boy*, Dunn said to himself. *Wait, motherfucker. Just wait.*

"And who were the other members of Team Two back on April the 6th, 1996, the day Howard Mills was arrested?"

"Detectives Michael Connolly and John Bailey, Detectives Frank Masselli and Victor Posteraro, Detectives Troy Anderson and Eric Bokina."

"And who was your superior in Team Two?"

"My immediate superior was Detective Sergeant Cary Carter. My commanding officer was and is Detective Lieutenant Theodore Groche," Gary clarified with a bored expression plastered across his face, answering Fox, yet fixing his eyes on Dunn.

"Thank you, Detective. Now, I'm going to direct your attention back to the day of April 6th, 1996, and ask you if you were working that day."

"That night. Yes."

"And what was your tour of duty that night, Detective?"

"I had a nine-to-five tour."

"And on this nine-to-five tour, did there come a time that you were asked by Detective Sergeant Carter to ascertain pedigree information from this defendant, Howard Mills?" Gail was pointing a finger at the defendant.

"On April 6, I was working the prisoner activity log. I believe it was on the seventh that the sergeant asked me to go in and secure pedigree info."

"And would you confirm that date from your notes?"

Gary glanced down at his notes. "Yes, it was the seventh."

"And would you explain to the jury what pedigree information is composed of?"

Detective York turned his head obliquely to his left, scanning the jury. He keyed in on the youngest, most attractive female juror seated in the first row. He spoke directly to her.

"Pedigree information is biographical data consisting of a suspect's full name, date of birth, work history, education, history of physiological and mental health as it relates to the arrestee, his or her parents, siblings—things of that nature."

"And did you in fact inquire of and record this information as given to you by the defendant on the evening of April the 7th, 1996?"

"Yes, I did."

"And in addition to the pedigree information that you secured from the defendant, did you come away with anything else?"

"Objection to, 'come away with,'" Profeta said, getting to his feet.

"As to form, sustained. You can rephrase it, Ms. Fox," Judge Best instructed.

"In addition to the biographical data that you received, did you obtain any other information from this defendant?"

"Yes."

"And what additional information did you receive?"

"I received a three-page voluntary statement from the defendant, confessing to the murders of Jane Doe/Medford, found in a garbage container along the side of a road; Danielle Louise Clarke, the young woman found on the conveyor belt in Brooklyn; and Claudia Rose Stetson, a.k.a. Darla Vasco, whose body was discovered in a Dumpster in Melville."

Staff reporters, sketch artists and spectators, one of whom was Robert Redler, focused on the men and women in the jury box. Twenty-two solemn faces, displaying discerning pairs of eyes, had shifted from Detective Gary York to the defendant.

Howard Mills hung his head and shook it slowly back and forth. Dunn put a hand on his client's shoulder, whispering in his ear. Howard nodded with a bit of encouragement. He set his head erect, looking the jury in the eyes. The majority of the jurors looked away.

"And how is it that you came to . . . withdrawn. Detective, why was it that Howard Mills voluntarily gave you a three-page written confession? I mean, did he just pick up a pen and start writing?"

"Objection," Profeta started, but Dunn waved his co-counselor off.

"Give me just one second, Judge?" Profeta asked the Court.

Should there be any lip readers present in the courtroom, Dunn shielded his mouth with his hand as he whispered behind Mills' back to Profeta.

"Are you withdrawing the objection?" Best asked Profeta.

"Yes, Your Honor," Profeta answered, rising and settling like a wave.

"Objection is withdrawn. You may continue."

"Do you want the question read back, Detective?" Gail asked.

"No, ma'am." Gary knew his script. "Mr. Mills didn't confess to anything until after I took the pedigree. Then he said, 'You treated me just beautifully.'"

"'You treated me just beautifully,'" Fox repeated.

"Yeah, they were bosom buddies by that point," Dunn interjected sarcastically, smiling and turning slowly to scan his audience of jurors and spectators.

"Your Honor!" Fox flustered.

Several spectators smiled back.

"Ms. Fox?" Judge Best questioned in deadpan.

"Yes, Judge. I object to Mr. Dunn's outburst. He's been admonished by the Court several times now for exactly this kind of behavior and it does no good. Maybe if monetary sanctions were invoked by this Court, Mr. Dunn might be kept in check."

Judge Best thought for a moment, signaling the court reporter that they were going off the record. "Before I rule on this—" He took a deep breath and leaned forward. "This has been a long and arduous trial for all parties concerned." He paused, deciding to lecture the attorneys before the jury rather than outside their presence or at sidebar. "As such, the Court has witnessed moments of less than satisfactory behavior from both sides, may I remind you, Ms. Fox. Fortunately, that comportment has been the exception rather than the rule. Fortunately, for Mr. Dunn, I do not view his interruption as an outburst nor a behavioral issue but rather as a lapse in judgment. Unfortunately, my patience is wearing thin. Furthermore, any suggestions of punitive measures, whether they be monetary or otherwise, will be so decided and directed by this Court. In other words, no threats or caveats or suggestions of any kind will emanate from the defense or the prosecution. Clear?" Judge Best gestured to the reporter that they were back on the record.

"Yes, Judge," Fox fired back, "but I just want the record to reflect that Mr. Dunn's outburst—excuse me, interruption is noted—"

"Objection is overruled. The remark is stricken from the record. The jury is instructed to disregard it. You may continue, Ms. Fox."

"Thank you, Your Honor," *for nothing*. "Detective, before we were rudely interrupted—" Fox let the words hang there.

Dunn turned and delivered a winning smile to his audience. Most of the spectators smiled back out of politeness, nervousness, or uncertainty. Danielle Louise Clarke's mother did not smile. Claudia Rose Stetson's father frowned and wanted to come across the railing and wrap his hands around Dunn's and Mills' windpipes while he crushed Profeta's with the heel of a boot—like a bug.

"I was asking you, Detective, how it came to be that the defendant gave you a three-page written statement, confessing to three murders after you took the pedigree information," Fox continued.

"After the defendant told me that I had treated him beautifully, I asked him why *this* had to happen. He said, 'I don't understand why.' I asked him if drugs had anything to do with *it*. He said, 'Absolutely.'"

"Let me stop you there for a moment, Detective," Gail stated before the defense would stop her with another objection. "When you asked the defendant why *this* had to happen and if drugs had anything to do with *it*, what were you referring to?"

"The murder of the three women he was being charged with."

"And was it clear to you that the defendant understood that you were referring to the murders?"

"No question whatsoever."

"Objection." Profeta stood five-foot six. "This detective is not a mind reader. He had no way of knowing what was in my client's head at the time."

"I have a good faith basis for raising this question, Your Honor," Fox retorted. "It will be made abundantly clear in just a moment that the murders were precisely what the detective and the defendant were talking about."

"Objection is overruled."

"Detective. What transpired in your dialogue with the defendant that left no doubt in your mind that the two of you were discussing the murders of the three women?"

"May I refer to my notes?" York asked the judge as he was supposed to do.

"Yes, you may."

Gary looked down at his notes. "When he said, 'Absolutely,' I asked him how often? He said: 'Every so often I got to hit somebody. I just explode. They don't do anything to make me mad. I just go into a rage.' Then I asked him—"

"Objection." Dunn was on his feet and pointing an angry finger at York. "Judge, he's reading straight from his notes. This detective knows better. He can look at his notes to refresh his recollection. He *can not* read from them. Please instruct this witness."

"All right." Judge Best went through the motions. "Detective, you can't read from something that is not in evidence. You can use your notes to refresh your recollection and then testify from memory."

"You bet," York snapped curtly, giving Dunn the evil eye before looking back down at his notes.

Gail wanted to cringe. "And did that refresh your recollection?"

"Yep. Then I asked the defendant what he used to hit the woman found in Medford. He said he used a five-pound weight, a dumbbell. A hammer on the woman found in Brooklyn. And a bat on the Melville victim."

Jack Stetson and Eloise Clarke were sitting together and crying quietly in the fourth row back, both parties having been told by the prosecution that any outburst or eye contact with the jury could result in a mistrial. Stetson had been a witness for the People during pretrial. Clarke had not. It took a great deal of restraint to control their emotions.

"And what, if anything, did the defendant do next?"

"In sum and substance, he asked me for a pen and paper."

"Had you said or done anything that prompted this request?"

"Yes."

"And what was that?"

"I told him that it was time to lift this heavy burden that he was carrying and to get things off his chest."

Howard sat quietly between his defense attorneys, sadly and deliberately shaking his head.

"And then you handed him pen and paper?"

"Not until he asked me for them."

"And then what happened?"

"He asked me to help him with the statement."

"And did you?"

"Yes. That's when I got paper and pen."

"Now, Detective. I'm going to . . . but first . . . . Ms. Presant, if you would put exhibit 135 on the presenter, please. Oh, and Detective, if you could indicate to the Court the person who you had this dialogue with on April the 7th of 1996."

"The defendant, Mr. Mills, right there in the plaid shirt and green sweater, sitting between his two attorneys," York said, pointing a gun-finger extended at arm's length.

"Thank you, Detective. Now, if you would read for us a copy of Mr. Mills' statement, which is in evidence," she instructed, staring sarcastically at Dunn, who grinned back at her from ear to ear. "Can we make that a little clearer, please? Good. Whenever you're ready, Detective."

Detective York read: "'I, Howard W. Mills, residing at 42 Willow Lane in Hicksville, picked up prostitutes on a regular basis and would return to my rental apartment . . . . '" Gary read on, relating in detail what he had said the defendant had said in that 8 x 8 foot interrogation room on the evening of April the 7th, 1996. The detective was nearing the end of the statement when it happened. "' . . . and each of these five girls was killed by me.'" No one saw it coming. No one caught it at that instant except Howard Mills. But it was too late. It was out there like a bucking bronco. And then it registered all over the place and even threw two jurors for a loop.

Five girls?

Mills was a maniac, and his lawyers had to calm him down.

A copy of the original document had not been changed to reflect *three girls*. It was supposed to have been altered from *five* girls to *three*. The jury wasn't supposed to know about the two additional Westchester victims. The mistake was of a serious nature and had the potential to result in a mistrial. At the very least, but at a much later date, it would be grounds, fertile ground for sure, for an appeal. But for the moment, the situation had to be remedied and fast, for the judge was not going to allow a mistrial at this late stage. Plain and simple. Too much time and money had been spent to date. Thousands of hours and millions of dollars. Ten million at last count it had been rumored. A mistrial was not about to happen. It was amazing that no one had picked up the error until it was read by York. Not the judge nor his law secretary. Not the prosecution. Nor the defense attorneys.

Or had they? Redler wondered.

The written statement with the word *five*, pertaining to the victims, had to be redacted. The jury was retired for the rest of the afternoon and told to report the following morning at ten o'clock. The issue would be decided. Howard Mills was instructed by his attorneys to apologize to the judge for his *understandable behavior.* The Court accepted with a nod and the equivalent of an okey-doke. It was unclear at that point what was on or off the record.

Nicholas Dunn announced to no one in particular that he was headed downstairs to the law library with Christopher Profeta. One of the court officers jokingly asked him if he even knew where it was. Profeta found and appreciated humor in everything. They all did, actually. It was how they held on to their sanity. It was how they got through their days and nights without going mad.

"The law library?" Profeta teased mischievously. "Not only does Nick have difficulty locating it, he can't even pronounce it correctly," the diminutive, elf-like lawyer goaded; which, if you listened to Dunn's pronunciation, was true enough. "Say, *liberry*," for the folks, Profeta needled with a giggle.

Dunn waved him off with a frown.

Chapter Thirty-Seven

Christopher Profeta was not smiling or joking the following morning. Out of the presence of the jury, the attorney asked Judge Best for a mistrial. He knew what the Court's ruling would be, but he was going through the motions as though he expected nothing less.

"Your Honor. We are asking for a mistrial based on yesterday's proceedings with regard to Mr. Mills' alleged written statement, which the defense maintains was coerced. Detective York's reading reference 'five girls' has had an effect that cannot be corrected. This situation is injurious and flagrantly prejudicial to the defendant." Profeta went on to cite case law for most of the morning, then wound up berating the judge's decision to insert '94, '95 girls (referencing the years of those murders) in lieu of the word *five* as if it were simply a clerical error. "You are duping the jury, Judge. You are manufacturing evidence, creating a fiction no less onerous than Team Two's tactics." Profeta was skating on thin ice. He wasn't headed toward any goal post, but merely maneuvering himself into a position whereby the puck might be slap shot across the line at some later date. "We oppose the insertion, Judge. Any insertion. We oppose the tampering of this document, the compressing or expanding of the space or the filling in of any blank. There is no cure, no remedy for this problem. And in the event that this request is denied and a guilty verdict rendered, we seek a separate sentencing jury for the penalty phase. Most respectfully, Your Honor, our client has a right to due process."

It was a consummate performance.

Howard Mills looked as though he were about to be handed the brass ring.

"Your motion for a mistrial is denied," Judge Best responded. "Your motion for a new jury at the penalty phase, should we ever get to that point, is denied. Are there any other motions, applications, or arguments to be heard before we proceed?"

"No, Your Honor," Profeta said, sitting back down quietly.

Howard Mills was buzzing back and forth between his attorneys.

Moments later, the jury was brought into the courtroom.

"Good morning, ladies and gentlemen of the jury. As I'm sure you recall, there was some confusion yesterday over the reading of the April 7th, 1996 copy of the written statement of Howard Mills. That copy was to reflect *three girls*, not *five girls* as was presented on the screen and read to you by Detective York." Best had not lied. The document *was* to reflect that precisely. But it hadn't. "Since that time, we have taken steps to correct that error." So far so good. "The new document reflects that correction. It reads, 'Each of the '94, '95 girls were killed by me.'"

Feasible but fraudulent, Robert Redler entertained.

A fiction heaped on top of fiction, Howard Mills certainly knew.

Formalities aside, ADA Fox called her witness back to the stand. Detective York strolled in and stood beside the bench. Gail had the feeling that he half expected the spectators and jury to bow to him.

"Detective, I remind you that you're still under oath," the court clerk stated.

"I stand reminded," York quipped, smiling past the clerk and staring back down at the defense table.

"Please be seated, sir."

York sank slowly down and back in the seat, his eyes set on Dunn's, mentally boring a hole between the attorney's sockets.

Dunn smiled up at the detective pleasantly. *Just you wait, you motherfucker. Have I got a surprise for you.*

Gail Fox had spent the morning having the detective reread and finally finish Mills' signed confession, covering some of the earlier testimony concerning Howard's younger brother, Jeffrey, and how he had helped Howard, most reluctantly, dispose of two of the bodies. *No snags, thank God,* Gail breathed with some relief.

"Thank you, Detective. No further questions," the prosecutor declared, about to close another chapter of direct-examination for her thirty-first witness for the state.

Nicholas Dunn stepped up to the plate. He placed his papers on the podium and moved the wooden structure forward a foot. "Good afternoon, Detective."

Gary looked to his right at the clock on the wall. "That wouldn't be for another few minutes, counselor." He looked back and down at Dunn.

Nicholas Dunn glanced at his watch. "Guess I'm a little fast for you, Detective."

"No. Maybe just a little slow in catching on."

The jury was smiling. Most of the spectators to either side of Robert Redler were smiling, too. Nicholas Dunn and Gary York were grinning at one another. The judge remained stone-faced. Redler wondered how the judge could keep a straight face as he had throughout most of the trial. Obviously, Judge Best saw and heard virtually everything. The horrific and the hilarious. Rarely did the trace of a smile or a froth-filled frown break upon the jurist's face. Robert Redler wondered if Jack Stetson or Eloise Clarke were smiling now. Probably not. Redler did not nor would not turn around to look. He hadn't drawn definitive conclusions. For the time being, he remained neutral. A group named Parents of Murdered Children had certainly taken sides. They were there to support the victims' families. Surreptitious supporters, such as one friend and two relatives of Howard Mills, who furtively entered and exited the courtroom, although infrequently, had most assuredly made early judgments, too.

"So, Detective," the defense attorney began his cross-examination. "I just have a few questions and then I'm done."

This time, there were not only smiles, but mild laughter. For anyone who had spent a day with Dunn at trial knew that a few questions translated into scores of inquiries.

Detective York put on his very best bored expression and examined his polished nails. "Fire away, counselor."

"Detective, you were telling Ms. Fox during her direct examination that you had certain conversations with the defendant concerning his younger brother, Jeffrey, helping dispose of two bodies. I'm sure you recall that. Yes, Detective?"

"Like it was late this morning, counselor," Gary said, glancing back at the clock. "And now it's early afternoon."

"So then, of course you remember Ms. Fox stating the younger brother's name with regard to that. Yes?"

"Yes."

"And what name did the defendant give you?"

"Jeffrey Mills."

"Jeffrey Mills?"

"That's what I just said."

"I know that's what you just said. But now I'm asking you what the defendant said when you asked him who helped him with the bodies."

"He told me Jeffrey helped him."

Dunn was smiling. "You knew that he had help, of course. Correct?"

"Believed, counselor," Gary York answered, stretching the two-word response out like a rubber band.

"And how did you arrive at that belief?"

Detective York dramatically turned his head and faced the jury. "I've been in Homicide for a while and handled a few bodies in my time. Sometimes it takes two or three of us to lift a dead body; hence the term, dead weight. I had my doubts that the defendant could handle the victim alone, lift her, and put her into a five-foot high Dumpster."

"So, you figured somebody helped him get rid of the bodies. Am I right?"

York craned his head back to the attorney. "You're right."

"And when you asked my client who had helped him, he volunteered a name?"

"Yes."

"And that name again, Detective?"

"Jeffrey Mills."

"Isn't it a fact, Detective York, that my client never uttered Jeffrey's name in connection to helping him with the removal or disposal of any bodies?"

"No, that's not true."

"No?"

"It's right there in his statement, counselor."

"I'm not talking about a *written* statement. I'm talking about an *oral* statement. Did Howard Mills ever, in your presence, or in the presence of any other detective from Team Two, that you're aware of, verbalize Jeffrey Mills' name in relation to helping him remove or dispose of any bodies?"

"I just told you—"

"No, Detective. You told me what was written. I'm asking you what was spoken by my client in that eight by eight foot claustrophobic walk-in closet you guys euphemistically call an interview room."

"Objection."

"Overruled."

"He may have."

"May have what?"

"He may have just written it down. I don't recall."

Christopher Profeta took out a handkerchief and sneezed; civilities were exchanged.

"Would it refresh your recollection if I were to suggest that you set forth a series of questions that you wanted my client to answer in writing, under the pretext that the room was bugged and as his savvy attorney you were ensuring confidentiality?"

"Objection, Your Honor."

"Overruled."

"That's preposterous," York responded.

"Is it not a fact, Detective York, that from the moment of Mr. Mills' arrest in Hicksville—his ride out to police headquarters in Yaphank, his interrogation by over a dozen homicide detectives from Team Two, Team One, as well as homicide detectives from other jurisdictions, spanning some sixty hours from arrest to arraignment, where he told the judge he had retained a lawyer, namely one Gary D. York—never once, in all that time, did he ever *speak* Jeffrey Mills' name with regard to helping him remove or dispose of bodies? Is that not a fact, Mr. Gary D. York, Esquire? Well, isn't it?"

"I object!" Gail Fox practically shouted.

"I object, too, Your Honor!" Nicholas Dunn bellowed back. "I object to—"

"All right!" the judge interceded.

"—to this impostor passing himself off as a lawyer before my client and promising him the sun and the moon and the stars, Judge. That's what *I* object to."

Judge Best was furious. "I'll see the attorneys at sidebar." He suddenly rose like an angry black bird, the sleeves of his robe taking wing as he stepped down from the bench and flew into a corner. The court reporter ran with her machine to keep abreast.

For the next two minutes, Judge Best cloaked his fury from

spectators as well as the jury. Anyone who wasn't in the well was in the dark. Anyone who wasn't ringside was completely out of the loop. Only those within whispering distance were privileged to the synchronized talkie. All others had to be satisfied with the semi-silent sideshow. But you didn't have to be a fan of slapstick to understand and appreciate the pathos and humor that were spontaneously being simulcast in that animated corner.

Dunn was figuratively being trampled upon. Profeta suddenly seemed six-foot-six by comparison, standing beside his partner. Best was beating his wings. The court reporter sat knee-high next to him, pounding away furiously upon the keys of her machine. The law secretary stood poised, leaning into the conversation, listening carefully rather than drinking in the scene with her eyes. She caught Redler's gaze and gave him half a wink without a change of expression. He liked her. She had shown him around the law library when he first came into open court. The woman was up for a judgeship. Super bright if not brilliant. Only problem being was that she would have to change her surname. Judge Jean Killem just didn't cut it, Redler entertained with amusement.

Dunn tried to say something but abruptly closed his mouth. The judge was in his face. Dunn nodded aversely, tried to say something again, then shook his head. Profeta pulled him aside. The group broke up.

From the witness stand, Gary York had lapped up the theatrics. Judge Best had given Dunn a little latitude and the attorney had blown it. He had crossed the line and incurred the judge's wrath. Detective York felt that he was in the catbird seat for now. He turned his head askew and followed Dunn's movements back to the podium, noting that the lawyer wasn't smiling anymore after having been taken down a peg or two.

Gail Fox and Elizabeth Presant sat back down at their table. Gail gave Gary a confident nod.

Judge Best resumed his position on the bench. "Objection is sustained. You may inquire, counselor."

Dunn continued. "Isn't it a fact, Detective, that from the time of Mr. Mills' car ride out to Yaphank, then having a myriad of detectives interrogating him and holding him in custody for a period of two and a half days, up to and including his arraignment, that my client never once, not a single solitary time, ever said, verbally, that his younger brother, Jeffrey, ever helped him remove, transport, or dispose of any bodies whatsoever? Did you *ever* hear him say that, Detective? Answer me with a yes or no. Now!"

"Objection, Your Honor."

"Grounds for the objection?"

"On three points, Judge. Number one, it's been asked and answered when this detective said that the defendant may have just written it down. Detective York said he doesn't recall whether Mr. Mills did or didn't."

"Now she's testifying for him, Judge," Profeta rose and spoke. "He never said that. He—"

"I'm not finished, Mr. Profeta," Gail snapped. "Judge, certainly Mr. Profeta can count. If I'm raising three points on objection and only finished one—"

"I'm objecting to her testifying for the witness, Judge."

"See, there he is interrupting me again."

"Mr. Profeta."

"Yes, Judge."

"Sit," Judge Best instructed as the attorney was halfway in his seat.

"I am sitting. When I'm standing, it looks as though I'm sometimes sitting, Judge."

Redler caught the trace of a smile starting on the judge's lips.

"Mr. Profeta."

"Yes, Judge."

"Shut up."

"Are we on or off the record with that?" Dunn wanted to know.

"You'll know immediately from what I have to say to you next."

Profeta giggled.

"Now. Mr. Profeta. Reference Ms. Fox testifying for the witness. I have on my laptop the detective's testimony. The detective indicated twice that the defendant '*may have just written it down*; once that he—that is, the detective—'*didn't recall.*' I believe you were in the midst of a sneeze. Would you like the court reporter to read it back?"

"No, Judge."

"Ms. Fox. Please continue."

Gail Fox didn't miss a beat. "Secondly, Judge, whether or not the defendant said it or wrote it is immaterial. And thirdly, Mr. Dunn is being argumentative in his questioning and demeanor by demanding that the detective answer him, 'Now!' Who does he think he is? It's improper and, quite frankly, Your Honor, does a disservice to this distinguished servant of the People."

Dunn wanted to puke right there at the podium but believed the judge would make him clean it up.

One only had to look at Judge Best to know that he was really mulling the objection over carefully. "While I'm quite inclined to agree with you, Ms. Fox, I'm going to overrule the objection *if* Mr. Dunn can tell me where he's going with this."

"Far afield, Your Honor," Fox now interrupted, seeing that the judge was probably not going to rule her way anyway. "On a . . . fishing expedition, Judge." She almost said a *fucking* fishing expedition. "That's where he's going with this."

"Mr. Dunn?"

"Where I'm going with this, Judge, is to the heart of the detective's credibility. Where I'm going with this is back into that 8 by 8 foot isolation chamber with my client and Detective York moonlighting as an attorney."

How dramatic, York thought.

"And how long do you plan on staying in this room and area of questioning, counselor?"

"Just a few more questions, Judge. Honest Injun."

"All right. Just remember our little talk."

"How could I forget?"

"The objection is overruled. Detective, do you want Mr. Dunn's last question read back?"

"Not necessary," York said with some annoyance, seemingly directed at the judge. "As I stated, he may have said Jeffrey's name reference helping the defendant move the bodies to the trunk of the car and then disposing of them, or he may not have. And as for the other detectives, I can't speak for them. I was alone with the prisoner when he wrote his statement."

"But you helped him. Yes?" Dunn insisted.

"I assisted him."

"Can you give me a for-instance?"

"Spelling," Gary answered, seeing where the attorney was headed.

"Words and phrases like, postmortem amputations? Bludgeoned? How about the word Dumpster with a capital D? Or did Howard Mills know to capitalize that by himself, Detective?"

Nicholas Dunn discerned the first sign of nervousness in their so-called 'distinguished servant of the People.' It was a slight but sudden movement in his neck. Something less subtle than a twitch. But there was also something far more obvious to most everyone present in the courtroom. The jury would have caught it had their eyes been closed, which they weren't. It was the detective's hesitation.

"I just told you. I assisted him. He was once a shop steward and quite proud of the fact. He wanted to be accurate."

"So you told him how to spell the word bludgeoned?"

"Yes."

"And postmortem, et cetera."

"Yes."

"And when you came to the word, Dumpster, you told him, 'Careful here, Howard. That's a tricky one. You spell that with a capital D. Not a lowercase letter.' Is that what you said? I can't hear you, Detective. You want to flick that finger and see if the microphone is on?"

"Objection."

"Overruled," Judge Best said without the slightest hesitation. "You can answer it, Detective."

"He probably picked it up from someplace," York stated, shifting uncomfortably in his seat. "Maybe he knew how to write it all along."

"So. You just assisted him."

"Yes."

"Didn't craft the letter for him to copy?"

"No."

Dunn was shaking his head, stepping past the podium, practically walking up to the witness. "You didn't have Howard Mills write out answers to your questions earlier and then—"

"Objection."

"Now I know what it feels like, Ms Fox. So, shame on me. Sorry, but I'm not finished."

"He's asked the detective that same question ten minutes ago, Judge."

"I'd like to hear the whole question, if you don't mind, Ms. Fox, so I know whether to sustain or overrule it."

"Sorry, Judge."

"Continue, Mr. Dunn."

"Thank you, Your Honor."

"Don't thank me yet," Best said, motioning the attorney to move it along.

"You didn't have my client write out answers to your questions initially, and then draft up a copy of a statement from which he copied down verbatim, which would explain the—"

"Objection."

"Overruled."

"But, Judge—"

"Sit down, Ms. Fox."

"—which would explain the capital D in Dumpster, among several other items."

"Objection to 'several other items.'"

"As to form, sustained."

"—which would explain the capital D in Dumpster, among several other *spellings*. Did you, Detective?"

Gail realized too late that she had fallen into Dunn's little trap. She had objected two, too many times, and all Dunn was doing was reiterating the point over and over again. The point she wanted the jury to forget.

"No."

"You wouldn't craft such a document stating what *you* wanted stipulated. Would you, Detective?"

"No."

"Nor would you lie under oath. You wouldn't do that either. Would you?"

"No, sir."

Sir? I rate a 'sir' from this detective, now? Dunn entertained. *Wait. You ain't heard or seen nothing yet, asshole. In a short while it will be, Sir Dunn.* But first he'd rattle the detective's cage a bit more, the attorney decided. *Let the jury see this detective slowly come apart at the seams*, Dunn entertained.

"Detective. You testified for the prosecution during pretrial examination, did you not?"

"Yes."

"The seventh witness as I recall."

"I'm not aware of the number of witnesses that testified before me at pretrial."

Where the hell is Nick going now? Gail wondered.

"Oh, by the way, Detective. All those other detectives who *interviewed* my client? What were they told when they asked him if he had any brothers or sisters?"

"It's like I told you before. I can't speak for other detectives."

"And that's because?"

"Because I was not directly involved with this investigation. I was working the prisoner activity log on April 6 as I stated earlier. And on the seventh, I was asked to go in and take pedigree information."

"You weren't asked to go in and secure a confession?"

"Objection. This detective already testified—"

"Sustained," Best said impatiently. "Move it along, Mr. Dunn."

"Sure, Judge. Detective. When you were in that eight by eight foot cubbyhole with my client, taking pedigree information, I'm sure you asked him whether he had any brothers or sisters. Yes?"

"Part of the drill, counselor," York said, staring up at the ceiling then back down at his nails.

"So the answer's, yes. Yes?"

"Yes."

"And what, if anything, did . . . withdrawn. You already knew the answer to that question starting out. Didn't you, Detective?"

Gary York started to say something, then stopped.

"I've seemed to cause you pause," Dunn submitted. "Be careful how you answer this, Detective."

"Counselor is making statements, not asking questions, Your Honor," Gail snapped.

"Respectfully, Judge. I think my statements may put the detective's entire testimony into question," Dunn stated.

"Is that an objection, counselor?" Best asked Fox, ignoring Dunn's comment.

"Yes, it is," the prosecutor affirmed.

"Sustained. Do you have a further question of this witness, or are you done, counselor?

"Is that a pun, Judge?"

"You're this close to being done," Best said in all seriousness, indicating the measurement of an inch between his thumb and forefinger.

"Sorry. Detective. You knew he had a brother who worked for the post office in Manhattan. Correct?"

"I didn't have direct knowledge of him. No."

"I'm not asking if you had direct knowledge. I'm asking if you had any knowledge of a brother before going into that room. Yes or no?"

"I knew about one brother. I didn't know about the other brothers at that time, or about his half sister."

"And when you asked him his brother's name, what, if anything, did he tell you?"

"Said his name was Jeffrey."

"He said, Jeffrey?"

"That's what he said."

"You're sure?"

"Sure as it's Tuesday afternoon."

"First time you asked him?"

"Right off the bat."

Nicholas Dunn reached inside a suit jacket pocket for a pair of eyeglasses and a sheet of folded paper. He put on his glasses, unfolded the paper and placed it atop the podium. The attorney remained silent for a full minute, studying the sheet. Finally, he spoke. "Then how come you have Lenny, with a question mark next to it written in your notes?"

York looked at Fox as though she might have the answer or at least raise an objection.

"Well, Detective?"

"Because one of the brothers' names is Lenny."

"Can you tell the Court which one?"

"The dead one. The one who committed suicide."

"When?"

"Some twenty years ago."

"But when you first asked my client what his brother's name was, he told you Lenny. Not Jeffrey. And initially you didn't know who Lenny was. That's why you wrote down, Lenny. With a question mark. Isn't that so?"

"Yes. I forgot. I knew there was a Jeffrey and just assumed he meant Jeffrey when I asked him about his brother. It was an honest mistake."

"But when you asked him his brother's name, he told you Lenny. Yes?"

"At first, yes."

"And every homicide detective who ever asked him about his brother got the same response in the beginning. 'Yes. I have a brother. His name is Lenny.' He was protecting Jeffrey then as he is today. The only way he'll discuss Jeffrey in connection with having helped him remove, transport and dispose of the bodies is in writing. Like he did with you initially, Detective. Like a child, he won't admit to it aloud, but it's somehow not as painful for him if he puts it down on paper, silently. Silently, he'll confess his brother's sins. But to this day, Howard Mills vociferously denies murdering anyone, maintaining his innocence as he had with you, Detective, on the night of April 7, 1996."

"Objection. Did I miss a question in that, Judge? Or is Mr. Dunn delivering his closing argument? No. He's off on a fishing expedition like I said earlier."

Well, Mr. Dunn?" Best asked, obviously agreeing with the prosecution.

It wasn't meant to be a question, and all the players knew it, including the jury. That's who Dunn's harangue was meant for. That's whose eyes he wanted to open—the jury's. The trial was near completion. The evidence, ostensibly, against their client, was overwhelming. The great irony being that there wasn't a single shred of it—not one piece, with all their forensic people and presentations concerning blood, human hair and cat hair, nylon and polyester carpet fibers and jute, yellow foam rubber particles, cleaning powders and plastic bags, finally bone and paint chips from unrecovered saw blades —which said proof positive that Howard Mills committed these murders and that Jeffrey Mills did not. As a matter of hard, cold fact, some of the evidence pointed to Jeffrey. And that's what the defense team of Dunn and Profeta was trying to do. Create a reasonable doubt in the jury's mind. That was their job.

But then there was that room at 42 Willow Lane in Hicksville. There was no doubt in the jury's mind that the murders took place in Howard's downstairs apartment. There was no doubt in anyone's mind that Howard Mills was involved and that he *probably*—that was the crucial crux of the matter—*probably* killed those women. And as there was no Jeffrey Mills before them to size up and factor into the equation, for that was certainly not the jury's job, they would *most probably* lay their verdict of guilty at Howard's door. Dunn felt it in his bones. Profeta knew it in his pounding heart. You could see it in the jury's eyes. The defense team's strategy at this point was to discredit this maverick cop. Both Dunn and Profeta believed they had adequately demonstrated Team Two's dubious testimony concerning Howard Mills' confession in that interrogation room during those grueling hours of questioning. But in light of all the evidence, seemingly pointing to Howard, the two attorneys believed that the tactics the police employed boiled down to two words. So what! Howard Mills had to be involved. And that would somehow be good enough for the members of the jury to convict.

If Nicholas Dunn and Christopher Profeta had any hope at all of having this jury see the light, remove any and all doubt from their minds as to Team Two's veracity or lies, it would be to discredit one of them, unequivocally, dramatically, once and for all, before their very eyes.

"I'm waiting, counselor," Judge Best said.

"We've been at this for a while, Your Honor," Dunn exhaled the words with feigned exasperation. "I want to move into another area before I finish up. I think this might be a good time to take a break, Judge." *The best is yet to come, folks*, Dunn swore, patiently biding his time. *You haven't heard or seen anything, heretofore*, he said and grinned inwardly.

"Good idea. We'll take ten minutes." Judge Best turned to the jury. "During this short recess, ladies and gentlemen, you must not converse among yourselves or with anyone else upon any subject connected with this trial, and you must promptly report to the Court any incident within your knowledge involving an attempt by any person to improperly influence any member of the jury. See you shortly."

Chapter Thirty-Eight

During recess, Nicholas Dunn and Christopher Profeta headed downstairs and outside the building so that Nick could get his nicotine fix. Their young assistant, Jimmy, followed closely on their heels. Nick couldn't go more than a few hours without a cigarette before climbing the courthouse walls. With his back to the wall, the sole of a cowboy boot against the bricks, he lit up a Lucky. Chris smiled and told Nick he had Gary on the ropes but that it was now time to clock the bastard. Nick agreed. One of Jimmy's important functions was to *read* the jury and report their reactions. Jimmy was to be on his toes for the next bout, studying each and every juror, alternates included—twenty-two faces in all—when Nick clobbered the cop to the canvas. Jimmy's take would be vital to their next course of action. Every round was programmed but could change in a heartbeat and usually did.

Nick offered Chris a cigarette as a Channel 12 News reporter closed in for a comment, a question, or both. Nick's offering served to subtly signal the appearance of an unwelcome party and would flag the beginning of many a comedic routine in order to blow the person off, as the media was back in town in force.

"Oh, no thank you, Nicky," Christopher declined when the newsperson was within earshot. "Gave it up when I hit puberty."

"Excuse me guys," the pretty newswoman interrupted.

"Stunted your growth, I see," Nick remarked, ignoring the reporter.

Chris shook his head in contradiction. "Height-wise, yes. Vertically challenged, I would have to agree. But I'm not horizontally restricted, Nicky. I have this perpetual hard-on out to here," he indicated, extending a hand the length of a yardstick.

Nick and Jimmy looked impressed.

"Excuse me, fellas," the woman persisted.

"By the time I was fourteen, I knew I'd better quit."

"Smoking?" Nick inquired.

"No, masturbating. Fourteen inches and still growing like a weed," Chris continued.

"Come on, boys. I've got a deadline. Grow up and give your favorite commentator a scoop," she pleaded.

At which point, Chris grinned and giggled and mischievously tried to grab Bonnie McKinley's butt.

Back upstairs, Chris, Nick and Jimmy headed into the men's room. Chris glanced under the stalls for eavesdroppers before strategies continued. Nick wet and combed his hair straight back, pondering an important point and strategy aloud. Chris and Jimmy emphatically shook their heads. Nick conceded. And then it was back to the courtroom to finish the bout.

"**C**ounselor, you may inquire," Judge Best stated after all formalities were concluded.

"Thank you, Judge. Just another question or two, Detective," Dunn said, pretending to look rather glum. "Earlier, I was asking you whether or not you testified at pretrial," the attorney continued with his cross-examination. "Do you recall my asking you that question?"

"Yes, of course I remember."

"You testified back in April of last year that you never saw my client chained and shackled to the floor of that eight by eight foot windowless void. Am I correct?"

"You're correct, counselor. Quite correct."

"Naked or otherwise?"

"He was never naked in my presence and certainly never chained or shackled to the floor."

"And the reason that you're certain he was never shackled to the floor, naked or otherwise, is because . . . . Well, why don't you tell us why? Will you do that for us, Detective?"

Gary York believed that the attorney was fishing in dark and deep waters and practically out of line. This was Dunn's last cast into the murky depths, he figured.

"Sure, counselor. That chain or shackle that you're referring to is a precautionary measure which we use in extremely rare instances to control an unruly or violent individual. Being that Mr. Mills was neither violent nor unruly, but rather cooperative, there was no need to utilize such restraints."

Nicholas Dunn studied Gary York. Carefully. The cop was back to being his cool, calm and cautiously optimistic self. His guard was down. Not completely gone but as down as it was going to get. Still full of himself like at the start of his testimony. Wordy. Articulate. *Like a lawyer. Just not as practiced,* Dunn entertained, biting the corner of his bottom lip for effect. *Not by a long shot.*

"So, that shackle and chain do still exist. Right?"

"As far as I know."

"As well as the steel ring in the floor, through which the chain is passed. Correct?"

"Correct."

"Yet, two other homicide detectives from Team Two, under sworn testimony, claimed they never saw such a chain or knew of its existence. Can you tell this Court why?"

It seemed a benign question. But Fox wanted Dunn out of that sphere of questioning altogether. "Objection, Your Honor. Pretrial was then and this is now."

"Judge, of the two detectives that I'm referring to, one also testified during the early stages of this trial."

"I'll allow it. Objection is overruled. You may answer, Detective."

"I already answered the counselor, Your Honor, in stating that the shackle he's alluding to is used in only rare circumstances. I, personally, can't recall the last time someone utilized it. So, it's quite possible that the two detectives you're referring to, Mr. Dunn, never used it and would therefore have no knowledge of its existence. Or it might have been so long ago that they've probably forgotten."

Good try, Gary-boy, but not good enough, Nick smiled to himself. "All right, Detective." Nicholas put his head down as if thinking hard. "Any idea where they store this in-house shackle and chain when it's not being used, Detective?"

"No idea at all."

Dunn withdrew a second sheet of paper from the shelf in the podium. "Detective York. I have here Detective Victor Posteraro's testimony dated March 28th of last year, in which he testifies during my cross-examination that the shackle and chain are stored and have been stored for as long as he can remember in a wooden box just outside the room; that is, the eight by eight foot interrogation room. Does that refresh your recollection as to where those items are kept?"

"Objection!" Fox blasted.

"Does it, Detective?" Dunn insisted.

"Once again, Judge. That testimony was brought out at pretrial. This is trial."

"Judge, Detective Posteraro was the only witness on Team Two who came close to answering my questions forthrightly," Dunn complained.

"So then let the defense call Detective Posteraro as a witness during this trial, Judge."

"Because we both know that he'd be out walking a beat on some busy boulevard if he did testify," Dunn barked at Fox. "Tell them why he was transferred, Gail. Tell them how far down the crapper his career would go if he agreed to testify, reluctantly or otherwise. Tell them, Ms. Prosecuting Attorney."

"You're out of order, Mr. Dunn," Best warned.

"Sorry, Judge," Nicholas quickly apologized. He was too close to the end to blow it now. He would probably be on report in just a moment anyhow. Or worse. Disbarment if they could prove what was about to happen next.

Gail Fox shook her head and smirked. "Detective Victor Posteraro put in for a transfer of his own volition, Judge. It had nothing to do with this case, any testimony offered in this case, or the price of eggs. It had to do with a family matter. And if Mr. Dunn would check his facts before shooting off his mouth, he'd know that, which he probably does but just wants this jury to think that there's something underhanded going on here. Well, that's just not the case." Fox sat back down, wondering if she really knew what she was talking about.

"All right," Best said calmly, seeing that the two adversaries had made their points and said their piece—for the moment, anyway. "I'll give you a little more rope to hang yourself, Mr. Dunn. But first tell me, within a light-year or so, how much farther do you have to travel?"

Dunn smiled and held up a thumb and forefinger, the width of a whisker between them.

"Objection is overruled. Please answer the question, Detective."

Goddamn boy's club, Gail Fox thought indignantly, looking to her left at her colleague who read her mind.

"It's like I said." *Asshole*, Detective York wished to add. "I have no idea where they store that chain."

"Yet you know it exists. Yes?"

"I'm sure it does."

"But if you had an unruly or violent prisoner on your hands tomorrow, you wouldn't be able to lay your hands on it immediately. Is that your testimony, Detective?"

Detective Gary York was smiling brightly. "Well, now that I know what you seem to know, counselor, the first place I'd look is in that wooden box just outside the interview room."

Many smiles lightened and brightened the courtroom along with York's.

"Just a moment ago you said that you, personally, couldn't remember anyone using that chain and shackle in the interview room. Isn't that what you said? The chain that gets put through a ring bolted to the floor. That's the chain and shackle we're talking about here, Detective. Yes? Are we on the same page?"

"That's what I said a moment ago. And, yes, we're on the same page, counselor."

"And would that include you, yourself, not using that particular restraint for as far back as you can remember?"

"Affirmative," Gary agreed.

"And is there a particular reason for that, Detective York?"

Gary studied the ceiling before he spoke. "I believe I may have indicated earlier that I remain on the outer fringes of an investigation, as I did this one. I usually handle the prisoner activity log. So I don't have much contact with a prisoner once he or she's brought into the interview room for questioning."

"Can you think of any other reason?"

"Just lucky, I guess," Gary answered.

"Lucky?"

"I guess."

"Isn't it a fact, Detective, that you're known as and called, 'The Closer' by your colleagues at the homicide squad?"

"Never heard the expression. No."

"Isn't it a fact, Detective York, that, like a salesman, you were to go in and get Howard Mills' signature on the bottom line?"

"Objection."

"As to form, sustained."

"Isn't it a fact, Detective Gary D. York, that your job was to go into that eight by eight foot interrogation room on the night of April the 7th, 1996, and secure a *confession* from this defendant?"

"My job was to go in and secure pedigree information."

"I see." Dunn gestured to one of the court officers seated in the well. "Raul, may I please have exhibit number 17A and B put up on the presenter? And while he's getting those, Judge, may I turn on the machine? It'll take a minute to warm up."

Judge Best motioned his approval.

"Thank you, Judge."

Gail Fox started searching through some records.

A moment later, Raul put the exhibit marked 17A on the presenter.

"Thank you, my good man," Dunn said appreciatively, having known the court officer for many years. "Now, if you'll look closely at the photograph, just to the left of center, you'll see a close-up of the welded steel ring fastened to the steel plate bolted through the floor. Maybe if you could blow that up for us a little better, Raul. Hold it! Right there. Perfect."

What is Nick's point? Gail wondered, rummaging through her notes and records while whispering to Elizabeth Presant.

Dunn shot a glance back to Profeta and beyond to Jimmy who sat still as a statue. "Now, you'll note that's the ring through which a phantom chain was passed, how so ever long ago. But of course there is no chain in this picture. Can you identify this picture for us, Detective?"

"It's the inside of the interview room."

Gail Fox and Elizabeth Presant were whispering excitedly back and forth. Something seemed wrong.

"Raul, if you'll put number 17B up for us next. Great. There is no chain in number 17A. But if you'll look very closely at number 17B, down in the lower right-hand corner of the screen—"

"Wait! Something's terribly wrong, Judge," Fox exclaimed and fumbled.

"Objection!" Elizabeth Presant cried out, bolting to her feet.

"Overruled."

Raul apparently saw the shiny item in evidence and, without having to be told, focused in on that particular area, isolated it, then zoomed in for a blow-up of the section of steel chain.

"See it?" Dunn was pointing, encircling the shortened length with his forefinger. "It's only several links. But there's your chain."

"But Your Honor, there is no number 17B like this in evidence."

Is now, Dragon Lady, Nicholas swore inwardly. "And if you'll look just a little to the screen's left, you'll note the tips of a pair of very interesting leather footwear, folks. Pretty expensive shoes at that. Designer Italian leather Loafers. Three hundred and fifty dollars a pair. I can't even pronounce the name. But I believe my learned colleague can."

Christopher Profeta rose and pronounced the designer's name, "Versace," then sat.

"I don't know how that picture got in here, Judge, or what it is," Gail barked.

"What it is, is a picture of the phantom chain, or at least a section of it, along with the tips and tassels of," and Nicholas Dunn was pointing to the shoes the detective was now wearing, "the detective's expensive leather Loafers. Detective Gary D. York's pricey leather footwear. The same shoes he's wearing right now. The same shoes he had on the night he misrepresented himself to my client as an attorney. The same detective who can't remember the last time he saw that chain."

"That's utterly ridiculous," Fox challenged. "Pure fiction. This doesn't prove anything. You can't say for certain whose shoes they are, or even who's wearing them, or when this picture was taken. And furthermore—"

"The date's right there on the photo," Dunn blasted.

"Let me see that," Fox demanded.

"All right, all right, all right! I've heard just about enough for now," Judge Best barked. "Obviously, there's been some kind of foul-up. I have no record of a number 17B either. Or we do, but this is not the one. I don't know how this photograph got into the mix, or even what it is. That said, I do not want you, the jury, to speculate on what this is or isn't either. I'm sure we'll need overnight to sort this out. And I want to see the four attorneys in my chambers immediately upon my excusing the jury till tomorrow morning."

"Most respectfully, Judge," Dunn interjected, "as to what it is, Detective York already testified that it was the eight by eight foot interview—"

"What the detective testified to, counselor, was exhibit number 17A, already marked into evidence, not number 17B, which has not.

Got it?"

"But 17B *is* that same interview room, Judge. I would like that put into evidence, and I'll bring in a photographic expert to ascertain that those shoes—"

"And I would like to lead a charmed life. But that's not going to happen," Judge Best blew.

"Judge, before this detective leaves the stand—"

"You'd like his shoes, Mr. Dunn?" the judge remarked.

"I was going to suggest—"

"That I loan him mine to walk out of here?"

"Judge—"

"My chambers, Mr. Dunn." Judge Best wheeled around and addressed the jurors.

"Ladies and gentlemen, I will ask you to please report at ten tomorrow morning for the continued trial in this matter. During the course of this overnight recess, you must not converse among yourselves or with anyone else upon any subject connected with this trial. You must not read or listen to any accounts or discussions of the case in the event that it is reported by newspapers or other media. You must not visit or view the premises or place where the offense or offenses charged were allegedly committed, or any other premises or place involved in the case.

"Prior to your being discharged, you may not request, accept, or discuss with any person the receiving or accepting of any payment or benefit in consideration for supplying any information concerning this trial. And you must promptly report to the Court any incident within your knowledge involving an attempt by any person to improperly influence any member of the jury. Have a good evening. We will see you tomorrow at ten a.m."

"Retire the jury," the court clerk announced solemnly, whereupon the jury was excused and escorted out of the courtroom.

"Detective, you may step down. We will see you tomorrow morning."

York was livid. He stood abruptly then swaggered through the hip-high door in the railing, continuing past the defense table while mumbling something barely audible beneath his breath. A steady sound emanating from the projection machine helped muffle the man's angry words. But Dunn read the detective's lips perfectly.

"Sounds to me like a veiled threat, Detective," Nicholas Dunn challenged, wishing and wanting to turn the detective's profane remark into something much more personal in that heated moment.

Detective Gary York stopped short, spun around to face the attorney and was immediately met by a court officer who politely opened the gate in the second railing then led the detective out through two sets of double doors.

"The matter is adjourned to tomorrow morning at ten," Judge Best concluded.

Inside the judge's chambers, the four attorneys sat. The court reporter had been dismissed, so the matter was off the record. Alongside the judge, Ms. Jean Killem stood. Poised. Ready to do patchwork or major surgery. Whatever the case required. It had been her brainchild to redact the language in Howard Mills' alleged confession, having changed *five girls* to read *'94 '95 girls*. All Judge Best did was apply the Band-Aid.

"All right. Let me hear it," Best demanded.

Profeta looked at Dunn.

"Hear what, Judge?" Nick asked innocently.

"Not a goddamn marching band, counselor, but how 17B, from another prosecutor's case file, that Riverhead knifing involving two nursing students, the deceased and the defendant, the latter of whom you're presently representing and the other whose death Detective York happens to be investigating, wound up in the evidence vault, *my* evidence vault, very conveniently behind exhibit 17A of Mills' case. Or am I expected to believe that that was just an extraordinary coincidence?"

Nicholas shrugged. "Beats the hell out of me, Judge."

"And I suppose, Chris, that you have no idea at all either as to how one photograph from one case got mixed in with another."

"Well, Judge, you have to admit the possibility of an honest mistake here. I mean, number 17B does follow 17A, and given the fact that you're the presiding judge on that case, too, maybe somebody was comparing apples and apples, and when they were finished, inadvertently put the wrong photograph into the case folder. Only thing I can come up with."

"And who do you suppose that somebody could be?"

"Got me there, Judge," Chris said.

"Nick?"

"Judge?"

"When did you just happen upon that photograph?"

"When I was going through the photos earlier."

"When, 'earlier'?"

"Yesterday, I believe."

"When, yesterday?"

"Early afternoon, I think."

"Around the time that the witness was reading the defendant's statement and this Court came unglued?"

"You mean the coerced and fabricated statement, Your Honor?"

"Don't toy with me, Nick. You did ask for those pictures of the interview room first thing yesterday morning. Right?"

"I did."

"And during yesterday's afternoon commotion, *you* could have *inadvertently* slipped the photograph from the Riverhead case into Mills' mix. Hypothetically speaking, of course."

"Motive and opportunity, Judge. Do I need a lawyer?"

"Only if I can figure out how you got your hands on that photo."

"Then until such time, Judge, could you release me in my own recognizance or into the capable hands of my attorney?" Nick suggested, resting his hand on Chris' shoulder.

"Judge, this is one of Nicky's nastiest, most underhanded tricks ever!" Gail jumped in. "I'll bet he damn well knew that *five* girls was in that document instead of the word *three*. And he somehow got that photo in, too. You know it, and I know it."

Elizabeth Presant nodded her head in agreement.

"Gail, I believe we're all guilty of letting that language get past us," Judge Best placated. "As for the photograph, you can't prove anything, nor can I. Nick denies it. Chris says he doesn't know from it. So what have we got? Nothing. Where do we go from here? That's the issue before us now. Any suggestions?"

Jean Killem started knocking the matter around. "Well, we have a jury that saw us screw up twice in two days. I suggest we simply level with them this time around and say what we know for sure at this point. And that's absolutely nothing," she stated emphatically. "We don't know how that photograph got into the mix. That's the simple truth. It's probably better for all of us if we leave it at that. We tell them that exhibit 17B is from another case and that it has no impact on this case whatsoever. Whether it is or isn't the detective's footwear is irrelevant and that they are to erase the issue from their minds. We move on from there."

"Sure, the damage has already been done," Gail said bitterly. "What the hell."

"Got a better way of handling this?" Best asked. "Any of you?"

"Absolutely," Gail blasted. "You hold Mutt and Jeff, over there, in contempt and launch a full investigation. That's how to handle it."

"We much prefer Edgar and Charlie," Dunn protested, whereby Profeta slid off his seat and up onto his partner's lap. Nick slipped a hand inside and up the back of Chris' jacket.

Elizabeth sighed and shook her head.

"As the judge just asked Gail, *Charlie*," Nick voiced, staring down at Chris, "Got a better way of handling this?"

"Sure do, counselor," Chris answered up smartly, flapping his gums while looking up with a wide-eyed expression into Nick's face, imitating the dummy from days gone by, the two attorneys parodying the famous ventriloquist act from the early fifties: Charlie McCarthy and his mouthpiece, Edgar Bergen.

"Well, do you want to tell this audience what you're suggestion is, *Charlie*?"

"Sure, *Edgar*. We put Gail on the stand tomorrow instead of the detective."

"And what will that accomplish?"

"It will show the jury how the prosecution tried to shift the blame our way, accusing us of being shysters who tamper with evidence when perhaps it was she and her cohort who included that picture to make us look bad before the judge. After all, it was Gail who first noted that something was amiss and Elizabeth who jumped to her feet and objected," the *dummy* reminded everyone, giving the two ladies the evil eye.

Elizabeth couldn't help but smile at the defense attorneys' vaudeville act.

Gail was not amused.

Jean covered up a grin with her hand.

And the judge, as usual, sat there stone-faced.

"And how do you propose I go about this business?" Nick asked. "What question could I conceivably ask Ms. Fox? And what response might I expect to elicit that would have the jury wondering about the lead prosecutor's repute?"

"You ask her how she came to be dubbed The Dragon Lady," Chris as *Charlie* chuckled, rolling his eyes around in his head while moving his mouth stiffly up and down as though it operated on a hinge.

"You know," Fox said, "if I ever do prove it was you who filched that photo from Peterson's file, I'll waive any 730 examination and have you declared insane myself," she promised, directing her comment to Dunn. "And as for you, you emaciated Danny DeVito, I feel that you had a very strange childhood, indeed."

Christopher Profeta clamped his mouth shut then opened it and giggled mischievously.

Judge Best looked sternly at the two of them before keying in on Nick. "I think it's time to put your dummy back in the trunk. Audition's over."

"Trunk?!" Chris cringed, snapping his head back up and staring in disbelief between his partner and the judge.

"Not to worry, *Charlie*." Nick smiled down reassuringly. "You can borrow the judge's robes, then tomorrow we'll do Dracula."

Everyone, including His Honor, laughed.

Judge Steven Best got up. "So then we're all in agreement. Jean's suggestion seems to be the best course of action. All right?"

Nick and Chris agreed.

Gail and Elizabeth assented reluctantly.

"Good. Now, how much longer you figure it's going to be with this witness, Nick? Or shouldn't I even bother asking?"

"I just have one quick question left for the detective, Judge."

"I'll bet it's a beaut."

"I want to ask him if he plans on using me for a reference for law school once they boot his ass out of the department."

"Gary York? Never," Chris responded. "The brass will move him ahead of Mick Connolly."

"Think so?" Nick reconsidered.

"Seriously, Nick," Elizabeth came into the conversation, testing the waters with a possibility. "Should we have our next witness here for the morning, or are you going to run this into the afternoon?"

"Who's your next witness?" Nick asked innocently.

Elizabeth looked to Gail.

"Tell him nothing, Liz," Gail stated firmly.

"Go ahead and play your silly little games, Gail," Nick said, turning to his partner. "Give you good odds, say three to one, that York dumps the Loafers and shows up wearing different shoes tomorrow."

"You're on," Chris accepted, sliding off Nick's lap and reaching into a back pocket for his billfold, withdrawing a twenty-dollar bill. "I'll bet the cocky bastard has tiny bells attached to those tassels as he struts back down the aisle."

Jean laughed.

"You want a piece of the action, Jean?" Nick asked Judge Best's legal eagle.

"Not in front of the judge, I don't," she countered with a smile.

"Put her in for twenty," Nick insisted. "She's good for it. You want Loafers or shoes by any other name?"

"Loafers," she mouthed silently, putting her back to the judge.

Nick shook his head. "Not to worry about the judge, Jean. He's going to have his wife call me tonight for a piece of the action." Grinning, Nick looked over at Gail and Elizabeth. "Wanna bet?"

"Well, I'm headed home," Judge Best said.

"You see, Steven can't even wait to have Evelyn place the call. You two dames want in or not?" Nick pressed. "But first I gotta see up-front money because you two are really good for nothing," he taunted rather ambiguously.

Chris giggled, handing Nick the twenty then putting his wallet away.

"And you two aren't exactly the Dream Team," Gail retorted. "Get a good night's rest for tomorrow, boys," she added. "You're going to need it."

"Good night, Judge," Jean bid.

"Good night, Jean. Boys and girls."

"Good night, Your Honor," the four counselors formally returned in kind.

Nick and Chris road the elevator down to the first floor.

"What are you going to ask York tomorrow?" was Chris' question.

"I'm just going to ask him if he had a nice ride out here. And when he answers me, I'll say, 'No further questions, Detective. Have a nice ride back.'"

Chris Profeta giggled then turned serious. "Think you may antagonize the jury?"

"I think I may have already done that, Chris. What do you think?"

Chris shrugged. "I think you're going to have to pay out a hundred and twenty bucks tomorrow."

"And the judge?"

"His wife won't call."

"Wanna bet?"

Chris smiled and reached for his wallet as the elevator doors opened to the lobby. "Hey, I just thought of something."

"What?"

"How come you get to hold the money?"

"I'm taller. Next question."

"How come I'm the one who's always got to look under the bathroom stalls for eavesdroppers."

"You're shorter."

The pair strolled out of the building together, discussing and imitating Detective Gary York's walk. Chris insisted that York *swaggered*. Nick swore the detective *strutted*. Both of them argued the fine shades of meaning concerning the two closely related words.

Chapter Thirty-Nine

"Hi, Ilona." Jeffrey Mills quickly closed the door from the cold.

"Jeffrey!" Ilona Alfold stepped from behind the beverage counter and took the man back away from the door where anyone could see. She gave him a hug followed by a peck upon a chilly cheek. "You startled me."

"My brother would always say the same thing," he said rather sadly.

"How is he doing?"

"Not so good. He's depressed."

"I'm very sorry to hear that."

Jeff hunched his shoulders then dropped them in indifference.

"What's the matter?" she asked with sincere concern.

"It's not so much the depression because he's always depressed. Been that way most of his life in fact."

"Then what?"

"It's . . . I don't know."

"Tell me," she coaxed, holding him firmly by the hand.

"It's his two attorneys."

"What about them?"

"They've gotten him to go along."

"Go along with what?"

"Their defense for Howard. Suggesting that I'm more involved than I am."

"What do you mean, more involved? Like how?"

"Like that I could have killed those girls. They're trying to create a reasonable doubt in the jury's mind that Howard didn't do it."

Ilona stared at Jeffrey in disbelief. "Wha*t*?" she said, putting emphasis on the t.

Jeff nodded his head, his eyes on the verge of tears. He could make himself cry so easily.

"How could they say a thing like that? Aren't they liable or something? Can't somebody stop them, sue them or something?"

"My attorney says they can say whatever they want for now and that we'll deal with it later."

"Later? What kind of an answer is that?"

"I don't know, Ilona. I really don't. But he says not to worry. To trust him."

"Not to worry? How can you not worry?"

"I'm more worried about Howard, right now. He's really down. I know him, and I know he really doesn't want to go along with them. But maybe he has little say in the matter. They're trying to save his life. My lawyer said something about that being part of their strategy or something. I was so upset I only half listened. It's coming to the end of the trial. Pretty soon the defense is going to call their witnesses like they did at pretrial."

"I don't know what to say, Jeffrey. I really don't. You want me to go with you to your attorney?"

Jeff was shaking his head.

"Two heads are better than one," Ilona pressed. "We can sort things out together. Maybe the three of us. I hope you don't think I'm sticking my nose where it doesn't belong, but I'm really concerned about you."

"I'm not even supposed to be discussing this matter with you. I don't mean you alone, Ilona. I mean anyone. That's what my lawyer said."

"Do you trust your lawyer, Jeffrey? Really trust him?"

"Not like I trust you, Ilona."

Ilona grabbed and held on to Jeffrey like a life raft. Jeffrey lightly stroked her hair.

"What is Howard saying exactly?"

"Like in the beginning. Says he admitted to bringing the girls home to his apartment, partying most of the night. Stuff like that. Still doesn't admit to killing them. Says he won't say who did, but that it wasn't him. He's admitted to the dismemberment, but that's all. Says the police tricked him into signing a confession. They promised him that he'd go to a mental hospital instead of prison. Help him get better. Told him he'd be cured and out in ten years. Maybe even less. Says one of the detectives pretended he was a lawyer. That's how they tricked him. His real lawyers are not saying anything about the dismemberment or anything. They're having him stick to his original story that he woke up after partying and just found . . . " Jeff was crying. "Just found them there. Each and every time."

Ilona held him closely, rocking the two of them to-and-fro.

"He says he'll ne-never tell anyone who did it. He's n-not going to take the stand. So the jury will either believe the story his lawyers are telling and acquit him, or they may n-not believe the tale. Then they'll either give him life in prison with no parole or, God forbid, sentence him to death because the state of New York has put the death penalty back on the books."

"I know."

"But he believes he's going to be acquitted and that his attorneys are going to help get him into a mental hospital for treatment. But first things first, they told him."

"Couldn't he have pled guilty to insanity or something like that? And then they'd have to put him away in a mental institution if the defense proved their case and won."

"That's just it. He won't plead guilty. And the Court found him fit to stand trial."

"Right. I'm sorry. I'm not thinking straight."

"I can't think straight either since this whole nightmare started. I'd just like to get away for a day or two and try and think things through."

Jeff waited for her wheels to turn.

"Listen! I got a great idea."

Jeff remained silent, wiping away his crocodile tears.

"Want to hear my great idea?"

She felt the nod against the side of her cheek.

"Then you got to say, 'Ilona, what's your great idea?'"

Jeff laughed through a sob. "Ilona, what's your great idea?"

Ilona stepped back and gazed into his eyes. "My idea is that we get away together for a weekend. This weekend. Day after tomorrow. Just you and me. We can talk. Or we don't have to talk. We can sit and think. And then I'll tell you what I'm thinking. And if you want to, you can tell me what you're thinking. But I won't pry. I can cook us a nice meal, and we can go out to eat, too. What do you think?" she asked with a cheerful smile.

"Where would we go?"

"How about the shore?"

"Shore?"

"Sure. The shore. Sandy beach. Water, stars and the moon. We'll bundle up and be alone together. Who's going to be walking on a beach in February? We can walk and talk and think. Are you off this weekend?" She was almost certain he was.

"Yes. Well, actually I get off Friday night at ten."

"Perfect, because traffic is a killer before then anyhow, my father always says."

Jeff smiled.

"Well, you haven't said yes, yet."

"Yes, but what about your father? And what about the store?"

Ilona opened wide her eyes. "You said yes! Oh, my God. We got a date. But next time you've got to ask *me* out, all right? I can only do this once. Say yes."

"Yes, but what about your father and the store, Ilona?" Jeff repeated.

"My father will be away for a week at a convention and then on a buying trip. I can get my mother to watch the store. She owes me big time," the teenager explained happily. "Besides, if she says two days are one too many, I'll tell her I'll more than make up for it over mid-winter recess because I have all next week off from school. How's that?"

"Are you sure?"

"Sure as sugar in a candy cane."

"What will you tell your mother?"

"A lot of little white lies and one very big black one."

"Ilona."

"Yes, Jeffrey?"

"I don't think it's a good idea you tell anyone about us going away together for the weekend."

"Who am I going to tell?"

"I don't know. A friend or somebody, I guess."

Ilona put her head down. "If you want to know the truth, you're the only friend I have. I don't have friends, Jeffrey. I have customers."

Jeff lifted her chin with loosely folded fingers. "I just want us to be careful until this is over. I don't want you dragged into anything. That's why I haven't had you over to the new apartment yet. It's best that no one knows about you and me until this trial business is over and done with."

Ilona nodded her understanding upon the bridge of soft flesh. He guided her chin in against his chest and held her head protectively.

"Still, too many people near the shore," he swore, stroking the back of her neck. "Even in February. How does the countryside sound?"

"Great!" For a second Ilona was afraid that Jeffrey was going to change his mind instead of her shore suggestion. She would have spent the weekend in a Dumpster with him if he had asked her to. "Where in the country?"

"I want it to be a surprise."

Ilona lifted her head and looked at him excitedly. He was taking charge. She knew in that moment that he was not simply the boy in a man's body that she had come to love. He could be strong, too. There was another side to him. She would pull him away from his problems if even for the weekend. When this was behind him, he'd be another person. She would help make him whole again. And maybe, just maybe, she could share in that celebration. Maybe, just maybe, he would think of her as truly his. She'd take things one step at a time.

"I love surprises," Ilona said joyously.

"This one you won't forget," Jeffrey promised. "This one will be one for the books."

"My God. You make it sound like you're going to go to a lot a trouble."

"Double trouble," he replied with a wide grin.

"So long as we're in it together," she boldly put forth.

"I know a very quiet spot. Nothing but woods and purple meadows filled with wildflowers."

Ilona looked at Jeffrey queerly. "This time of year?"

Jeff had a sad and distant stare starting on his face, but caught and covered it with a little laugh. "I guess you'll have to close your eyes when we get there and imagine it. But it is quiet. That I promise you. No one around this time of year. Yet it's near enough to the beach, too, if we decide."

"Is there something wrong, Jeffrey? For a second you had this million-mile-away look in your eyes."

"I was just thinking about Beth."

"Uh-oh. Old flame. Had to open my mouth."

Jeff smiled and shook his head. "She's my half sister."

"I didn't know you had a sister, Jeffrey."

Jeff nodded. "The most wonderful sister in the whole wide world."

"Will I get to meet her one day?" Maybe she was asking too many questions. Maybe she was just talking too much. She never in her life had the gift of gab. And now, all of a sudden, she had nonstop running of the mouth. "Sorry."

"What are you sorry about, Ilona?"

Ilona looked down at the hardwood floor. "For months I've been trying to get you to, you know, spend some time with me. Every time I see you, I wonder if it will be the last. Now here we are planning to go away together, and I make it sound like I want to rush in and meet the entire family. I just get carried away."

"That's nothing to be sorry for, Ilona. Sorry is said for when you do something bad or wrong and then realize you hurt someone you really care about. I told you once before that you could never do anything wrong. I know this about you, Ilona. I don't know how I know, I just do."

Jeff was back to staring down at his shoes.

Ilona shook her head in wonderment, marveling over the man. She had never met anyone quite like him. His sensitivity made her into a molten mess from the moment he stumbled into the store, literally, and almost knocked her down as she was busy dusting off cans and bottles. *Come to think of it, he never said he was sorry*, she recalled. Instead, he had said, *Excuse me, ma'am. I can be so clumsy at times. Are you all right?* And then he just stared down at his shoes. Her very first impression of him was that he was slow, or maybe even partially blind, or both.

"Would you like to meet her? I know she'd love to meet you."

"Really?"

"Really, Ilona. Perhaps soon."

"Jeffrey?"

"Yes."

"I have to say something. I was going to wait and tell you later, but I can't." Ilona was about to cry.

"What is it, Ilona?" Jeff asked, seeing her anxiety. He held her close.

"I think I'm falling deeply in love with you," she declared and wept quietly, summoning forth her words in a whisper, praying that she didn't sound like a foolish school girl—though, that's exactly what she was—a part time student at Stony Brook University, about to spread her wings and fly.

"Well, then you keep thinking about it and let me know when you know for sure because I fell in love with you the first moment we met."

Ilona's shoulders were shaking. In slow motion, she closed her arms tightly around him and would not let go.

Suddenly, the front door opened. "I can see that I'm going to have to help myself this time out," someone said at the threshold, closing the door quickly behind her. "Brrrr."

Jeff recognized the woman immediately, although she was well-covered with hat, scarf, coat and gloves. The last time he had seen her was in the middle of July. Middle-aged woman. Very pretty, in fact.

Ilona looked over in surprise. It was the same woman from the time Ilona stood in the center of the store with her eyes closed, disbelieving Jeffrey when he had told her that a customer had entered.

Ilona went over to the woman and gave her a hug as if she were a long-lost aunt instead of a brand new customer. "I didn't have a chance to say hello to you last time. I haven't seen you since the summer. But I wanted to thank you for the nice things you said, especially a personal comment you made that I know came from the heart."

"Life is so short and precious, my dear. You'll realize that later on in years. That's why I said what I said. I usually don't give people advice. Who really takes it anyway?" she said with a sigh. "Who even listens? Certainly not most young people today. But for better or worse, I feel I have to say this, too. And that is, always follow your heart, my dear. The head confuses things so badly. There. I said it." She gave Ilona two quick pats on her shoulder. "And the reason you haven't seen me is because I lived in the city and just moved here permanently. Now, if you haven't moved the seltzer or the chips, I think I still remember where everything is. I'm having some lady friends over this evening to help me unpack, so I suppose I'll need some diet soda. Do you have cans on sale? And may I mix them? Like, say three Cokes and three ginger ales. Or am I being a nuisance?"

"Usually, we tell customers, 'only by the case,' but you may mix, match, or do anything you like. And when you come back and I'm not here, you tell my mother or father that Ilona said it was okay." Ilona extended her hand.

"I'm Roselyn. Roselyn James." She took and held Ilona's hand.

"I'm very pleased to make your acquaintance, Ms. James. Ilona Alfold. And this is Jeffrey." Ilona was careful not to mention Jeffrey's surname—whether she was new to the neighborhood or not.

"Call me Roselyn, please, Ilona. Jeffrey," the woman greeted, smiling and shaking his hand.

"Then Roselyn it is," Ilona agreed. "Come, Roselyn. Let me help you. Chips, seltzer, diet Coke and ginger ale. Yes?"

"Yes, thank you."

Ilona was pleased with the way the day was turning out. "And I want you to try my homemade dip. On the house. You want to get that for me, Jeffrey? You know where it is."

"Sure, Ilona." Outwardly, Jeff went happily down the aisle. Inwardly, he was steaming. The woman was sure to remember him now. Still, he was pleased that Ilona hadn't given the woman his last name. That would have been the last thing he would have wanted her to know. Still and all, he'd have to think things through very carefully.

"Where's your new place?" he asked abruptly, taking the item from a refrigerated compartment, carrying it over to the counter.

"Just around the corner. Why?"

"Well, I recall last time that you didn't have a car, and I don't see one now. So I thought maybe I could help you carry home your package or deliver it later if you'd like."

"That's very sweet of you, Jeffrey. But I can manage just fine." Roselyn James turned to Ilona. "He's one in a million," she said in a low tone. "Believe you me, I know."

Ilona nodded knowingly.

After Roslyn James left, Jeff and Ilona made final plans. She would rent a vehicle for the weekend; he would take care of their lodging.

Chapter Forty

Roselyn James' apartment bell rang several times before she answered.

"Who is it?"

"Hi, Ms. James, it's me. Jeffrey. From the beverage store."

"Oh, dear," she said with some surprise. "What is it, Jeffrey?"

"Ilona said she was too quick in letting you get away. She sent me over with some extra dip. Realized you might need more if you were having people over later like you said."

"How did you know where I live?"

"Ilona called information," Jeff lied, "and asked the operator for a Roselyn James; new listing. Then Ilona finagled the address from her. Lots of James' listed, but only one R. James, a block away. Ilona wanted to surprise you."

"I don't believe you two," Roselyn declared in shocked delight, unlocking and opening the door the width of the chain. "It's freezing out and you came over here to bring me more dip?"

"Yes, ma'am. Ilona insisted I come. But I don't mind. Really I don't. Remember, it was me who wanted to help you carry your packages home in the first place," he reminded the woman, handing the item through the door.

"This certainly isn't necessary, but thank you so much. And

thank that sweet, dear girl of yours, too."

She wasn't about to ask him in.

"I will." Jeffrey turned and started to leave. "Oh, Ms. James?" Jeff faced about.

"Yes, Jeffrey?"

"Could I trouble you to use your bathroom real quick? Feel like my bladder's about to burst. Couldn't go before I left the store because a customer was using it. And I think Ilona's closed the store." Jeff consulted his watch. "Yep. Six o'clock sharp."

Roselyn looked abruptly over her left shoulder and then to her right, like she was checking out base runners on first and third. "I just moved in, Jeffrey, and I've got cartons all over the place. If you're sure you won't mind the mess," she hedged momentarily, sliding the chain off its track and inviting him in, "and if you promise not to look around."

No wedding band or ring on either hand, he noticed.

"I promise to keep my eyes straight ahead." Jeffrey crossed the threshold, stepping into the apartment.

"Right this way." She led Jeffrey past the long line of boxes, through the living room, directing him down a long hallway. "First and only door on your left. And please excuse the clutter. I've got stuff everywhere."

"Not at all. As a matter of fact, I moved into a new place, too. Been there for a while. And guess what? I have boxes I haven't even touched. Sitting on the floor in the middle of the living room."

"But men can do that," Roselyn generalized. "We women are supposed to be more together," she went on, speaking from the end of the hallway. "Excuse me a moment, Jeffrey."

Roselyn went back to the front door and secured it.

Jeffrey stepped into the bathroom, quickly scanning the area. A single toothbrush in its holder. One hairbrush and a large comb. Several hairs found on both items. Blonde. Wearing a pair of leather gloves, he flushed the toilet to cover the sound of his opening the medicine cabinet. No men's razor or toiletries or any articles that would indicate a male partner or roommate of any sort. Ms. Roselyn James positively lived alone. Ah! Except for the telltale box on the floor; the very first box that Ms. James must have set down after moving in. A litter box parked adjacent to the sink. Roselyn had a cat. He hoped it was a scaredy-cat and wouldn't make much noise.

Jeff came out of the bathroom, faced right, then with eyes half closed, started back down the hall toward the living room. "I'm not looking around," he called out.

Roselyn stood smiling before the alcove kitchen. Her back toward him.

"Jeffrey."

"Yes, ma'am?"

"I want you to meet somebody." Roselyn turned around.

Jeff popped open wide an eye.

"Jeffrey, meet Tabitha. Tabitha, meet Jeffrey."

Roselyn was holding the cat in her arms.

"A calico," Jeff whispered. "Oh, what a precious pussycat."

"Do you like cats?"

Jeff didn't answer directly. "I have a cat named Orbit."

"Male or female?"

Jeff popped open wide the other eye. "You know, I never looked!" he answered kiddingly.

Roselyn James began to peal with laughter.

Jeff reached forward and gave Tabitha a scratch behind an ear. "Hi, calico kitty cat. What a pretty girl you are." The black, yellow and white fur-ball turned its head and looked up at Jeff plaintively, then closed its eyes and purred. "Yes," Jeff continued on in baby talk. "I can see you're really mommy's little girl. Yes you are, sweetheart."

"Oh, she likes you, Jeffrey," Roselyn crooned, cradling the cat and giving it a gentle rock from side to side.

Jeff reached back and lifted the corner of his coat. He withdrew his wallet.

Roselyn wondered what he was up to, staring down at the billfold curiously.

Still wearing leather gloves, Jeff flipped clumsily through several photographs. "Close your eyes. It's a surprise. Don't open them until I tell you to. Promise?"

Roselyn realized he probably had a picture of Orbit that he was just dying to show her. "All right," she agreed, tilting her head back and staring blindly at the ceiling the way Ilona had when the three first met. "But then you have to go because I have people coming tonight, and I have to shower and get things ready."

"Eyes closed?"

"Yes, Jeffrey. My eyes are closed. And I'd bet Tabitha's are closed, too."

"Good."

From out of nowhere, Jeff plunged a blade into Roselyn James' throat and cut across her windpipe. The cat was gone before the woman ever hit the floor. And so was Roselyn. Gone for good.

"Sorry, Ms. James. But I couldn't take the chance of you saying, 'The last person I saw Ilona with was a very nice man named Jeffrey.'"

Jeff stepped around the corner and into the alcove kitchen where Tabitha was hiding behind a plastic-lined trash container. The killer exchanged his leather gloves for a pair of nitrile disposables, opened the refrigerator, then removed the items Roselyn James had purchased from the beverage store: diet Coke and ginger ale, seltzer, chips and dip, along with the larger container that Roselyn had just put away.

"Subject to connection and fingerprint analysis," Jeff declared. He was talking to the cat.

Jeffrey went over to the trash container when Tabitha suddenly shot past him.

"Fraidy-cat."

He reached into the garbage and removed two brown paper bags in which Ilona had packed the items. Jeff looked to make sure that the register receipt was there, too. It was. He packed up all the items neatly within the wrinkled bags.

Before Jeff left the apartment, he helped himself to the cash in Roselyn's handbag, then grabbed her set of keys to double-lock the door. He'd be back in short order, but he'd have to move quickly, first heading off to collect a couple of important items before returning. Jeff made a quick adjustment to the thermostat so that he wouldn't later forget. He thought of everything; he was thinking well ahead.

Chapter Forty-One

Ilona picked Jeffrey up at the Hicksville train station. Jeff was the last passenger to step off the new double-decker diesel. The moonless sky and frigid temperature sent folks scurrying toward their vehicles. The brim of Jeff's cap shielded his features from what little light lit the platform. For a moment Ilona didn't recognize him. For a second she thought that he had stood her up. Jeff signaled for her to pop the trunk. He threw in a duffel bag then went around to the driver's side and gave Ilona a quick kiss on the cheek.

"Shove over, pretty lady. I'll drive."

"I really don't mind driving," she swore. "In fact, I love it. It's not every day I get to drive around and see the towns."

"How can you see anything? It's pitch black."

"I see you, silly."

"And I see you, pussycat."

"Pussycat? You never called me that before."

Jeff smiled.

"I guess you got Orbit on your mind. I'm sure she'll be fine. Come on, get in."

"You sure you want to drive?"

"Absolutely," she said in a tough-guy, *Rocky Balboa* tone.

"Okay. Suit yourself," he submitted, walking past the front of the rental to the passenger side, opening and closing the door quickly from the cold.

She leaned over and gave him a good hug and a better kiss than she had gotten. "I love you, Mr. Mailman," she swore, rubbing the tip of her nose against his.

Jeff laughed. "I'm not a mailman, Ilona. I keep telling you. I'm a mail handler."

"Well, you're my *male* handler, Mr. Mail Person, and I'm awaiting a special delivery. How's that?" And with that announcement, Ilona put the car in gear and they were off and running. "Which way?"

"You're driving, Ilona."

The train pulled away. Up went the gates. Everyone was gone.

"Which way, Jeffrey?" she repeated.

"I said, you're driving."

"Then I'm just going to drive you around in circles until you tell me, Mr. Mail Handler."

Ilona drove around in circles before Jeffrey complained that he was getting dizzy.

"You've been running me in circles since the day you stumbled into my life. Remember? I'm just giving you some of your own medicine back. What do you say to that?"

"Turn here."

"That's better."

The two of them were giggling like school children.

"Got a radio in this heap?"

"Broken."

"You're kidding."

"Nope. But I know how to fix that, Mr. Postman."

"You do?"

"Yep."

"How's that?"

Ilona began singing. "*I wrote a let-ter for the post-man*. Come on, come on," she encouraged, giving him a playful slap on the shoulder. "I know you know the words. I can just picture all you guys sitting around a bunch of mailbags with your coffee. Morning, noon, and night. Crooning away. I'll give you one more shot." Ilona cleared her throat:

"*I wrote a let-ter for the post-man*," Ilona sang.

"*He put it in his sack*," Jeff picked up.

"*But ve-ry ear-ly next morn-ing—*"
"*He brought my let-ter back.*"
"*He wrote upon it—*"
"*Re-turn to sen-der.*"
"*Ad-dress un-known.*"
"*No such num-ber.*"
"*No such zone.*"
"*We had a quar-rel.*"
"*A lov-er's spat.*"
"*I'm sor-ry—*"
"*But my let-ter keeps com-ing back.*"

Ilona and Jeff were singing and laughing up a storm. She had delivered her lines in alto. He had accompanied her in baritone. They were acting positively nuts.

"Please keep your eyes on the road, Ilona." Jeff was tittering. "Neither one of us wants to wind up dead. Right?"

Ilona leaned to her right, lifted herself briefly, and smacked him on the left cheek with two quick kisses, never taking her eyes off the road.

Jeff gave her two rapid-fire kisses in return. "Okay. Slow down. Up there, you bear left."

"Why did the Polish hunters turn their vehicle around when they approached the road sign while driving through the mountains?"

"I don't know, Ilona. Why?"

"Sign read, BEAR LEFT."

Jeff laughed himself silly.

"Never heard that one? Or are you just humoring me?"

"No. I never heard that one before. But I got one for you. Ready?"

"Ready."

"Why is it that they don't have labels on prescription bottles in Poland?"

Ilona thought for a moment then shrugged. "I give up. Why?"

"Because they're still trying to figure out how to get the bottles into the typewriter," Jeff delivered the punch line with a light punch to her shoulder.

Ilona practically went off the road in a roar. Guffawing. Gaining control of the wheel but hardly herself. After a minute, she finally got ahold of herself and took a deep breath.

"That's a very funny joke, Jeffrey. Got any more?"

Jeff shook his head. "Too risky. I don't want anyone laughing over my grave."

"Silly." She gave him a love-tap on his shoulder with her fist. "So. What's our destination? Where am I headed?"

"Told you before. It's a surprise."

"Give me a little hint."

"East. Make a right up ahead."

"That's not a hint. That's a direction. I want a hint."

"East *is* a hint."

"How far east we gonna go?"

"A good ways."

"To the North Fork?"

"Yes."

Ilona was bouncing up and down on her seat with excitement.

"Are you going to be a lot of trouble on this trip?" Jeffrey questioned.

"Who, me?"

"Yes, you."

Ilona shook her head and remained silent for a good sixty seconds. "How far east?"

Jeff remained silent with a smile on his face. At least she thought it was a smile. It could just as well have been that shit-eating grin of his, she considered. It was hard to tell while he was staring straight ahead.

"Okay, then don't tell me. Let me try and guess." Ilona reached past him and opened the glove compartment, removing a folded map. She switched on the interior overhead light.

"Oh, boy. Now she's going to read a map and drive." Jeff was shaking his head.

With a finger, Ilona traced a line north of the train station, then east through Riverhead, which spearheaded the north and south forks of Long Island, then east along Route 25 through the first town.

"Aquebogue?"

Jeff simply shook his head.

"Is that a no? Or are you just tired and disgusted of this game already and going to give in and tell me what I want to know? *Now!*" Ilona questioned, putting on the bitchiest timbre she could muster behind a well-concealed smile.

"What happened to the shy, retiring girl I knew?" Jeff asked timidly, going along for the ride.

"Devil took her over," Ilona answered in a voice that took one back in time to the little girl in the movie, *The Exorcist*.

"Watch that rabbit in the road," Jeff teased.

"Fuck the rabbit, Jeffrey!" Ilona continued in her spooky tone. "Jamesport?"

Jeff was honestly taken aback. Never once in all the months he had gotten to know her had she ever uttered a profanity. Never once over the course of years in observing her with other customers did she even say hell or damn. Not only was it out of character for Ilona to utter a curse word, it was downright diabolical. He wanted to trash her mouth right then and there.

"Jamesport?" Ilona repeated.

Jeff took a breath and shook his head. He was seeing another side to Ilona that he did not like—kidding around or not.

"What about Laurel?" she pressed. "Is that where we're going?"

"Further east," he said.

Ilona ran the tip of a finger through Mattituck, Cutchogue, Peconic, Southold, Greenport, East Marion, Orient and Orient Point, noting that those towns were all in the Township of Southold. Just like Calverton, Baiting Hollow, Wading River, Riverhead, Aquebogue, Jamesport, and Laurel were all part of Riverhead Township. She was getting the lay of the land. Ilona tapped her finger upon the town of Southold. That had to be it. '*Believe me. East is a hint*,' Jeff had said. Riverhead was out of the running because they would be heading east along the North Fork. She thought about Howard sitting in Riverhead Jail, and a chill took hold of her. She shook Jeff's brother from her mind and concentrated on where they were and where they were going.

"I think I know," she said with certainty.

"Really?"

"I get three guesses."

"You had three guesses."

"No, sir. You didn't answer up to Laurel, and it's too late. I say Southold. What do you say?"

"No."

"Nooo?"

"Nope."

"But you said east was a hint."

"It is."

"But you're not going to tell me where?"

"You used up your three guesses and part of my patience."

"How patient is the other part?"

"So-so," he answered, twice rocking his hand in a manner of indifference.

"That much?" she needled.

"My turn to ask questions."

"All right."

"Did you consume an alcoholic beverage before you left the store?"

"No, sir. High on love. Next question."

"Tell anyone where you were going?"

"I don't *know* where I'm going."

"You know what I mean. Did you tell anybody that we were going away together?"

"Nope."

"Swear?"

"I just did a moment ago, and I thought you were going to have a cow because of a rabbit."

"Did you?" Jeffrey reiterated.

"No, I did not tell a soul that we were going away together."

"Take a swear."

Ilona raised her right hand. "I swear. There. Happy?"

"Write anything down in a diary?"

"A diary?"

"I'm the one asking questions. Remember?"

"No friend, no diary, no one. Not a soul."

"What did you tell your mother?"

"Told her I was staying over a friend's house and that we were working on a project for school."

"And if your mother calls this person?"

"I'm covered. Besides, she won't."

"Ever?"

Ilona hit him playfully with the map. "Not unless you kidnap me. Got any plans like that?"

"I'm still asking the questions."

"You had more questions than I did."

"Who's this friend whose house you're supposed to be staying over?"

"A girl in my accounting class."

"Thought you said you had no friends. Just customers. Remember?"

"She's an acquaintance. I asked her for this favor."

"She know anything about me? Like that I work for the post office? Anything at all?"

"All I said was that I was going away with a boy in my bio class and did she think she could cover for me just in case my mother called. She said no problem, that all my mother would get is an answering machine because her parents were going to Maryland for the week. Now stop worrying." She put down the map and took his hand. "No one in the world knows about you and me. And that's the truth. All right?"

"Cross your heart?"

"Cross my heart and hope to die."

Jeff smiled and began to relax.

"Except one."

Jeff looked at her strangely.

"God," she explained. "I have to confess that I told God all about you."

"God is good."

"Glad you approve."

"You talk to God, do you?"

"All the time."

"And does He answer you?"

"He did this time."

"How do you mean?"

"You're here next to me at this moment." She squeezed his hand.

Jeff stared straight ahead. "Howard talks to God all the time, too."

"Does he say that God talks to him?"

"He says that God is a little upset with him right now."

"Little wonder."

Jeff nodded.

"How about you?"

"What? Talk to God?"

"No. Moses. Of course, God, silly," she teased.

"There is another side to you, Ilona. I just know it."

Ilona reached above and switched off the interior light. "The dark side," she sounded in a throaty *sotto voce*.

"Sick girl," Jeff said, shaking his head slowly back and forth while staring out the windshield.

But not as sick as Howard, she wanted to say, but thought better of it. "So what about you? You speak to God, or pray?"

"*Prey*," Jeff answered discerningly, smiling over at Ilona. "I do a lot of *preying*," he toyed.

"Praying's good." She returned his smile.

The two turned quiet. Jeff was truly beginning to relax. Neither of them said a word for the next few minutes. They were traveling east on the Long Island Expressway. Jeff switched on the overhead light and picked up the map between them.

"What?"

"You said you want to know where we're going."

"You're lost, and you need a map? My goodness, Jeffrey."

"No, Ilona. I'm not lost. Just want to show you where we're headed."

"Really?"

"Really and truly."

"Won't it spoil my surprise? Maybe I don't want to know now," she continued teasing.

"Believe me, you'll be surprised. But maybe you really don't want to know. All right?"

"Kidding, kidding, kidding. I want to know. I want to know."

"Christ."

"What?"

"You'd think they'd give you a map light and a radio that worked in this jalopy."

"Lucky we have heat. I told them I wanted something mechanically perfect. That I didn't want to break down in February—" *in the country*, she almost slipped. Not immediately realizing that she had told the woman at the rental agency exactly that. Jeffrey would have had a canary, she'd bet. "Anyway, they only had two cars left. This and a Sherman tank. I guess everyone is trying to get away this weekend."

"Heat I don't care about. I can deal with the cold."

"Uh-oh."

"Uh-oh, what?"

"Our first disagreement. I have to have it warm. Not hot, but warm."

Jeff ignored the comment. "I don't know how you could possibly see these towns on the map. The print is so damn small."

"My mother says I can see grass grow. Anyhow, I'm twenty

years younger than you," she declared, wondering how he would take to the subject of their age difference.

She had been testing him here and there with her silliness and a little bit of bitchiness thrown in for good measure. *Temperate* was one of her new vocabulary words in English class that week. The instructor had asked his students to use the words he had assigned in as many different senses as possible. Shit! She had done it again, she realized. *Mr. Jeffrey Mills is a man of temperate habits and fine character,* Ilona had written as part of her assignment and handed it in. Oh, well. No real harm done. It didn't say they were seeing one another. Jeffrey was just one of many customers if it ever came up. And why would it? She wouldn't bring that blunder up either. He was so sweet to want to keep her out of his problems until this mess was behind him. But she did think that he was being a bit paranoid. Then again, considering the circumstances, it was understandable.

Jeffrey set aside the map. "Twenty years younger!" he said, studying her in profile.

Ilona nodded, staring straight ahead and trying not to smile.

"Are you saying I'm an old man who's practically blind and needs his specs? Is that what I'm hearing?"

Ilona shook her head while trying to keep herself from laughing.

"Is that what you're saying?" Jeff repeated, wrapping his lips around his teeth as if talking past his gums like his former neighbor, Mr. Hammond. "Is that what this has come down to? Because if it has, you can let me out right here," he demanded kiddingly. "I'll take a bus."

"Do you think you'd be able to see one coming?" she exploded in laughter.

"No. But I'd bet I'd be able to hear it and stop it."

"How?" She was laughing hysterically.

"With my foot."

"Your foot?" Ilona was practically sliding off the seat.

"Yes, my foot."

She was trying to catch her breath. "How can you stop a moving bus with your foot, silly?"

"Haven't you ever heard of a bus *stop*?"

Ilona gave him a look with the craziest of eyes. "That is so corny. Can't you do better than that?"

"How about a bus *trip*?"

"Stop it. That's so silly. You're the oldest, silliest man I know." And Ilona was loving every second of it.

"So, when you calm down, this old man will tell you where we're going."

"There. I'm calm. Now, tell me."

He held the map between them and pointed. "Three towns past Southold."

"Give me back the map."

He handed over the Hagstrom. "There. There. And there," he pointed.

"Greenport. East Marion. Orient. All the way out there?"

"Actually, a little further." Jeff traced a line with his finger, and Ilona almost went off the road.

"Shit!"

"Got the wheel, Ms. Twenty-Twenty?"

Ilona gave a nervous laugh. "Sorry. All the way out to Orient Point?" she questioned, glancing up and down between the map and the road.

"Yep."

"What's out there?"

"My sister's place."

Ilona was silent for a few seconds. "We're staying at your sister's?"

"Yep." Jeff reached up and shut off the overhead light.

"Is your sister there?"

"She's away right now."

"Away where?"

"South."

"Florida?"

"Not that far down, but she *is* south of us," Jeff revealed quietly.

"You seem funny when you talk about Beth."

"Do I?"

"Uh-huh."

"Hum. I'll have to watch that."

The two continued heading east.

"Well, you have a choice," Jeff said, before they headed along the Fork. "We can either go through the towns along Route 25 that you pointed out, or we can take Sound Avenue, which the locals call the North Road. It's too dark to appreciate the farmland and the vineyards, though. But if we head through the towns, I can point out some nice restaurants and places of interest along the way."

The subject of food came up, and Jeffrey told her about his favorite places for pizza—certainly not in connection with the Dumpsters behind the restaurants where he and Howard had deposited several bodies. Surely not the ever-popular Fisherman's Rest in Cutchogue. Greatest place on the entire Island for thin-crust pizza, with its single Dumpster opposite the ice machine in back. *Yet, because of the time of year, perhaps a convenient place to dump a body*, Jeff mused. *Yes, closed for the season.* For Sicilian pizza, Howard's favorite was the famous Umberto's in New Hyde Park, back west. Too much traffic even at night to ever risk depositing a body there—for sure. Howard and he preferred the rural areas of the East End to dump their victims.

"Food is my downfall," Ilona confessed. "I live to eat. Not the other way around. However, if I didn't control my urges, I'd be a two-ton Annie."

"You look just fine, Ilona."

"Potato chips. I could eat a big bag myself. And you, of course, know about my homemade dip."

"Onion, right?"

She smiled. "Not exactly."

"Then what?"

"Secret."

"You sound like my sister."

"How do you mean?"

"She makes the best Italian sauce and won't tell anyone her secret recipe."

"Honestly?"

"Kid you not. She services one restaurant out there and makes the guy a small fortune. He boasts that *his* sauce is too good to be called sauce. He calls it Gretta's Gravy. Gretta's his wife."

Ilona nodded. "Is this restaurant in Orient Point?"

"Uh-huh."

"What's the name?"

"Carlos', with an apostrophe."

"Don't know. But then again, I wouldn't know the names of any of the restaurants out here."

"Never been out this way?"

"Never. Been to a few places close to home along the shore with Mom and Dad. That's about it. Led a pretty sheltered life right up to now. This is the first time I've ever been away from home alone."

"Your father doesn't know you're gone?"

"You kidding? He'd have a conniption."

"Gotta let you go sometime."

Ilona smiled and nodded. "I filled a cooler with some special treats. I'm going to make you a very special meal. I don't know if I can compete with your sister, but I'll bet you'll be surprised. And if you want, we can go to Carlos', too. My treat."

"Do you like pizza, Ilona?"

"Do I like pizza? Does the pope live in the Vatican?"

"I don't know, Ilona. I'm a Jew."

Ilona gave a nervous little smile. That was another issue she wanted to discuss. Religion. But first, pizza. "To me, pizza's like that potato chip commercial, 'I bet you can't eat just one.' In truth, I could eat a pie by myself. I love pizza. I adore pizza. Actually, I worship pizza. And speaking of worship, are you a practicing Jew?"

Jeff was surprised by the question. "I practice what I preach, Ilona."

"And what is it that you preach? Hum? Tell me, pretty please."

"That the world belongs to those who seize the day," Jeff said without hesitancy.

"Wow!"

"Wow, what?"

"Pretty remarkable statement from someone who seems so shy."

"Doesn't mean I can't have these thoughts just because I'm timid at times."

"And at what times are those?"

Jeff shrugged. "Times that I'm around you. Time it took to get to know you."

"Think you know me, Mr. Mills?"

"Pretty much, I guess."

"What do you know?"

"I keep telling you, Ilona."

"Tell me again, Jeffrey. I want to hear it in the dark."

"That you're very special, Ilona. That there is no other like you in the world."

"I chose *you*, Jeffrey T. Mills, and made you fall in love with me."

"No, Ilona. I chose you."

Ilona was so happy that she could have died right there in that brief moment of joy and not be the sorrier, for she could envision no greater gift than the gift of Jeffrey's love. She started to cry.

"Did I say something wrong, Ilona?"

Ilona shook her head. "Nothing but all the right things, Jeffrey. Nothing but the nicest things I've ever heard."

"That's good, Ilona."

"You're good, Jeffrey."

Indeed, Jeff knew that he was as good as it got. "That's a very nice thing to say, Ilona."

"Did you notice that there's no moon tonight, Jeffrey?"

"I know."

"So, I'm going to sing you up one."

"Really?"

"Old song; my mom's favorite." Ilona started singing again. She had a pleasant voice. "*When the moon hits your eye—*"

"*Like a big pizza pie,*" Jeff joined in without prompting.

"*That's amore.*"

"*When the world starts to sing—*"

"*Ring-a-ling-a-ling, ring-a-ling-a-ling* . . . or something like that," Ilona sang so happily.

"*That's amore.*"

"But I don't a-know the rest of the words."

"Who-the-hell-a-cares?"

"'Cause we're not Italian." Ilona could not remember having a better time in her life. Jeff seemed to be having a good time, too.

"Jeffrey, did you experience prejudice growing up Jewish?"

"Actually, I thought I was Italian until I was six or seven. The whole neighborhood was practically Italian."

"How did you learn that you weren't?"

"It was when I went home and asked my mother why her spaghetti sauce didn't taste like Angelo's mom's sauce." Jeff paused. "Angelo was my neighbor and childhood friend growing up."

"So, what did your mother say?"

"She smacked me in the head for insulting her cooking. My father said it was jar sauce and healthier for you. My Aunt Sadie later told me it was plain catsup. Catsup from a bottle. She told me how the Italians flavor everything with pork. 'Against our religion,' she would say. 'What religion is that?' I asked her. 'Jewish,' she said. 'You're a Jew, Jeffrey.' 'What's a Jew?' I asked.' 'You. Now eat your spaghetti like a good Jewish boy.' 'But I thought I was Italian,' I protested. 'You are, you are,' she'd explain in her nonsensical way. 'From eight to four

Mondays through Fridays you're Italian. All day Sunday, too, if you like. But on Saturday, you're a Jew. Now eat up your spaghetti, and stop with the pushing the sauce to the side.' She served her spaghetti the same way as my mother. Some spaghetti. Mush. Some sauce. Some Jew. On Sundays, Mom would cook spaghetti with raw chicken. I don't mean raw, raw. I mean burnt on the outside. Hardly cooked on the inside. That was her idea of medium rare meat, when questioned." Jeffrey was silent. Surprisingly, it was the longest statement she had ever heard him deliver.

"Who cooks meat like that?" Ilona asked with the look of disgust on her face.

"Mom."

"Yuck."

"My brothers and I didn't know any better. Not until I had chicken over Angelo's house years later."

"What about your father? Didn't he say anything?"

"It seemed whatever she did was fine with him. When Dad died, Mom became deeply depressed." Jeff did not tell Ilona that his father had committed suicide, as did Lenny a short time later. "I remember her being mostly depressed, but with Dad around she wasn't as bad. She remarried almost immediately after his death, which seemed to shock no one in our family except us kids. One day she came home and said, 'Guess what? I have a surprise for you. I'm married!' Just like that. Howard hid in the closet when she brought her new husband home. A taxi driver. A gambling man. Loved the horses. Eventually, he taught Howard everything about horseracing. Mom became pregnant right away and had Beth. Premature. Beth was born blind. From what I understand, all babies are blind at birth. But Beth had a rare eye disease. Mom and the lawyers claimed one thing; the hospital claimed another. Anyhow, that's how Beth came into the picture."

"You had a younger brother who committed suicide, or so the papers said. Lenny."

Jeff nodded, not saying anything for a moment.

"You all right?"

"Just thinking how bad Howard took it when he found Lenny."

"Sorry. I shouldn't have brought it up."

"Sorry? Don't be sorry, Ilona. Howard's the sorriest of all. Wants to die for what he said to Lenny."

"What did he say?"

"Lenny went to him in a state of depression after Dad's death, saying that he wanted to die, too. Howard told him to go kill himself. And just like that, Lenny did."

"How?"

"Booze and pills. Same night. Howard found him in the morning. Blames himself, of course. Day in and day out. Only peace he'll ever find is when he kills himself, or if the state finally does it for him."

Ilona looked at Jeffrey sadly.

"So. You sure you want to get involved with such a dysfunctional family? Suicide. Murders. Dismemberment. Blindness. History of severe depression on both sides of the family. I didn't tell you my father's aunt died in Pilgrim State. Double whammy. When I was a kid, and the family talked about the Great Depression, rarely did it have anything to do with the economic crisis of the thirties. They were mostly talking about Aunt Sarah on my father's side. Ronald, my other brother, and I would visit her every now and then. That was another riddle unraveled for us the first time we went to visit Aunt Sarah at the mental hospital. 'Shh, shh,' Aunt Sadie would say. 'You don't say nothing about no mental hospital or your Aunt Sarah, hear? The neighbors wouldn't understand. When you talk about the hospital and your Aunt Sarah in the same breath, you say Pilgrim's Progress.' 'What's that, Aunt Sadie?' we'd asked. 'That's a book you'll read in school one day.' 'What's it about?' 'About morals and truths and such nonsense like that. It's all in a convoluted language or something. Which is how I want you two to talk when you talk about your poor Aunt Sarah. Hear?' 'We hear you, Aunt Sadie,' Ronald and I would say. 'Such good boys. Now finish up your spaghetti and go outside and play.'

"Play was our salvation, Ilona. Pilgrim's Progress became part and parcel to the Great Depression. Our family had a dark secret. Our family is positively nuts."

"Does Ronald ever get depressed?"

"Actually, he's as sane and as solid as they come."

"And you?"

"As hard as they come."

"You are not, silly. You're as soft as a pussycat. A real pushover." Ilona gave him a gentle shove, and Jeff fell off to the side. "Sit up straight," she demanded. "I won't know if I'm going right."

"Just stay straight ahead."

"I said, sit up!"

Jeff started to rise, his arms outstretched like Frankenstein. He was going for Ilona's throat.

Ilona gave a gasp, followed by a nervous giggle. "Stop scaring me like that. Come on. I don't know where I'm going, Jeffrey."

Jeff ignored her, leaning against the door.

She gave him three good punches in the leg. "Sit up. Sit up. Sit up, I said."

Jeff slowly turned his head to the left while making the squeaky sound of a door on a rusty hinge. He fixed his eyes on Ilona.

"Will you quit it?"

Jeff opened and closed his mouth, but nothing came out.

"Good. Now, behave."

In an instant, Jeff had his hands around her neck and throat. In the next moment, he planted a kiss on her lips. Ilona gripped the wheel and drove blindly ahead, gasping for fear of a head-on collision before swerving back into her own lane.

"Oh, you *are* a crazy person, Jeffrey Mills! I don't need a family member to tell me that. You're absolutely certifiable."

"Yeah, but I'm not depressed."

Ilona glanced over at Jeff, and the two of them laughed all the way through Aquebogue.

When the pair hit Cutchogue, Jeff told her to slow down and make a right into a driveway before a restaurant.

"Here?"

"Yes."

Ilona made the sharp turn and pulled partway up the drive. "It's closed, Jeffrey. Everything's closed. It's after one in the morning and freezing out there. What are we stopping here for?"

"Cold pizza," Jeff joked. "I just want you to remember this place. You said you like pizza. The best thin-crust pizza in the world is served right here. Pull around back."

"What's the name of this place?"

"Fisherman's Rest."

"My uncle's a fisherman. He keeps a boat in Freeport. How did you find this place?"

"Just driving through one evening."

Ilona drove past an ice machine off to the right, then around back through the parking lot.

Jeff glanced over at the large green Dumpster to the left. "You can go right around here and back out to the road."

"Who lives there?" she asked, pointing to the house set back a hundred yards rear of the restaurant.

"Owner and operator."

"Pretty convenient. Just roll out of bed, and you're at work."

"Sure is."

"Pretty deserted looking. Desolate, in fact."

"Pretty observing, Ilona. Fact is, they're away on vacation now. Not a soul around in February."

"Too bad. We could have stopped on the way back if they were open. Remember, I'm the pizza aficionado."

"Well, I might just dump you off here on the way back."

"Oh, yeah?"

"Yeah."

"Then I just might hang around until they open for the season."

"You might."

"Might say, I'd be in my element."

"Might be right."

"I love pizza almost as much as I love you, Jeffrey Mills."

"I have a feeling you like pizza more."

"Nope."

"Yep."

"You'll see."

"See what?"

"Nevermind. You'll find out soon enough."

"You gonna make me a pizza?"

Ilona was shaking her head and smiling. "I'm gonna make you whole again."

"I didn't know I was broken."

"There are a few things you don't know about yourself, Mr. Mail Handler."

"Oh, really?"

"Yep. And a few things you don't know about me."

"Such as?"

"You never even asked me my major at college."

"I didn't?"

"No."

Jeff looked down at his lap as if embarrassed. He shook his head. "Sorry, Ilona."

"No, Jeffrey. You set sorry aside for when you do something bad or wrong and then realize you hurt someone you really care about.

289

Remember? Your words."

Jeffrey looked up at her. "You're a good listener, Ilona."

"That's exactly what my psychology professor says, Jeffrey!" Ilona responded brightly. "I've gotten straight A's on all my papers and tests so far. How's that?"

"Pretty impressive. *Now* I remember my asking you your major and your telling me psychology," Jeff fabricated.

Ilona shook her head emphatically. "You never asked, and I never told you. I also have an excellent memory. So there."

"Think you do?"

"Uh-huh."

"Want to test it?"

"Sure."

"Okay. I'm going to give you three nouns that I want you to commit to memory. Ready?"

"Ready."

"An airport. A yellow apple. And Thomas Jefferson. Got them in your head?"

"That's it?"

"That's it. Later, I'll ask you to recall them."

"That's so easy, silly."

"We'll see. So. How are you doing? Want me to drive?"

"No, I'm fine," she answered and yawned. "Where are we?"

"Coming into Peconic."

"That means we still have Southold, Greenport, East Marion, Orient, and then you said a bit further to Orient Point," Ilona rattled off the top of her head. "I think I saw *an airport* on the map in Mattituck, just south of town. So we'd probably have to fly pretty far south in that direction for *a yellow apple,* and if you could file a flight plan for me, Jeffrey, I could probably pick out the Memorial on the way back; *Thomas Jefferson's*, that is. That's how I'll remember those three nouns later on when you quiz me. Association." Ilona sat staring straight ahead, grinning proudly from ear to ear.

Jeff stared at her in awe. "And now you're scaring *me*, Ilona," Jeff swore, moving away and bracing himself against the passenger door.

Ilona laughed, pulling him back toward her. "And now you know why I don't have any male friends my age. I scare them all away, Jeffrey. Am I going to scare you off, too?"

"This old coot?"

"You're not that old, silly," she assured him.

"Yeah, well, when I helped ol' Tom draft his Declaration of Independence—"

"Was that you?" she interrupted. "And all this time I thought it was Martha."

"No, it was me, Ilona. Martha was upstairs taking a bath."

"You are the funniest, silliest, loveliest, craziest man I know."

"Would you care to analyze me when we get to my sister's?"

"We'll have to have a consultation first. But I must warn you; my hourly fee is steep."

"Well, then can I just get the Alfold Discount Beverage Center discount until I see your degree up on the wall next to the Budweiser sign?" Jeff asked with a twinkle in his eye.

Ilona's sides were splitting.

Chapter Forty-Two

It was 1:45 a.m. when Jeff and Ilona pulled up in front of the condominium on Orient Point. Jeff was now driving. Ilona was leaning against his shoulder. It was cold outside. Dark. It had started to drizzle.

"We're here." He switched off the engine and removed the keys.

Ilona sat up straight then stretched.

"Tired?"

"Happy tired," she answered, covering a yawn. "How about you?"

"I'm fine. You did most of the driving."

"Raining." Ilona looked around. "Place is beautiful."

"You can't see anything now. Wait until morning. The view will take your breath away."

"You take my breath away."

He gave her a peck on the cheek. "Pretty bird."

Ilona gave a, "Peep."

Jeff laughed. "I'll get our things later. Let's just go on up."

"Someone's coming."

"Doorman. Or in this case, doorwoman. Wait here a second." Jeff stepped out and quickly closed the door. "Good evening, Katie."

The woman stepped up and held out both hands, catching the

cold light rain in her palms.

"I usually tip after services are performed," Jeff kidded.

Katlyn smiled. "Pretty lady you got there."

"Aren't they all?"

Katlyn stooped forward and opened Ilona's door. "Good evening, ma'am."

"Good evening." Ilona slid over and out, stretched again, craned her head back, extended both hands palms up and allowed the misty rain to hit her hands and face for a second or so. "Brrr!"

"My sentiments exactly," Katlyn said.

"Katie, can I leave the car here for a few minutes? I just want to go up and let the lady in."

"You bet. Sure I can't help you with anything?"

"We're fine."

"If you need anything, just ring." Katlyn smiled, turned around, then went back inside the building.

"I just need my pocketbook for now, Jeffrey."

Jeff stepped smartly to the rear of the vehicle and opened the trunk with a key. "Yes, ma'am."

"Why didn't you let her take our things up?"

"The truth?"

"Always."

"I don't want to give her a tip."

Ilona shook her head. "I can see I have my work cut out for me."

"Analysis isn't an overnight affair, Doctor Alfold."

"Hum. I'll reserve comment," she said, staring down curiously at his duffel bag in the trunk.

Jeff handed Ilona her handbag.

"You know, if you took your bag in one hand, and I took my suitcase in the other, and we carried the cooler between us, we'd have everything in one trip."

"Then I wouldn't be able to hold your hand," he said, closing the trunk, locking the doors, then taking hold of her hand. "Come. I think you'll be wild about the place. I wish you could see it in the spring and summer. Outside and in. Flowers everywhere. You'd think you were attending someone's funeral."

Jeff unlocked the deadbolt as well as the lock below it. The two went in together, hand in hand.

The entrance was unusually warm for anyone to be away on vacation was Ilona's first thought. She figured he had phoned ahead, reminding herself of her fisherman uncle who would dial a series of numbers from his home, or anywhere for that matter, drive a good distance to his boat and, *voilà*, the air conditioning was running; the cabin was nice and cool by the time he got there. Very cool idea, indeed. Jeffrey probably had Katlyn or someone from maintenance adjust the thermostat earlier, upon request. Whatever. Just so long as the space remained nice and cozy and warm.

Jeff hit the light.

"SURPRISE!" a dozen people shouted. Twelve men and women put a finger to their lips.

Ilona had both hands covering her mouth. "Oh, my God!" she managed, and then began to sob.

"Shh, shh," a tall black man said, raising a long thin finger before a pair of protruding lips. The other hand held his erect penis in a fist. He stood completely nude. Muscular yet lean. Scholarly-looking, yet mean. "Not one fucking word, or Katydid will do you in a single pop," he promised, making a plosive with a finger to his mouth, pointing to the woman whom Ilona had just seen downstairs.

Katlyn stood half clad in leather from the waist down. In her right hand, she held a pistol with a silencer running half the length of the barrel. The weapon was pointed at the center of Ilona's chest.

Ilona wept uncontrollably, praying that this was all some sort of perverted joke. "Take me ho-home this minute, Jef-frey," she cried. "Pl-lease." Ilona's chest and shoulders heaved as everyone in the room laughed. "This can't-can't be happening." Ilona wept bitterly. "Let me go." She looked over helplessly at Jeff and knew. Knew she was going nowhere. *But why?*

"What happened to all those giggles, girl? Hum?" Jeff asked, removing his hat and coat.

"WHY?" Ilona screamed and was immediately knocked to the floor.

Katlyn had the muzzle of the gun pressing firmly against Ilona's left eye. The black man had taken Ilona's legs out from under her with one swift foot-sweep. Another finger of warning met the young woman's lips.

"You scream like that again, and Katie will whisper your death." Jeff held out his hand. Palm up. Katlyn placed the pistol in it. Jeff walked over to one of the couches and snatched up all three bolsters, lining them up like soldiers. "On the count of three."

Everyone in the room whispered, "One, two, three, SURPRISE!" anew, as Jeff fired a round from the .22 caliber pistol. The bullet ripped through all three cushions, the last of which Jeff picked up and dropped beside Ilona.

"Get up."

Ilona got to her feet.

"See that fellow standing behind the Haitian?" Jeff pointed past the black man. "We call him Nec because he has a strange and erotic attraction to corpses. We don't understand it necessarily, but then who are we to judge? He's simply here to clean up and play with the uncooperative. Nec, Ilona Alfold. Ilona, Nec. You'll get to meet everyone in a bit. Most of my friends here tonight are from S & M clubs around Manhattan. Nec just flew in from Orlando."

Nec stood naked except for socks and shoes and held a tapered wooden club. The kind you use to put big fish out of their misery.

"Why, Jeffrey?" Ilona whispered, her head and body convulsing in total disbelief. Shivering as if she were standing naked in the frigid February air.

"Get undressed," Jeff ordered, handing the gun back to Katlyn before taking off his shirt and shoes and pants. There wasn't a shy bone in his six-foot body as he pulled off his black bikini briefs.

Ilona shook her head. "No."

Half of the group oohed and aahed in an expression of surprise. The rest remained mute. Their anticipation mounting, evident in their eyes. Nec's were glazed yet remained focused.

Jeff smiled and removed his undershirt. "You will do everything I tell you to do."

Ilona was shaking her head *no* and trembling.

"Oh, yes! And I'll explain why. Because if you don't, you're going to die. Very slowly. Very painfully. You're obviously not too afraid of Katie's gun. How about Nec's little bat? Not the one that's hanging between his legs, but the one he's holding in his hand."

Everyone in the room laughed but Nec, Jeff and Ilona.

"Care to join our club? Or be clubbed?"

Ilona was taking in short, quick bursts of air through her nostrils before she drew the courage to open her mouth and speak. "I'm a virgin, Jeffrey. I was saving myself for you. I love you. I don't hate you. Even now. You're sick. You need help. The help of doctors. Take me out of here, now. Let me help you get the help you need. It's not too late."

There was mumbling and grumbling throughout the room, but Ilona tuned them out.

Jeffrey smiled most sadly and silently shook his head, seemingly unaware of the others in the room. He took a moment before he spoke. "It's far too late for that. It's far too late for me as well as everyone in this room. We've crossed the line somewhere back there in time. Once you cross that line, Ilona . . . but enough said about that. Here's the deal. We have, every now and then, but not often enough, a slave auction block. You're the slave. Tonight, I'm the auctioneer. And these anxious ladies and gentlemen are here to do the bidding. One will offer the highest bid and have his or her way with you. Any way he or she wants. One hour. The rest of us get to watch. Unless we're called upon to assist. And then you get to meet my sister, Beth. Oh, yes. She'll be here later this evening." Jeff had to pause for the hearty heartfelt applause from around the room. Katlyn flounced between Nec and the Haitian, jiggling her ample breasts. "Given the fact that you said you're a virgin, and believe me we'll soon find out if indeed that is the case, this has encouraged me to start the bidding at one thousand dollars instead of the customary five hundred." Another series of oohs and aahs and a boo thrown in rose from the group.

"I'm nineteen, Jeffrey." The tears were streaming down Ilona's frightened face.

"Guess I missed a birthday somewhere along the line there, bitch. Now take your fucking clothes off."

Ilona shook her head again. "Come near me, and I swear to God I'll scream my head off. Someone will hear. Someone will call the police."

Jeff cupped a hand behind an ear as if listening by the door before he began delivering his monologue, mocking Ilona's empty threat. "Listen, Officer," Jeffrey acted out. "I'm sorry. We're just having this little party and one of our guests got a wee bit carried away. Won't happen again. What's that you say? You recognize someone in the party? A fellow officer? Oh, you mean, Glen, over there. Glen, could you come to the door for a moment and clear this matter up?"

Half of the half-clad and naked men and women grabbed and threw on togas, robes, and wraps. A man in slacks and no shirt went over to Jeff.

"Glen, would you mind showing Ilona your credentials?"

Glen reached into his right hip pocket and removed his badge.

"One of Greenport's finest before they were disbanded and

became part of Southold Town Police. Officer Townsend, Ms. Alfold. Ilona, meet The Man."

Glen gave a little grin from eyetooth to eyetooth. "It's nice to make your acquaintance, Miss. I hope I'm the highest bidder tonight. I really do." The cop put away his badge. The shield was real, and so was Glen—a Southold police sergeant.

"One scream is all you get, Ilona. Now, get undressed. Do exactly as you're told, and you may see the light of day."

Ilona wept bitterly, removing her scarf, gloves and coat.

Chapter Forty-Three

A vehicle from Suffolk County Laboratory, Division of Forensic Sciences, pulled up and parked directly behind a similar SUV from Nassau. The corner concrete apron in front of the apartment building on Brittle Lane in Hicksville looked like a motor pool. Forensic hair and fiber specialist Peter Danowski stepped on the frozen lawn, crossing the yellow crime scene tape. A uniform came forward; Peter nodded to the man.

"Go right on in, sir," the police officer said to Peter. "Someone will direct you."

"Thanks."

Peter went into the building, and a suit walked him up four flights of stairs, explaining that the elevator was off-limits while tape-lifts and vacuuming were still being conducted.

"Walt upstairs?"

"Yeah, waitin' on ya."

The detective led the specialist upstairs, down the hall and into Roselyn James' studio apartment.

"Hey, Peter."

"Hiya, Walt. Whatta we got?"

"Lots of blood. Nasty slice across her throat. Seems someone knew what they were doing. Place is sterile. Every print we lifted so far either belongs to the tenant, the handyman, moving men, or the super. We're moving pretty quickly on this. We got a couple latent prints on the toilet tank cover. But I wouldn't hold my breath. Probably the asshole plumber who set the new bowl. Pretty sloppy job."

"Weapon?"

"Gone."

Peter went over to the large stained section of blood-soaked carpeting. "Who's the donor?"

"Roselyn James. Fifty-four-year-old Caucasian. Lived alone. Just moved in from Manhattan. This morning we moved her out. Recently divorced."

"Husband a possible?"

"Nah. Guy's living it up in Europe."

"Could be a contract murder?"

Walter looked at Peter rather queerly. "You're reading too many detective novels, fella. Lighten up. You're a scientist, just like me. Leave the speculation to the dicks. Besides, the woman loved him; *he* walked out on *her*."

"So?"

"So a guy's not going to have his wife iced who he recently got away from—unscathed."

"Why not?"

"Why?"

"Yeah, why? There're rules now?"

Walter looked from Peter over to a homicide detective standing off in a corner. "Tell him why, Timmy."

Detective Timothy Sosan looked up from his notes, smiled, then addressed the two forensic scientists. "Why don't both you guys quit your gabbing and do what you do best. Tell him what you got, Walt, so I can get the hell out of here and solve this case."

"Yeah, yeah, yeah."

"Why am I here, Walt?" Peter asked.

"Surprised?"

"A bit."

"Nobody told you?"

"Nobody tells me shit."

Walter Weber had a gleam in his eye. "You're not going to believe what I found, Peter."

"So why are you about to share whatever it is you discovered?"

"Why? Because you did such a crackerjack job with the Mills

evidence—in spite of the fact that you guys claimed jurisdiction and took everything out from under our noses. I want you to help us out so that *we* can now take most of the credit," Walter explained in a very civil tone, passing the first of four small, clear plastic evidence envelopes to the man.

"What are these?"

"Number one—exemplars taken from Tabitha, Roselyn James' cat." Walter held up the second envelope. "Number two—cat hairs from the couch over there. Number three—cat hairs I found on the sleeve of the victim's sweater. Those hairs from the couch and the sweater are inconsistent with Tabitha's because Tabitha's a calico: black, yellow, and white. But these unknowns appear consistent with Orbit's; that is, a defined gray and brown. And number four—my friend, are fibers I also found on the couch," he concluded, handing it over with the others. "Note, and tell me that it doesn't give you a rush."

Peter unbuttoned his coat and held the fourth evidence envelope up to the light. "So?"

"So? So it's orange. Do you see an orange anything anywhere in this room? Go up and down the hallway, alcove kitchen, bedroom and bath and you won't. And it's polyester, Peter. And it appears relatively new. Not worn. Ring a bell, baby? So. All I need from you, Peter my boy, is to compare these cat hairs and polyester fibers—which I'd bet your bar tab are from a certain cat and make of carpet—with the known fibers and hairs that you have locked away in evidence, and then tell me if we have the evidence we need to take this fucker, Jeffrey Mills, down for the count—once and for all."

Peter shook his head. "You're reaching, Walt. First off, there are a million carpets out there with orange poly fiber. You know yourself we couldn't call it a *match* even if it came from the same carpet you think it came from. All we could say is—"

"That it's *consistent*. I know, I know. Tell me something I don't know. Like how long is it going to take you to get back to me on this?"

"We're going to convict Howard Mills in part because the light blue-gray nylon carpet we found—"

"—at 42 Willow Lane, Hicksville, County of Nassau, Peter. I repeat. Nassau."

"—was well-worn, had jute and other debris commingled with it, and *matched*, the known fibers found on the Melville victim, at least in our minds and microscopes. Still, we couldn't just waltz into court and say they're identical. But what we could and did say is that the known and unknown samples were quite significant in that they went well beyond the point of being consistent. The jury understood that."

"You're lecturing *me* on language and the law, Peter?"

"No. What I'm saying for the benefit of Detective Sosan over there, who might go off half-cocked, is that the poly fibers you have here, in and of themselves, mean very little. Now, tell me what else you guys got."

"Proximity to Jeffrey Mills' new digs," Timothy Sosan offered.

Peter smiled and shook his head.

"All Jeffrey did, Peter, was move from one side of the tracks to the other," the detective continued. "He lives several blocks from here. That and the fact that we can't find him. He's not at work, home or his usual haunts."

"Such as?"

"OTB, just like his brother, Howard. Wanted the weekend off. Usually grabs the overtime on Sunday. Cut out Friday evening. He has no wheels now. Yet, nobody knows where he is."

"So you think he may have murdered the woman and is hiding out?"

"What I think is that I have to have a talk with him when he surfaces."

Peter looked back at the door. "No forced entry."

"Nope. She probably knew him and let him in. Or they came in together."

"Take anything?"

"Money and keys out of her purse."

"And he slits her throat? How much?"

"A relative and some friends say she never carried much cash. She withdrew fifty dollars from an ATM machine Thursday afternoon. So she probably did a little shopping. Had some close lady friends and a relative coming over that evening to show off the new apartment and help her unpack. They knew something was wrong when she didn't answer the door or her phone. The superintendent tried to open the door, but the key was broken off in the top lock. He called the police and a locksmith."

"She have keys to a car, Timmy?"

"You working my case, Peter?" Tim asked with a questionable smile. "I don't need another partner. What we need is your help with the fibers and hairs so that when I do find him, I can bring him in. Sweat 'im. Can't bluff 'im. Gotta be on solid ground here."

"Thought this guy's a pussycat. Rolled over on his brother. Not that we needed him, you understand."

"Come on over here," the detective said. "Show you how slick this guy thinks he is."

"Maybe it's a gal," Peter needled.

"Maybe it was your mother," Tim threw back.

"Now, now, Timmy," Walter chided. "Let's be nice. Remember, we need this Suffolk/Nassau surfer for the moment."

"See this thermostat?" Tim walked Peter over to a far wall. "It was set to the highest. Windows were all steamed up."

Peter understood perfectly. "Trying to throw off the time of death."

"Figuring normal room temperature, the M.E. placed her time of death at around late Thursday afternoon," Timmy expanded. "Possibly earlier if not for her ATM withdrawal, which would give Jeffrey Mills a questionable alibi because of when he left work in Manhattan that day. Anyhow, he left a broken key in the door to hold up the works. Quick grab at cash to maybe make it look like a robbery. Went to work Friday. Cut out around ten p.m."

"You don't think it could have been a random robbery?"

"She knew something, Peter. And Jeffrey wanted her dead."

"What are you saying here, Timmy? Let me hear it."

"What I'm saying is what I've been saying all along. Jeffrey Mills is more involved in those murders of prostitutes than you guys give him credit for."

"If that's so, then factor in the clean and proficient slice your middle-aged victim received here against the bloody beating those girls had gotten. *Knifing* versus *bludgeoning*." Peter weighed each word in the palms of his hands as if he were trying to balance a scale.

Tim took Peter's hands and gently pressed the specialist's palms together, covering the man's hands with his. "Jeffrey Mills is simply covering his tracks."

"Yeah, but he knows about trace evidence by now, or should," Peter said to Tim and Walt, staring them both in the eyes. "Would he be so dumb?"

Both men simply shrugged.

Peter studied the two of them. "What else you guys got?"

Tim glanced over at Walt then addressed the question. "Gave you quite enough. I'm not going to lay out my whole case for you."

Peter scratched his head before he spoke. "Fair enough."

"You may want to take your own exemplars from Tabitha for comparison before you leave, Peter."

"Where's this cat of hers?"

"Waiting for you in the bathroom," Walter replied, handing him a pair of tweezers.

"Got my own tools, and I'll collect my own exemplars, thank you." Peter headed for the bathroom.

"Peter."

"What?"

"You're not going to find a single gray or brown hair on that cat," Walter assured him.

"Yeah? What did you do, Walter?" Peter called back. "Pull out all the suckers before I got here?"

Walter laughed heartily.

A few minutes later, Peter flushed the toilet and came out of the bathroom holding Tabitha.

"You weren't doin' funny things with that cat in there, were you?" Walter asked with a disgusted look on his face.

"What are you guys going to do with this cat?" Peter wanted to know. "Seriously."

"James' *good* friends couldn't take her. Some friends. Neither would the relative. I asked," the detective said. "Guess we'll send her to the shelter."

The Suffolk County scientist shook his head and looked Walt dead in the eye.

"Don't even think about it," Walter spoke up.

"I want you to take Tabitha home with you, Walt," Peter insisted, scratching Tabitha behind her ears.

"Give me a fuckin' break, all right?"

"I mean it, Walt."

"And who the hell are you to tell me what to do?"

"The guy who's going to compare those orange poly fibers for you, Walt. The guy who's going to examine these cat hairs and help you with your case."

"I think he's got you by the short hairs," Tim said, laughing away like a loon.

"But that's blackmail," Walter protested. "That's not fair."

"Oh, no?" Peter stated categorically.

"No. You Suffolk guys come here and take over like you run the damn—"

"Stop! All right? You know what the score was. Two of the bodies turned up in Suffolk. Medford and Melville. We didn't steal your thunder. Look. You may be right about the fibers and cat hair, and maybe you'll make a case. I'll tell you what, Walt. If the carpet fibers turn out to be consistent, and Orbit's hair is actually what you found here, I'll take the cat back from you and find it a happy home. If you're wrong, Tabitha's all yours."

"You're all heart, Peter."

"Deal?"

Walter Weber looked at Peter cautiously. "How soon?"

Peter handed over the cat. "Tonight."

"You're a hard man, Peter Danowski," Walter scowled.

"And you're a pussycat, Walter Weber. If you *are* wrong, I'd better see Tabitha at your spring barbecue. I don't want to hear a bunch of excuses."

"If I'm wrong, you may not get an invite for an inspection, wise guy."

"You want me to look around a little, while I'm here, Walt?" Peter asked politely and sincerely.

Walter turned to the detective. "Show him the way out, Timmy. And here," he scowled, handing the detective the cat.

"No, thank you, Walt. I'm allergic."

"Ah, go on now and get out of here. The two of you," the Nassau hair and fiber expert groused as Tabitha squirmed in his arms.

"Walt, please put down the cat. And see that he keeps his word, Timmy."

The detective smiled. "Come on, Peter. We'll go down together."

Chapter Forty-Four

It was a bitter cold night. Saturday. The wind whipping across the Sound made it seem Arctic-like. A ghostly figure stood staring out the large picture window but couldn't see a blessed thing. The room was pitch-black, thermostat set at forty. Safe enough to keep the pipes from freezing.

"Hi, Ilona."

Ilona said nothing. Ilona was freezing.

"Hi, Ilona," the voice called out again.

Her naked body sat propped up at the base of the cushionless couch. She was shivering fiercely from fear as well as the cold.

"Wasn't that something how not one but two officers came to the door last evening? You see how Jeffrey thought of everything? He couldn't go to the door himself, you understand. That's why he sent Glen and Katie."

Ilona was shaking like an unfurled flag in a sixty-mile-an-hour wind. She was bound and gagged with strips of silvery-gray duct tape.

The figure stepped away from the window and turned around as a huge cloud mass unveiled a silvery moon that seemed to complement the person's gown and shoes. Jeff stared directly at the floor as he spoke in a feminine tone. "You don't know the trouble we went through to get you here, dear. A lot easier when Howard and I simply picked up prostitutes off the streets. Families who didn't know or care about the girls' whereabouts or business as we went on about ours."

Ilona now saw the form standing not twenty feet away from her as she listened to the soft and strangely familiar voice.

"Poor Jeffrey had to silence Roselyn James after following her home from your beverage store so that she couldn't identify him as the person intimately seen with you—twice—before your, shall we say, disappearance."

Through swollen eyes from crying, as well as a recent beating, the nineteen-year-old stared disbelievingly at the ghost-like image. Ilona shook her head and body violently. She thought she had no tears left to shed, no strength remaining in her bruised, battered and violated body to shake off anything save the numbing cold; certainly no worthless wish to offer up yet another muffled scream to be thwarted by the sticky adhesive mask of duct tape. Still, Ilona summoned forth periods of intermittent courage, which somehow overrode her fear.

Nec appeared from out of nowhere in seemingly a nanosecond. He stood in his underwear. Confronting Ilona. Tapered club in hand.

"Go back inside, darling. Please. It won't be too long. Ilona and I are having a rather one-sided conversation. Go on now."

Nec disappeared into a shadowy edge of the room.

"Sorry about him, Ilona. And I never ever say I'm sorry. But in your case, I truly am." The figure slowly closed the distance between them. Abruptly, the high heels stopped. "I can see why Jeff liked you. I'm sorry he had to draw you into the middle of this messy business. Oh, but before I forget. I'm Beth. Jeff promised you'd meet me. So here I am." Jeff smiled handsomely.

The tears were streaming down Ilona's silvery-taped cheeks. She firmly shook her head.

"What? Think you can see right through me, don't you, Ms. Twenty-Twenty?"

Ilona tried to kick her feet out, but they were tightly bound to a foot of the heavy couch.

"How did you enjoy the auction last night? I'll bet you've never been to one like that! To tell you the truth," the silhouetted gray ghost whispered, "none of us knew what we were going to do if Nec was high bidder." Jeff laughed lightly and elegantly.

A broken cloud formation covered the moon for a brief passage, and the silvery-gray gown shone in and out of the shadows. The ghostly figure moved even closer. Ilona could see that the formal evening wear

Jeff wore was actually stark white as were the shoes—eerily white and blinding albeit no other light was cast upon the room. The moon alone now illuminated the moment of madness. The figure stood tall and trim and bore long, dark brown hair. Jeff tilted his head and smiled prettily before he sang:

"*When the moon hits your eye, like a big pizza pie, that's amore.*" The ghost gaily gathered up a corner of the gown then glided past Ilona before pirouetting around to the back of the couch. "*When the world starts to sing, Ring-a-ling-a-ling, ring-a-ling-a-ling, that's amore.*"

Ilona lay shivering frantically. She wanted her mother and her father. She wanted the warmth of her happy, humble home in Hicksville. She'd be good. A good Hungarian girl. She'd listen to both her parents. She wouldn't tell any more lies. She begged God to listen to her silent prayers. She begged Jeffrey not to kill her. She begged with pleading eyes.

Jeff felt with his foot for the lead-filled bat lying on the floor behind the couch. He smiled and adjusted his wig then caressed the clip-on earrings, stepping around, bending forward from the waist. "They're Beth's," he whispered lovingly into Ilona's right ear. "I know all Beth's secrets, Ilona. I know the secret to her sauce. Three varieties of tomatoes: plum, beefsteak, and Roma. But the real secret lies much deeper than that. The real secret is in the soil. When she'd be out there planting at midnight to two o'clock in the morning, it didn't matter if a nosy neighbor knew, because Beth had the perfect cover. Not only the cover of darkness, but of being blind. Who'd honestly suspect what was in the wheelbarrow that Beth would push from the greenhouse to her gardens? Or more precisely, who'd even suspect *who* was in the barrow? Her seducers are the secret to the soil, Ilona. She'd lure her lovers down from Greenport to her greenhouse on a lovely spring or summer evening and permanently cure them of their lust. Most of them were migrant workers up from Central and South America, working the farmland along the Fork. They'd ride their bicycles, hitchhike, or walk for miles to steal a kiss before getting *laid*," Jeff divulged. "Get it?" he said, speaking in a now normal, informal tone. "Of course, she'd dig a hole deep enough so that the dogs couldn't get to the corpse. She'd expand on the advice given by one of her favorite radio talk show hosts. A fellow who had a gardening hotline. 'Always dig a ten-dollar hole for a one-dollar planting,' he'd say. Beth went him one better. 'Always dig a one-hundred-dollar hole for a ten-dollar-a-day laborer,' she'd kid.

"Do you know how many Chicanos, Guatemalans, Ecuadorians and the like are planted right outside that window, Ilona? In the hundreds. Yet, she had a fit when Howard and I came by the greenhouse one night with a single dead prostitute. Can you imagine? I said to her, 'What is this, sis? A male-oriented mortuary?' Howard liked that joke. But Beth could just drop in anytime on Howard and run the show, keeping him happy several times a year. He'd do anything for her. But when I asked him for a few dollars, he'd smile and shake his head. Hand me one story after another. He's loaded, Ilona. He's going to go to his grave a rich man. And guess what? He's only *thinking* about making me his beneficiary. He's worth millions, and there is no beneficiary as it stands presently! I was so afraid of that; otherwise, I would have killed him a long time ago. I had to kiss his ass for bail money, Ilona. Imagine? He said that *he* couldn't get out on bail with all the money he had, so why should he help *me*? He actually said that! I had to beg him to have his attorneys set up an account for me. I'm trying to convince him to turn everything over to me. What good is all that money doing him? His life is over, one way or the other. I wouldn't let all that money just sit there collecting dust along with daily compounding. When this is all over, I'm going to take a distant trip.

"By now the authorities believe that Beth has taken an extended vacation. Her gardens are a mess. Actually, she never left. You might say that she's the centerpiece of what was once the source of her thriving little business. I paid her a visit shortly after the police interviewed her. I told her that we should go away together after Howard's affairs were finally settled. I told her we could live together like king and queen. That we could trust one another because we both had plenty of beans to spill. She laughed and said that if anyone was going away when this was over, that it would be she and Howard; that is, if he got acquitted, which she seriously doubted, intending to do some serious traveling no matter how things turned out. If need be, on her own. 'Solo,' she told me.

"I gave her ample opportunity, but I can't say I was surprised. Like Howard, I knew that I'd miss her terribly. That's why I've been planning ahead for years. I not only can look like her, Ilona, I become her. I can sign her signature perfectly. I can perform any task she could do around this apartment. Whether in daylight or the dark. Once upon a time, or two, in Howard's downstairs apartment, he even believed I was Beth. Well, now she's actually right outside that window, soon to be pushing up daisies and dandelions. You should have seen Beth's expression when she came in and smelled her own perfume. In the bedroom she smelled a rat. She knew she was going to die, she did. I gave her a fair chance though, Ilona. I used an aluminum bat. Her one scream aroused a half a dozen neighbors and even the doorman. When I was sure she was silent, I stepped out of my jumpsuit, straightened my hem and hair, took the rat by its tail, then marched through that front door and deposited the carcass in a planter by the elevator, assuring everyone that the situation was well under control." Jeff laughed "Two tenants actually moved out that same week. Of course, it was I who brought the dead rat for cover. Clever? Yes?

"Well, it's about that time, Ilona. You'll be taking several secrets of your own to the grave. You can tell Saint Francis for me when you see him that I know we'll have a score to settle when we meet because I really hate that fucking cat, Orbit. You can also tell him that I took care of all the pussy along Jamaica Avenue, and in no small way helped clean up the streets, ridding them of garbage. I kept Orbit simply for convenience and cover. The ladies loved that cat, Ilona. It put their guard down right away. Crazy cat, though. Runs in the family, I guess. Runs all around the room in circles." Jeff swung the bat in an arc, high above Ilona's head. "You never did get to meet Orbit, did you? You'd have liked her a lot, too."

Ilona was twisting and turning at the foot of the couch. She shook her head insanely.

"No, what? You wouldn't have liked Orbit? Or, no, you really don't want to die?" Jeff smiled. "Tell you what. Remember our little game in the car? Huh? Of course you do. You remember everything. Well, if you can remember the three nouns I gave you back then, I'll let you go free. Fair enough? You can walk right the hell out of here. How's that? All right?"

Nec stepped out of the shadows and shook his head.

"Don't worry yourself, Nec. It's a safe bet. And what's fair is fair. I'm going to cut a slit in the tape across her mouth. If she screams, you club her. And I'll even go to bat for you," he assured the man. "But if she names all three nouns correctly, she walks. A deal's a deal."

"I don't like it," Nec said.

"Why?"

"She looks smart."

"She is smart. And last night she acted smart or otherwise she'd be dead right now. But fear has clouded her thinking, I'd be willing to wager." Jeff was staring down at Ilona. "Want to take the bet, my pet?"

Ilona nodded her head quickly.

"Good. See, Nec? You've got to offer a person hope. Because without hope, you might as well be dead. Howard has high hopes that he's going to be acquitted. I have hope that I'm going to end up with a fortune and not have to share it with anyone because I believe I'm going to inherit everything. It's the way our mother set things up, but with a stipulation; that clever bitch. You hope I wind up hitting a home run so that you can take Ilona into the bedroom and do your thing. And poor Ilona, here, now has hope of getting out of here alive. See what I'm getting at, Nec? Life's a gas."

Nec shook his head while Jeff removed a knife from the sleeve of the gown. Ilona took a sudden breath through her nose, and her nostrils bowed inwardly. He made a lateral incision in the tape between Ilona's lips. A little trail of blood trickled down her chin.

"Any order you wish," Jeff promised. "Whenever you're ready."

Nec was standing ready with his club, waiting for Ilona to scream.

"Thomas Jefferson," Ilona whispered just as clearly as she could.

"Go on, go on," Jeff said encouragingly.

"Yellow apple," Ilona continued, new tears mixing with the line of bright red blood.

"Yes!" the mail handler said enthusiastically. "One more and you're home free."

"Airplane," Ilona concluded, wriggling forward against her restraints, praying to God Jeff would keep his word.

"Oh, I'm so sorry, Ilona. I truly, truly am."

Ilona was throwing her head up and down, up and down.

"No," Jeff assured her. "That's not what I said to you in the car."

But Ilona was insistent, sobbing a little too loudly through the tape. Nec raised his club. Jeff gripped it and held it back.

"Shh, shh. And listen. The noun was airport, not airplane. Stop and think. Remember what you said?" 'I think I saw an airport on the map in Mattituck, just south of town.' Your very words." Jeff was smiling. "Recall that now?"

Ilona recalled the recitation and lowered her head, trembling uncontrollably. Jeff was correct. She didn't want to see it coming. Her whole body quivered violently. She knew that she was a moment away from death. All hope left her being, and she shrank squarely against the corner of the couch.

"Ilona. Listen to me. Don't despair. You did very, very well. Two out of three. Your professor would be proud." Jeff lifted the wig from his pate and set it neatly upon the couch. He unclipped the earrings from his lobes. Lastly, he gently removed the green contact lenses from his eyes. "Look at me, Ilona."

Ilona lifted her eyes.

"Why, I'm surprised you even know your name, silly," he swore as he brought the bat down solidly and cracked the top of the teenager's skull.

Ilona went limp.

Nec went to work with his own tapered club.

Jeff finished the job with the lead-filled wooden bat. "Bye, Ilona."

Chapter Forty-Five

"Hi, Jeff."

A bit startled, Jeff turned around. "Yes?" He looked past the man's shoulder to a taller figure standing behind him, closing the driver's door to the sedan.

The man directly in front of Jeff displayed a badge. "Detective Sosan, Nassau Homicide," Tim said solemnly. "This is my partner, Detective Waverly."

Detective Waverly gave Jeff a little wave. "Jeff."

"What do you want with me?"

"We want to have a little talk. Just the three of us." Waverly was smiling. Sosan was not.

Jeff shook his head. "It's late, fellas. And I got to be at work tomorrow."

"Tomorrow you don't report till twelve noon," Waverly reminded him. The smile was gone.

Jeff stared down at his shoes. "I'm sorry, but my lawyer says I can't talk about the case with anyone unless he's present."

"Oh, that case," Sosan responded. "No, we're here to talk about another case. We're here to talk to you about Ms. James."

"Who?"

"Ms. Roselyn James, Jeff. You know. The lady with the cat."

Jeff shook his head. "I don't know any lady by that name with a cat."

"How about Tabitha?"

"I don't know that lady either," Jeff said coolly, "and it's late and freezing out here."

"Mind if we come inside?"

"I told you. My lawyer said I can't talk to you."

"He means those Suffolk fellas, Jeff. We're your good ol' hometown Nassau boys." The smile reappeared on Waverly's face.

"Can't." Jeff started to walk away.

Detective Sosan put a hand on Jeff's shoulder and looked back to his partner. "Tell him."

"Tabitha was Ms. James' cat. Orbit let us know you were there in the woman's apartment," the cop said flatly. "We have enough to hold you. To take you in and talk."

"Do you have a warrant?"

"How about my boot up your ass?" Waverly suggested.

"I'll be sure to pass that remark on to my attorney."

Sosan put his other hand on Jeff's other shoulder. "Turn around."

Waverly put the suspect's hands behind his back and slapped on a pair of cuffs. "Get in the car."

"I've got to feed my cat," Jeff insisted. "I've been away the whole weekend."

"We know. You've kept us waiting."

"What about my cat?"

"Come home early next time," Detective Tim Sosan suggested.

"I'm going to sue."

"Your prerogative," he said.

"Your money," Waverly added.

"I want to call my lawyer."

"And wake him up at this hour?" Sosan got into the back seat with Jeff.

"I want to call him now."

"Just dial M for murder one. We'll put you right through." Bill Waverly picked up the car mike.

"You guys are making a terrible mistake."

"But we learn from ours," Sosan remarked. "Now, sit there and be quiet."

Detective William Waverly radioed headquarters.

0300 hours, and Jeff's attorney marched into police headquarters wearing a heavy coat and earmuffs.

"I'm Kevin Casey, and I want to see my client, Jeffrey Mills."

The desk sergeant looked up nonchalantly from a report. "Name again?"

"Kevin Casey, attorney. Here to see Jeffrey Mills. Here's my card."

The cop picked up a pen and made a notation. A moment later he phoned upstairs. "Kevin Casey for Mills. Right. Right." The man hung up.

Kevin Casey stood there for a good thirty seconds before he spoke up. "Well? You want to tell me what's going on?"

The sergeant looked back up from his report. "Detective Sosan will be coming down momentarily."

"Sosan," Casey mumbled. "And his sidekick, Waverly, no doubt," the attorney grumbled under his breath.

"Problem?" the police officer asked, his eyes fixed on the report in front of him.

"Three o'clock in the morning is my problem, Sergeant."

The desk jockey said nothing, putting the report aside then shuffling through another set of papers.

Quiet for a Sunday night, the attorney thought. Then again, it was actually Monday morning. *Shit.* He had to be in his office by eight. Court at 9:30 a.m. Casey turned around as he heard footsteps coming down the stairs. Sure as the temperature was in the teens, the two appeared. Sosan and Waverly, looking just as tired as he.

"This couldn't wait?" was Casey's initial comment.

"And it's nice to see you again, too," Sosan said, folding a stick of gum in his mouth.

"Hey, Kevin."

Kevin Casey just shook his head at Waverly.

"Fuck you too, counselor."

"Go run a coffee errand or something and let me speak to Timmy alone," Casey complained.

"Why, so he won't have a witness to a deal you'll later deny?" Waverly said through a smirk.

"No, for kicking his ass for getting me out of bed."

"I didn't get you out of bed, Kevin," Sosan clarified. "Your client did that all by himself."

"What's this all about?"

"Murder one."

Kevin Casey grinned from earmuff to earmuff. "The James woman, right?"

The two detectives looked at one another, then back at Casey.

The lawyer laughed incisively and shook his head. "A no-brainer, my classic comic sleuths. She's on the news. Hicksville. Transplant from the city. I was asking myself how long it would be before you guys rounded up *all the usual suspects*, with my client heading the top of the list because of bad publicity and proximity to her apartment. If there were a murder in a distant country today, you'd probably try and make it stick tonight. And I'm losing a night's sleep for this?"

"How about a fifteen-minute walk to her apartment from Jeffrey's?"

"How about you give me something more material than that?"

"How about you come upstairs with us?"

"How about pressing the elevator button?"

"We're up on the second floor, Kevin. You getting soft?"

"I'm not walking a single flight. I'm too old, cold and tired."

"Maybe your client should have gotten himself a more youthful mover and shaker," Sosan tormented the man.

"Maybe his boy should have hired Dunn and Profeta," Waverly suggested, hitting the elevator button.

"Too busy," Sosan said, shaking his head. "They'll be preoccupied with appeal work well into the next century."

"Then I guess Jeff is stuck with Father Time, here."

"Have your little laugh now, boys. But my client will be leaving here with me within the hour."

"We'll see." Sosan winked at his partner.

The elevator doors opened, and the three stepped out to the hallway.

"You doin' this pro bono, Kevin?" Bill asked. "Out of the goodness of your black heart?"

"You doing this because you guys got upstaged by the Suffolk boys and girls?" Kevin countered. "Or is your department just a glutton for punishment?" he retorted as the elevator doors closed behind them.

"What's our punishment gonna be, K.C.?" Sosan asked. "Another frivolous suit? Just a friendly reminder that you still haven't collected on the first one."

    Kevin Casey just smiled. "This better be good."

The attorney spent ten minutes with the two detectives and fifteen minutes alone with his client. Five minutes later, the four of them sat in a small conference room down the end of the hall.

    "Jeff."

    "Yes, Mr. Casey?"

    "Remember what I told you. You don't answer any question we haven't covered unless I tell you that it's all right. Understand?"

    "Yes, Mr. Casey."

    Casey smiled. "Then let the games begin."

    "Where were you this weekend?" Sosan asked.

    "Me?"

    "No, your counselor," Sosan replied sarcastically.

    Jeff seemed embarrassed and sat staring down at his shoes. "I . . . I was at a friend's house."

    "Friend have a name and address?"

    "Yes, sir. And a phone number, too, if you care to check."

    "We intend to."

    "Oh . . . I just remembered."

    "Remembered what?"

    "I can't give it out."

    Sosan smiled politely. "That's okay. Name and address will do."

    Jeff looked across at his attorney. Kevin Casey gave a nod.

    "Katlyn Land. We call her Katie."

    "Who's we?"

    "Everyone at work."

    "At the post office?"

    "Yes."

    "She's employed by the post office?"

    "Yes, sir."

    "Got her home address?"

    "1411 Kingston Avenue, Hicksville."

    "Apartment or private home?"

    "Apartment."

    "That's over by the cemetery," Waverly offered.

    "Where were you Thursday?"

    "At work."

    "And what time did you leave work on Thursday?"

"Three o'clock."

"That's three in the afternoon?"

"Yes."

"You're working seven a.m. to three p.m. these days."

"Yes, except Fridays."

"And what did you do when you got home on Thursday?"

"I didn't go home."

The two detectives locked eyes for an instant.

"Where did you go?"

"Katlyn's."

"You went directly there from work?"

"Yes, sir."

"Walk?"

"We rode in her car from the train station. Then we went back to her place," Jeffrey flat-out lied.

"What time did you get home that evening?"

Jeff looked to Casey.

"Tell him, Jeff."

"Like I told you before. I didn't go home."

"At all?"

"Not that evening, no."

Detective Timothy Sosan studied the suspect's face and body language. Jeffrey's facial features were alike yet unlike his brother Howard's. Same shape head and nose. But as Howard's countenance was rough-hewn, Jeffrey's was as smooth as alabaster. Jeffrey Mills had perfect skin.

"Go to work next day? Friday?"

"Yes, sir."

"She go to work, too?"

"Yes, we rode the train in together."

"Same schedule?"

"Work schedule?"

"Yeah."

"I work late on Friday. Saturday and Sunday if I want the overtime. But Katlyn and I wanted to spend the weekend together. So we left work together and went to her place."

The detectives knew Jeff's work and train schedule. They had checked his hours for Thursday and Friday with an inspector at the Manhattan post office on John Street. The detectives knew nothing of a Katie or Katlyn Land.

"What time did you get to Katlyn's home Thursday, after the two of you got off the train?"

"Around five-fifteen. Maybe five-thirty."

"Drive straight there, or did you stop someplace along the way?"

"Drove straight there."

"And?"

"And what?"

"What did you do?"

Jeff shot an embarrassed glance across to his attorney.

Casey nodded.

"I . . . can't," Jeffrey flustered in a shaky voice.

Casey shook his head and grinned. "He's embarrassed to tell you that he fucked her brains out as soon as the two of them made it through the front door."

"I'm asking *him* the questions, counselor," Detective Sosan snapped.

"And I'm just helping him over the rough spots, Detective. So cool your jets. She's a married woman with a husband doing a tour a duty somewhere in the Middle East. Get the picture, Timmy?"

Tim Sosan did, indeed. A *reluctant* alibi witness at the very least. The most damaging kind. Especially from a woman who had something to lose along the line. Anything from a reputation to custody of the kids—if she had any. The kind of woman who would nevertheless get on the stand out of a sense of justice or the fear of committing perjury, not adultery, mind you, and *reluctantly* tell the truth.

Casey was grinning as if reading Sosan's mind.

"Is this true, Jeff?" the detective asked.

"Yes, sir."

"And you're saying you were with this woman from Thursday morning till when?"

"Until the time you stopped me tonight, put me in handcuffs, and that guy over there said he'd put a boot up my ass."

Casey looked over at Waverly, who sat silently.

"Well, Detective Waverly certainly has a way with words," Casey offered sarcastically. "You have to excuse him, though, Jeff. Underachiever. High school dropout. Authority complex," the attorney confided behind a smirk.

Waverly's face went red. "Fuck you."

"See how easily you can get under his thin skin?"

"And I asked this detective if he had a warrant. He had no right putting me in handcuffs."

"We're going to take care of all that, Jeff. Let me assure you."

"I sure hope so."

"Giving them the benefit of the doubt, though, they reasoned they had cause. So let's hear them out. You can answer their questions, Jeff, being the fine gentleman that you are. Unless I tell you otherwise. All right?"

"Yes, sir."

Sosan was getting a knot in his stomach. Casey was acting too damn confident. Not his usual low-key self. Somehow the detective sensed that this pettifogger wasn't blowing wind.

"You spent the entire time together since Thursday, you were saying," Detective Tim Sosan continued.

"Except for the time I went home to feed my cat and pack a small bag because I was spending the weekend at Katlyn's."

"When did you pack a bag and feed your cat?"

"Friday, after we got out of work."

"Sure it wasn't Thursday afternoon when you got home?"

"Positive."

"How come so sure?"

"Because I figured I'd be staying at Katlyn's for the weekend. Late Friday evening, I went home, cleaned out the cat's litter box, and put out enough food and water Orbit would need for the rest of the weekend. I wouldn't leave her alone for three days straight."

"And this Katlyn will tell us that you were with her since Thursday morning, from the time you two arrived at the train station, till the time the two of you left for work the following day. Then the rest of the weekend. Is that what you're telling us?"

"I really don't want her involved. But Mr. Casey said I don't have much of a choice. If you have to call her, she's going to tell you the truth."

"Anybody see you at her home? Anybody come by?"

"Somebody rang the bell. And somebody called. But she didn't answer either time."

"Any reason for that?"

"We were in bed." Jeff put his head down. "We wanted to be alone."

"Afraid it might be another boyfriend?" Detective Waverly

questioned.

"You don't have to answer that, Jeffrey," Casey said.

"What times did the bell and phone ring?" Sosan grilled.

Jeff searched the ceiling before exhaling a sibilant column of air. "Had to be somewhere around five thirty for the doorbell and seven for the phone."

"Why, 'had to be'?"

"Because around five thirty we got into bed. And at seven, Katie wanted to watch the news. I went in to take a shower."

"Thursday, p.m.?

"Yes, sir."

Tim Sosan reached for a folder in front of him. He opened it and showed the suspect a crime scene photo of the victim's face.

"Ever see this woman?"

Bill Waverly watched Jeff's reaction.

Jeff looked down. "Oh, my God! No, sir."

"Take a good look, Jeff. Weren't you in her apartment Thursday afternoon?"

"My client already told you he never saw her, along with his whereabouts for Thursday, Friday, Saturday and Sunday, Timmy."

"I think your client's lying, Kevin."

"It's your thinking that concerns me, Detective. I'd be careful," the attorney warned through a yawn.

"Tired, Kevin? Let's see if we can keep you up and interested." Tim turned his attention back to Jeff. "We told your lawyer, here, that we found cat hair in the victim's apartment that matches Orbit's. You have a gray and brown cat that is significantly different than the victim's cat, Tabitha."

"Hooray! Exhibit number one entered into evidence," the attorney interrupted with a sarcastic laugh. "Say nothing about that, Jeff. Next, Timmy."

"We have orange polyester fibers from your carpet, also found in the victim's apartment."

Jeffrey shook his head. "Not from my carpet. I don't have an orange polyester carpet—anymore."

Casey studied the two detectives looking at one another blankly. "Duh, fellas," the attorney funned and grinned.

Detective Sosan's face drained of color. "Say what?" He was staring confusedly at Jeffrey. Sosan had physically seen the carpet from Jeff's old apartment picked up and taken to his new digs well over a year ago. The detective also knew that it had been reinstalled less than a week later. He had even spoken with the carpet man who laid it. *Was Jeff lying? Stalling? What the hell was going on? Why would he have picked it up? And when?*

"I had an orange carpet from the old apartment and— Oh, Mr. Casey, should I tell them? You told me not to say anything. May I talk?"

Kevin Casey was all smiles. "Till I tell you to say good night to these two mental midgets and take you home."

Jeffrey smiled handsomely. "I had the orange carpet pulled up from my old apartment and put down in my new place."

"Pulled it up when?"

"About a year ago. But Katlyn didn't like the color, so she had it removed and bought me expensive green wool wall-to-wall."

"When?"

"Installed the following month. You can check."

Waverly looked away in disgust.

"And that, my Nassau ninnies, concludes exhibit number two," Kevin Casey vaunted.

"Those carpet fibers could still be from his old apartment," Waverly said defensively.

"As might a speck of dust from Cleopatra's tomb," Casey jabbed good-naturedly. "Just be sure and tell the judge and D.A. when that carpet in question was removed from my client's present place of residence. Over a year ago! Which wouldn't prove anything anyway if it hadn't." The attorney was shaking his head in disbelief. "Do you know how many carpets those fibers could have come from, Timmy? Do you have any idea how many places your cat hairs could have originated? I wouldn't want to venture a guess. You have nothing, fellas." Casey formed a circle with a thumb and forefinger. "One big, fat goose egg, guys. But what my client has . . . " he paused for the full effect, "is a solid alibi."

There was a full five seconds of silence.

"Get your coat, Jeff. I'll drive you home."

"Hold on, Kevin," Sosan ordered. "Mr. Mills is not going anywhere just yet. I want to speak to this woman, Katlyn Land."

"She just went to bed a little while ago like I was trying to do before you picked me up," Jeff snipped at the detective.

"I couldn't care less if she hasn't slept in a week," Tim Sosan stated angrily.

"You could speak to her in the morning, Timmy," Casey

suggested.

"I'm not finished questioning Mr. Jeffrey Mills."

"Then finish up."

Tim gave Kevin a cold look. "Cool your heels, counselor. You're going to be here awhile."

Waverly grinned.

Kevin Casey leaned back.

Jeff sat quietly by. Pissed.

Sosan folded another piece of gum into his mouth and combined it with the other. "How'd you get home tonight?"

"From Katlyn's?"

"That's where you said you were."

"She drove me."

"How come you were walking when we picked you up?"

"Katlyn dropped me off near the apartment. We try and be discreet."

In truth, Jeff had left Ilona's rental car at a nearby park then started walking home. Jeff and Katlyn had their stories straight. Katlyn had even helped Jeffrey with Ilona's body, lifting and dropping the heavy duffel bag into the Dumpster in back of Fisherman's Rest in Cutchogue.

Sosan's questioning went on for another twenty minutes, going over Jeffrey's story, trying to trip him up. Rather than spend the night in jail, Jeff agreed to call Katlyn's unlisted phone number and have her speak to the detectives. If necessary, she would be asked to come into headquarters. But Katlyn did not pick up the receiver. She was probably fast asleep. The matter was put over until the world awoke. Jeffrey was being held until such time. Casey promised Jeff that as soon as the detectives spoke with her, and the story checked out, he'd have him home. Jeff then insisted that they all ride out to Katlyn's apartment, immediately, and wake her up.

The detectives declined.

Jeff bellyached. "These guys aren't going to talk to her first thing in the morning before she goes to work," he whined. "You know that, and I know that. And if they insist on seeing her, they're certainly not going to run into Manhattan on my account. It'll be tomorrow night before I get out of here. And I'm going to lose a day at work. As it is, I'm on their shit list. And who's going to take care of my cat?"

Tim Sosan loved it when dirt bags whined and whimpered. The detective knew he had real trash sitting before him. He also knew that this piece of filth was going to walk tomorrow. Walk away free and clear. Furthermore, he knew he'd be told by his immediate supervisor to step back. Especially after Kevin Casey got finished with him.

"I'm going to handle this, Jeff," Casey assured his client. "Heads are going to roll. In the meantime, you'll keep your cool. All right? Now, tell Detective Sosan he has permission to give me your keys from your property bag. I'll head right on over to your place and take care of the cat. How's that?"

Better Casey with the keys than the police, Jeff thought. Not that any home was secure from illegal entry, he surmised. *Thank goodness that the apartment was free of contraband.* "Fine, Mr. Casey. Thanks."

The attorney gave Jeff a couple of manly slaps on the shoulder. "You'll be fine." He turned to the two detectives. "God help you if I hear that one hair on his head fell out of place," Casey warned, pointing a finger at each of them. "I mean it, boys."

Had there been no witnesses in the room, including his own partner, Detective Tim Sosan believed that he would have broken the feisty old man's finger on the spot.

Suddenly, the door to the room opened.

"Sorry, guys. There's a call for you, Timmy. It just can't wait. Woman's hysterical, but she's not a hysterical woman." There were near tears in the desk sergeant's eyes.

"Make some sense, Bones."

"Their daughter. Never called the whole weekend."

"Whose daughter?"

"The Hungarian couple with the beverage store over on Newbridge."

"Jane and Janos Alfold?"

The cop nodded. "I been talking a blue streak to her since Saturday afternoon. Daughter never called; she was supposed to be back home tonight."

"That store's a block away from the James woman," Waverly clarified.

"See? They'd have had you out of bed for this one, too, Jeff," the attorney affirmed.

Detective Sosan and Jeffrey Mills locked eyes.

"She says she's going to call the governor's office in the morning. She's already called the mayor's office in Manhattan and left a message. *Newsday* too, I think. She's a nice lady, Timmy. Not a nut."

"I know. I know the daughter. Goes to school with my kid. Tell

Mrs. Alfold I'll call her back in two minutes."

"She won't hang up this time."

"Tell her I'll be there in a minute, Bones. Bill, take this asshole outta here and lock him up. Get his keys from Mike and give them to Casey. Now, amscray. All of you. And don't forget your earmuffs, old man."

When everyone cleared the room, Tim Sosan took the gum from his mouth and stuck the wad beneath the wooden tabletop. He unwrapped another stick and fired it into his gob. "Bullshit and elephant dung," he muttered. "And then there's Kevin Casey and his fucking clients." He kicked the leg of his chair. Hard. "Fuck."

Detective Timothy Sosan knew it would be the cat hairs, not the carpet fibers, that would possibly incriminate Jeffrey Mills.

Chapter Forty-Six

Robert Redler was on long-distance to Florida, speaking with his old-timer, retired private investigator friend, Emiel G.

"The mother, Sophie, wanted a daughter as her second child but was disappointed and depressed when Jeffrey was born. So, she dressed him up like a girl, long curls and all, till around the age of eight. Later in life, he'd dress up on his own in women's clothes," Emiel explained. "Like one of them whatchamacallits? Transvestite fairy fellas. We got them down here, also, I hear."

Redler laughed. "What'd you think? Some sort of northern thing?"

"Yeah, well in my day, we didn't have many of them floatin' around as much."

"You probably did but just didn't realize it is all. You probably even dated one and didn't even know it," Redler teased.

"Oh, I'd know, all right. First date I'd know."

"You would not. Back then you guys wouldn't even unhook a brassiere until you had an engagement ring on their fingers. Who you kidding anyhow?"

"You don't know what you're talkin' about, Rob. First off, the women down here don't have and never did wear brassieres. Cars wear brassieres today, across the grill. Secondly, I've had more successes on first dates in my Model-Ts than Rudolph Valentino had female fans."

"I didn't think the automobile was around when you were."

"Whattaya think, I got laid in a horse-and-buggy?"

"I was going back even earlier in time."

"To what?"

"Something with a stone wheel."

"Cute." The old man laughed and steadied his glass of orange juice. "But I'll tell you one thing right now. I had more fun in them Ts than I do my Continental. Kids down here today smash up sixty thousand dollar automobiles like they were drivin' bumper cars. Mercedes, Corvettes, Mustangs, Thunderbirds. Then they go out and buy a new one a week later. One kid last week bought the farm when he hit a stone wall doin' ninety. Ninety miles an hour! Can you imagine? At least when I hit somethin' back in the Stone Age, feathers flew, chickens squawked, and your hat flew off. Not your goddamn head."

"Nostalgia's nice, Emiel. But it is my nickel, you know."

"Phone call used to be a nickel, you know."

"So was a pickle. Tell me more about Jeffrey Mills."

"Jeffrey's a strange one all right."

"Whole family's strange."

"Nuts would be hittin' the nail on the head."

"Lay it on me, Mr. G."

"Well, for openers . . . you're gonna love this. The half sister, Beth Tracy, was especially close to Howard. Fond would be a more suitable term. Very fond. Jeffrey Mills was insanely jealous of their relationship. He was as keen on her as she was on Howard. Beth was a nice lookin' kid from what I hear. Matured early. Jeff would dress up like her and pretend to be blind like her. Nothing malicious or mean-spirited. He wasn't teasing her or trying to be a clown. He wanted to *become* her, not *act* like her, his aunt said."

"Which aunt?"

"The one who hung up on you. Sadie."

"She talked to you?"

"That's right. You see, Rob, you don't know how to talk to people yet."

"I see."

"See, that's what I mean. A little abrupt. A little too cute with folks. Sudden."

"Sudden?"

"Sudden. You've got to give people a chance to talk."

"I do."

"You think you do, but you don't."

"At twenty cents a minute, maybe you're right."

"And don't attach a dollar value to every deal you do."

"If I can get my information and be off the phone in four minutes flat, I won't," Redler kidded.

"You gotta learn to relax around people. Let them know you care. Not, 'Hi, Emiel. Whattaya got for me?' like ya did as soon as I picked up the phone. See, I know you. I know you care. But they don't know you like I know you. All they know right off the bat is that you want something."

"Uh-huh."

"You're hopeless."

"No, I'm not."

"No, you are. When I spoke to that woman, she was as nice as pie."

"Personally? I thought she was nuttier than a fruitcake."

"She is. But that's not the point. You still have to be nice to people. Start off with something that they may be able to relate to."

"Okay, Emiel. What did you first say to that old cow that made her melt and confide in you?"

"Oh, that's easy. I asked her if she ever rode around in a Model-T."

Redler was pleased that the old man couldn't see him smiling. "Did you ask her if she ever lay down in the back seat of one?"

"No, but after we met, I did ask her why she was wearing a bra."

"And?"

"And that night she removed it and in the morning hooked it to the grill of my Continental."

Redler's sudden burst of laughter had him spill a portion of hot coffee he was sipping.

The old man swallowed his orange juice and smiled. "So, anyhow, this guy's got some serious problems, Rob. Loves the ladies and likes to dress up like one."

"He violent?" Redler questioned, blotting his flannel shirt with a dishtowel.

"Don't know. The aunt doesn't seem to think so. But guess what?"

"The aunt's violent."

Emiel put his glass down. "Beth Tracy."

Redler threw the dishtowel and watched it land in the sink. "Beth Tracy?"

"Very violent as a kid. Aunt said she seemed to outgrow it. But a neighbor saw things a bit differently."

"I'm listening."

"Well, the neighbor watched her grow up and made an interesting observation. Said it was like the girl kept herself in check."

"Not sure I follow."

"Well, I'm gonna tell ya."

"So tell me."

"See what I mean, Rob? You get a little too abrupt every now and then. Anyhow, what the neighbor was saying was that Beth was quite a precocious little girl. Blind but actually brilliant. She knew how to read adults real well. Would modify her behavior to suit a particular situation. She'd test you. She learned to hide her true feelings. For instance, there was this young girl Beth's age. Ten at the time. They got into an argument, and the other girl pulled Beth's hair and kicked her in the shins. This neighbor witnesses a most remarkable scene, she says. Little Beth Tracy admonishes the girl's behavior in what the woman called, 'truly adult terms,' with Beth explaining that such '*conduct* and *comportment*,' those are the kind of words the neighbor said Beth used, was 'most unbecoming, most unladylike' for a young girl her age, a girl she wanted to call her friend. The woman said the girl was so taken by Beth's reprimand that she started to cry and apologized a hundred times over. She said Beth smiled and told the girl that they could still be friends and suggested that they take a walk together in the woods. The two of them went off, hand in hand, laughing. That was the last anyone saw of the girl. When Beth was questioned, she said they walked out of the woods together to a road. Her friend went one way, and she went the other. Beth said she turned and heard her friend getting into a car that had stopped for her. And then the car took off. But the neighbor thought she heard something strange when the two girls first entered the woods and were out of sight. A strange sound. Like someone trying to catch their breath but couldn't. And then there was silence. That girl completely vanished, Rob. Never heard from since. Maybe some maniac did pick her up. Maybe not. No one knows. Case remains unsolved. Neighbor has her suspicions though."

"Doesn't prove she's violent."

"Want to hear another one?"

"Bear shit in the woods? Ferret fart in a furrow?"

"Wouldn't that be a burrow?"

"Whatever."

"Twelve years old. Beth's walking along the side of some rural road, tapping it with her cane, making her way to town when two bullies approach and start picking on her, teasing her about being blind. You know how mean-spirited kids can be. They were calling her names and tossing pebbles at her. She caned one of them across the mouth and broke some teeth. The other boy rushed her head on, and she just tossed him aside like a rag doll, kick-boxing her way around his body like she had eyes in the back of her head. Finally, the boy had enough and ran away. The one with the broken teeth took the chain he used to lock his bike and went after her, whirling this weapon in the air above his head. Fella told me it was like watching a ballet in fast motion, the way she took the boy down. Had the chain around his neck like it was a garrote. She would have strangled this kid to death if the postman hadn't come along and made her stop. She tried to take him on, too, until she realized who he was."

"Neighbor tell you this story?"

"Postal fellow himself who had the route back then. Retired now, of course, with less than six months left to live. Throat cancer. Know who else confirmed the story?"

"Nope."

"The boy who ran away. Retired police officer. Said it was the most humiliating moment in his life, getting his ass whipped by a girl. A blind girl, no less. Two years younger than he and his friend. Said he and his toothless crony probably deserved what they got. He said the pebbles they were tossing led to small stones, then rocks. Although they weren't trying to hit her with those larger missiles. Just scare her. But he also said that she kept leading them on, showing absolutely no fear. Calling them chicken-shits and mamas' boys and fags. He said that each blow he received from his beating was followed by a taunt. Each punch and each kick landed with such precision. She actually told him what she was going to do to him before she did it. She told him on the last kick that she was going to break his nose. And she did just that."

"Jesus. You saying now that maybe she can see?"

"No way. Nohow. What I told you first time out still stands. She's blind, Rob. Blind as a bat. No question about that. And like a bat, she seems to have a sort of sophisticated sonar system. A sixth sense, or in her case, a well-developed sense of *seeing* blindly."

"Kind of like that blind kung fu master who taught his student, what's his name?" There was a pause in their conversation. "You know who I mean. Played by David Carradine."

"I don't know, Rob. I don't go to the movies. Haven't been to one in thirty years."

"It was a TV series."

"Don't have any interest in them either. Haven't had a set in over twenty years."

"Thought you had one on your boat."

"You're probably thinking of the radar screen. You wanna hear the rest or not?"

Redler smiled an inch away from the receiver. "I want to hear."

"The really spooky part?"

"Yes, Emiel. The really spooky part."

"She carried a bat around for a while."

"A bat?"

"Yeah, a bat. The kind you swing. Not a flying mammal. Don't get stupid on me now."

"You did say spooky, you know," he prompted.

"I'm getting to that. Only it was her mother who clubbed the family's gardener when Beth was fourteen. Man was twenty-four."

"Christ."

"Mother had said she caught him molesting Beth, chased him with a bat but that he ran away. Beth stuck to the same story."

"What happened?"

"A deputy sheriff found the guy six months later."

"Found him where?"

"Not in any flower bed, which would have been poetic justice. No. The mother had planted him smack in the center of a tomato garden. Beth's garden. Her mom grew flowers. The daughter grew tomatoes. The mother confessed, and the county sheriff and the court later ruled it a justifiable homicide. Shortly after that, Beth disappeared."

"Disappeared where?"

"Somewhere in South America. Then she turned up in Central America. Then finally, the North Fork of Long Island, where you told me she's disappeared again."

"Yep. Without a trace."

"As far as the aunt knows, last anyone heard, Beth was still living on Long Island."

"I wonder if she's living at all."

"I've turned up nothing on that, and believe you me, I've been looking under rocks."

"You've turned up some good information, and I appreciate, Emiel."

"I'll appreciate eighty-four bucks. Going to start moving the boat around next month."

"Sounds like you did a lot of running around for eighty-four bucks."

"Well, to tell you the truth, Rob, the aunt and I kinda worked things out. She wanted some information on her nephew, Howard, which I provided, in exchange for two meals a day and a roof over my head before she sent me packin' with a doggie bag for the trip back."

"Mind my asking what she fed you?"

"Spaghetti mostly."

"With catsup?

"How'd you know?"

"Little research on my end."

"Just remember to acknowledge me in that book you're writin'."

"Maybe I'll make you into a major character; bigger than life." Rob smiled fondly. He loved the old man.

"I am a character. You're a character. Simply write it straight."

"Sound advice."

"If you're feelin' a little guilty, put another ten in the envelope," Emiel suggested.

"Done deal. Call me when you got something."

"How about Aunt Sadie's family recipe? Only one written in her book."

Robert Redler laughed completely through his last mouthful of coffee, hung up the receiver and, again, blotted his flannel shirt with another clean dishtowel.

"Shit."

Chapter Forty-Seven

Down the end of the hall from her office, the chairperson of the English Department at Stony Brook University sat at the head of an oval table in a small conference room. To her left, seated in clockwise fashion, were Nassau County Homicide Detectives Tim Sosan and Bill Waverly; the president of the college and its attorney; an adjunct English instructor who taught an English 102 section and was Ilona Alfold's Tuesday/Thursday morning mentor for the spring semester; a teary-eyed female student and classmate in Ilona's accounting class; lastly, but certainly not least, Suffolk County Homicide Detective Gary York. The student was asked to return to her class and instructed to keep their conversation under wraps. She nodded and, without a word, left the room.

"I believe she has told us everything," the chairperson said matter-of-factly.

The lawyer sitting directly across from her nodded as did the president.

"I spoke to her professors, and they all assured me she is a forthright young woman," the president said with assurance. "I'm quite sure she left nothing out," he added, reiterating the chairperson's assessment.

"I concur," the instructor offered. "I had Cynthia in my 101 class last term, and she was one of my finest students. Very mature. Most thorough. It's not surprising to me that the two girls were acquainted. Yes," he reaffirmed. "I'm most certain she's been candid here. It's Ilona's assignment that is even more telling," the instructor continued.

The instructor had everyone's attention as he had earlier. They all had a copy of Ilona's last written assignment. Each person picked up the paper and put it back under their noses. They all focused on the word *temperate* and the way in which Ilona Alfold had used it in context: *Jeffrey Mills is a person of temperate habits and fine character.*

Detective York suppressed a smile. Detective Sosan wanted to puke. Detective Waverly smirked.

"Do you have something further on this, Jason?" the chairperson asked the instructor.

"Yes, I do. I recall something Ilona said in class last semester. She mentioned a man who came into the beverage store on a regular basis. A customer who enjoyed fine beer and ale. When she talked about him, it was like she was in a trance. It might sound a bit silly, but I had the distinct feeling that Ilona was infatuated. Nothing that she said specifically, as I remember. It was all written in her eyes."

"You have a copy of any of her papers from that semester, Jason?" York asked.

"No, sir. Detective Sosan asked me that before. Like all essays, tests and other assignments, I grade them and hand them back to the students. And I don't recall anything further that could help you out, gentlemen. I'm truly sorry."

"You have nothing to be sorry for, Professor. You've been a great help," Tim Sosan said. "Believe me."

"I *concur*," Bill Waverly offered. "Not trying to be a wise guy, Teach. Just trying to improve my vocabulary as we go along," the detective kibitzed.

"You're doing very well, Detective," Jason professed, offering up a brave smile.

"Thank you, Jason," Waverly accepted politely.

"If you do remember anything else," Sosan rejoined, "no matter how insignificant you might think it is—"

"I'll be sure to give you fellows a call. I have your cards."

The chairperson stood. "Thanks, Jason," she said, and the instructor took his cue.

"Ma'am, do you mind if my partner and I and Detective York

use this conference room to finish up here?" Sosan asked, making quick work of dismissing them all.

"No. not at all," the chairperson invited with a sweep of her hand. "If there is anything else you need, I'll be in my office." She pushed in her chair.

The president and the attorney did the same. Handshakes concluded the meeting. The detectives were getting down to cases. Waverly quietly closed the door and returned to his seat.

"What do you think?" Sosan asked.

"I think Ilona fed her girlfriend a story about spending a weekend with a boy in her bio class," York said flat out. "I think Ilona was with our boy, Jeffrey Mills. That's what I think."

"Me, too," Sosan agreed.

"I concur," Waverly conjoined in his smart-alecky style.

"So what've we got?" Sosan asked rhetorically, laying it out before them. "We got a woman at the car rental agency who remembers Ilona saying that she wanted something 'mechanically perfect,' that she 'didn't want to break down in the *country*.' Odometer reading shows one hundred sixty miles, which corresponds with the agent's record. Eighty miles each way if they didn't drive around sightseeing. And with that rain we had, it would seem unlikely. Which way did she go, guys? Which way did she go?"

"A straight run and back would put her near West Point if they were heading upstate," Waverly theorized. "Then again, they could have headed out to Jersey."

"I took an uneventful trip out to the end of the North Fork last spring to interview the half sister, Beth Tracy," York offered. "Mileage would basically work for either Fork; from Hicksville to Orient Point and home, or Hicksville to Montauk and back."

"Mrs. Alfold said Ilona loved the shore. We've got people covering the areas along the parking fields at Jones Beach. Christ, she could be anywhere. She could turn up in Newark, God forbid," Waverly half-kidded.

The three detectives batted facts and speculation back and forth.

"At least we know she didn't book a ferry to Connecticut."

"That's not to say she couldn't wash up on that shore."

"Maybe Jeffrey just told her the country in case she slipped and said something to someone. Jeff meets Ilona Friday night and switches gears. Changes the game plan. Man thinks ahead. Like that thermostat business you told me about, Tim," York said.

"I guess we should be thankful he didn't mess with the odometer. For whatever that's worth," Sosan said with a sigh.

"Too bad we didn't know about this paper right away instead of after mid-winter recess," Waverly complained, holding up a copy of Ilona's class assignment.

"Let's count our blessings we've got it at all. It establishes a connection. Nothing that would hold up in court, of course, but coupled with Jason's comments and Janos Alfold's statements about his daughter's behavior whenever Jeff was in the store tells us that there was more than just a passing interest on Ilona's part."

"Yeah, but Kevin Casey will argue that Jeff was told to stay away from the store and apparently does because her father never saw him after that," York stated.

"I say Jeff was in that store and met Ilona when he knew the old man was away. The James woman comes in who could later identify him. Maybe she catches them fooling around or something. He follows Roselyn James home and whacks her. My feeling is that Jeff planned on killing Ilona and wanted no witnesses around who saw them together."

"Suppose ten people happened into the store and saw him. He's going to kill all ten, Bill?" Sosan said, playing devil's advocate.

Bill Waverly shook his head. "It was around closing time. Six p.m. Place doesn't get a lot of traffic at that hour. James woman walks in. She sees something, I'm telling you."

"*Neither* parent has seen him in their store since the time Janos Alfold told Jeff to take a hike. And they didn't recognize the woman as a customer. Besides, there's nothing in her refrigerator or pantry that puts her there. We got *ogots*," Sosan concluded, grabbing his crotch for effect before leaning back in the chair.

"I think Jeffrey took whatever she might have bought in the store the hell out of her apartment after he killed her," Waverly insisted. "Hell, if he's thinking clearly enough to turn the thermostat up to ninety, for cryin' out loud, he's not going to leave a link like that in a chain of evidence for us to follow. Whatever Roselyn James bought in that beverage store, Jeff got rid of, I'm telling you."

"Another thing," Sosan threw out for consideration. "The James woman was killed sometime late Thursday afternoon. Ilona didn't cut out of town till Friday night. It's not like Roselyn James was the last person to see her."

Waverly looked to York for support. "Is my partner thick, or what? What I'm saying, Tim, is that the James woman was the last person to see Ilona with *Jeffrey Mills* before they went away the following day. We're talkin' a good twenty-four hours before Ilona signed out that car."

"Car's clean, Bill."

"I know, Tim. So was James' apartment, except for the carpet fibers and especially those questionable cat hairs. I can't understand why it's taking Walter Weber's team so damn long."

"Because DNA comparisons on cat hairs is a relatively new science," York clarified. "And because of that, a good defense attorney like Kevin Casey will certainly try and create a reasonable doubt in a jury's mind. Even if we do have a match."

"If only we had gotten into Jeffrey's apartment for a look-see while he was in our custody and we had his keys, we might have found something," Sosan said.

Gary shook his head. "You'd have found nothing; just as you'll find nothing if and when you do find Ilona. Find her dead, I'm afraid. After ten days she's not going to pop up and tell us she ran off and got married because her father's one strict son of a bitch."

Tim Sosan nodded in agreement. "If we only had this information earlier and gotten the cooperation we needed, that is, authorization and manpower, and went through every Dumpster in a radius of eighty miles, every recycling plant and garbage dump in the area, looked under every rock, we'd have found her. And you're probably right, Gary. We probably wouldn't have any more than we have right now. Jeffrey Mills is by no means a genius. What he is, is smart. Smart enough to have you Suffolk County boys think that his brother, Howard, committed those five murders. And believe me, there are more bodies out there. Many more. No, gentlemen. Howard Mills did not kill those women. You guys rushed to judgment back there in Suffolk County. Oh, he dismembered those bodies like he said. And as far as I'm concerned, he deserves whatever a jury decides. Sick or not sick, Howard Mills is simply better off dead or locked away for good. And that's exactly what Jeffrey wants. He knew you'd hang his brother's ass. He helped set him up."

"Gotta ask you at this point, Gary. Do you think Jeffrey Mills killed all those girls?"

"I really can't say for sure, Bill. Like I said, I had a few questions for their half sister, Beth Tracy. Disappeared without a trace. Her rent's been paid on the condo through March. Maybe she'll surface soon."

"What does your gut tell you about this case, Gary?" Sosan questioned.

Gary York smirked. "That no matter who killed those girls, Howard Mills is going to take the fall. Too much time and money invested for it to go any other way. *Mucho* millions."

"Think the jury will convict?"

"Slam dunk. Can't not. Evidence is overwhelming."

Sosan nodded. "Death penalty? Your gut notion, Gary."

"Never know. But if I had to bet, I'd bet the jury will vote for the needle over lockin' 'im up and throwing away the key."

"Really think Jeff killed Roselyn James?" is all Bill Waverly really wanted to hear for now.

"I do."

"You see, I told you he was on the same page, Tim. So, you truly think he took out Ilona, too? And I don't mean for just a date."

"I think he's a very sick puppy with a cat. I also think he may have purposely planted those cat hairs and orange fibers Walter Weber found in James' apartment."

"What?" Waverly asked quite skeptically.

Sosan held his tongue.

"It's the way his mind works," Gary York explained. "He'll throw you a little bone so you won't take a big bite out of him. He'll take a little heat so that you don't wind up burning him altogether, like he did with his brother, admitting to helping Howard dispose of the bodies right off the bat. No pun intended. His lawyer tells him to keep his trap shut and then walks out of our building. Just like that. Jeff's mouthpiece wasn't with him five minutes. That's it. Believe that? Had to be in court, or so he said. Jeff couldn't wait to tell Mick Connolly what his involvement was."

"Still a serious charge. He should have gotten several years," Sosan said.

"Normally, yes. But there's nothing normal about this case. All the D.A. wanted was a warm body to offer up to the god in Albany. First death penalty case on Long Island in twenty-one years. Patterson will leave the D.A.'s office in a trail of glory. His son steps in as a young judge to finish the chapter. That's the way daddy wrote it. The script is set in stone. They don't want Jeffrey for those murders. He cooperated. They've got their scapegoat. The scuttlebutt is that there's a family fortune sitting in an offshore bank. Another rumor has it that an even greater fortune is locked up in some Central and South American concerns. A huge fortune, in fact. Jeff is trying to convince Howard to turn everything over to him immediately if not sooner, or at least make him beneficiary. Then all Jeff has to do to collect is survive his brother, Howard."

"And what if Howard receives life in prison—no parole? What about the appeals? That could go on for a decade. The state's not going to kill Howard overnight. Could be a long time before Jeff collects a dime."

"Good point, Tim. And what I can tell you is this. With the kind of money that's at stake, arrangements could be made where Jeff would borrow against that prospective fortune today and pay the piper tomorrow, at exorbitant interest rates to be deducted from the principle at such time, rest assured. I have it on good authority it's a gamble that a certain Columbian cartel is willing to take. That's Jeff's worst case scenario. However, if he can convince Howard to sign over the estate, Jeff's hit a home run. Howard never touched a nickel of that money in over twenty years, and the estate has grown exponentially. From what my sources tell me, we're talking tens of millions, conservatively."

"Jesus."

"So why would Jeff risk fucking things up with Roselyn James and Ilona Alfold?" Waverly questioned more to himself, although they all knew at least part of the answer to that question. Sick is sick and you let it go at that. The rest was for psychiatrists and psychologists to explore.

Gary York answered straightaway. "Our boy just has to kill, is all."

Bill Waverly and Tim Sosan nodded in silent agreement.

"Once again, Gary, what about these cat hairs and carpet fibers you say he may have *planted* for our benefit?" Waverly questioned anew. "We're talking a murder charge. I don't know if I buy into what you're selling here. Why would he do that?"

"To show you that he's in control. As you said, he's no genius, but he believes he knows enough about trace evidence to keep you on your toes. There's that pet shop near the beverage store. Puppy mill and cats galore. Inside, they've got one of those scratching posts for cats. Guess what the board is covered with?"

"Orange polyester carpeting," Tim Sosan answered quietly.

"Correct. He made you guys look bad when you learned that the original orange carpet was pulled up from his old residence, laid down in his new apartment, then replaced with new carpeting. You'll soon learn, I'd wager, that the cat hairs Walt found, although gray and brown, will not be a match to Orbit's. Not even close."

"Can't we just bug his fucking place? 'Cause I know he's telling all this business to his cat," Waverly blew.

York smiled. "I'll bet you dollars to doughnuts Jeff took precautions to be on the safe side and to drive you guys crazy. He probably showered at a place other than his own apartment or Katlyn Land's as a precautionary measure after killing Roselyn James, then discarded the clothes and shoes he wore. Then he planted those hairs from a cat of similar color to Orbit, along with those orange carpet fibers. And when forensics came back negative on those orange carpet fibers, I'm sure you had more than Kevin Casey warning you to keep your distance. I'll bet you got some flack from your lieutenant. Correct?"

"Got a real good ass-chewing," Sosan conceded.

York nodded. "Got mine chomped when I started delving deeper into Beth Tracy. I'm telling you this business is in the hands of the politicians now. Not the police, per se. If you understand that, you'll make it through your twenty and get the hell out."

"Before I do, I'm gonna nail this guy," Waverly swore. "You're not just gonna look the other way, are you, Gary? You gonna keep diggin'? You're not gonna stop and bury your head in the sand, are you, pal?"

"Why don't you let him answer?" Sosan suggested.

"He's too fuckin' stubborn to let this thing go," Bill Waverly insisted. "I can see it in his eyes."

York smiled. "I'm up to my ass in alligators on that high school student stabbing case back in Riverhead. Black on black."

"Ever use the N word?"

"Never."

"Not a fuckin' thing to worry about, Gary. Mark my words," Waverly joked.

Gary York laughed. It felt good to laugh again. It felt good to be around guys who understood . . . understood that there was a lot of garbage out there. But when your face got rubbed in it and your own people were standing with one foot on your neck, it was time to let loose. He knew exactly how these two detectives felt.

"Ask you something, Gary?" the lead detective questioned.

"You can ask."

"Got a plan?"

"Probably better than the teachers' union," York quipped, "but not with the time off those slackers get."

Tim Sosan and Bill Waverly laughed heartily, then pulled their chairs closer to the table, leaning forward.

"Care to share?" Sosan pressed.

Gary York studied the two before he spoke. "Tell me all about this Katlyn Land."

"Thirty-eight, twenty-six, thirty-eight," Waverly said with a straight face.

York didn't crack a smile. "Tell me more."

"I believe she'd alibi a snake," Sosan said emphatically. "Comes from a good family. Solid. Old money."

"What's she doing living in Hicksville and working for the post office?"

"Asserting her independence, although I think her parents laid down some ultimatums. Spoiled brat rich kid. Always got everything she wanted. Mommy and daddy finally saw the light and booted her ass out sometime ago. Yet, Katlyn has some serious funds and has supported Jeffrey's spending habits, including his legal fees."

"She got a sister?" Gary half joked.

— Book III —

March 4, 1999
5:20 p.m.

Chapter Forty-Eight

It was late Thursday afternoon when the Suffolk County jury arrived at a unanimous decision and found Howard Mills guilty of one count of first-degree murder and two counts of second-degree murder for the bludgeoning deaths and dismembering of three women. Howard sat at the defense table, expressionless, as the verdict was read.

Jeffrey was ecstatic, having heard the report on the six o'clock news. Now that Howard's life was virtually over, it would prove easier for Jeff to convince Howard to relinquish his holdings, or so Jeff hoped. He and Katlyn celebrated with champagne and his favorite ale. Phase one was over. Phase two—the penalty phase—would be the jury's decision to either sentence Howard to life in prison without the possibility of parole or death by lethal injection, the latter being the worst case scenario, for a decade of uncertainty would prove unsettling. In that event, Jeff wished he could be the one to make-ready the plunger and other paraphernalia if only to ensure the death benefit clause firsthand. Zing went the strings of his heart. He was happy, hopeful and horny.

Jeff handed Katlyn a strap-on dildo and disappeared into another room to change. She set the lights low, put on a Vivaldi tape, then got undressed.

Jeff's progress was slow and meticulous. A metamorphosis in the making. Jeff was evolving. He was practically pretty. A creature to behold. A songbird. A bird of prey. A contradiction in terms of itself. A silent note he held before putting on a padded bra then slipping into a white gingham nightgown and a pair of black and white spiked heels. *S/he* put on a brand-new wig, the precise color of Ilona's shoulder-length, light brown hair. Jeff had never seen Ilona in earrings, so the hermaphroditic figure brushed them aside, reaching for a contact lens case. *S/he* opened it and removed a pair of soft, tiny plastic disks, placing them over the cornea of each eye. Blue as the sea on a sunny day and about as bright. Brighter than Jeffrey's. *S/he* was ready. The transformation was complete. Ilona's ghost opened the door and emerged from the second bedroom, walking across the hall and into Katlyn's quarters, standing at the threshold of the dusky doorway.

"Wow!" Katlyn exclaimed. "You look positively wild. That really you?"

"It's still me, silly. I just put on a little weight."

"You look exactly like her."

"And unlike Beth, I can positively see."

Katlyn smiled. "Can you see this?"

"I can see that you have your hands full," *s/he* giggled girlishly. "Is that all for me?"

"Why don't you come on over here and see, up close, for yourself."

Ilona's look-alike stepped into the room.

"God, you're good. Her own parents would be convinced. I'm telling you, you look just like her."

"I am her, Katlyn. At least I am for tonight. Maybe tomorrow I'll be you."

"And I'm not Katlyn at this moment, either, *Ilona*. Can't you tell? At the moment, I'm Jeffrey Mills."

"I love you, *Jeffrey*," *Ilona* sounded, turning around and pulling the cotton nightgown up around *her* waist.

"I love you, too, *Ilona*."

"I'm so cold."

"Come close."

Ilona was shivering. "I'm a virgin," *s/he* whispered.

With one hand, Katlyn held *Ilona* down firmly upon the bed. With her other hand, Katlyn reached for an open tin of aromatic salve from the nightstand. "Shh," she said ever so softly. "Shh."

Chapter Forty-Nine

Nicholas Dunn seemed shaken over the jury's verdict. Just outside Judge Best's courtroom, Christopher Profeta's voice quavered as he spoke to reporters.

"We're not going to comment on the verdict. There is still a lot of work to be done at the next phase of this trial."

Jack Stetson, the father of Claudia Rose Stetson, aka Darla Vasco, shed tears of joy over the victory of the verdict. Detective Michael Connolly hugged the California resident and told him, "We're almost there."

Stetson told Robert Redler how he remembered his little girl sitting on a chair in back of him and running a comb through his hair . . . so many years ago it seemed that he felt it was in another lifetime.

Assistant District Attorney Gail Fox and her co-counsel, Elizabeth Presant, glowed as they glided from the courtroom. Gail took center stage in the hallway before the microphones and cameras.

"I'm very pleased with the verdict," the lead prosecutor announced. "We're now ready for the penalty phase."

Redler found it interesting that the jury foreman had sent a note to the judge just hours before announcing the verdict, requesting that their accommodations be changed as they were neither happy with the rooms in which they were sequestered, nor the meals being served in the restaurant. The judge had addressed the note and informed the jury that because of the voucher system, which the court was mandated to follow, he could not alter the procedure and accommodate their request. A nice way of saying that they were shit out of luck, Redler entertained. With a frown followed by a nod of reluctant acceptance, the foreman acknowledged the judge's instruction. Three hours later, the jury came in to read the verdict that should have begun with, *We, the jury, will positively be home for the weekend* . . . . But Redler would be the first to admit that he was a cynic, thereby, giving the jury the benefit of the doubt. Nevertheless, with tongue in cheek, Rob told *Newsday*'s staff writer, David Culver, that he expected tomorrow's headline to read, **Runaway Jury**.

Culver smiled but said nothing—as was his style.

F riday's headline on page three read: **Convicted of 3 Murders**, with a picture of Howard Mills adjacent to it.

The trial was scheduled to resume in the middle of the month, at which time jurors would hear further testimony from additional witnesses for the defense, relatives most likely, who would try and save Howard's life. The prosecution would, of course, challenge those folks, in essence by saying to the jury, 'So what? Howard Mills killed those women. He must pay with his life.' But first, Judge Best would interview the jurors to determine if they were still of an open mind and had not already decided in advance what sentence the defendant should receive before hearing *all* testimony in addition to closing arguments from both sides.

Rarely would a juror, after having invested months of his or her time, admit that their mind had, indeed, been made up befittingly beforehand. But better *that*, Redler entertained, than having it made up for them. Besides, having an on-board determination at that late juncture, so long as it wasn't voiced or recorded in stone before all testimony and arguments were heard, was healthy, the writer believed. It showed that one had weighed the evidence, drawn a conclusion for one's self at that particular point in time, and was now ready to weigh any mitigating factors against such evidence. But to declare one's mind a tabula rasa at the penultimate hour was ludicrous—certainly either delusional or downright dishonest. *Take your pick*, Redler contemplated. *That's our criminal justice system in a nutshell.*

As far as Redler was concerned, the prosecution did not prove its case. Oh, there was no question that blood from at least three women was found on the walls and floor and furnishings of that apartment at 42 Willow Lane in Hicksville. No question at all. The question was, did Howard Mills do the killing? Again, the prosecution did not prove that point conclusively in Redler's mind. Not beyond a reasonable doubt. Not even close. But what the prosecution did prove to Redler was that they had the perfect patsy. The fall guy for all seasons.

Chapter Fifty

On Sunday, March 7th, Howard Mills, tried to commit suicide in his jail cell. Judge Steven Best had issued a gag order, and the attempt was kept under wraps until reported in *Newsday* five days later. Howard Mills' brother, Ronald, had been notified earlier. Jeffrey Mills had not. Katlyn called Jeff at home with the news as she had been going through the morning paper at breakfast.

"Have you heard?" Katlyn asked, figuring he might not have, for Jeffrey had neither cable television nor a radio in his apartment. Too, she knew he didn't read the newspaper until she would hand him hers at the train station most mornings.

"Hear what?"

"About Howard." Her tone gave nothing away.

"What was I suppose to hear?" Jeff reckoned it was a problem with Howard's medication, for the defense had accused the prosecution of using its influence to persuade jail officials to take Howard off his Zoloft so that he would act irrational before the jury and bury any chance their client might have of receiving life in lieu of death if he flew off the handle or started climbing walls. *It was always something*, Jeffrey reflected.

"He tried to kill himself last Sunday."

Orbit was brushing past the leg of a table and came within an inch of Jeff's foot when suddenly the cat screeched and went flying across the room, hitting the far wall.

"What the hell was that?" Katlyn hollered into the receiver.

"What the fuck do you mean, *tried* to kill himself?" he blew. "How?"

"Oh, yeah. Like it comes as some sort of big surprise to you. He's been trying to do it since he was thirteen. Recall what you told me? Paper says he tried to cut his throat with a razor."

"That's bullshit. We're so fucking close," Jeff shouted angrily. "So fuckin' close, and they're gonna let him kill himself?"

"How does it work if he does?"

"How does what work?" Jeff asked, his mind a good thirty million dollars away.

"The inheritance; you as beneficiary if Howard commits suicide versus the state pulling the plug. How does that legal shit go down then?"

"If he commits suicide before I convince him to sign everything over to me, I'm shit out of luck. The estate goes to the state of New York. End of story."

"Well, if Howard's still mad at you, couldn't you convince him to sign everything over to your cat?" she toyed. "Better be good to Orbit, Jeffrey dear."

Jeff went into a sheer rage before he could speak again. " . . . I'm going to break your fucking neck when I see you. Understand me?"

"But you said you had this whole thing figured out."

"I didn't figure on this. He's supposed to be on suicide watch twenty-four hours a day. Especially since he has a history."

"Well, can you find out for sure what's going on from your guy?"

"Don't even think or talk that shit on the phone. All right?"

"Tap, tap, tap. Paranoid, paranoid, paranoid."

"Pick me the fuck up. Now!"

"It's still early, Jeff."

"So what the fuck you doin' up?"

"Apparently keeping you informed of what's going on. Aren't authorities supposed to call and let you know about something like this?"

"Probably called Ronald. Me, they tell shit."

"Howard's lawyers or Ronald wouldn't call you?"

"Well, Katydid. It's not exactly like Ronald and I are loving brothers. Dunn and Profeta kept me as far away from Howard as possible, implying to the jury that I'm the possible killer of those prostitutes. That was their defense. That was their strategy. And I had to tell the police what I had to tell them. So of course Howard's still mad. You gonna come and pick me up, or what?"

"Pick you up for what?"

"Breakfast."

"I'm having breakfast now."

"So you'll watch *me* fuckin' eat."

"I suppose you want me to bring you something."

"Coffee and a bagel."

"You want the paper?"

"I won't get the truth from the paper."

"Why not?"

"For starters, you don't try and kill yourself with a razor. They're safety razors. Specially designed. That's a bullshit story they're handing the press. Took them a week to figure out something to say."

"Says here that, '. . . after the correction officer seized the razor, Mills used his fingernails to cut his face and neck.' I guess he was trying to finish the job he started on his throat."

"You're not listening, Katie. You can't do anything lethal with those razors, I'm telling you. And attacking yourself with your fingernails is a lot like holding your breath to try and suffocate."

"So what do you think happened?"

"Either he got his hands on some pills, his favorite trick, or he tried to hang himself."

"You know who you better call."

"You better shut your fuckin' mouth."

"Tap, tap, tap. Paranoid, paranoid, paranoid," Katlyn repeated and giggled.

"I'm gonna tap your ass when you get over here, bitch."

"Like I did yours, Jeffrey?" Katlyn kept giggling.

"Fetch my fuckin' breakfast, bitch."

"Eat my dick," Katlyn howled with laughter.

Jeff hung up. "Stupid bitch."

Jeff was doing one-arm pushups when Katlyn arrived at the front door of the apartment with bagels, doughnuts, coffee, hot chocolate and a copy of *Newsday*. She tapped her foot against the door as her hands were full. Jeff took a good minute to answer.

"Tab, tap, tap," she teased, giving the door another little kick as he pulled it open.

"There is a fuckin' doorbell, dumbbell."

"You see my hands are full, asshole?"

"Then push it with your fucking Jew nose."

Katlyn marched into the room past Jeff, setting the items down on the Formica table off the alcove kitchen. As she turned, Jeff shot the heel of his hand hard against the side of her jaw. Katlyn's body hit the same wall as Orbit had a half hour earlier. Instantly, the young woman withdrew a weapon from beneath her coat: a cold, steel-blue aluminum receiver Colt MK IV/ Series 80 Commander (Lightweight). She held the pistol before Jeff's wide and angry eyes.

"I asked you to hold that piece for me. Not carry it around like a tampon."

"You fucking chauvinist pig."

"What are you going to do with that, Katie? Huh? Wake the neighborhood before ten o'clock?"

"Don't you ever call me a Jew, you skinny fag, or they'll be scraping your so-called brains off the fucking ceiling. And I wouldn't care if it was midnight or noontime. You understand?"

"I didn't *call* you a Jew, Ms. *Kike* Land. I said, push the bell with your fucking Jew nose. Now put that away before I get pissed and stick your head in that oven and set it to hi broil."

Katlyn pushed off the safety and cocked the hammer back completely. "Open your mouth, Jeff." Katlyn had the sights aligned between the mail handler's lips. She stood several feet away.

"I'm a Jew, too, you know," Jeff declared and scowled, showing his perfect teeth.

"Well . . . you don't treat me like a nice Jewish boy should," she frowned, holstering and securing the pistol with a leather strap. "You treat me mean, and I can have anything or anybody I want, I want you to know."

"You can't have this cock unless you beg," Jeff snapped, stepping forward while raising an open hand before her face.

Katlyn went to kick him in the crotch, but Jeff backhanded her across a cheek. She shook it off and laughed in his face. Jeff closed his other hand into a fist and delivered a powerful blow to her temple. Katlyn went down like a rock. Orbit ran from behind an overstuffed ottoman, disappearing around the couch.

"Don't you ever talk like that on the phone again. Don't flirt with fucking death, like Beth."

"See, I didn't even have to beg for your brutality, you bastard," Katlyn swore and laughed aloud. "You're really such a fucking wimp."

Jeffrey pulled her roughly to her feet, and the two embraced.

"Now serve me my fuckin' coffee, cunt."

Chapter Fifty-One

Late that evening, Jeff learned that his brother's suicide attempt was not life-threatening. Nothing could have been further from the truth. Although Howard had indeed been on around-the-clock suicide watch, he did manage to make a noose for himself by tying both ends of a long-sleeved flannel shirt about his neck, pulling and securing the end to a pant leg through the loop, then joining the other leg to the sleeve of his sweater. Climbing the iron-barred wall of his solitary cell, like a gibbon on a junglegym, Howard attached the other sleeve to a high, horizontal steel bar before he jumped. With tears of joy in his eyes, Howard hung there happily until a guard spotted the figure suspended near the ceiling, rushed in and summoned others. Collectively, they took Howard down from his quasi-makeshift gibbet. Shortly afterward, Howard Mills went into a blind rage, clawing and tearing at his face and throat with fingernails and a safety-razor. Howard was out of sorts, and it appeared as though the penalty phase of the trial was going to be delayed.

From that moment, Nicholas Dunn and Christopher Profeta had reported that their client was being most uncooperative; hence, the delay.

Two days later, Howard Mills had a visitor.

"Hello, Howie."

Howard was crying before he ever looked up and saw his younger brother, Ronald, seated across the dividing barrier.

Ronald Mills was crying, too. A thick Lucite block served as a window between their worlds. Ronald picked up the telephone receiver adjacent to the window and repeated his words, signaling for Howard to do the same.

"Hello, Howie. Please pick up," Ronald pleaded, gesturing with the phone.

Howard shook his head.

"I still love you," Ronald declared, holding the receiver out to his side, mouthing the words. "You're still my brother," he added loudly, his shoulders fluttering like a leaf caught in a steady wind. "I love you dearly," he swore and wept.

Howard couldn't bear to see his brother sitting there crying like that. He could hear the muffled moan.

"Why did you come?" Howard shouted, wiping away his tears with a swipe, but more kept coming. "Please go home," he whispered in the next breath.

Ronald couldn't hear him, but understood. He shook his head. "I love you, brother."

"I love you, Ronnie!" Howard blared.

And with that pronouncement, Howard started to strangle himself, both hands wrapped tightly about his neck, thumbs pressing solidly against the larynx, trying desperately to crush his trachea.

Stunned, Ronald watched his brother's face go from pale-white, to crimson, to blue before the visitor started smashing the receiver violently against the plastic block.

A corrections officer walked casually over to Howard as the prisoner suddenly dropped to the floor.

A security guard rushed over to Ronald, took the receiver from his hand, then escorted him quickly and quietly outside the area.

In the wake of Mills' suicide attempts, the penalty phase of the trial was delayed on three separate occasions. The jail-issued razor story—a safety implement that could only cut stubble and not one's throat—was the only account reported by the media. Robert Redler learned from a source what had actually transpired. The guard who was supposed to be watching Mills in solitary was busy doing something else at the time. When the correction officers had cut Howard down from the bars, the prisoner was down to his skivvies. What went unreported and covered up by administrative officials was particularly upsetting to Redler. He certainly didn't condone but completely understood their actions because of what had recently occurred in the neighboring county.

The Nassau County corrections facility was having their own share of problems concerning the recent death of an inmate that the administration chose to present as an accident, allegedly unrelated to the brutal beating the young man suffered at the hands of correction officers. Instead of treatment, the junkie received the jailers' own brand of medicine, dispensed as a result of the prisoner complaining too loudly and too often for his methadone. Hence, the Suffolk County facility would take whatever steps *it* could to keep bad publicity from reaching the doorstep of the People. The Suffolk matter would be handled internally.

Not surprisingly, Dunn and Profeta requested a new jury for their client, referencing the penalty phase, arguing that the well had been poisoned and that those looking down into it had become prejudiced because of the testimony given by Detective York concerning the two crimes for which their client had *not* been charged. The attorneys' contention, coupled to the horrendous photographs the prosecutors presented and that the judge allowed, depicting the dismembered women, served only to inflame the jury. Judge Best denied the defense's request.

In the interim, Howard had been interviewed by several state psychiatrists at the jail and also at Kirby Forensic Psychiatric Center on Wards Island off Manhattan. The doctors found him fit to continue with the proceedings. One psychiatrist for the defense saw it quite differently, of course. Dunn and Profeta announced that Mills was no longer cooperating with them whatsoever since his conviction and had attempted suicide on more than one occasion.

Quite frankly, Howard was stunned by the fact that the jury had found him guilty in less than eleven-and-a-half hours over a two-day period, believing that the jurors' unsatisfactory accommodations had, in large part, prompted the sudden verdict only hours after learning that Judge Best could not oblige the group with better meals and lodging. Pundits had seen potential problems with even more delays in the works, but on the fifteenth of April, six weeks after their client's conviction, Nicholas Dunn and Christopher Profeta sat on either side of Howard, who was reluctantly ready to continue with hearings, outside the presence of the jury.

A psychiatrist for the state had called Mills' action "a suicidal gesture." Profeta argued that the doctor breached ethical conduct as well as Howard's constitutional rights by using Mills' confidential file to their client's detriment. Judge Best wrangled with Profeta over case law, accusing the attorney of misleading the court. A hot half hour ensued. Best ruled Profeta's arguments irrelevant, telling the attorney to address the issue in appellate court. "The doctor's ethics are irrelevant as far as I'm concerned," the judge had said.

Another week of hearings between doctors and attorneys continued in order to help the judge decide whether or not Howard Mills was competent to proceed (although it was so settled in the arbiter's mind already, Redler firmly believed). Too much was at stake. Not necessarily a person's life, but time lost and millions of dollars spent to date at taxpayers' dollars with the clock still ticking away indifferently.

There was a lot of psychobabble presented by the state's doctors that really boiled down to the fact that their decision to declare Mills fit to continue was largely based on Howard's ability to correctly add two plus three and acknowledge that Bill Clinton was the President of the United States, furthered by the defendant's ability to recall three nouns presented in a much earlier evaluation: *an airport, a yellow apple*, and *Thomas Jefferson*—an evaluation that Howard had shared (prior to pretrial) with Jeffrey during a brief visit. In truth, Profeta and Dunn themselves had recalled but two of the three nouns and were arguing that point, which only helped to support the opposition. A joke or two was made during the hearing at Mills' expense, and Redler truly wondered if the entire business was a rigged game right from the start, consummate actors—each and every one—playing out a loose-lipped script. All but the defendant sat tight-lipped at the table, disgusted with the entire proceedings.

Putting such sport aside, the two defense attorneys suddenly turned serious, sending up a series of similes and metaphors like columns of smoke.

"Your Honor, Howard has crashed. He is like a baby seal on the ice, letting the hunters club him," Profeta drew.

Claudia Rose Stetson's father's shoulders shuddered at the word *club*.

"He's like a vegetable," Dunn delivered. "This is not a human being sitting here. We are dealing with a truly crazy man who will not help us help him. His depression is so severe that he is incapable of helping us save his life."

Of course, Howard *was* suffering from severe depression, Robert Redler frowned, for the two defense attorneys had just figuratively clubbed their own client but a moment before. Robert Redler felt sad. But not for one second did the writer forget about Mills' victims. Rob's sadness was more affected by the system itself rather than any one individual. That certainly had been evident in the writer's article published in *The Southampton Press*, strongly suggesting that the police audiotape and videotape suspects' alleged confessions. Soon it would be time for the author to write another.

One week later, Judge Best ruled that the defendant was mentally competent to proceed. Fit as a fiddle, in fact. On Thursday, April 22nd, seven weeks after Howard's conviction, twenty-two jurors once again returned to court. And, yes, they remained open-minded and had not yet sealed the defendant's fate is what, in essence, each juror told the judge. The jury would ultimately decide—after listening to further testimony from witnesses who would be called by the defense in order to try and save a man's life—as to whether Howard W. Mills would live out the rest of his natural life in a cell the approximate size of a Ping-Pong table, or be laid to rest for all eternity via a lethal fluid injected into a vein. But if the twelve men and women of the jury could not *unanimously* decide Mills' fate, the Honorable Judge Steven C. Best would be given the honor.

On Sunday, April 25th, Jack Stetson traveled into Nassau County to attend the ninth annual Candlelight Vigil of the Long Island Chapter of Parents of Murdered Children and Other Survivors of Homicide Victims, which was held at the Temple of Israel in Lawrence. A rabbi spoke at the nonsectarian meeting, drawing an analogy between the shattered lives of its victims and a shard of glass in the sea: "In the beginning, the glass cuts deeply," he stated, "but over time the edges dull. They can no longer open a wound, but the edge was not supposed to be there, for the glass was meant to remain intact. There is a wound, but over time it doesn't hurt as much, yet it is always there," he finalized.

That Monday, Jack Stetson was back in court listening to the whispered words of wisdom from Gail Fox, who warned him not to react vocally or visually to any testimony by Mills' relatives as Dunn and Profeta would ask to have him removed. Fuming at that instruction and questioning his rights, Jack sat quietly by and listened to Ronald

Mills' plea to save his brother's life. Later, in an interview, Jack Stetson told Robert Redler that he was moved by the brother's words, that he felt sorry for the families involved, but that he wanted to see Howard Mills dead.

Ronald Mills' love for his brother was "unconditional," the witness had said through a letter he had written on Howard's forty-second birthday, two weeks before the arrest, trying to restore their childhood relationship. Jack Stetson's hatred of Howard, too, was unconditional. Ironically, Ronald and Jack had been looking to repair relationships with loved ones. For Jack, it was too late. His daughter was dead. Ronald Mills had read from his heartfelt letter, then spent the rest of the afternoon talking about Howard's horrific childhood. Outside the courtroom, Stetson told *Newsday*'s David Culver, in brief, about his own childhood:

"My own mother left me when I was four, and my father died an alcoholic. I was beaten as I child. But somewhere along the line, I learned right from wrong."

Over the next few days, testimony was heard from Howard Mills' relatives, a co-worker/friend, and acquaintances.

Relatives spoke mostly about the mother's neglect.

The co-worker/friend talked about the time Howard had come to her defense when two male postal employees were sexually harassing her and using profanity.

A female administrator of the medical unit at the correction facility who was acquainted with Howard testified that he'd been to her office several times, unescorted, unshackled, unhandcuffed, and posed no threat. She said that she felt at ease around him.

The commanding officer of internal security at the jail testified that not once in three years since Mills' confinement had the prisoner been written up for a single infraction.

Dunn and Profeta hoped that such positive testimony given by jail personnel would pave the way and instill confidence in the jury as exhibited by the former first deputy commissioner of the New York State Department of Correctional Services, whose opinion it was that Howard W. Mills would be a model prisoner.

Another gentleman, the former state commissioner of corrections, seconded that endorsement, elaborating on the exiguous living conditions that Mills would likely experience if sent to a maximum security prison instead of a grave.

Last but not least, on the 5th of May, the jury was given the arduous task of deciding whether Howard Mills would lead a rather harsh existence in an upstate prison, working long hours each day before returning to a rectangular cell only ten percent larger than a table tennis board, furnished with a combination toilet-sink, a metal bed welded to a wall, and a small writing table, versus a six-foot deep rectangular hole in the ground for all eternity.

Still and all, the jurors first had to juxtapose the mitigating factors, that is, Howard's direful life, against the aggravating factors, meaning the fashion in which he (as it was now determined) murdered his victims. Jurors were then to run those elements through their own minds both individually as well as collectively for consideration, further calibrating particular components such as the significance of postmortem dismemberment, to which the Court remained mute in its instruction in categorizing the particular aspect of *similar fashion* as an aggravator for which Mills might receive the death penalty.

Wow!

It became abundantly clear to Redler that a simple weighing of factors upon a scale was not the instrument of consideration at all. Firstly, there was nothing simple about weighing over two dozen mitigators alone, aggravators notwithstanding. Secondly, it wasn't a question for untrained minds to even consider if they were truly to work within the guidelines set by the Court, for the problem was not in its complexity but rather in its impossibility because the brainpower required to reckon and render an impartial decision would have to be on the order of IBM's super chess computer, Deep Blue. Only a sophisticated processor, not a lay lamebrain, would do, Redler had decided for himself.

Profeta put it aptly when he apprised Judge Best that, "those kinds of mental gymnastics are impossible to make," referring not only to the jury's task at hand, but more specifically to what would be withheld from them prior to deliberation.

Redler saw the whole Mills business as a most complex case. Too intricate to be put into the hands of laypersons. Too many facets. Too many variables made complicated by a system that insisted on seeing itself and have others view it as fair, just, and, consequently, civilized. Robert Redler believed that all America, let alone the courts, was going to one day civilize itself into a primitive state of semiconsciousness, if it hadn't already. There were solutions. Much simpler solutions. But that would be for another article and another time, the writer ruminated.

For the time being, the lay jury—in lieu of professional jurors— would just have to do the best it could with what it had. It would first have to decide individually what those mitigators were and what weight to attach to each. Collectively, its members would have to agree that the aggravator(s) outweighed the mitigators before they could consider death. If no agreement could be reached unanimously in that regard, the jury must opt to spare the defendant's life. In inverting the elements, that is, if the jury felt that the mitigators outweighed the aggravators, a vote could still be taken to save Mills' life. Only in the event that unanimity could not be established with respect to a sentence of life or death would Judge Best hand down a ruling: a minimum of twenty years to life; a maximum of fifty years to life. Best declared that he would inform the jury regarding such an outcome. That announcement became another bone of contention for Profeta, who pointed out that such an advisement would prompt the jury to decree a sentence of death for their client.

The following day, Christopher Profeta gave a persuasive and poignant closing argument before twenty-two jurors. With tears in his eyes, he spoke of Howard Mills' childhood in comparison to his own Catholic upbringing and the nurturing he received from his stepmother; the breaks in life he had gotten; those that Howard had not. He spoke about Howard's years of mental illness, his neglectful mother and her psychological disorder and depression. He spoke about the suicide of Leonard Mills and the pronounced affect that the event had and still has on Howard Mills' life. And then the attorney took a profound breath before continuing.

"This crime cannot be excused by the arguments I make to you. This crime cannot be justified. This is about whether there is an absolute necessity for the taking of a human life." Christopher Profeta spoke softly and slowly, pausing between each sentence so that the mini messages would sink in. "This is about whether justice can be tempered with mercy. Sparing Howard Mills' life is not the same as forgiving him for what he did," the attorney said.

Not having lost sight of the fact that the accused stood convicted, Robert Redler sat somewhat confused as to the reason why Profeta now spoke in condemnation of his client, even though Mills had, did, and would maintain his innocence. It was the reinforcement of Profeta's nullifying rhetoric that troubled Redler. Phrases such as, "This crime cannot be *excused*," or, "This crime cannot be *justified*," or words like "*sparing*" versus "*forgiving him*." It was tantamount to saying, 'You're right. Our client **is** guilty.'

"But let us not dispose of one of God's children," Christopher Profeta declared. "I believe he has a soul. I believe he is redeemable. Howard Mills will still be punished severely for what he did."

And when Profeta finished with his emotionally charged and painfully paced monologue, the prosecutor moved into her own. In no uncertain terms did Gail Fox excuse pure evil, damning Mills for the brutal bludgeoning deaths of Jane Doe/Medford, Danielle Louise Clarke and Claudia Rose Stetson, reminding the men and women seated in the box of judgment of the victims' dismemberment and demeaning disposal, demanding that the members of the jury do their civic duty and discard society's trash. Fox's form of justice was tempered with hate. A hate for Howard W. Mills and for what he had done.

"To allow somebody who has intentionally killed three people to walk this earth is unjust," Fox put forth deliberately. "You know that death is not only appropriate, it is the only just penalty for what this defendant did. To ask for anything less than the death penalty under these circumstances would be defending the undefendable, excusing the inexcusable, forgiving the unforgivable, justifying the unjustifiable. These were disposable human beings to this defendant. Pick them up. Beat them up. Cut them up. And throw them away forever. May God damn Howard Mills for all eternity," Fox concluded in her cheerless closing prayer.

A few minutes later, at 12 p.m. sharp, the jury left to deliberate.

Just outside the courtroom, all cameras and microphones were pointed at Jack Stetson as Gail Fox and Elizabeth Presant had no comment. Dunn and Profeta were still inside. Brushing aside his tears, Jack Stetson said what he had to say.

"I just wish I had the opportunity to plead for my daughter's life. If I could have gotten her life without parole, I would have gotten her life without parole. And if Howard Mills does get the death penalty, they won't chop him up and throw him on a garbage heap."

Three hours later, the jury returned with their verdict. The jury foreman stood and read from a sheet of paper: "We, the members of the jury, individually and unanimously, sentence the defendant to death."

Simultaneously, and most ironically, Stetson and Mills signaled their sensation with clenched fists: Howard's, symbolizing the agony of defeat; Jack's, the ecstasy of victory.

Chapter Fifty-Two

In a dimly lit corner of a small, seedy bar in Greenport, two men sat at a table opposite one another. The taller of the two held an inch of whiskey in a water-spotted glass. The other man took a sip from a green bottle of cheap warm ale. The late hour had little to do with their quiet conversation, for the establishment was closed. Closed to the public, indefinitely. Closed by the Board of Health. Closed by the building and fire inspectors by order of the Court. Jeffrey Mills felt relatively safe.

"Wish they kept some Grolsch back there," Jeff said.

"You could wish your life away," Detective Vic Posteraro remarked.

"I can't believe they came in with a verdict so fast."

"The evidence was overwhelming. They had to say to themselves, then probably each other, 'Enough's, enough. We've been at this far too long. Let's take our lives back. Let's get this over with once and for all.'"

"Still, I thought they'd take the weekend for appearance sake. Or at least stay Thursday night into Friday."

Vic sipped his whiskey then shook his head. "Their last three or so hours were like their last four months. Being sequestered for even a single night seemed an eternity to them, probably feeling like prisoners themselves. They wanted out. Not another night. Certainly not the weekend away from family and friends. Believe me."

"Well, you called it, Vic. I'm just surprised."

"It's not like they feel they didn't do their job. At that point, there was really nothing to decide. They were of a single mind. Or at least most of them were. Maybe one or two needed a little prodding. Usually do. Then they quickly fall in line. It's not like Henry Fonda in *Twelve Angry Men*. At least not in Suffolk County, it's not," Vic said and laughed lightly. "Juries generally take their job pretty seriously. In this case, most of the members had their minds made up a long time ago. DNA did it for them. Slam, dunk. So why dwell over the issue of life or death? The brutality of the acts blew any lingering doubts away. And then there was the real motivator to move them into action and get them home for the weekend."

Jeff looked puzzled. "Motivator?"

Vic nodded. "Sunday is Mother's Day, Jeff. Or did you forget?"

Jeff laughed long and hard, finally taking a long pull on his ale before smacking the bottom of the bottle upon the chipped Formica tabletop.

Vic smiled. "You did forget."

Jeff continued laughing. "Well, I may have forgotten Sunday is Mother's Day, but I sure as hell haven't forgotten dear ol' Mom and all her money, may she rot in hell." He raised his brew toward Vic's whiskey.

The detective clinked the bottom of his glass against the neck of Jeff's bottle. His partner in crime. "I'd say by this time next year you could be celebrating Son's Day," Posteraro posited.

Jeff liked that idea a lot. "But first I'll have to declare it!" he exclaimed, pondering the proposition as if half serious. "Then the year after that, I'll declare Daughter's Day," he added and giggled girlishly, "to honor *all* loving children."

The gleam in Jeffrey's eyes made the cop uneasy. A lot of things made the detective uneasy of late.

"What about Katlyn?" Vic asked, cutting to the quick.

"Sleeping out there in the car. Feel bad that she has to go," Jeffrey said so sadly, solemnly returning his thoughts back to the business at hand.

"Do her quickly and quietly. You're not dealing in the dark anymore. They're onto you. Watching you like a hawk."

"Well, I can assure you that no one followed me here if that's what you're worried about."

Vic shook his head. "No, Jeff. *I* can assure *you*. You can assure me nothing but fifty percent, partner. I told you not to involve her from the beginning. She's positively nuts. You're nuts for having told her anything."

"She is . . . was my soul mate."

"You were a fool. You trust no one."

"I have to trust you," Jeff confided.

"There, you have no choice. And up to a point, I'm trusting you, too. It's a small but necessary risk I have to take. But you increase that risk when you party and fuck around with dames like that. You keep your mouth shut and your killing urge in check until the real check clears. Got it?"

"Maybe *you* can take care of Katydid for me?" Jeff toyed.

"No, you're going to squash that bug all by yourself. After that, you're on your own."

"I'm on my own now. No?"

Vic reached down for the case next to him. "With just a little bit of help to help you pull this off." The detective opened the case and took out a medium-sized plastic box covered with lots of little holes, setting the item upon the table between them.

"What's in that?"

"Mostly maggot larvae."

Jeff moved back in his chair. "What the hell do we need maggot larvae for?"

"*You* need them, not me. Now, let's go over the times again. You leave Hicksville for Southold at eleven a.m. You put your so-called soul mate out of her misery up there on Soundview Avenue, like we planned. Half past noon. You know the wooded lot. Do her any way you like. But then I want you to give her a good slice, deep in her belly. A nice long cut. It's going to be very warm later. Set her body out in the sun. Naked. Not in the shade. Not underneath a tree or anything that might create a shadow later on. You pull her to that field. Then I want you to open this case, take out the box and containers. Dump the contents of the smaller container of larvae all around her abdomen and let nature take its course. In the larger container, you'll find some beetles and other bugs. You'll empty them in her hair. But first—" Vic waited for Jeff to expound on earlier instructions the two of them had rehearsed.

"You'll have someone call the Southold Police Department at eight a.m. sharp, saying a girl was heard screaming for her life. The caller hangs up."

"But has given the wrong location, sending the police a mile to the south," Vic elaborated.

"That is, if they even bother checking."

"The point being that the call's recorded. At two p.m., an hysterical caller will say that a woman's body was discovered in a field off the wood lot. Gives the exact location. Doesn't want to get involved. Hangs up. You're back home in Hicksville by then."

"Just back up a bit. What's with the insects?"

"It's all about establishing time of death. I'm giving you the perfect alibi."

"Cool."

"Just make damn sure that several people who can identify you see you in Hicksville before eight a.m., and then again around eleven a.m. before you leave for Southold. Make a scene in front of one or two witnesses so that they'll remember you. Anything so they won't forget. Got all that?"

"Got it. Tell me more about this bug business." Jeff seemed fascinated.

"Really want to know about this stuff?"

"I'm broadening my horizon, my man. I like to know a lot about a lot of things."

Vic smiled. "Well, depending on ambient temperature, weather conditions, humidity, et cetera, et cetera, forensics experts can accurately determine PMI; postmortem interval. When someone dies, there are chemical changes that take place in the body almost immediately, and insects pick up on that right away. Flies. Beetles. Creepy-crawlies. It will appear as though Katlyn was killed during the first instar, meaning the initial period of postembryonic larvae growth; that is, within the three-hour window when you are seen in Hicksville."

"Got you."

Vic finished his shot of whiskey.

Jeff took the last swallow of ale before getting up to grab another bottle.

Vic took hold of Jeff's wrist. "One's enough. You've got a job to do."

"What are you, my keeper?"

"Might be if you lose your head. Want to spend some more time in that eight-by-eight answering a million questions like your brother did?"

Jeff laughed. "Well, you ain't working Suffolk County any longer, partner."

"That's right. Nobody there to protect your ass. You'd probably draw Connolly or York."

"Lovely boys. Where did those two go to cop school? Probably attended some Nazi summer camp as teenagers."

Vic wore a serious face. "Two smart detectives. Believe me, Jeff. That's why we have to stay a step ahead," he said, tapping the plastic container before pushing it across the table.

Jeff took hold of the box. "Feels cool."

"Packed with Dry Ice, gel and certain chemicals to preserve the larvae and retard odor."

Jeff nodded his understanding. "But why'd you pick the Southold area and police?" Jeff asked, studying the box like it was a Rubik's Cube.

"One of their boys took a forensics entomology course at Penn State last May. Learned how to collect the critters. Preserve them. Stuff like that. He's got the duty this afternoon. Just dying to use his newfound knowledge, I'd bet."

"Tell me more about this forensics stuff," Jeff pressed.

"Well, considering the forecast, about a quarter hour after you put Katlyn to rest, flies will start to gather and lay their eggs. A few hours later, larval matter will form. We're just jump-starting the process. Making it seem as though she was killed while you were back in Hicksville. Like I said, you've got yourself a three-hour window; eleven to two," the detective repeated. "You'll be back in Hicksville around two, two-thirty. It will appear as though those critters had been crawling around Katlyn's body since early morning. Be sure to stay within the speed limit. You don't want to get pulled over with this case."

"Gotcha."

"You'll dump it along with Katlyn's clothing, the paper jumpsuit, hat and nitrile gloves I gave you."

"Dumpster at the old Boy Scout Camp in Southold, on my way home."

"Right."

Katlyn stirred the moment Jeff slammed down the trunk.

"How did it go in there?" she yawned as Jeff climbed behind the wheel.

"Like clockwork."

She yawned again and stretched. "What time is it?"

"It's after midnight," Jeff noted, realizing that his Katydid had twelve hours left to live. He looked at her strangely.

"What?" she questioned.

"Nothing."

Jeff received a good punch in the arm. "Ow!"

"Don't tell me *nothing*," she chided.

"It's a surprise," he offered, turning over the engine and pulling out slowly into the pitch-black night before putting on his high beams.

"I want to know, now!" she demanded, hitting the heel of her hand hard against the top of his shoulder.

"Hey! That hurt."

"Better tell me," she warned.

"Okay, okay. We're going on a field trip in the morning."

"It is morning. A field trip?"

"Uh-huh."

"How early?"

"Eleven o'clock sharp. You pick me up."

"Where are we going?"

"The woods."

"Where in the woods?"

"Grandma's house."

Katlyn laughed. "Be serious."

"Around you?"

"I'm a very serious person, Jeff."

"Uh-huh."

"I am."

Jeff said nothing.

"What kind of field trip and why?"

"Bug collection, because they're there."

"Bugs?"

"Yes, bugs. Insects. We're going to experience nature and all its splendor. Study the little bastards. See what makes them tick."

"Speaking of ticks, the woods are full of them. I don't want to get Lyme disease."

"Then wear a light-colored long-sleeved shirt and pants so you can spot them. You'll be fine."

"Yeah, right. What woods?"

"You're beginning to bug me, Katydid."

"But I'm still your little grasshopper, aren't I?"

"Till the very end," Jeff swore.

"Ah, so sweet. So, where?"

"Southold."

"Southold?"

"That's what I said."

"That's right near here."

"Yep."

"But why come back out this way again? We got woods closer to home."

"What's the matter? Don't you like it out East?"

"Not especially. Give me bricks and concrete and I'm in my element. You know that I'm a city girl at heart."

"In a few hours, you'll be my Sunday kind of girl."

"It is Sunday." She poked him hard in the ribcage.

"Stop that."

Katlyn laughed.

"If you like the city so much, why did you pick the suburbs?" Jeff asked, heading back west on Route 25, switching to low beams.

"Spite."

"Whattaya mean?"

"Wanted to be far enough away from dear ol' Mom and Dad so they couldn't *bug* me. Get it?"

"Why Hicksville?"

"Just to see the expression on all their faces when they had to finally tell my grandparents." Katlyn giggled. "'Hicksville?' Grandma and Granddad had said rather affectedly, disbelieving their ancient ears. 'Our granddaughter is residing in Hicksville? Good Lord.' And all my newfound friends in Hicksville wanted to know where TriBeCa is. 'TriBeCa?' they questioned, putting on a perplexed look. 'Where or what in the fuckin' world is that?' they'd ask. 'Trendy little place in Greenwich Village,' I'd tell them, 'where you can get a cup of java, a blintze, and *The New York Times* at two in the morning.' They'd look at you like you had three heads. They know of the Village, or think they do. They have a mental picture of a bunch of beatniks, hippies and sugarplum fairies from the sixties."

"Just don't pull any kind of crap and tell me later that you went to visit your mom on Mother's Day. You pick me up at eleven o'clock sharp. Hear me?"

"Fine. Now tell me why we're really going to the woods."

"Picnic."

"Really?" Katlyn said excitedly.

"Really."

"Just the two of us?"

"You and me."

"Are you gonna fuck me in the forest?" she asked coyly.

"Gonna fuck you real good."

"Alone? None of our funky friends?"

"None of our funky friends."

Katlyn seemed pleased. "Why Southold? You didn't answer me that."

"We're going someplace special for dessert after our picnic."

"Where?"

"It's a surprise."

Katlyn made then raised a threatening fist.

"All right. Johnny's."

"Who's that?"

"Now you sound just like the people from Hicksville you were making fun of."

Jeff received another shot in the arm and the car swerved.

"Cut it out! There's a time and place for batting each other around."

"Tell me."

"It's a carhop kind of fifties place. Broads come out in short skirts and roller-skates."

"Are we gonna have ourselves an honest-to-goodness kind of date?" she asked, bouncing up and down on the seat like a little kid. "A picnic and a special place to go afterwards?"

"Yes, but now you ruined the surprise."

"Maybe I'll surprise *you*."

"How do you mean?"

"Maybe I'll pick you up wearing a miniskirt and roller skates."

"What about the ticks you're so fucking afraid of?"

"You can pick them off me one by one," she said happily. "How's that?"

"Just wear something that I can slip you out of easily."

"How about just roller-skates?"

"Perfect," he agreed with a laugh.

"Pick you up in front of the apartment at eleven a.m."

"Not the apartment."

"Then where?"

"Around the corner in back of 7-Eleven."

"Why there?"

"Vic says they're watching me like a hawk. Police don't need to know our business. I'll pick up some things there for the picnic. Enter through the front, exit through the rear, just in case they're on my tail. "

"I can do that on the way over. I don't mind."

"Just be there at eleven."

"You sure? It's a bit of a walk."

"Positive. Besides, I need the exercise."

"You're going to get a workout in the woods," she promised, reaching over and putting her hand on his crotch.

"So are you," he pledged. "So are you."

Chapter Fifty-Three

It was a pleasant Sunday morning with the mercury already approaching seventy degrees Fahrenheit. Janos Alfold entered his beverage store through the rear of the building and went behind the counter. It was 9 a.m. Sunday business hours were from noon till six. Normally, the merchant would not arrive until 11:30 to open and set up, but nothing had been normal for the distraught man and his hysterical wife since the middle of February when their darling daughter, Ilona, had suddenly and mysteriously disappeared. From that moment in time, the woman had sat home with a broken heart, refusing to leave the house, waiting by the telephone for a call from Ilona that would never come. In March, the Hungarian man had suffered a mild heart attack.

Stepping brazenly into and through the back of the beverage store, walking right up to the counter, Jeffrey Mills greeted the merchant. "Hi there, Mr. Alfold."

Janos Alfold's heart skipped more than just a beat as he swung around furiously. He wanted to smash and bloody Jeffrey's mouth. That was the man's first impulse. The second was to grab the gun he kept behind the counter and kill Jeffrey Mills on the spot. Alfold immediately came around the counter, heading for the front of the store, unlocking and throwing open wide the door. "Get out!"

"I beg your pardon."

"I know it was you," Janos Alfold said.

Jeff ignored the comment. "I just came by after what I thought was a decent period of time to personally tell you how sorry I am," he said, standing there with his hands in his pockets, staring down at his shoes.

"I know it was you," the man repeated.

"I'm sure you and your wife received my sympathy card, but I just wanted to let you know in person."

"I spit on your sympathy card, Jeffrey Mills. Like I want to spit on you." The man's face was filled with hatred and as red as the Red Dog beer poster hanging on the wall in back of him.

"Hey, Janos. You old goat," a burly customer called out from the threshold. "I don't want to hear, 'No beer before twelve o'clock,'" he kibitzed with his friend. "Your door's wide open, Janos."

"Maybe she just ran away from you," Jeff said in a low voice just loud enough for Janos Alfold to hear before the shopkeeper's friend stepped inside the store. Jeff shook his head sadly, still standing there looking down at his shoes. "I'm truly sorry, sir," he said politely at a level he knew that the husky patron heard. Jeff gave Janos Alfold a furtive little wink.

With both hands still in his pocket, Jeff was lifted off the floor by the owner and thrown against a pallet piled with cases of beer.

"I KNOW. I KNOW. I KNOW IT WAS YOU," the proprietor screamed at the top of his lungs. "YOU!"

The beefy customer took a second to collect his wits then swiftly stepped between Jeff and Janos. Jeff was picking himself off the floor as Janos lunged forward and met an immovable force.

"Janos! Stop it. What are you doing, man?"

"He killed my Ilona. He killed my little girl," Janos swore and wept. "He came here on Mother's Day to torment me. I *know.* He's sick like his brother, Howard Mills."

Jeffrey was shaking his head. "I came here to tell this gentleman how badly I feel. I sent the family a sympathy card three months ago, but I felt I should come here personally and see if anything was new—if the police heard anything—if there was anything I could do."

"He's a liar, Andy. Ilona trusted him. And now she's gone. He killed her. I know. The school knows. The police know. But they can't do anything because he's got a liar lying for him. He killed my baby. Look! You can see it in his eyes. He's evil. Let me go, Andy. Please." Janos Alfold was fighting to get away from his friend. Not to get at

Mills directly, but to get behind the counter where Janos had just placed his handgun. "Please. I have to go home to my wife this Mother's Day and share her grief. She hasn't stopped crying in three long months. Ilona was our only daughter. Our only child. Our very own flesh and blood. I want to give my wife a present. Instead of a bunch of roses, I want to give her that killer's head." Janos made a final attempt to break away. "He killed her, Andy," Janos Alfold swore and struggled.

Andy shook Janos to his senses. "Now stop! You don't know that she's dead." The husky man turned to Jeff. "You! You better get out of here. And don't come back. He don't need no more trouble, and neither do you."

"Yes, sir. I was only—"

"I said, get!"

Jeffrey was gone in a hot second, heading back toward the 7-Eleven for a second cup of coffee and bagel that morning. He had told the clerk earlier he'd left his wallet at home. Jeff had time to kill before Katlyn would arrive. Maybe he'd accidentally spill the container of coffee on the counter, insist on cleaning it up, apologize profusely, then hand the clerk a five-dollar tip for trusting him and for all the trouble he caused.

Oh, Jeffrey would have alibis galore.

Chapter Fifty-Four

Jeffrey and Katlyn parked in a secluded area near a marsh off Sound Avenue in Southold, then walked into the woods. It was a splendid day. The temperature was now in the mid-seventies, much to Jeff's liking. The woods were cool. Katlyn thought it was a perfect day. She wore loose-fitting white cotton pants with the bottoms tucked into ankle-high designer boots, a tight-fitting long-sleeved beige print top, which showed off her ample breasts. Katlyn topped her outfit off with an ostentatious, large-brimmed flowered hat.

"I'm perfectly happy today," Katlyn announced, taking Jeff's free hand and pulling him through a line of white and gray birch trees.

Jeff resisted, making her pull all the harder. "Think you know where you're going?"

"Come on, you. You promised me a picnic."

"I did. Indeed, I did."

"So, come on."

"No, this way." Jeff took the lead and pulled her to his right. "Grandma's house is this way, little girl."

Katlyn held on to her hat as they ran along a path. "Slow down. You trying to kill me, or what?"

"Let's go," Jeff insisted. "Where are your roller-skates? I thought you were in such an all-fired hurry."

Katlyn started singing on the trot. "*I got a pair of roller skates. You got a brand new key.* How does that song go, Jeff?"

"Don't know. Keep your voice down. We don't want to let the world know we're here."

"Why? We on private property?"

"Land has got to belong to somebody. Right?"

"I didn't see any posted signs."

"See any wanted signs?" he teased.

"Yeah, yours."

"Profile or full face?"

"Ass end up."

"Funny girl."

"Funny looking picnic basket," she remarked.

Jeff glanced at the case. "This?"

The pair slowed their pace to a walk.

"Yeah, that."

"This is not our picnic lunch."

"What?"

"These are the bugs I was telling you about last night."

"I thought we were *collecting* bugs."

"We'll be adding to the collection."

"Jeffrey. What about the picnic lunch you promised?"

"Business first."

"How long is this nonsense going to take?"

"Fifteen minutes, tops."

"Swear?"

"Swear."

"Cross your heart and hope to die?"

"Jews don't do that."

"Sure they do."

"Do not."

"Do too."

"Not."

"They do, Jeff. Especially if I tell them to."

"Show me how."

"What?" Katlyn scrunched up her face.

"Show me how to do it."

"Are you kidding?"

"I'm serious."

"You never crossed your heart and hoped to die as a kid?"

"Hoped to die, I didn't," Jeff swore.

"You know how."

"I don't. Really. Show me, and then I'll know."

"This is so silly."

"Okay, then don't."

"All right. I'll show you. But then *you* have to do it. Fair is fair."

"Fine. You first. But let's wait till we get close to that field."

Katlyn looked to where Jeff was pointing. She squinted down through the timberline. "What do we do down there?"

"That's where I'm going to release the bugs."

"Are we going to create a plague and blight a farmer's crop, Jeff? Is that what this is all about?"

"Yes. I tried to tell you in the car last night, but you went back to sleep."

"I *did* not."

"Did too."

"Not."

The two of them laughed away insanely, starting down the hill. Katlyn let go of his hand as they neared the bottom.

"When I asked you about the little buggers, you changed the subject twice. That detective friend of yours tell you not to tell me?"

"Nothing like that at all."

"Then how come—" Katlyn slipped and fell on her backside with a thump. "Fucking rocks all around this place," she fumed. "When you said woods and picnic, I had this park-like setting in mind."

"You going soft on me?" he questioned, offering his hand.

"Not at all," she said, taking it and pulling herself up, kicking a rock with the toe of her boot. The rock that tripped her. "Shit!" The same rock that just put a scar in the tip of her boot. "Goddamn it! These are five-hundred-dollar boots. Fuck!"

"You mad?"

"Fuckin' A, I'm mad."

"Then I want you to do what I do when I get mad."

"What? Kick the cat?"

"I want you to say, piss, shit and corruption. Go on. Say it."

Katlyn stared at Jeffrey as though he were a lunatic. "Say what?"

"You heard me. Piss, shit and corruption. Say it."

"Look at my motherfuckin' boot," she said loudly.

"Keep your motherfucking voice down, and say, piss, shit and corruption, quietly."

"It's Mother's Day, Jeff. All the motherfuckers are with their fucking mothers having an early dinner right about now. So don't get your bowels in an uproar. This is what's going to make me feel better." Katlyn kicked the rock with the toe of her other boot. "There! Might just as well have a matching pair. One good one isn't going to do me any fucking good."

"Feel better?"

"No."

Jeffrey stooped and set the case down in back of him. He started to pry the rock up with his fingertips. It wouldn't give. He worked the other end, inching the stone slowly back and forth. Finally, it came free.

"What are you doing?"

"How many questions do you ask in the course of a day?"

"Tell me."

"I'm going to show you what I do when kicking and mouthing off doesn't work." He held the large rounded stone in the palm of his hand out at arm's length. "You've heard of a pet rock, I'm sure."

"Uh-huh."

"Well, this is *Bad Rock*. And this is where we have our little talk."

Jeffrey made a nasty face, staring along the length of an outstretched arm, one eye closed, facing Bad Rock head-on.

Katlyn was amused.

"Bad Rock, you busted my lady's boots. And you're gonna have to pay."

Katlyn crossed one leg in front of the other, set an elbow in her palm, placed her chin in the other, then grinned the width of the brim of her hat. Her brown eyes were alive with laughter.

"Now, I don't have a lot of time left here because in a hot moment my Katydid's gonna want out of the woods. Been buggin' me about a picnic since we stepped foot out of the car."

Katlyn was laughing lightly, covering her full lips with the tips of her fingers.

"This is what we call a showdown in this neck of the woods, Bad Rock," Jeffrey declared, opening his hand, palm up, repositioning Bad Rock past his right ear as if about to cast the stone as a shot put.

Katlyn ran all ten fingers between the brim of her hat and her ears, taking and curling two wisps of hair behind them.

"Katie."

Katlyn was all ears.

"Katie, I don't want you to have to see this."

He didn't even have to tell her. Giggling, Katlyn turned around.

With the force of a wrecking ball, Bad Rock demolished the back of Katlyn's head. She fell forward onto her face and lay there as still as a stone. Her flowered hat came to rest not two feet away from her.

"Head. Stone. Flowers." Jeffrey giggled. "Headstone, flowers," he punned. "Sorry, Katie. But I have to drag you off to a potter's field in your five-hundred-dollar boots. At least you're as good as out of the woods." From a jacket pocket, Jeff withdrew and unfolded a wheat-colored paper jumpsuit and hat, along with a pair of 12-mil shoulder-length nitrile gloves. He grabbed and pulled his *grasshopper* by her hair. "See? You're not the only fashion plate. Come along now, Katydid. Got to get a move on. This is no picnic for either of us. Let's go." Jeffrey struggled with her dead weight.

With the bug case in one hand, and Katlyn in the other, Jeffrey made his way down the slope and partway into a field of newly planted cover crop. The sun was high overhead and hot. He had little trouble pulling off her boots. Undressing Katlyn as quickly as he could, he ran a Buck knife with a six-inch blade from her sternum to her pelvic bone, wondering what sort of sick pleasure his brother Howard derived from postmortem amputations. "Freaky guy, my brother Howard," Jeffrey projected. "And Nec, another strange dude with a serious disorder," he reflected. "My man said *deep*, Katie. And don't worry about no ticks. I mean, *any* ticks," he corrected himself, suddenly concerned with his grammar. "They can't hurt you now."

Jeffrey was not inhuman. He truly did feel a tiny bit of sorrow for his poor Katydid, measured by two true tears. To say he felt nothing just wouldn't be fair. Genuine remorse, however, was quite another matter. Guilt was not part of Jeff's makeup. Jeffrey was sad because Katlyn had taught him so many things. She had been teaching him to act refined. Not to use double negatives when important people were around. He was truly saddened because he would no longer have a mentor who would help him pick out a fine wine at South Fork's upscale Villa Paul restaurant in Hampton Bays, or get off on instructing a waiter or waitress to hold the label up when pouring a one-hundred-dollar bottle of claret. Jeffrey was most melancholy because he'd miss Katlyn's monthly handout until his own windfall blew in—hopefully. Jeff was glad that he had held on to a good part of what Katlyn had set aside for him for a rainy day.

A moment later, Jeffrey simply laughed away his tears.

So, Jeff was short on sad and long on selfish. *So what?* he told himself.

Jeffrey carefully opened the case and removed the box within. Lifting its lid and uncapping the smaller of two breathable containers, he found a mass of white maggot larvae. He dumped the contents onto the center of Katlyn's gaping, bloody belly wound as Vic Posteraro had instructed. Small packets of Dry Ice and other items were held firmly in place by plastic ties. Next, Jeffrey opened a screw-top sectioned container of beetles and other insets, releasing them throughout Katlyn's bloody head of hair. "There. Just pick up after myself, and I'm out of here."

Jeffrey put the empty containers and box back inside the case. He picked up Katlyn's boots and clothes, sticking them into a plastic bag. In less than a minute, he was heading back into the woods— singing quietly:

"*Don't mean a thing if you ain't got that swing. Doo-wop, doo-wop.*"

Chapter Fifty-Five

Howard Mills sat on the floor in the far corner of his cell; not that the adjective *far* denoted distance, for the space he occupied was 8 x 6 feet. The correction officer who sat right outside the steel cage watched him like a bug, for the Suffolk County Department of Corrections didn't need the kind of publicity and shakedown that the Nassau County facility was undergoing over the recent beating death of an inmate. Howard was off his medication and behaving quite erratically. All he could think about was death and the peace that it would finally bring. But it was hard to concentrate on anything let alone the concept of eternal rest, especially with guards standing over him twenty-four hours a day.

"Hey, Howie. You know what I find amusing? The confinement throughout your life," one of the correction officers tormented his charge. "Think about it. Your one-room apartment in Hicksville was the size of a walk-in closet from what I read in the papers. The guard shack you worked out of from time to time had the dimensions of a bread box from what I hear. Then there's the eight-by-eight foot confessional the homicide detectives had you in, in Yaphank. I've seen that one for myself. Now, this cell. Tad bigger than the one you'll find at the Clinton Correctional Facility in Dannemora, where you're headed. Spittin' distance from the Canadian border. Sixty square feet for your accommodation. Which will still be a damn sight bigger than the box they're finally going to put you in before they drop you into a hole. Eighty-four by twenty-eight by twenty-three. I'm talkin' inches, chump."

The officer waited for a reply. Howard Mills offered none.

"Anyhow, it'll be years before they put the needle in your arm. Ever ask yourself why they even bother to sterilize it? Huh? Not very talkative lately. Not since the verdict," the correction officer simpered. "I wonder when the judge is formally going to sentence you. One delay after another. I don't understand it myself, Howie. Jury found you guilty, convicted you, then sentenced you to death, yet you got to wait for the judge to make it official. Makes no sense. Pure waste of time and money. So here I am, and here you are. Personally, I'd have let you hang there. Be done with it. Save the county a bundle. As it is, you've cost the taxpayers a fuckin' fortune. Millions of dollars. I'm a taxpayer, Howie. How do you think that makes me feel? I pay taxes so that we keep you goin' until the state decides to kill you. What's wrong with this picture? Who's runnin' the asylum? Tell you the truth, I think you're saner than some of those bureaucrats who're runnin' the show. They may not bash someone's brains in and cut them up, but they're killin' us just the same, Howie. Chokin' us till we can't breathe no more."

Howard turned and looked up. "If they didn't find people like me to stick in here, you wouldn't be sitting out there and drawing a paycheck. How about them apples?" He stood up. "Ever think about that?"

The officer got up from his chair. "Sure I thought about it. But what I'm talking about is the waste. For instance, after Judge Best formally signs your death warrant, they're goin' to try your ass up in Westchester County. Another friggin' trial for two more women you wasted. Does that make any sense? They can only kill you once. Right?"

"I didn't waste anyone."

Sergeant Jim McQueeny looked at Howard for a Long Island minute before the officer opened his mouth again. "You know? You fuckin' guys gall the hell out of me when you talk that shit. You're the kind of fuckin' punk who will go to your grave sayin' you didn't do it. You know goddamn well you did. So why don't you be man enough to admit it, at least to yourself, and make your peace with God before it's too late? Before God says, 'Howie, you can kid those around you, you can even kid yourself, but I know you know the truth in your heart of hearts. So come clean before I sentence you to eternal damnation.' He's the real Judge, Howie. Lord over all this earthly bullshit. Denial will be your downfall. And I do mean—down. Think about it. You're going to have lots of time to think. No one can save your ass here. Too late for that. Jury sealed your fate on this end. What I'm talking about is down there in a hereafter called Hell." The correction officer pointed to the floor.

Howard Mills looked at McQueeny for a hard minute, mulling over the officer's supposed well-meaning words of advice.

"Number one, I never killed anybody, Sergeant. Number two, I'm going to beat this thing on appeal."

"Really? Then how come you tried to kill yourself? And where did they get all that evidence? Huh? Manufacture it?"

"No. They got it from my room. But that doesn't mean I killed anybody. All it means is that they were killed in my room."

"You mean murdered. In cold blood. Beaten beyond belief and dismembered. You denying you did that?"

Howard shook his head. "No. Not the dismembering part. But I never killed anyone."

"Then who did, Howie? Tell me. It doesn't really matter now."

Howard turned away from the man and slid back down in the corner.

Jim McQueeny just shook his head. "You're a strange one, Howie."

Howard Mills took a deep breath and wept. His heart ached at the thought of Beth. *Why hasn't she come to visit me? Why?* he wondered. *Why?*

Chapter Fifty-Six

Jeffrey Mills stood completely naked, his hands and feet shackled with a length of chain joined to a steel bolt fastened to the floor of the 8 x 8 foot interrogation room at police headquarters in Yaphank. Jeff was high on confidence. He wasn't about to be intimidated. Not at any price. The prize assets that awaited him the police would not fathom no matter how deep they delved—he believed. Jeff was in the catbird seat. Being chained hand and foot was simply the cost of doing business. A temporary setback.

"Did I not tell you he had a puny putz?" Detective Mick Connolly harassed, pointing a gun-finger at their prisoner's privates from less than three feet away. "Another gelding we got here, John."

Detective John Bailey smiled. "You called it, Mick. You sure as hell did. This guy's prick belongs on a stunted pygmy. Fuckin' girls had to have laughed their heads off when they saw that puny thing. Probably why he finally bashed Katlyn's brains in. Think his lawyer could use humiliation as a possible defense?"

"Nah," Mick rejected. "If the defense ever brought in pics of his prick, they'd play right into the prosecution's hands."

"How so?" Bailey went along as straight man.

"Well, The Dragon Lady would accuse Kevin Casey of altering the photo array with an airbrush. Not enhancing but downsizing Jeff's dick as a sympathy ploy. Defense'd be the laughing stock. Jeff, here, is a schtuper with a putz the length and thickness of a golf tee—ain't nobody gonna believe this wee wee," Mick went on mercilessly. "Your mother ever catch you masturbating, Jew boy?" Connolly turned back to Bailey. "She probably told him, 'That ain't even a pig in the blanket, so stop acting like you're holding a forbidden ham.' At age five, John, my Saudi father told my Syrian mother that I was destined to be a nomad because wherever I went I had my own portable pole and tent; a perpetual hard-on with which to hide a harem. Personally, I think Casey's gonna go with an insanity plea for Jeffrey boy, here."

"Why?"

"Because he's fuckin' crazy. Plain and simple. That's why. Whole fuckin' family's bats."

John Bailey shook his head. "You're wrong there, Mick."

"How so?"

"Juries ain't buyin' into that happy horseshit anymore. Especially out here in Suffolk County. Why do you think Dunn and Profeta went the other route with Howard?"

"Yeah, I guess you're right."

"You know I am, Mick."

"Hey, asshole," Jeff remarked, "you're making one big fucking mistake. When my lawyer gets here, he's going to run your balls up the flagpole. He's going to sue this county for a fucking fortune. Now, I'm going to say it one more goddamn time. I want that phone call that I'm entitled to, and I want it now. You ain't dealing with my brother. You're dealing with me, clown."

Mick stood looking into Jeff's eyes for a few seconds before a cupped hand caught the suspect behind his head and snapped his face forward, smashing it forcefully into the cop's forehead. Jeff went down like a rock, rattling chains and handcuffs as he fell out of the way of a foot that missed his head by an inch.

"I'm neither a sad nor happy clown, maggot. I'm just really pissed," Mick Connolly declared, bringing back his foot for a second attempt.

As Mick's foot came forward, Jeff lifted a leg along with the chain, catching the cop off balance. In a flash, Jeff shot his body atop the detective's, and with tenacious gnashing teeth, bit the fleshy lobe of Mick's right ear. Mick screamed in anguish; Jeff shrieked with a vengeance while Bailey pummeled the prisoner's kidneys. With blood pouring from his right ear, Mick managed to wrap a powerful arm around Jeff's neck and squeezed with all his might.

Jeff was on his back and gave a muffled laugh. "Hear me better now, clown?" Jeff droned. "One fuckin' phone call, bozo."

John Bailey had stopped punching the suspect and, instead, drove his size twelve shoe into Jeff's side—again, and again, and again, until several homicide detectives rushed into the room and separated the beaten body from the flailing, beefy leg of the big man. Howling in pain but loving it, Jeffrey Mills was released from the shackles, then dragged roughly from the room and down the hallway. Detective Sergeant Carter started shooting orders, and Team Two turned into a whirlwind. Jeff was hauled around a corridor and out of sight.

"You're gonna pay dearly!" Jeff screamed. "Kevin Casey will *fold* your fucking tent," were the last words Connolly could clearly hear.

Detective Gary York went marching down the hall after Jeffrey Mills and his escorts.

"Where in hell do you think you're going?" Carter called after him.

The homicide detective ignored his immediate supervisor.

"Jesus H. Christ," Carter complained, starting down the hall and around the corner after him. "Come back here."

York caught up to the group and stepped ahead of the lot.

Standing to one side of the prisoner, Eric Bokina warned Gary off as Troy Anderson blocked York with a shoulder. Nevertheless, Gary stood toe to toe with Jeff.

"What did you just say back there, Mills?" York demanded.

"Cool it," Anderson snapped.

The prisoner raised his head and immediately recognized Detective Gary York. Jeff knew who he was and what he had done to his brother. How he had tricked him. Jeff smiled past his pain.

"I said, you're all gonna pay. That my lawyer's gonna fold this fucking tent, dickhead. That's what I said."

Carter walked up and put his hand on York's shoulder, but Gary shook it off. Gary was shaking his head. He was in Jeff's face.

"No, fucker. First off, you and your lawyer are going to soon see that the circus is back in town. Secondly, you're not going to see your asshole attorney for a spell. I've got a surprise for you, fuckface. I'm going to blow your fucking mind."

Jeff spit in the detective's face before the two were wrenched apart. Lieutenant Theodore Groche came up to the group. Both he and

Carter took Gary aside. Eric and Troy led Jeff away.

Gary went inside his jacket pocket and withdrew a handkerchief, wiping the spittle from a cheek.

"You all right?" Theo asked.

"Never better, Lieutenant," Gary answered. "Never better."

"Come. We'll go to my tent and talk," he ordered with a smile.

Carter gave Gary a wink along with a show of support, lightly punching the detective's shoulder. The three cops headed back down the hall.

Jeffrey Mills was back in the interrogation room, fully clothed but cuffed and shackled to the floor. Detective Gary York walked in alone and took a seat at a table out of biting, kicking and spitting distance of the mail handler. The detective acted as if the prisoner wasn't even there. York busied himself with paperwork. After ten minutes, Jeffrey opened his mouth.

"Think you're gonna pull one of your stunts with me? Huh? Gonna tell me that you're Casey's co-counsel?" Jeff forced a smile. "Think I'm stupid like my brother? Huh? Gonna try and trick me into signing a confession? You guys ain't even smart enough to send in another clown." Jeff launched into song while his back and sides were splitting with pain: "*Send in the clowns. Where are the clowns?*" he crooned. He had to stop. He was breathing heavily through his nose. "Oh, how you're gonna pay," he said after a pause. "When my lawyer and I get finished with you jokers, you're gonna have to dissolve this county. We're gonna bankrupt Suffolk. We're gonna make you boys bleed."

Gary continued with his paperwork, paying no attention to Jeffrey Mills.

Five minutes later, the door to the room flew open. Detective Victor Posteraro fell across the threshold. Mick Connolly, his right ear bandaged, stood over Vic. The trembling detective got to his knees and, with hands cuffed in back of him, worked himself into a corner. Vic was bleeding from his nose and mouth. Gary York put his pen atop his paperwork and stood. He walked over to the cowering figure and smashed a Versace Loafer into the man's ribs. Vic let out a cry and quickly folded himself into a fetal position. Gary drove his other shoe into the back of the cop's neck. Vic screamed as his head hit the bottom of the wall.

A second later, Detective Frank Masselli stormed into the room.

He appeared haggard and was sweating profusely as if he had just come off a treadmill.

"Get out," he said to Gary. "You too, Mick. Go on."

Mick looked dumbfounded.

"I said, get out. Both of you," Masselli tried to say calmly but couldn't.

Mick was shaking his head. "You don't tell me to get out. I'm running this—"

"HE WAS MY PARTNER!" Frank Masselli screamed, grabbing up a chair. "Now get out. I have some things to take care of here."

"Put down that chair, Frank. I can't let—"

"GET OUT!" Masselli went after Mick Connolly with the chair.

Mick backed up to the door. Gary got out of the way, moving along the wall. "Don't do this, Frankie. Please. Let us handle this. It's not worth it. I know what you're gonna do, and I'm telling you it's not worth it."

"We're gonna have to take you down, Frankie," Mick said. "You know that. Listen to Gary." Masselli was shaking his head. "Frankie. Please," Mick pleaded. "I know we don't like one another very much. Maybe not at all. So why should you listen to me? Right? But listen to Gary, Frankie. All right? Our voice of reason. Maybe the one thing we do agree on. Okay? You take out Vic, we can't help you. I was gonna take him out myself. But I thought about my wife and what I'd be putting her through. I know what you're capable of. We all do. But I'm telling you, fella, it's just not worth it."

"Look," Gary interrupted. "I promise you this piece of shit is going to pay dearly, like Jeffrey here. But *we* know when to stop. You don't. I swear to you that Bailey will administer punishment that Vic will remember for a long time. Not here, but on the way to his arraignment. Let the state take care of the rest. We got 'im," he stated, pointing to Posteraro lying curled up on the floor, "along with this piece of garbage who thinks he's Tyson tangling with Holyfield," he said of Jeffrey Mills. "We got them good. They're both going down for the count and then up to Dannemora for a decade before at least one of them meets his Maker. Think about that, Frankie. Jail time followed by ten long years in prison, just for openers. No maybes about it. We've got them stone cold."

Jeff wanted to say that they had crap. Another ruse of theirs. But he really wasn't sure about anything. For there was his partner in crime, Vic, cowering in the corner. What had the crooked cop told them?

Nothing, Jeff prayed. Prayed to God, he did. Vic was smart. Surely he'd keep his mouth shut. Too much to lose. Both their lives if they weren't careful.

Detective Frank Masselli cooled his heels and put down the chair, nodding in agreement. "All right. Okay. I just want to talk to Vic, is all. I swear. Alone. Five minutes."

Mick looked at Gary.

Gary nodded in the affirmative.

"Five minutes, Frankie," Micky swore. "Not a minute more. We'll be right outside that door. You move on either of them, and it might be you who goes to the hospital. I ain't fuckin' with you, Frankie boy."

Frank Masselli nodded again. "Five minutes."

Mick and Gary stepped from the room, leaving the door ajar. Frank knew that they would, indeed, be watching. He took the chair and placed it a foot away from Vic, locking him into the corner so that his former partner couldn't move even if he had wanted.

"Want to know how I got a line on you, Vic? What made me suspicious from the start? I mean besides that high-and-mighty attitude of yours; all that better-than-thou bullshit." Frank Masselli took in all the blood, watching the man cowering before him.

Vic turned his head toward the wall.

"You can't even look at me, can you?" Frank turned his head and looked at Jeffrey Mills. "What the fuck are you looking at, cocksucker?"

Jeff immediately looked away. He was hurting.

Frank turned his attention back to Vic. "We were all up by the train station in Hicksville. You and me, partner. Mick and John. Dan Fowler and Max. We had to come up with an excuse for Dan and Max to be snooping around the line of cars along Marcy, in case someone came by that morning. I suggested looking for lost keys. Remember? But you topped that one without a second thought," Frank said, snapping his fingers. "'Contact lens,' you said. Just like that. 'Be like looking for a needle in a haystack,' is how you phrased it." Frank looked back at Jeff. "That's what this nutcase is all about. Contacts. He wears them when he kills. Gary had a lead on the lens and lens case that Artie held in the property room. The missing contact aroused Gary's curiosity. You know Gary. Leaves no stone unturned. He worked it till Theo told him to back off. Lieutenant saw it as a total waste of time. Afraid Gary might throw a monkey wrench into the entire works concerning Howard's trial. Gary developed other leads. Working them on his own. Guess what he came up with? You, Vic. You had contact lenses on the brain. The missing one from the lens case after Howard was arrested. Only it wasn't Howard's. It was Jeff's. That missing lens was on your mind, too, Vic. Just like Gary." Frank shook his head so sorrowfully. "Soon you'll be just a sad memory, pal.

"And now I'm getting to the good part. I should really let Gary tell you. But this is almost as good as getting off by kicking your head in instead. Gary can place you and Jeff at a certain bar in Greenport. How's that?"

Jeff shot a glance at Vic. Vic was shaking his head.

"What? You don't believe me? Gary has it all on tape."

Vic began to cry, and his shoulders shook.

"Oh, yes. Every fucking word. Let me give you the highlights. Buzz words, baby. Let me see your face when I rattle some of them off. Oh, come on. Give me at least that satisfaction. I won't tell you if you don't look at me. And then you won't know if I'm bullshitting or not. You know that half our business is bullshit, Vic. Howard certainly knows that now." Frank glanced over at the ashen face of Jeffrey Mills before returning his attention to Posteraro. "LOOK AT ME, VIC!" Frank roared.

Vic turned and looked up into the crazed eyes of his former partner. His colleague. His friend.

"Buzz words. 'Maggots and beetles and bugs,' Vic. Ring a bell? How about, 'fifty percent, partner.' That jog your memory?"

Vic was moaning.

"How about you over there in bracelets and chains, Mr. Solid Alibi? Think you're covered? Not. And I'm gonna tell you why. Your alibi window is off by many hours, jerk-off. Know how come, asshole? Because the maggot larvae you deposited on Katlyn Land's body pinpoints her time of death approximately twelve hours after the two of you left Orient By The Sea Marina and Restaurant on Saturday night at eleven o'clock. Not that Mr. Fix It, here, didn't know what he was doin'. It's because we switched boxes and bugs on you when you were catching a few zees before Katlyn picked you up Sunday morning. Know how we managed that, shithead? With a duplicate set of car keys that Detectives Sosan and Waverly of Nassau Homicide had copied before handing yours over to your attorney, Kevin Casey," Detective Frank Masselli lied. "Recall? We have half a dozen witnesses who saw you leave the restaurant with Katlyn Land. Matter of fact, you two closed the place before your meeting Vic at that closed-down bar-and-grill in Greenport. The way it's going down, Jeff, is that you killed Katlyn shortly after dinner last night at that wood lot in Southold. Got an alibi from eleven p.m. Saturday till the wee hours of Sunday? I'm telling you all this because I know you're trying to broaden your horizon," Masselli added with a smirk.

"What was my motive, dickhead?" Jeffrey screeched.

"She was a blabbermouth, fuckface. You had to silence her. We know all about Howard's offshore bank accounts, properties and your mother's other investments. Money was your motive, Jeff. Big money. We know all about your scheme. Think we're backwoods bumpkins out here in Suffolk County, boy? We've known about the money for a year."

"You're so full of shit about everything. You're saying I killed Katlyn and that you knew about it beforehand. Like you're really gonna let something like that ever happen, huh?" Jeff laughed in pain. "You know how stupid you'd look in a court of law?"

"Of course you're right on that account, Jeff. We're not going to present any of that business about the meeting or the box of bugs. Don't need to. We're just gonna let you hang yourself. Maybe literally. Like your brother tried to do. We're going to give you lots of rope for that. But you're dead wrong about not letting us let Katlyn Land die. She's got a history, I'm sure you know. Maybe you don't. Want to hear?"

Jeff said nothing.

"'The Death By Chocolate Killer.' Ever hear of her? She poisoned cakes, ice cream and candy. Victims turned up dead whenever she happened to be in Maryland with her parents, some years back. Authorities down there are positive it was her. Can't prove it, though. Then a former Greenport cop wound up dead in his apartment after a lethal dose of chocolate chip ice cream," Masselli fabricated. "Day after Ilona Alfold disappeared. Coincidental, Jeffrey?"

The door to the room opened. Gary and Mick stepped back in.

"Guess my five minutes are up, boys. Vic. I got so many things I want to say to you, but I'll just sum it up like this. You're as good as fuckin' dead. You were my partner, man. And now you're his. I trusted you with my life out there. Right up to the end. You were too smart for your own good. For what, Vic? Money that neither of you will ever see."

Frank got up from the chair and left the room, brushing past Mick and Gary.

Jeff's head was reeling and hurt as much as his body.

Chapter Fifty-Seven

It was the day after Mother's Day.

Picking up the receiver from a pay phone on Love Lane in Mattituck, Robert Redler deposited several coins then punched in a seven-digit direct number. It was a perfect spring morning. Seventy-two degrees. Not a single cloud in the sky. It had been a busy night. He was so nervous that he misdialed. Redler cursed his carelessness, redialed and waited anxiously as the phone rang.

"Homicide, Sergeant O'Toole."

"Good morning, Sergeant. And it is just that," Redler said, trying to relax.

"You sound like you're at the bottom of a canyon. Speak up."

"About the best I can do," Redler lied, holding a handkerchief over the mouthpiece and further disguising his voice by speaking low and languidly. "Detectives Connolly, Bailey or Masselli around?"

"Who is this?"

"Someone who has very important information regarding the Howard-Jeffrey Mills matter."

"Connolly's retired; the other two are not here now. I can give them a message."

"Fine. Tell them to go out to Beth Tracy's condo—"

"Hold on a second."

Redler was getting more anxious by the second.

"Go ahead."

Redler figured he was being recorded. He paused. "Yes. Tell them to go out to Beth Tracy's condominium in Orient Point. She has gardens in—"

"And what?"

"What?"

"You said to go out to Beth Tracy's condo in Orient Point. To do what, exactly?"

"Dig"

"Dig?"

"Yes, dig."

"Dig for what and where?" The voice was downright nasty.

Redler took a breath and pushed the cop's button. "You getting this down, or just jerking me around?"

"No, you're jerking me around," the man said with a sigh.

"Tell me what I just told you from the beginning or I'll hang up and call back when Bailey or Masselli are around, or when I know I have someone who can take a fucking message without becoming exasperated." Acting tough was one way the writer dealt with his nervousness. He didn't care for the man's tone.

There was a long pause.

"You still there?" Redler asked.

Another voice came on the line. "Connolly here. What about Beth Tracy?"

Redler recognized the voice from the homicide detective's many days on the stand during pretrial and trial, as well as from the conversations they had in the hallway outside the courtroom. Small talk. About boats and marinas. About his novels. About things the detective couldn't and wouldn't talk about. Robert Redler prayed that his own voice was sufficiently masked. "I was just told you were retired."

"Retired for the night. And now I'm wide awake and listening."

"I see. You know Beth Tracy's condo on Orient Point, Detective?" Redler asked, feeling a bit relieved his anonymous message was being acknowledged by a key player.

Mick Connolly was dedicated. The man *had* been retired, retired for a month, yet the man was there. In the courtroom, the hallway, upstairs in Gail Fox's office, and now back in the squad room.

Commendable. Dependable Mick Connolly. Redler liked the man a lot.

"Go on," Mick said, neither affirming nor denying that he knew the place, for the police were used to asking the questions and getting answers. Not the other way around. Cop-speak, Redler reasoned. Noncommittal, to say the least.

"Tracy's gardens out back. Not necessarily the tomato gardens, but the flower beds. Start your digging around there. Bring lots of men and shovels and body bags for bones." Redler trembled as he spoke. "I don't know if you're going to need earthmoving equipment. Graves are all bunched together—if you'd even want to call them that. I started digging in the center, working outward toward the Sound. I'd say a mass graveyard from the little I uncovered. It's in your hands now. Gotta go."

Redler hung up the phone and hurried down the block. He was sweating and shaking like a leaf.

Chapter Fifty-Eight

Nicholas Dunn and Christopher Profeta paid a visit to Howard Mills at the Riverhead Jail. The convicted killer of prostitutes stood shackled and cuffed, looming out at them like a nasty bird tethered within a cage; in this case, a holding cage. Howard stood staring at the ceiling as though he were considering sudden flight.

"Please look at me, Howard," Dunn said. "If you won't look, then at least listen to us."

Howard suddenly appeared parrot-like. The stretched-out bright green sweater belied his most foul mood. The disheveled red and yellow untucked shirt hanging off to his side took on the semblance of a broken wing. With crusted, crested mussy hair standing on end, a caricature artist would have captured Howard's comic likeness along the lines of a cockatoo, giving prominence to a hooked-billed beak. But there was nothing humorous about Howard's situation or the new developments concerning his half sister, Beth, and his brother, Jeffrey.

"Please, Howard," Profeta joined in. "What we have to say to you is probably the most important thing we have ever said to you or any client to date. Please listen to us."

Tears were forming in Christopher Profeta's eyes, and they weren't of the crocodile kind. The attorney was not on center stage or in the courtroom. Yet, he was in the middle of a melodrama greatly magnified by circumstances that few folks might have imagined.

"'Please, Howard' this, and 'please, Howard' that," Mills mimicked. "'Most important. Most important.' NOW?" he questioned, displaying what little was left of his sanity. Howard raked his head hard along the vertical shafts of steel as though they might be musical bars. And on that note, the wounded bird collapsed.

"Goddamn you, listen," Profeta barked.

"God damn me," Howard shrieked aloud with laughter.

"Beth Tracy is dead!" Dunn snapped. "Get a grip on that."

Howard immediately put a finger in each ear and made pretty bird-like music in his head, twisting his upper torso back and forth for a full two minutes. Suddenly, he stopped.

"Did you hear me?" Christopher Profeta stated. "Beth is dead!"

Howard said nothing, lying on the floor while staring at the ceiling. Numb. Numb was good for Howard. Howard loved being numb. Numb, dumb, numskull.

Nicholas Dunn kicked one of the bottom bars. "We can turn this around for you, Howard. Give us that chance. There are new developments in this case. Please try and cooperate. Don't let Jeff get away with this."

"Let me tell you why he *is* going to get away with this if you let him," Profeta rejoined. "Let's talk about something you can relate to. Let's talk money. Let's talk about the price tag for your death. You're good with figures, Howard. Figure this. Two-and-a-half million is what's being conservatively touted as to monies spent on this trial so far. That's a deflated bullshit number to quiet the public. Try five. Five million dollars, Howard. And by the time we're finished with the appeal, it's going to be more like ten. Ten million bucks. Just to house you on death row will cost New York State more than double what it costs an ordinary prisoner per year. Twenty-eight thousand dollars for Collin Ferguson; more than sixty thousand for you. You're exceptional, Howard. You're the first prisoner on Long Island in over twenty years to receive the death penalty, and the third in the state. You're going to be expensive to kill. But let's go with the conservative figure that Suffolk and the state say they spent to date. Two and a half million dollars. Not marbles, Howard. Greenbacks. The politicians here, meaning Patterson and his people in the district attorney's office, and those under the governor's dome upstate, don't want Howard W. Mills to turn out to be a ten-million-dollar mistake. Not at any cost. Understand? Unless you level with us, and I mean tell us everything now, they're going to find a way to kill you fast. They'll save a bundle in the bargain, but just as important, they'll save face. Your execution may come in the form of a beating, an overdose, a so-called accident. God only knows. I know that's what you think you want, but it's not what we want to see happen. You're not an evil person, Howard. You're sick. Nicholas and I made a mistake in not entering an insanity plea right from the start. Hindsight is twenty-twenty. We can't turn back the clock. But we can enter in new evidence. You've kept quiet to protect Beth and Jeffrey. Jeff killed her. We believe that Beth killed those women in your apartment. We also believe Beth killed many men out in Orient Point. So, now the truth, Howard. But I'm going to try and make it easier for you because I'm going to go first. It's true confession time." Christopher put his head down. He felt ashamed. "I never really believed you were innocent, Howard."

"Nor did I." Nicholas added woefully.

"Neither of us believed you until now. We're defense attorneys, and we defended you to the best of our abilities. In light of what we now know, we didn't do a very good job." The tears were falling freely down Christopher's face. The attorney searched the ceiling for the right words to turn their client around. "Please help us move forward, not backward, Howard. Please, for God's sake, tell us what you know. You can't hurt Beth now. If I know Patterson, and believe me I do, he'll go for the death penalty with respect to Jeff. You can't protect either of them any longer. But you can help us hand you back your life. If you did the postmortem amputations and Beth and/or Jeff did the killing, then Nick and I have a chance to turn this conviction around."

Howard hadn't batted an eye or changed his expression since the moment he sunk to the floor.

Christopher Profeta never felt more helpless in all his years as a defense attorney as he did at that moment. Wiping the tears away on the sleeve of his jacket, he said good-bye. "I'm terribly sorry, Howard."

"Bye for now, Howard," Nick said softly.

"Nick, Chris," Howard sat up and called out sadly as the attorneys started to leave.

Profeta spun around.

"What's the day and month?" Howard asked morosely.

"Second Tuesday in May," Nicholas answered.

"The eleventh to be exact," Chris Profeta answered. "Why?"

"I didn't get my tax return in on time again. Do you think I'm in trouble with the government?"

"We'll take care of it for you like we did last year," Nick came back.

"Just the same, do you think you can get me the forms?'

"Short form, correct?" Nick humored their client.

Howard smiled his multimillion-dollar, million-mile-away smile. "Probably won't need the long form unless I decide to give everything away to Jeffrey." Howard wasn't acting.

"We'll see, Howard."

"I know you will. One quick question? I know you're both very busy. Chris, you're talking to that male elementary school teacher arraigned on sexual abuse charges of an eight-year-old female student of his. Nick, you're interviewing that black female high school nursing student accused of murdering another here in Riverhead," Howard stated, referring to Profeta's and Dunn's pending cases.

"You're well-informed and right on top of things, Howard," Nick answered straightaway. "What's your question?"

"It's why I'm really here, isn't it? Taxes."

Neither of the attorneys responded.

"That's okay. I'm still gonna tell you about the nursing student and the schoolteacher."

"Tell us," Chris said.

"They're both innocent."

"How do you know?" Nick asked good-humoredly, grinning like a Cheshire cat.

"The nursing student told me so herself. And the elementary school teacher? Got it through the grapevine."

"We'll take that under consideration. Right, Nick?"

"Goddamn right we will."

"Gotta go now, Howard," Chris said. "Chin up, hear?"

Howard raised and stretched his neck toward the ceiling, holding the position in the holding cage until a correction officer came and removed him, escorting the prisoner back to his cell.

Chapter Fifty-Nine

Homicide Detective Gary York marched smartly down a long hallway at headquarters, heading toward a small room used as a storage area. Rows of dusty cardboard filing cartons along with boxes of cleaning supplies filled the cluttered space. ADA Gail Fox followed the cop to a holding cell. Jeffrey Mills sat fully clothed, his wrist handcuffed to a steel bar. Except to be taken to the bathroom twice in the past seventy-two hours, he had not left that cell.

"Messy place, Jeff," York tormented. "And you're beginning to stink. Get up, asshole. Can't you see there's a lady present?"

Jeff got to his feet, running a metal handcuff up the rusty steel bar as he rose. "This is illegal. This is the United States of America. And you, lady, are an assistant district attorney."

Gail looked at Jeff icily.

"Well, now that everybody knows one another and where we are, what say we get down to business?" Gary said without expression. "Don't want you saying later on that Ms. Fox misrepresented herself as a dominatrix and forced you into signing a false confession. Although, if I put a whip in her hand this instant, I think she'd have you on your hands and knees."

"I ain't signing nothin'."

"You mean, *anything*. And of course you're going to sign.

You're going to sign a confession to the murders of Beth Tracy, Roselyn James, Ilona Alfold and Katlyn Land. And you can thank Ms. Fox that she's not going to push for an indictment concerning other women you likely killed in your brother's downstairs apartment at 42 Willow Lane. We're just going to let that business sit the way it is."

"You're nuts."

"Jeffrey. I'm a Suffolk County homicide detective. Of course I'm nuts. It's a prerequisite. It's on my résumé. Difference is I have a license to behave this way. So do my colleagues. You see, we're organized as a team. But you're operating out there as a renegade. Oh, I know you had your little group and all. But they're all disbanded now. Glen, your Greenport crony, is on a slab in the morgue. But I'm sure you know that. Nec, as you named him, was detained at the airport near his hometown. And your buddy, Vic? Nothing worse in the world than a dirty cop. Now, guess what your pal Posteraro went and did? He gave you up, Jeff. Nec gave you up, too, as well as the rest of your sick little group. So. Here's what you're going to do."

Jeff was shaking his head. "Doin' nothin'. Sayin' nothin'. Telling you for the hundredth time, and now in the presence of this assistant district attorney, that I *demand* to call my lawyer."

"You demand?" Gary questioned with a sick, slick smile, glancing over at a large yellow Rubbermaid bucket holding a heavy-duty plastic wringer and smelly mop. "If we didn't have you dead in the water, Jeffrey, know what I'd do? I'd put you through that wringer over there," he swore. "Know how many confessions I've gotten by the mere mention of that thing? Know how many times maintenance had to come up here to mop around a guy who pissed and shit in his pants when I put his head in that clamp? Or maybe I simply forgot about him for a day or three. 'Gary's mop-up operation,' word went out. If we didn't have you dead to rights, that's where your head would have been days ago."

"You got nothin' or you wouldn't be here now. You can threaten all you want. All you got are the words of a bunch of freaks, if you've even got that."

"How about Vic's words and your own on tape like I told you before?"

"Like you told me," Jeff recited with a laugh. "Like I really believe what you say."

But they sure as hell had snippets of Vic's and Jeff's conversation, the man in custody could not deny . . . whether the words were from a recording device planted in the bar-and-grill in Greenport, or from the mouth of the cop who ostensibly gave him up, Jeff could not be sure. Thank God he had Kevin Casey on retainer, Jeff breathed easily. Thank God he could afford Kevin Casey—all thanks to Katlyn. *How in God's name did Vic slip up?* Jeffrey wondered. *It couldn't have been because of a contact lens as Detective Masselli had said*, Jeff pondered. *Or could it?* Vic could run circles around these guys. He was one of their brightest, Casey himself had said. Jeff considered if Vic's transfer to West Babylon was voluntary, like he had said, or if *The Team* had actually pushed him out for one reason or another. Jeff was running a wee bit worried but refused to show it.

"You guys are full of shit and deceit. You guys are bad news bears. If you told me it was bright daylight out there, I'd figure it would have to be midnight. For what you did to my brother, you ought to be fired from the force."

"Whatever it takes to get psychos like you off the streets. But you're right. I wouldn't believe me either if I were you. That's why the assistant district attorney is standing here beside me. She's going to lay it out for you. I'd listen to her very carefully, Jeff. If you're smart, you'll take the deal. If not, you can tell the illustrious Kevin Casey that you had your chance but blew it. He won't be able to help you at that point. It'll be too late. Of course, I had to make a deal with the devil because of certain problems with the tape. Nothing to do with its quality. Clarity as sure as your guilt. But there's always that concern over admissibility. So, now we've got Vic's written confession in addition to your accomplices' voluntary statements—all rolled into one neat little package."

Gary York pointed to the Manila envelopes that Gail Fox was holding protectively in her arms.

"We made several copies of Vic and you discussing the deal. One for Casey if need be," Gary continued. "Don't really want to put Vic at that bar-and-grill in Greenport unless we have to. Bad PR. We try and handle these things internally. Not that he's going to walk away from this and everything's going to be hunky-dory, because it's not. He's about to officially lose his job, his pension—everything he's worked for so hard. He's going to do a little time. His lieutenant's doing the paperwork right now."

Keep your mouth shut, Jeff told himself. But he couldn't. "What kind of paperwork?"

"A deal's been cut. The top gun has, of course, fired him from the force. He'll never work the job again. He's practically an inmate as we speak."

Jeff looked sick.

"To tell you the truth, when Vic gets out, I don't think he could get a job at BJ's, checking receipts and customers at the door. Not when his commanding officer gets through with him, he won't."

Detective Gary York was, in effect, telling the man standing before him that Vic Posteraro would one day see the light of day at the end of the tunnel, but he, Jeffrey Mills, would not. Was he expected to simply turn in his civvies—for what? A promise of life in prison without the possibility of parole in lieu of death? *Was that the deal? Had to be. Were they positively nuts?*

"I want to hear for myself exactly what you have on tape," Jeff said, smirking and calling their bluff, but wondering whether the snippets of conversation Connolly had recited referencing the clandestine meeting with Vic was the product of a recording device secreted in that defunct bar-and-grill on Front Street in Greenport, or from a traitorous mouth. God forbid the meeting had actually been taped.

Jeff's lawyer could certainly deal with a corrupt cop's confession as a made-up pack of lies. But a surveillance operation involving his and Vic's recorded conversations was certain to spell disaster. Jeff's mind was spinning. *Piss, shit and corruption*, he lamented silently.

Gary York smiled inwardly, knowing exactly what was running through their prisoner's mind. "Really want to hear the tape, Jeff?"

Jeff nodded nervously.

"Actually, I was going to play this for Kevin Casey when he got here. But the district attorney's office thinks it's a bad idea. Still, if you insist, I'll play it just for you."

"I insist," Jeff said, swallowing hard.

"I'm going to have to go get it."

"Yeah, right. Go do that, and I'll wait right here for you," Jeff soured, raking the handcuff noisily along the vertical bar.

Gary York and Gail Fox turned and headed for the door.

"And tell your bitch there to bring me back a cheeseburger and a brew," Jeff called out. "Tell her I had two cups of tea and four soda crackers in . . . in I don't know how many days, you fuckin' prick," he cried out in anguish. "And I ain't sayin' or signin' nothin', hear?"

"You'll say, you'll sign, you'll see," Gary called back. "Oh, you want fries with that?"

"FUCK YOU!"

Within an hour, Detective Gary York and ADA Gail Fox returned to the storage area. Gary had Jeff's food request. A moment later, Detective Troy Anderson appeared with a small tape recorder.

Gary handed Jeffrey a bag containing a cheeseburger and a paper boat filled with French fries. Next, he handed Jeff a bottle of Grolsch.

"This one's on me, Jeff," Gary offered.

Gail Fox still held the Manila envelopes in her arms.

Detective Anderson fussed with the recorder while Jeff unwrapped his prize with one free hand. He took a good-sized bite out of the burger, put it down and, with his thumb, popped off the halfway opened bottle cap, watching the busy detective all the while.

Troy switched on the recorder, and Jeff took a long pull of the brew.

The sound of heavy chairs being set down then dragged along the floor was heard. Troy fast-forwarded the tape:

Wish they kept some Grolsch back there.

You could wish your life away.

I can't believe they came in with a verdict so fast.

It was Jeff's and Vic's voices on the machine. Troy pushed a button and advanced the tape.

—they quickly fall in line. It's not like Henry Fonda in Twelve Angry Men. At least not in Suffolk County, it's not.

Clearly, the voice was Vic's. Troy advanced the tape well ahead. Jeff recognized the sound of glass clinking.

I'd say by this time next year you could be celebrating Son's Day.

But first I'll have to declare it. Then the year after that, I'll declare Daughter's Day. Jeff heard himself giggling. *To honor all loving children.*

What about Katlyn?

Sleeping out there in the car. Feel bad that she has to go.

Do her quickly and quietly. You're not dealing in the dark anymore. They're onto you. Watching you like a hawk.

Well, I can assure you that no one followed me here if that's what you're worried about.

No, Jeff. I can assure you. You can assure me nothing but fifty percent, partner. I told you not to involve her from the beginning. She's positively nuts. You're nuts for having told her anything.

She is . . . was my soul mate.

You were a fool. You trust no one.

I have to trust you.

There, you have no choice. And up to a point, I'm trusting you, too. It's a small but necessary risk I have to take. But you increase that risk when you party and fuck around with dames like that. You keep your mouth shut and your killing urge in check until the real check clears. Got it?

Maybe you can take care of Katydid for me?

No, you're going to squash that bug by yourself. After that, you're on your own.

I'm on my own, now. No?

With just a little bit of help to help you pull this off.

What's in that?

Mostly maggot larvae.

What the hell do we need maggot larvae for?

You need them, not me. Now, let's go over the times again . . . .

"Got all that, Jeff?" Gary mocked as Troy stopped the tape.

"That doesn't prove nothin'," Jeff chomped. "You hear me? Nothin'. All that is is a conversation. Bunch of words." Jeff took another swig.

"You like that beer, huh?"

"Ale, asshole. And what the fuck's it to you?"

"Oh, nothing," Gary answered.

"Just because some guy on that tape asks for a Grolsch, and you hand me one, doesn't mean dick."

"So that's not you on that tape?" Gary questioned with a winning smile.

"Could be anyone."

"Hum. Well, then let's clear this up once and for all." Gary turned to Troy. "You want to bring me the box you and Eric recovered from that Dumpster by the old Boy Scout Camp in Southold?"

"Sure. Be back in a moment." Troy handed the tape recorder over to Gary.

Gary turned back to Jeff, their eyes locking on one another in sheer hatred. Jeff's face was ashen.

"Savor that burger and brew and fries, buddy. You haven't seen or heard anything yet," York assured Jeffrey. Gary and Gail exchanged knowing glances.

Jeff put his cheeseburger down then moved the bottle aside; he couldn't swallow. Jeff was suddenly sick with dread. Gary and Gail stepped aside and made small-talk about a motion in another case while they waited for Troy.

A few minutes later, Troy returned carrying a box with many tiny holes that looked exactly like the one that Vic had removed from a case when he placed it upon the table in the Greenport bar-and-grill, the box that Jeff had indeed discarded in a Dumpster in Southold.

"Troy, why don't you show Jeff and Ms. Fox just how ingenious we are here at headquarters and how we retrieved a second tape recording," Gary invited.

"Sure thing," Troy said, inverting the box and sliding out a panel that formed a false bottom. He removed a tiny recording device.

"This was set on voice-activated," Gary explained. "As soon as any significant sound is picked up, the machine starts. Sound stops, it stops. Six hours of recording time. Nothing out of James Bond, or anything like that. You can pick up something similar in Radio Shack. Except that this one is much more sophisticated. Super sensitive. And therefore, *mucho dinero*."

Once again, Troy fast-forwarded the tape.

The whirring noise unnerved Jeff.

The detective hit STOP then PLAY.

—oddamn it! These are five-hundred-dollar boots. Fuck!

Troy spun the tape ahead rapidly.

Jeff accidentally knocked over the rest of his ale.

"Last one, asshole," Gary said and laughed.

Troy pressed the advance button.

Been buggin' me about a picnic since we stepped foot out of the car . . . . This is what we call a showdown in this neck of the woods, Bad Rock . . . . Katie, I don't want you to have to see this.

Katlyn's giggling was followed by a sudden thud.

Head. Stone. Flowers. Headstone, flowers. Sorry, Katie. But I have to drag you off to a potter's field in your five-hundred-dollar boots. At least you're as good as out of the woods . . . . See? You're not the only fashion plate. Come along now, Katydid. Got to get a move on. This is no picnic for either of us. Let's go . . . . My man said deep, Katie. And don't worry about no ticks. I mean, any ticks. They can't hurt you now . . . .

The machine seemed to run on forever before Jeff's voice was heard anew.

There. Just pick up after myself, and I'm out of here. . . . Don't mean a thing if you ain't got that swing. Doo-wop, doo-wop.

Jeff's face was white.

"We watched you put the box in the back seat when you came out of the wood lot in Southold. I had a bet with one of my colleagues that you'd have another conversation with yourself before you dumped the box along with Katlyn's clothes," Gary confessed. "Lost a sawbuck on that wager, I did."

Jeff looked at Gary York as though he were nuts.

"Eat up, Jeff. I don't think you even touched those fries."

"Mr. Mills." It was the first time Gail addressed Jeff since she had questioned him during his arrest three years ago, along with Howard. "We have a deal for you. It's cut-and-dried. Life or death. It's a one-time offer. Nonnegotiable. Take it or leave it."

Jeff forced a laugh. He tried to act tough. He felt as though he might crap in his pants. "I want my lawyer," Jeff asserted.

"That's certainly fair, and it is the law," the assistant district attorney said. "I wanted you to hear this tape, though, before you called your attorney. I know you're not going to believe it when I tell you that we had all intentions of having you hear this days ago. But we've been extraordinarily busy with the discovery of a lot of bodies on the East End of the Island, in addition to working on four death penalty cases. One of which may be your own. To be especially blunt, Mr. Mills, I don't think Mr. Casey is going to take your case considering what he has learned over the past few days from several sources. The reason I say that is because he only handles cases that he feels are winnable, or at least have a good chance of a favorable plea offer. I could be wrong, but I believe your hope for an acquittal is doomed to failure from the start. It would be like putting all your money, and I'm talking every penny you have, on a long shot. You wouldn't do that, now, would you? Because in addition to losing all your money and declaring yourself broke, the odds are that you're going to lose your life as well. I'd give anybody interested very good odds on that. And as far as getting a good attorney to handle this capital case that we're building against you, I'd say you'd be hard-pressed to find anyone truly qualified. You know yourself that the death penalty law is relatively new. Anyhow, be my guest and call your attorney and see. But once we play portions of that tape for Casey, the deal will be withdrawn. You'll have your day in court. I'd wager a hundred-to-one that the outcome will be death by lethal injection. I can only remind you how things turned out for your brother, Howard."

All three figures stood before Jeffrey T. Mills. Standing in judgment.

"Your fingerprints are on the bottle of ale taken from the bar-and-grill in Greenport, Jeff," Gary added. "Vic's fingerprints are on the glass of whiskey. So don't tell me or your lawyer that the two of you weren't there because we have photos of the both of you entering and leaving the bar. We have other pictures, too."

"I have some crime scene photos for you to look at and initial and papers for you to sign off on, Jeff," Fox said. "It's true confession time." She tapped her bundle of Manila envelopes lovingly. "Give you one hour to decide. Beth Tracy, Roselyn James, Ilona Alfold and Katlyn Land had no choice in the matter. One hour, Jeff." Gail walked away. Troy followed after her.

The prosecutor hadn't gotten more than ten feet before Jeffrey Mills started ranting and raving.

"YOU BLACKMAILING SONS OF BITCHES! THE PACK OF YOU. YOU WON'T GET AWAY WITH THIS. I CAN HIRE A *BATTERY* OF LAWYERS. I CAN BUY THE VERY BEST. YOU'RE MAKING A VERY BIG MISTAKE. I'LL BANKRUPT THIS COUNTY. SUFFOLK WILL BE A WASTELAND. WAIT AND SEE IF I DON'T MAKE IT HAPPEN."

"One hour, Jeff," The Dragon Lady called back. "One hour."

"Only problem is, Jeff, that attorneys like Casey have no layaway plan for the likes of you," Gary stated. "This is not some bullshit case. We're talking four counts of murder one. Casey and his co-counsel will want a *bigger* chunk of dough than what you have on hand from Katlyn. You won't be able to pay the consultation fee, let alone a retainer. That's because we came through with flying colors. We delivered, kid."

"FUCK YOU!"

"You're never going to see any of those millions, fella. Not a single dime. Not where you're going. And if by some fluke you happen to gain control of the empire, you'll have two choices. You can either sign it over to your brother, Ronald, who probably deserves it more than anyone else in that *meshuga* family of yours—that the right word, Jeffrey?—or leave it to your cat. And speaking of your cat, Kevin Casey still has Orbit and your keys. He'll probably tack on a boarding fee to your tab in addition to his retainer if he takes you on at all," the detective said, reinforcing the prosecutor's words.

"If he still had my keys and cat, he'd know where I am," Jeff reasoned. "And he'd be here."

"Not necessarily. But someone did tell him you may or may not be calling his office within the hour."

"You knew about Katlyn, and you let her die? Set me and Vic up?"

"Careful, Jeffrey. Sounds like you're on the verge of a full confession. Should I get Ms. Fox back here with her papers?"

"I ain't going down alone, by God. I'll tell you that."

"Of course you're not. Vic's an accessory to murder. He's going to do some time."

"Some time? And you want me to spend the rest of my life in a fucking cell?"

"Or in the ground. Couldn't care less."

"Fuck you."

"Let me say this, Jeff. You can either take the secret to the grave, or you can spin the yarn upstate, which nobody's going to believe anyhow. You and I both know that Howard didn't do any of the killings. Correct?"

A tiny smile curled at the corners of Jeff's mouth.

"Beth did and you did," York elaborated. "You'd dress up and pretend to be her. Yes? Well, Suffolk County and the state are going to see to it that Howard doesn't die. For his role in some of those murders, meaning postmortem amputations, he's going to spend the rest of his natural life in prison. The appeals process will prove to be one big charade. Your brother probably belongs in a nut house, but that wasn't in the cards because of how Dunn and Profeta played their hands. Had they known that he was truly innocent of those murders, things probably would have turned out differently. But it is the way it is for now. State has to save face, but at the same time, it's going to do what it believes to be just." Detective York put his head down for a moment, reflecting. "Tell me something. Doesn't it give you some peace of mind to know that your brother isn't going to die for crimes he didn't commit?"

Jeff didn't say a word.

"I see. About as much concern for Howard as you have for your cat. Right?" York slowly shook his head. "What makes guys like you tick? Tell me. I'm at a loss. I really don't get it. Is it simply in the genes, meaning that you're preprogrammed from the start? Or is it a seeming sickness that you cultivate because of something that went haywire in your life? Huh?" The detective waited for a response. "Can't or won't answer that?"

"You tell me something. What kind of cop are you who misrepresents himself as a lawyer and promises to get my brother into a mental hospital if he cooperates and signs a false confession? What kind of cop are you who lets Katie die in order to set me up? Will you answer me that?" Jeffrey asked, swiping a tear or two off his cheek.

"That's easy," York answered freely. "The kind of dick who knows how to rid the streets of garbage."

Chapter Sixty

Detectives Mick Connolly, Frank Masselli, Eric Bokina, Troy Anderson and John Bailey were seated on either side of a conference table at police headquarters in Yaphank. Detective Sergeant Cary Carter sat at one end. Detective Lieutenant Theodore Groche, commander of the homicide squad, sat at the head of the group assembled before him.

"Jeff will go for it," Mick said confidently.

"Then why did Jeff make that phone call to Casey?" Anderson asked.

"Because he feels he has nothing to lose at this point, that Gail will still offer him the same deal. And if Jeff does tell Casey about the box and the meeting with Vic in Greenport, two things are going to happen. One: Casey's going to dismiss the whole story as delusional; a piece of fiction on his client's behalf in order to launch another cop conspiracy. Casey might even think that Jeff told Howard to make up that story about Gary passing himself off as an attorney," Mick conjectured with a big smile. "Two: If Casey does buy into Jeff's story, we create the fiction. What meeting? What tape? What box?"

"What corrupt detective?" Masselli added with a chuckle.

"We can't use any of the stuff anyways," Mick Connolly continued.

"Maybe we could alter a portion of the tape if we have to," Eric suggested. "Do a voice-over on Vic, or take him completely out of the picture, claiming that some mystery man, like Deep Throat in the Watergate investigation, later wrote everything down—saying that Jeff did all the talking. Sort of like the game Gary played with Howard."

"Yeah, we'll just go dig up Rose Mary Woods for you," Bailey kibitzed, alluding to President Nixon's secretary who may or may not have *inadvertently* erased incriminating taped conversations in the Oval Office as they pertained to the Watergate scandal.

"Enough with the digging," Anderson balked. "Beth Tracy's flower gardens proved to be a virtual cemetery. I feel like I belong to the gravedigger's union."

"I'll second that," Mick said.

"You?" Carter countered. "You walked around holding a shovel in one hand and your ear in the other. How the hell do you dig like that?"

"Malingerer," Mick's partner swore.

Theo sat back smiling, taking it all in. After a minute of good-natured back-and-forth bantering, the commander spoke up. "Let's hope Mick's right. Let's pray Jeff will go for it. What Gail told Mills upstairs is probably true. I don't believe Casey's going to take the case. Jeff doesn't have the necessary funds. And if he somehow manages to come up with the money, Casey's going to tell Jeff to take the plea, even without hearing any portion of the tape," the lieutenant affirmed. "The depositions alone, coupled with Southold's entomological evidence, are enough to bury Jeffrey Mills. He has no alibi for either Katlyn Land or Ilona Alfold. He killed his alibi witness when he murdered Katlyn Land," Theo summarized. "If he mentions Vic, the meeting, the box or the tape, I'd have to agree that it sounds like one of the most farfetched stories I've ever heard."

"A fucking fairy tale," Mick put in. "Like Humpty Dumpty."

"I told you before that's a nursery rhyme," Bailey came back at him.

"When did ya ever tell me that?" Mick challenged with a grin.

"Nevermind."

"Just what I thought," Mick concluded.

Theo got up and placed both palms on the table. "All right. Let's see where all this goes. As soon as Casey gets here, you give me a call. I don't think he'll be here much before two o'clock because he's still in court. Meanwhile, let's see if Jeffrey Mills has had time to think things through. You never know. Let's see if he bites . . . if you'll pardon the pun, Mick. Eric, why don't you go up and see our boy. Put on some of that innocent schoolboy charm of yours. I think Jeffrey Mills has just about had it with the rest of you fellows."

Everyone seated around the table smiled and nodded in agreement.

Jeffrey Mills had held out for his attorney. The two sat in the 8 x 8 foot interview room. Jeff's hands were cuffed in front of him. Kevin Casey was shaking his head and staring at the ceiling, then down at his briefcase on the table, and finally at the floor.

"I can't help you if you don't level with me, Jeff."

"I'm leveling with you."

"Bullshit. They've got a half a dozen written and signed depositions from witnesses who place you at your half sister's apartment in Orient Point with Ilona Alfold."

"Do they have a body? No. So what do they have?"

"Five people who saw you with Ilona shortly before she disappeared; another who says he saw you kill her."

"They're all nuts."

"What they say on the stand and how they're perceived by a jury will determine whether they're nuts or not. Ole Gundersen, a.k.a. Nec, could seal your fate."

"You'll make mincemeat out of that guy. He's a necrophiliac! He's got a criminal record."

"He hasn't killed anyone. He sneaks into funeral parlors and cops a feel. Plays with the dead. He says you clobbered her. He fiddled with Ilona for an hour afterward while you cleaned up. Then the two of you got her out of there. That's his statement."

"He's in custody. He'll say anything. How can they put a guy like that on the stand?"

"I'm telling you they will. Along with the other five."

Jeffrey was chewing up the corner of his thumb.

"Why don't you tell me what happened, Jeff. It's your only shot. The prosecutor's going to link you to Roselyn James through Ilona Alfold, establish motive as she'll do with Beth Tracy. Money. Millions of dollars waiting in the wings. People do outrageous things for a lot less. Forensic folks say you have no alibi concerning Katlyn. She was killed a lot earlier than what you're telling me. There are witnesses who saw you leave the Orient By The Sea restaurant with her late Saturday night."

"And I'm telling you we were together most of the night and into the next day."

"Not according to the lab report."

"Fuck the lab report, and fuck that forensic shit! Can't you see they're setting me up?"

"Who's setting you up?"

"The police. That Detective York. And that other guy."

"What are you talking about?"

"They switched boxes."

"What boxes?"

"Jesus, Mary and Joseph."

"Didn't know you switched affiliations," Kevin Casey joked.

"Funny. You gonna listen and tell me what to do?"

"That's what I get paid for."

"All right. Then listen. But you're not gonna believe this."

"Why don't you start from the beginning? I want to hear it straight."

Jeff nodded, relating the story in part as it pertained to Detective Victor Posteraro. The client told his attorney how the disgruntled cop had first approached him, slowly building trust and carefully laying out a scheme as to how the two of them could, with the right connections, get their hands on a veritable fortune. Howard's. Vic hadn't told Jeffrey anything that he didn't already know. Jeff had known for a good many years what had to be done to put himself in the catbird seat. The fat cat. The cat's whiskers. *Número uno.* The cat's meow. As a matter of fact, Jeffrey had been working on his own connections in that regard for quite awhile, slowly building bridges from America to Central America and down into South America. He had contacts of his own. The smell of considerable money and property drew a few corrupt officials out of the dung heap. But establishing trust was not as simple as adopting the adage that there was honor among thieves.

By way of analogy, mixed with a bit of hyperbole, Jeff realized that thieves—secreted along the fringes of foreign outposts—would steal the eyes out of a blind man, replace them with cat's-eyes, insist that the handicapped now had 20-20, then charge the sightless patient for a transplant operation. And if one didn't pay up, especially after a syndicate's time and trouble and *trust*, it would literally sever the head of the defaulter, perhaps shrink it, then possibly sell it as a trinket on the black market. The head in question would more than likely be his, if he weren't careful, realizing that he wasn't dealing with petty thieves but rather a highly organized criminal organization.

Rarely would a gringo's proposition pass the garrison and reach those in ultimate authority. Those in power, serving invisible masters, usually sought to do the corrupting for the cartel.

The contacts that Jeff needed in the lending institutions, too, were off limits. Some of them were offshore as well. Vic's purported network of promoters promised to pave the way and get the job done expeditiously, provided that Jeff could handle Howard, one way or another—inheritor and sole beneficiary.

As a mail handler with contacts via the postal service, Jeff had Victor T. Posteraro meticulously checked out through a most notorious source. Resourceful and untouchable was a certain Columbian drug lord. What Jeff didn't know but should have was that this Central American contact was a businessman who would offer his services to the highest bidder; favors and friendship notwithstanding. Vic's credentials as an underworld operator proved impeccable. Jeff's fears had been assuaged.

Jeffrey Mills was careful to tell his attorney the story in limited scope. No names, aside from Vic's, or specific details. Jeff was not stupid. It had taken him years to cultivate his contacts. He told Kevin Casey only what he had to tell him to show that there was, indeed, a crooked cop in their midst. Jeff went on to tell the lawyer about Saturday's late night meeting at the defunct Greenport bar-and-grill. About the case and box containing maggot larvae, insects and the planted audiotape recorder. He told him about Vic's arrest and his bloody beating in that very room, about some kind of deal being worked out whereby the detective would do "little time" for his culpability. Jeff finally finished his incredible story then sat back in the chair, awaiting his attorney's advice.

Kevin Casey sat motionless, staring at his client as though he bore two heads.

"Well?" Jeff said.

"Well?"

"Yeah, man. Like what the fuck are we gonna do? They want me to confess to four murders, or they're gonna stick a needle in my arm. Vic fucked up, gave me up, and they've probably offered him a sweetheart of a plea for his cooperation against me."

Kevin Casey shook his head in disbelief and sheer disgust. "Jeff, look at me. What are you trying to pull?"

"Whattaya mean, what am I trying to pull?"

"Is this your way of telling me you want to shoot for an insanity plea?" Casey postulated.

"What the hell are you talking about, insanity plea? I'm talking about a crooked cop who they're gonna use to try and bury me, Kevin."

Kevin Casey shook his head. "Detective Posteraro is not going to testify against you, Jeff."

"Whattaya mean?"

"Detective Posteraro is a detective with the First Squad in West Babylon."

It was now Jeff who was shaking his head. "He *was* with the squad there, Kevin. Haven't you been listening to me? His commander is doing his papers as we speak; he's been fired from the police force. He's—"

"Whoa, Jeff! Time out." Kevin Casey formed the letter T with his hands. "Detectives York, Anderson, and Bokina have been telling me that you've made specific allegations referencing Detective Posteraro as a corrupt cop, as you're doing now. Is that correct?"

"I just told you. He *is* a corrupt cop."

"And they beat him in your presence, you said?"

"Kevin, where was your head when I was telling you what went down? Listen to me," Jeff said excitedly. "They switched the box of maggot larvae and beetles on Vic after our meeting, giving me a different window of time. A much earlier one. I'm telling you, they set me up."

"Beetles?"

"For her hair."

"Katlyn's?"

"Goddamn it, yes!"

"You're telling me that they set you up and—"

"Somehow framing me for Katlyn's murder," Jeffrey hedged.

Casey sat and didn't say a word.

"I know it sounds crazy, Kevin, but that's exactly what they did. It's the only way they figured to get at me."

"By framing you for Katlyn Land's murder?"

"She was expendable. They figured her for the Death by Chocolate Killer, anyhow."

"The who?" The attorney couldn't help but smile.

"Murders that took place in Maryland."

Kevin Casey was back to shaking his head again. "You're losing

414

me, Jeff. Let's back up to Vic Posteraro for a second."

Jeff was getting angrier by the second. "Yeah, let's."

"I just spoke with Detective Victor Posteraro at the First Precinct Bureau in West Babylon, about an hour ago."

"So? I guess that's where they're holding him."

"He was at is desk when I spoke to him."

"What?" Jeff looked positively bewildered. "What are you talking about? They arrested Vic. They beat the shit out of him, and Connolly threw him in here with me. Aren't you listening? Then that York piece of shit went to work on Vic. Kicked the crap out of him, like one of them did to me. He was bleeding, man. Then Vic's old partner came in and started reading him the riot act on how he got the goods on him and me. So don't sit there telling me he's sitting at his desk in West Babylon. More likely a hospital bed with a few cracked ribs."

Kevin Casey sighed. "Look."

"No, you look! Something's very fucking wrong." Jeff's head was swimming. He looked like he was going to faint. "Fuckin' ale."

"Ale? What ale?"

"A strong lager from Holland. Can't you see what they're trying to do, Kevin? York gave me a Grolsch yesterday."

"A what?"

"A Grolsch. Eric Bokina gave me two today. Probably slipped me a Mickey."

Kevin Casey was connecting the dots: Grolsch and Lieutenant Groche; a Mickey and Detective Mick Connolly. Either his client was, indeed, delusional or simply laying the groundwork for an insanity plea.

As Jeff continued explaining, he realized how preposterous his story sounded. He was beginning to get an inkling as to what was going down when suddenly the door to the interrogation room opened wide. The homicide detective was standing at its threshold.

"Hello, Jeff. Mr. Casey. How are we faring here this afternoon, gentlemen?" Detective Vic Posteraro asked with a straight face, his gold badge hanging officially off the breast of his suit jacket pocket.

Frank Masselli stepped into the room behind his former partner. "Gentlemen. We making any headway here?"

"You motherfucking bastards," was all that Jeff could muster.

"That's most ungrateful," Masselli offered. "And here Detective Posteraro came all the way from West Babylon to wipe your nose for you, trying to be a nice guy and help you out like he tried to help Howard. And that's even after some of the nasty things you said about this detective."

Detective Gary York stepped into the room carrying a medium-sized brown paper bag. He went right up to the table to where Mills and Casey were sitting and started unpacking the contents.

"Here we go, Jeff. Got everything you ordered. Chicken chow mein, an egg roll, roast pork fried rice, and the soup's right down here on the bottom. Egg drop/won ton mix. Oh, and a can of Coke. Jeff eats better here than I do at home, Kevin. Glad you're here to see that we take good care of our guests. Jeff's going to eat us out of house and home." York peered into the empty bag. "What!? No fortune cookie? Well, I can fill you in later on that account." Gary spent the next thirty seconds opening the containers for his prisoner. "Think I can trust you with these utensils, Jeff?"

Gary didn't have to wait but a millisecond for the answer as the entire contents on the table went flying through the air. Kevin Casey fell off his chair as Frank Masselli and Vic Posteraro grabbed and held Jeff down.

"Can't be too good to these people, Casey. They take advantage," Gary said calmly.

Kevin Casey, Esquire, couldn't hear a word over his client's screams. Gary helped the attorney from the floor. Casey grabbed his briefcase, completely covered with Chinese food, then headed quickly for the door.

"YOU FIND YOURSELF ANOTHER LAWYER!" Casey shouted at Jeffrey Mills.

Jeffrey quickly considered the man's advice. "YOU'RE FUCKING FIRED, FUCKER!"

"Amounts to about the same thing," Gary said evenly to the attorney. "Maybe even better this way."

"I'LL BUY MYSELF SOME REAL TALENT, NOW! YOU'LL SEE!"

A few seconds later, Jeff was handcuffed with his hands in back of him, left leg shackled to the floor.

Chapter Sixty-One

Time dragged slowly for those connected with the Jeffrey Mills matter. As far as the public knew, Jeffrey had served his time for having helped his brother, Howard, dispose of bodies. They knew nothing of Jeff's more recent arrest and questioning by police. Bail had been set at one million dollars.

Having learned of Beth's murder, Howard Mills had relinquished the entire estate to his brother, Jeffrey. Jeffrey Mills disappeared off the face of the earth. No one was talking. Those who had the answers, buttoned up. Others who likely knew part of the story remained tight-lipped, speculating among themselves. Bosses and employees at the post office on John Street hadn't seen or heard from Jeff. The rumor mill started running at breakneck speed through the middle of June. One source said that the police were holding Jeffrey incommunicado. Another proclaimed that Jeff had taken a plane to Bolivia. Yet, another insisted that the bail provision had allowed Jeff to divide his time between staying with his younger brother, Ronald, in Hempstead, Long Island, and his Aunt Sadie in Texas. Ronald Mills flatly denied that Jeffrey was staying with him. And after nothing noteworthy turned up, there were those who speculated that Jeff had taken his own life.

It was nearing the middle of July, and not a word about Jeff was to be found in any local or mainstream newspaper. Not a syllable was aired. The focus was on Howard Mills. Howard was presently the center of attention.

There were those who thought this day would never come. Howard Mills entered Judge Steven C. Best's courtroom for the final time, minutes away from the formal sentencing for the murders of Jane Doe/Medford, Danielle Louise Clarke, and Claudia Rose Stetson. Howard looked a mess and was directed to take a seat between Nicholas Dunn and Christopher Profeta. Their client wore the same familiar clothing. Only this time, the green sweater assumed no particular shape as it was stretched out widthwise to its limit and hung off Howard's shoulders like a shawl. A crumpled shirt draped a pair of soiled and wrinkled khaki pants. Adding insult to misery, it was clear that a comb hadn't touched Howard's filthy, oily hair in days. Nor had the prisoner shaved. It was twelve minutes past ten in the morning, July 12th, 1999. The twelfth of never was at hand.

At 10:14, Jack Stetson was asked to come forward, step up to the podium, and address the defendant for the purpose of delivering an impact statement. Mr. Stetson rose from his seat at the rear of the courtroom, went swiftly through the gate in the railing, then up to the podium. He set down a 3 x 5 lined index card before him, but the man needed no reminder of what he had to say. The tiny card merely served as a point-by-point indicator in case he lost his cool. Jack adjusted the portable wooden platform squarely to meet Howard Mills' eyes.

Actually, Howard had to crane his head ninety degrees, looking over his left shoulder in order to meet the man's angry gaze.

Dressed in a black suit and dress shoes, Jack Stetson began his statement.

"I waited a long time for this day. Since December 11th, 1995. As I sat in this courtroom, day after day, I wanted to come up to you and break your neck over that railing," he said, pointing to the three-foot-high partition behind him. "And believe me, I could have. But I thought about my family, my wife and daughter, and what it would do to them. I'm not like you, *Coward* Mills," he continued. "You've committed crimes that are beyond human comprehension." Jack wiped away a tear. "If I do something in the course of life I like, well, I keep doing it. If I do something I don't like, I stop. You, *Coward*, enjoyed what you were doing, or you wouldn't have repeated it. Your lack of remorse is despicable." The man paused. "I have scars on my heart and in my mind that will remain forever. I have a vision of my Claudia as a beautiful angel, but she has no goddamn hands," he swore through a tremble. By 10:17, Stetson was totally in tears. "I pray to God each night that when I wake that vision will no longer be there. But it still returns."

Summing up his sermon, Stetson wrapped both hands around the corner of the pulpit as if it were Howard Mills' neck. "You don't deserve to live. I want to be there when they give you your injection. I want to envision you burning in hell."

Jack's younger daughter, Belinda, took to the podium. She was a pretty woman in spite of a heavy foundation of makeup and blush. She had Claudia's classic features. Belinda spoke to Howard directly, hardly above a whisper. She made clear how her sister's murder affected the entire family, ascribing particularly poignant passages to her father's physical and mental health and how she had watched him wither over the past three-and-a-quarter years. In a subdued manner, the woman told Howard that she didn't know him but hated him for the things he had done to her family, inclusive of the other victims' families that had suffered by his hand. In a well-nigh dispassionate tone, Belinda flat-out informed the defendant that she would love to be there when he got his injection.

A moment later, Howard was told to rise.

With a business-as-usual appearance, Judge Steven C. Best peered down at the defendant and formally pronounced sentence: "Howard Willis Mills, you are hereby sentenced to be put to death in a manner in accordance with the laws of New York State. May God have mercy on your soul."

Howard was near collapse and took his seat. Disheveled and haggard, the defendant was asked by the judge if he had anything to say. Still sitting, Howard spoke.

"Yes, Your Honor. And that is that I am innocent. I've said that since the beginning. I understand how the families of the victims feel. I'd feel the same way if anything happened to a member of my family. Most recently it did." Howard hung his head and wept, picturing his beloved half sister, Beth, buried deeply in the center of a flower bed. "I did not do these crimes. God knows that, and that gives me peace of mind. I am not a coward."

Judge Best signed the execution warrant, which was handed down to the defendant by a court officer. Howard was set to die by lethal injection on August 30th, 1999—although many of the people present in the courtroom knew that it would be years before the order would be carried out. Robert Redler knew, too, that the appeals and legal proceedings, wrangling and maneuvering, would be the cogs of the gears throughout the years that would grind that machinery to a halt. Several key players believed that the death penalty would soon be repealed because of the way in which juries were instructed by judges. Those in the seat of power positively knew that the new death penalty law would be declared unconstitutional.

The new New York State death penalty law, concerning Long Island, would now focus on its next victim. It would be a day laborer from Shirley, who had raped and murdered a thirty-two-year-old high school art teacher and track coach from the Patchogue/Medford area. Redler knew her father from the Moose Lodge where he kept his boat.

Redler's heart went out to the victim's parents and their entire family. The deceased's father and his son-in-law attended the trial virtually every single day. It was a constant reminder for the writer that the world was anything but fair. Far from it, in fact.

Redler was pulled from his thoughts by the voice of Jack Stetson calling out to Howard Mills as the prisoner was being led from the courtroom.

"I'll be there the day you die!"

Chapter Sixty-Two

Emiel G. stood impatiently at an outdoor phone booth located near a local bar on the Indian River in Melbourne, Florida . . . waiting for Robert Redler to pick up the receiver at his home in Riverhead, New York. The old man was agitated, looking nervously over one shoulder and then the other.

"Come on, Rob. Pick up, damn it," Emiel snapped. A gliding, ghostly gull circled high above the boatyard, banking right then left before swooping low—as if homing in on the recurring rings. "Be home, boy . . . shit."

Redler finally picked up the phone. "Hello?"

"Don't say anything. I'll do the talking. You just listen and answer yes or no. Get in your car and call me from a pay phone at the lodge. Coins. Lots of them. No calling card. I'll be at the watering hole. You got the number?"

"Not in my head, but handy."

"Good. Have Joey B. page me."

"Everything all right?"

"If everything was all right, I'd be on my boat fishin' or girl-watchin'. Now move." Emiel hung the receiver on the hook.

Redler gathered up a slew of quarters and hustled out of the house and into his vehicle. Four minutes later, he was at the pay phone in the parking area of the Moose Lodge. He dialed a private number at a bar in Melbourne. The phone swallowed up a heap of silver. The connection was made, and the proprietor picked up. "Yeah?"

"Joey B.?"

"Whattaya sellin'?" the grating voice questioned.

"Emiel there?"

"We got a lot of Emiel's here. Who wants to know?"

"New York."

"Never heard of it."

"Emiel G. there or not?"

Redler waited a New York minute before his friend got on the line.

"Rob?"

"What's going on?"

"He's here."

"Who's there?"

"Jeffrey Mills."

Redler took a deep breath and let it out slowly. "What's the story, Emiel?"

"Big!"

"Where's he holed up exactly?"

"Flew into Miami two days ago. They got him stashed in the Glades. Exactly where, I don't know."

"Who's got him stashed?"

"Several Central and South Americans, along with a couple of retired agents who are making a federal case out of this."

"What? Why? How are they and the feds involved?"

"Waiting for a wire transaction to go through from a central bank in the Bahamas. Howard Mills turned everything over to Jeff."

"Howard's a basket case. What about diminished capacity? Howard lawyers can't even talk to him from what I'm hearing."

"Jeffrey's got a team of lawyers setting things in motion and running interference for him. So he's out on bail again. Only this time, he's flown the coop. No extradition where he's headed. He'll of course forfeit a million, but that's chump change because money talks and bullshit walks, Rob. Suffolk County could care less 'cause they couldn't make anything stick. Couldn't get him to confess."

"What's this estate worth, Emiel?"

"Fifty million, cold cash—not including red-hot real estate properties in Central America; mostly, Columbia. Not to mention several other garden spots in South America. We're talking close to a billion bucks all told."

"What about Howard Mills? I believe he's innocent of murder, Emiel. How can Jeffrey Mills get away with this?"

"You listening to me? You never listen. Fifty million American. You could buy a Third-World country for that. Jeffrey's buying his freedom. Some kind of charade is being set in place to appease the powers that be in your lovely state. Not that it couldn't happen anywhere. New York's not going to undo what it's done concerning Howard Mills. Period. Howard signed over everything. There was a lot of legal maneuvering and posturing, but when the smoke cleared, a deal was cut. Jeff is going to be living somewhere in Central or South America. That's all I know at the moment."

"Can you document any of this?" Redler asked excitedly. "Can you throw me a crumb? I know a few people at *Newsday* who will listen to me. Maybe let me do the story." The writer's mind went off in several directions at once. *What country and where exactly would Jeffrey Mills take up residence?* Redler was writing the news in his head.

"Now, you listen to me, and you listen very carefully. You have that other death penalty case going on in Long Island. The Shirley roofer who murdered that teacher. They're going to be entering the sentencing phase soon concerning that guy. Jury convicted him. Yes?"

"Yes, but—"

"But nothing. You've got to listen to me on this one, Rob. With both ears, even though you've only got one of them planted to the phone. Am I getting through to you?"

"Say your piece."

"Take a look around you. You're at the pay phone at the lodge. Right?"

"You running paranoid on me?"

"Anything missing from the picture that was once part of the scene?"

"What are you getting at?"

"Your boat that went up in flames four years ago."

"What about it?"

"That was just a warning."

"From who? A nineteen-year-old white piece of trash who liked playing with matches?"

"Yeah, five minutes after you not only finished winterizing your vessel but spring commissioning it, too—putting fifty some hours into it, you told me—compounding and waxing. Isn't that just a little too coincidental? Doesn't that tell you something?"

"Like what?"

"Like that you were being watched."

Redler had, in fact, considered a myriad of theories, one of which was that he was, indeed, being singled out; that is, until the ADA working the case assured him that the troubled young man had set many fires to homes, garages, boats, cars and businesses. A pyromaniac. The detectives who had arrested the perp told the writer that the kid was positively bonkers.

"Why am I being watched?"

"Well, you do have a way of pissing off the wrong people with your prose. You'd agree?"

"And you didn't in your day? And what does that have to do with the Howard Mills case? Nothing, that's what. As a matter of fact, it was the boat burning business that brought me to the courtroom where I learned that Howard Mills was ten days into pretrial with the lead detective on the stand. I didn't even do a piece on the trial until it was well under way."

"And what pieces concerning two Long Island felons did you write about awhile back?"

"Keith King and Lee Coulter. Two convicted rapists who were ultimately released from prison."

"Because?"

"They didn't do it."

"Don't get cute. Because why, exactly?"

"Because DNA excluded them as the rapists. That's why."

"Right. And who blocked their release for a year-and-a-half?"

"Where we going with this?"

"Answer me, please"

"Patterson."

"Your infamous Suffolk County D.A."

"The point of all this?"

"What was the other story you did recently on DNA? Can't even pronounce it."

"Mitochondrial testing."

"You haven't bothered to link up the common denominators yet, have you?"

"What common denominators?"

"All the burnings and all the stories concerning the new state-of-the-art DNA testing—mitochondrial—or however the hell you pronounce it."

"Said it fine. Tell me what you mean."

"Surprised you haven't figured it out for yourself."

"Me, too. So tell me. This is costing me a fortune."

As if on cue, a recording came on asking the caller for his weight in silver—or so it seemed. Redler deposited more quarters.

"Every car, home, garage, boat, business—and I left out a plane at Gabreski Airport on the south shore in Westhampton Beach—that went up in smoke was owned and or operated by writers, mostly freelance, who did stories on the criminal justice system, especially stories involving questionable police practices and especially DNA evidence that questioned the guilt of felons convicted in the Suffolk County Court under Patterson's reign of terror."

Redler turned and looked over his shoulder to where his boat had sat on boards and blocks shortly before it had been set on fire four seasons ago.

"It appears now that several of those so-called felons were framed," Emiel continued. "Some convictions were the product of questionable police work, while I'm sure others were convicted simply based on the mishandling of forensic evidence commingled in the lab. My guess would be that many more men and women sitting in your upstate prisons are going to be proven innocent in time. The mainstream press isn't casting aspersions or pointing fingers in a particular direction like you mavericks manage to nail down in the local papers. But Patterson's scrambling like a hermit crab right now. His underbelly is exposed, and he's seeking shelter wherever he can find it. Still, he's lashing out. His office is tainted. You know that. I know that. He's no one to mess around with at the moment. He's made a deal with the devil if my source of info is correct—and when have you ever known me to retract anything I've ever written or said?"

"Never, Emiel." And it wasn't that Rob was being cute.

"Good of you to note. So here's what you're going to do."

"Now hold on a second, Mr. G. If there's a story—"

"No time, except for you to listen up. You're going into that roofer's sentencing. When's it scheduled?"

"Planned on it anyways. Twenty-eighth of this month. Why?"

"Because you're going in there, and when they ask you how the Howard Mills book is coming along, you're going to tell them it's going great guns. That you're almost finished but you've abandoned the idea of a nonfiction account because it's too convoluted, protracted and incredible—contrary to what you're telling everyone you're going to do. Also, you'll tell them that you can't wait to get started on that Shirley roofer slash teacher case, and that you have an agent interested. Too, you'll tell them how you've been spinning your wheels writing articles that are taken with a grain of salt, that fiction is your vehicle to let the truth be known. Because let's face it, Rob. Woodward or Bernstein you're not—meaning that you don't have the resources, connections or backing. A factual account without the right contacts hasn't got much hope. Do like I tell you, and maybe they'll let you live."

"Come on, Emiel. Why don't *we* do the story? Forget about your fish and funky women. Nobody's gonna touch you down there."

"You're so naive, Rob. Part of your charm, I guess. Nobody's gonna touch this story. Not as fact, anyhow. No one's gonna write it, let alone you or me. This is a story that has to be told in terms of fiction. It's not just about big money, Rob. It's about an American institution—the criminal justice system of the United States of America. Best in the world, we believe. Just imagine conditions in other countries. This is a story about Suffolk County saving face. It's to be a story about the lies, conniving and cover-ups that have come to light over the course of darkness for many years, Rob. Go write it, but as fiction."

"I can't believe you're walking away from a story like this, or that you refuse to dump what you know into my lap. I can't believe this, Emiel."

"You know enough right now."

"Give me the name of your contact. Let me follow up."

"Listen to me for the last time."

"I'm listening. I always listen."

"It's time for us to get off the line. Bye, Rob."

Redler set the phone down gently on the receiver although he felt compelled to have slammed the conversation to a close.

Before leaving his favorite watering hole, Emiel had a Myers's rum and Coke. Original Dark. Double. Lemon and lime. He drove the few blocks back to the boatyard, parking at the far end of the adjacent marina as he always had. *Parking ol' Betsy out of harm's way*, he would invariably say—away from people who parked too close to one another, throwing car doors open with abandon—creating unnecessary nicks, scratches, scrapes, dents and gouges made by rods and reels, aluminum gas cans, or props affixed to hand-carried outboard engines.

Emiel G. locked the Lincoln Continental then headed in the direction of his boat. A shiny black sport-utility vehicle with dark tinted windows appeared from behind several cars parked close to the entrance of the marina. The SUV suddenly picked up speed, aiming directly for the old man who saw it and tried to get out of harm's way. The mass of metal swerved into him, solidly smashing flesh and bone with a sickening thud as the forty-four-hundred-pound murderous machine quickly fled from the scene.

Chapter Sixty-Three

Emiel Grinsberg's ashes were taken out to sea just south of Merritt Island. It was a hot July day. Emiel's family had made the necessary arrangements, and Robert Redler had said his good-byes following a quiet service, vanishing for a spell to his old friend's sacred watering hole. He sat for a time on one of the bar stools, trying desperately not to cry into his beer. After a cold brew, he decided to order something stronger. "Excuse me."

"Another beer?"

Redler shook his head. "Myers's Rum and Coke. Original Dark. Double. Lemon and lime. Please and thank you."

The barmaid looked at him without expression, turned around and took the bottle down from the shelf. She measured out a double shot, poured it over ice, hit the dispenser for Coke, then plopped in a wedge of lime and lemon.

Robert fixed his eyes on one of the overhead fans.

"Only one person I know orders that drink like that," the heavyset woman said, sliding the glass in front of him.

"And that person is dead," Redler said matter-of-factly.

The woman nodded. "You a relative?"

"Friend."

The woman nodded again. "You went to the service?"

"Yep."

"I had my kids this mornin', then got stuck here. I think they already put his ashes out to sea."

"That's where they were headed."

"Didn't go?"

"Just immediate family."

"Sucks. 'Cause many times friends are closer than family." The woman wiped the area in front of him with a sour-smelling dishrag, wrung it and opened it, draping the cloth over the edge of the sink behind the bar. "You from around here?"

"Nope."

"Didn't think so. Know most of the regulars. Know most of his friends, too."

Redler raised his glass and toasted the woman as if her pronouncement were a remarkable thing to note. Robert took a good swallow. *Whoa! Strong.*

The woman smiled and went down to the far end of the bar to a customer who stood between two stools, quietly sipping the last of his Scotch. She poured him another before coming back past Redler, disappearing down a hallway. Less than a minute later, she returned with a barrel-chested six-foot-three fellow. He nodded, said something to the woman who then busied herself back at the other end of the bar. Redler recognized the gravelly voice. The man stood directly in front of the out-of-towner.

Redler held the man's gaze. "Yeah?"

"You Redler?"

"Whattaya sellin'?"

The man grinned "You're Emiel's friend."

"I know a lot of Emiels. Who wants to know?"

"Yeah, you're the one from New York, all right."

"Never heard of it."

"You that writer, or not?"

Redler put his hand halfway across the counter before it disappeared into the big man's mitt.

"Joey B.," the fellow said, pumping the little paw. "I own the joint. Emiel gave me the down payment on the place a thousand sunsets ago. Wouldn't take a penny back until I was well on my feet. Bet you never knew that."

Redler shook his head.

"That's the kind of guy he was," the proprietor said, staring directly into the writer's eyes. "That was no hit-and-run accident, you know. That was a *hit*."

Redler nodded. "Was he on that phone over there in the corner?" Rob questioned.

"No, you called directly into the back on my private number. Bernice over there told him he had a call. He took it inside. After you guys hung up, he had a rum and Coke then left. Headed back to the boatyard. Never made it from his car to the boat. They hit him in the parking lot next to the marina. He was trying to warn you."

"He told you?"

"Didn't have to. I was standing right there."

Both men studied one another for a moment.

It was Redler who looked away. Guilt overcame him.

"He loved you, Rob. Didn't want to see you hurt."

"And because of me he's dead."

The owner smiled and shook his head. "No. Not you. Me."

Redler looked up and held the man's stare. "What do you mean?"

"I'm his contact."

"Jesus Christ." Redler took a gulp of his drink. "Should we even be talking here? I mean this place has got to be bugged," he said, lowering his voice to a whisper and gesturing toward the guy at the end of the bar.

Joey B. simply shook his head. "I had the place swept for e-bugs late last evening and then again before we opened up. I have some people covering the area outside, looking over anyone suspicious. Guy at the end of the bar is one of mine. Only bugs in here are the kind that crawl," he assured Emiel's friend.

"Who the hell and what the hell are you?" Redler asked uncomfortably, pushing his glass aside.

"Owner of this bar like I told you. Also, the gatekeeper of secrets up until a day or two ago, I guess."

"Secrets that got Emiel killed."

"That would be fairly accurate as I just told you," the bear of a man responded. "But you've got to understand he was directing you out of the line of fire. You have no idea how hot this whole Mills business has become."

"I just left the funeral parlor and listened to a speech delivered by a minister who offered me no words of comfort. Telling all of us how senseless and tragic my friend's death was. So please don't stand there and tell me how hot this Mills business has become unless you're going to tell me what this business is all about."

Joey B. grinned. "And if I were to do that, you'd be dead, and so would I before you ever filed your story."

"So much for sweeping this place for e-bugs," Redler said with a frown.

"Nothing to do with that. You see, I'd have to kill you myself. Then certain people would know why I had to do that, and I'd be dead as well. Then Bernice and my buddy over there would be listening to a eulogy and trying to make sense out of another senseless and tragic death. Mine. I say mine because I don't think either Bernice or my friend over there would be attending yours. So, as Mr. G. would ask you, 'Am I getting through to you?'"

"Things are about as clear to me as a fog bank," Redler replied, squeezing the wedge of lemon and then the lime above his glass, roiling the liquid together with a thin red stirrer.

"Well, then let me give you a better picture of who comes through that gate." Joey B. pointed to the door. "Sammy The Bull Gravano, once upon a time an underboss for John Gotti. I recall you did a couple of pieces on Gotti and one on Gravano after he left the witness protection program. Gravano went from here into hiding. We put him on a boat. Guess whose boat took him out of here? Since then a deal's been cut among several factions whereby he's out of hiding; living beside and liking his neighbors next-door. He killed nineteen people that we know about and lives his life with celebrity status. But he'll be back in bracelets before long. You see, the feds and the bad boys hardly ever mix it up together. Like oil and vinegar, they coexist. But to accomplish a greater end, they both know when it's time to toss the salad. I provide the bowl, the fork, the spoon.

"Jeffrey Mills is seemingly small potatoes," he continued. "Fifty mil is really chump change. Those real estate properties, however, are another story. Just shy a billion. Anyhow, your state fucked up concerning Howard Mills. Jeff and his half sister, Beth Tracy, were the killing machines. Only the state's not going to show you the egg on its face. Its problems are also being compounded by new DNA testing. Twenty-seven so-called serious felons are soon to be released from New York State prisons because new evidence has excluded them as murderers, rapists and the lot. Guess how many were tried in Suffolk under Patterson?" Joey B. didn't wait for an answer. "Better than two thirds. No surprise to anyone when you figure that the confession rate the Suffolk boys obtain is ninety-eight point something percent.

"Some of those convictions were the result of planted evidence. Most were not but were the product of dubious police and prosecutorial work, based on preconceived notions, unreliable eyewitness testimony, or faulty forensic findings. Patterson abused his office by putting undue pressure on his people and the police to secure convictions. It's about to bite him in the ass. You're not going to see that in any sort of print unless you publish it yourself. Guaranteed I'd read your obit in some local paper. Patterson made it under the wire of scrutiny this past election, but he's as sure as out next time around. What he's doing now, as you probably know, is grooming his son for a Suffolk County Supreme Court judgeship in exchange for stepping down. What I do, Rob, is deal with the devil to bring about the desired result for the good of the People. Sometimes men and women who have committed one or many murders may walk so as to prevent others from committing political genocide. Get the picture?" Joey B. put his hands out, palms up. "I weigh the scales of justice. Myself and others like me."

Redler took another sip. "Who killed Emiel is what I need to know."

"Feds? Flunkies? Somebody somewhere in between the top and bottom of the frenzied feeding column. You and I will never know." Joey B. placed one palm above the other. "The deck is stacked."

Redler was feeling sick.

"Let me tell you how dangerous you are to them." Joey B. ran himself a short river of seltzer in a water glass. "You're not drawing a salary. No one is paying you to write. You write what you want whether you get paid or not. And it gets published. Not in the mainstream presses. But you're making a dent. You're making some people very nervous, Rob. And then you sank your teeth into this Howard and Jeffrey Mills business. You went from pissing off the Suffolk police with your article on audio and videotaping confessions to exposing the fallacy of certain forensic practices. Fine. But you're pointing fingers, too. Do that in your fiction writing if you have to do it at all, like Emiel strongly suggested. Not in *The Southampton Press*. Not by speaking out on the Mills cases at a round table discussion on Channel 12 News, as we learned you're scheduled to do."

"Who's we?"

"Go home now and write your novels like Emiel told you to. You're in way over your head. I'm speaking for Mr. G. when I tell you this. Go home and write about the roofer-teacher slaying. Oh, and by the way. He really did do it. Murdered that poor young woman. That's a fact. Tell you another. No one on death row is going to die by way of lethal injection in the state of New York. Costs too much. They'll change the law before appeals run out. You'll see."

Redler threw down his drink in three quick swallows before he turned to leave, putting down a twenty. "I'm going home like you said. I'm going home to start a massive book. I'm going home to write a dozen articles for newspapers and magazines for little or no money. I'm going on the tube."

"It won't be a boat or a car or your home that they're going to burn next time out, Rob."

"No, when I get done, *they're* gonna wanna burn the book."

"Meaning what?"

"Meaning nonfiction. Meaning a tome filled with fucking facts."

"You dig them up, they're gonna bury you."

"We'll see."

"Your funeral."

Chapter Sixty-Four

Robert Redler sat across from William Franklin, the assistant to the *Newsday* publisher. They were discussing, in detail, how the new mitochondrial DNA testing gave forensic experts the ability to extract DNA from a single strand of hair, whereas before the breakthrough, it was necessary to have a root end of the shaft for analysis. Not too often did a perpetrator leave behind that kind of calling card.

"You realize, of course, that many convictions were obtained throughout the eighties and nineties," the writer emphasized, "especially in Suffolk County, because these forensic folks were permitted to testify that, 'Yes, the exemplars taken from the head and pubic area of the defendant are *consistent* with those found on or around the victim's body.' Couple that to erroneous eyewitness testimony, and bingo! The defendant's goose is cooked. *Consistent*, Bill. Microscopically, they only had what the police and prosecutors would misconstrue and plant in the jury's mind as a proof positive *match*. Look at these numbers. Like DNA testing, the results don't lie; it goes to the integrity of the evidence. Suffolk County's rate of conviction is alarming. Don't let them juggle the statistics. It is what it is. Close to thirty overturned convictions in the state. Two thirds of those prosecuted were right here in Suffolk under Patterson's regime. Let me do the story, Bill. Please."

William Franklin shook his head. "Rob. Number one, we have our own people on this mitochondrial testing. As a matter of fact, Linda's doing a piece on convicted rapists who were exonerated in New York State. And as for pointing a finger at Patterson, you simply don't have enough here." Upon his lap, the tall, well-spoken black man tapped the pages of Redler's outline. "Quite frankly, I don't think I'd let you go ahead with this even if you did have more to go on. Know why? It doesn't mean crap because Patterson's office is going to argue that an aggressive prosecutor is certainly going to nail down more convictions, overturned or not, and that a jury decided a defendant's fate. Not District Attorney Patterson. Too, the police had probable cause to arrest, the confessions were voluntary, conceding only in some cases that the admissions may have been the result of overzealousness on the part of the police."

"How do you translate deceit on the part of the police and the prosecutor's office into overzealousness?"

"Come on, Rob. Deceit's permitted. You even said so yourself in one of your articles. Remember? 'Chicanery's okay,' you said."

"Fine. How about misleading versus outright lying. You and I both know they crossed the line. Detective York misrepresented himself as a lawyer to Howard Mills, promising to warehouse him in a mental hospital instead of a prison cell."

"Prove it."

"Jeffrey and his half sister, Beth Tracy, killed hundreds of people, Bill."

"Prove it."

"The powers that be let Jeffrey Mills walk."

"Prove it. Ostensibly, Mills jumped bail."

Redler was getting nowhere. "If you'll allow me to go back in time," he pressed, "the cops planted evidence by going into Keith King's garbage, swabbing semen from a condom onto the alleged victim's clothes."

"Prove it."

Redler stared at the ceiling. "The government was behind the killing of my friend, Emiel G."

"Prove it."

Redler went for broke. "Patterson made a deal with the devil to keep people like you from having the truth be known."

"Again, prove it," William said, without betraying a trace of resentment in his voice or eyes. "Prove any of the above, and I'll let you write your story. Otherwise you're no different than the people you're accusing of underhandedness."

"Let me do the story without directly pointing a finger. Just the facts. Let the readers decide."

"Like I told you. We have our own people."

Disgusted, Redler stood, shook the man's hand from across the desk, then quietly exited the office.

Chapter Sixty-Five

Jeffrey Mills sat next to a dark-haired, light-skinned shapely young girl. She was all of sixteen and a bit drunk. The bartender came over, looked at Jeff, then poured the teenager another *aguardiente*, a popular Columbian liqueur. She thanked her companion in English, which was limited to about a dozen words, took a sip, then sang softly in the American's ear. She did not need music. Drunk or not, her voice was beautiful. Jeffrey loved this land with its sun and sky of red. He loved this little bird crooning in his ear. He knew none of the words but delighted in their satiny syllables. Sure and sexy. He believed it was a ballad. Jeff was learning refined things. Jeff was becoming a country gentleman in a foreign land. He sat there quietly, staring down shyly at his expensive leather boots, heels locked onto a rung of the wooden bar stool.

Minutes later, after staring into one another's eyes for an eternity, oblivious to the small crowd who filled the room, Mónica led Jeff away from the bar and back onto the outdoor patio. The night was clear and filled with millions of stars, along with a stark sliver of silver moon. Jeff pointed to the heavens. Mónica looked up in wonderment as Jeff scrawled an S across the face of the firmament before slashing two vertical lines through it.

"Dollar sign," Jeff explained, then hastily finger-painted the sky full with them. "I have one peso for every star you see tonight," he declared. It was certainly a stretch because Jeff was patiently waiting for significant funds to clear. He reached for his golden, diamond-studded money clip and withdrew a thick wad of bills, holding them up against the stars. "*Mucho dinero*," he declared. "Millions and millions of dollars; like the stars."

"Ah," the pretty girl caught on and laughed. "*Ven*," she summoned. "*Baile conmigo*." She opened her arms for one more dance.

"Last dance," Jeff swore. "And then we leave."

Mónica seemed to understand.

The two walked from the cafe in the tiny village below the Cordillera Oriental, Villavicencio. Southeast of Bogotá. It was a perfect time of year. May of the new millennium, 2000. A year for every bloodstain found at 42 Willow Lane by the police and forensics people, Jeff exulted sillily . . . now thousands of miles from a place that never really felt like home. Mónica was a good many kilometers away from her home. She couldn't care less. She was having a fling. Jeff held her hand as if he were holding on to that of a small child. He thought he heard movement behind him, but when he turned around, it was only the sight and sound of a cat. Twice the size of Orbit. Completely black . . . unless it was a phantom's shadow creeping along in the night, Jeff considered, wearing a cautious smile. Daytime travel through the continent for Jeff proved to be the land of countless llamas, cattle and crops.

"Come," Jeff said, pulling Mónica along. "I've got a million and one things to attend to. But you're my number one tonight. *Número uno.* Yes? He put the tip of a finger just above her breast. "*Tú.*"

"*Yo?*"

"*Sí, tú.*"

Mónica rose to her tiptoes and pecked Jeff on the cheek. She thought he was the dreamiest of all the men she had ever met. A rich American, no less. In truth, money was not as important to her as friendship. She felt at that moment their relationship had developed into something far more special. Mónica had been falling in love since the moment Jeff picked her up at a marketplace just outside her hometown that morning.

Mónica so reminded him of Ilona.

"*Like tak-ing can-dy from a ba-by*," Jeff sang as they strolled along a beaten path.

Mónica was so excited, for she had recognized the American

song.

"*Ike ta-keen can-dy from a ba-by*," she mimicked phonetically.

"Hey, you have a pretty good ear," he rejoiced, for he couldn't be happier at that moment. Freedom along with a virtual fortune was practically his.

The pair walked hand in hand for over a mile when Jeff suddenly grabbed Mónica by an ear and pulled her off the path. Mónica cried out in sheer surprise.

Drawing a knife from the top of his boot, Jeff released the blade with the press of a button. *Flash!* Grabbing a handful of her shoulder-length hair, he threw the young girl roughly to the ground.

"Back home I had to bash them in the head to keep them from screaming," Jeff remarked, gently running the back of the blade above the bridge of her nose. "I didn't know what I was missing. I even like your shrieking better than your singing," he swore in utter exhilaration. "From a mile away I bet you sound like a bird of prey." Jeffrey pointed the tip of the blade below her left eye.

The teenager screamed again.

"I'm going to cut you up like ribbon and watch you bleed. *Sí?*"

Mónica shivered and shook her head as if she clearly understood.

"You see, murder is a universal language," he went on, letting go of her hair and reaching into a shirt pocket for his contact lens case. "It's kind of like fucking with or without music because you don't need any words." Jeff deftly put a lens into his left eye. The other into his right. "There."

Mónica was trembling. Rattling off Spanish a mile a minute. She couldn't believe her eyes. Why was he doing this? The moment begged for an answer. She pleaded for a reason. What had she done wrong?

Jeffrey grinned. "Sorry, but Spanish is not my native tongue, bitch."

"But you do understand plain English, don't you?"

The voice came from somewhere behind Jeff.

Jeff spun wildly about.

The form stood in the shadow of the tall grasses, bushes and trees.

Jeff took a step forward and laughed. "I know this looks kind of crazy, but my girlfriend and I were just having a little argument. And then we make up. It's just a game we play," he explained. "Sex gets fucking wild," the killer elaborated. Jeff took another step toward the stranger.

The figure stepped from the dark vegetation and into the penumbra.

Jeff saw the arm extended through his light-collecting contacts, the menacing pistol pointed toward the center of his chest. The intruder was wearing what appeared to be a pair of skintight latex gloves.

"You've got this figured all wrong," Jeff went on. "Let me tell you what's going on here. Please."

"Toss that knife over here and kneel down. Now."

Jeff let out a rushing breath of air as if he were really annoyed instead of truly scared, biting down on the rim of his ten-thousand-dollar diamond ring. "Goddamnit, tell him we were only fucking around." The bon vivant broke the second or so of silence. "See? She's so upset with me she can't even speak. She's all right. Everything is fine. Right, sweetheart? Tell him, my pretty dove."

Mónica crawled on her hands and knees, away from Jeff. The killer started to make his move.

"Stop!" the stranger ordered, stepping completely out of the shadows, beneath the splinter of moonlight.

Mónica froze on the trail.

The unfamiliar figure summoned the girl with his finger, signaling her to move closer to him.

Jeff took a step toward Mónica.

The gunman cocked the hammer of the pistol, raising the sights from the center of Jeff's body to a point between his eyes.

Mónica fell numb.

"Just a little hammer on this pistol, Jeff. Not like what you used to clobber those women with back home. But when this one comes down, it's going to take your head clean off your shoulders. Now, drop the knife. I'm not going to tell you again."

The ex mail handler turned profile, giving the gunman a temple for a target before Jeff suddenly wielded the knife and made a lunge for the girl.

The foreigner firmly squeezed the trigger. Like a little red planet, the side of Jeff's head exploded there in the dim moonlight.

Jeff immediately fell to the ground.

The girl scrambled toward the high, green, grassy brush. Mónica moaned and sobbed and shook for a full minute before the stranger could even approach. He was fearful that she was in shock. Finally, she allowed him to help her to her feet.

The man reached deep down into Jeff's right pants pocket, removing an item.

"Come. We've got to get out of here, and fast."

Mónica surely understood.

Chapter Sixty-Six

The American sat alone at a bar near the airport in Cali. He loved what little of the land he had seen since his visit to Villavicencio. He loved the flatlands as well as the Andes Mountains. He was sure God was watching over him from somewhere high in the Cordillera range. He was sorry to have tainted its soil with the likes of serial killer Jeffrey Mills. He hoped that the authorities would simply write the motive for the murder off as robbery. He was happy that Mónica was safe and sound and back home with her family where she belonged.

"What can I get you?" the bartender asked in English.

The foreigner smiled warmly. "Dark rum and Coke. Top-shelf. Make it a triple. Slice of lemon and lime."

The man looked at the stranger and smiled warmly. "Heading back home?"

"Yep."

"Have a chance to see our lovely country?"

"Sure have."

"A triple 'cause you're sad to go?" The bartender measured out three shots over a tall tumbler of ice, then ran a little Coke. He reached for a wedge of lemon and lime and added it to the mix.

"Nope. A triple because I'm celebrating."

"Celebrating all alone?"

The visitor squeezed the slices of lemon and lime above the rim of the glass. "I'm not alone."

"Oh?"

The writer raised his glass toward the blue sky just outside the huge panoramic picture-perfect windows. It was a beautifully bright and sunny afternoon. "Got my good friend and God close by. Got their light upon my shoulders." The American threw down his liquor in a single swig and stood.

"*Dios mio!*" The bartender smiled and shook his head.

The customer put down a twenty and waved off any change. He headed toward the door and out into the day.

On a short walk to the airport, the American saw a boy of eight or nine years of age. The foreigner carefully unfolded a handkerchief, went up to the youngster and handed him a thick wad of bills held in place by a golden, diamond-studded money clip—the shape and symbol of a dollar sign.

"Here, put this away. Keep that in your pocket and take it home to your parents. You speak English?"

The child looked up in amazement but didn't say a word.

"*Para tus padres.*"

The lad lit up like a light bulb and nodded his head in short order. "*Sí.*"

"*Bueno.*"

The youngster firmly formed a fist around the folded wad of American fifties and hundreds, pushing the clipped bills deep within a baggy pants pocket, disappearing around a corner before the stranger could change his mind.

Robert Redler smiled satisfactorily, heading home to write his book as Emiel had wished . . . in the form of fiction.

— Epilogue —

Memorial Day Weekend
2000

It was a cloudy but comfortable early afternoon. Nassau's forensic hair and fiber expert, Walter Weber, had his Weber grill fired up and ready for his guests. Sausages, marinated ribs and chicken, frankfurters, hamburgers and slices of deli cheese sat in nearby coolers along the back deck. Packaged rolls, paper cups, napkins, and plastic utensils lined one side of a serving table. Along the other side was a row of fixings: salad dressings, sauces, mustard, catsup, salt and pepper; trays of onion, tomato, cucumber and leaf lettuce. Big bowls of homemade coleslaw, macaroni and potato salad took up most of the space in Betty Weber's refrigerator. Numerous desserts took up the remainder. A large aluminum keg of cold draft beer stood elevated atop a potting table just outside the kitchen doorway leading to the deck. Across the lawn, beneath a railing, sat gigantic galvanized tubs filled with ice that contained bottles of soda as well as imported and domestic bottled beer; a bottle opener hung from each tub. In one corner of the deck, sitting upon two sizable inverted clay flowerpots, stood magnums of red and white wine respectively clustered in plain and iced-filled pails; a corkscrew hung from each pail.

"There is only one thing we have to worry about running out of," Betty Weber said to Arlene Danowski.

"Beer, dear?"

"Never."

"Ah, ice."

The hostess smiled and nodded. "The meats and cheese could go to hell in a hen basket, but the beer better be cold for our boys."

"Got that right. Peter even carries around his own insulated beverage holder for his suds. God forbid he took the wrong size today. The one that holds cans slips off those slender bottles."

"Walter hates cans, so I hope Peter brought the one for bottles. Better yet, there's a giant keg of draft out there."

Arlene smiled. "I carry both holders for backup." The woman pointed to her pocketbook.

"You sound like me. I carry around a pepper mill in my handbag. God forbid we're in a restaurant and the server's running around searching for the item, or they don't have one on hand. It's just easier that I have my own. One evening, I'm returning from the ladies room when Peter's dinner arrives. Peter can't wait two seconds, so he starts rummaging through my bag and pulls out a can of mace without thinking or looking. 'Close, but no cigar,' I tell him just in the nick of time. 'That's pepper spray, darling, not the pepper mill.'"

Betty Weber was laughing and picturing the scene. "I hope you never encounter a situation where you're approached by a pervert and pull out a pepper grinder in lieu of your mace, my dear."

"No chance of that ever happening. Believe me."

"How come?"

"I just carry around the can of repellent to appease and assuage Peter's concerns."

"You're kidding me, right?"

"No, I'm not."

"And if you ever found yourself in a compromising situation?"

"I'd blow the sucker away with my snub-nosed revolver." Arlene tapped the small of her back beneath the jacket. ".38 Special. I'm not going to screw around with any can of mace," she assured the hostess.

"I think I'm missing a beat, Arlene. Why even carry mace around if you're not intent on using it. Unless, of course, you're telling me that Peter doesn't know you carry a weapon."

"Oh, he knows all right. He just doesn't think I'd really use the piece on a piece of garbage. Figures I'm really safer with my mace. Yeah, right. My handbag's somewhere out of reach. But my weapon is right here and at the ready."

Betty nodded appreciatively. "I have a pistol packin' pocketbook, but I'm going to think about what you're saying."

"You better, girl. And you'll be better off for it. Believe me. If you don't mind me asking, what are *you* carrying these days?"

"Sig Sauer P232."

Arlene nodded knowingly. "9 millimeter kurz/.380 caliber. World Class sidearm, Betty. I also started with a 9 mm./380 Walther PPK. Great for concealment; caliber comes up short on firepower, though. I want to knock the fucker down and put his lights out permanently. Pistols jam, Betty. What am I gonna do then? Dig for my can of mace? Revolvers are the way to go; .38 caliber. I'd love to see you upgrade. Sidearm on your person; perfume in your bag. Think about it."

Detective Gary York stepped into the kitchen. "Think about what?" he questioned rather nosily.

"What color curtains would go best in my bathroom, Gary."

"That's where I'm headed, Betty. I'll let you know what I think. Point me in the right direction."

"Through there and to your left. Did you forget from last year?"

"I'm lucky that I remembered how to get from Suffolk into Nassau, let alone your home or bathroom."

"You didn't come with Mick and John?"

"Came with Frank, who can barely see over the steering wheel and doesn't know how to read a Hagstrom."

"Yet, he knew how to read the riot act to a certain someone out there helping Walter with the grill," Betty Weber reminded Gary, referring to the act Frank Masselli and Vic Posteraro pulled on Jeffrey Mills.

"That he did, by God. The only problem with that show was that Vic couldn't get the bogus blood out of his expensive necktie, shirt, suit or fancy footwear. Still can't. And to add insult to injury, his lieutenant tore up the request for reimbursement."

"Just like your lieutenant tore up your power of attorney and promissory note for Howard Mills' quarter mil," Betty reminisced with a hearty laugh.

Gary smiled brightly. "Listen, gotta piss like a racehorse. Talk more to you ladies in a minute."

Before a smoking barbecue, Walter Weber and Vic Posteraro stood cooking up a storm, taking orders for rare, medium and well-done burgers, along with hot dogs.

"I want two slices of cheese on my burger," Mick Connolly

ordered, stepping up to the grill.

"Would that be two on top, two on the bottom, or one top and bottom?" Vic asked with a straight face.

Mick stared at Vic with annoyance. "Now that you mention it, I'll have two on top *and* two on the bottom," Mick decided.

"You want a roll with that?" Vic went on.

"Listen. Don't be a wise guy. I'm still trying to get you compensated for your clothes and shoes. All right?"

"Yeah, right."

"You didn't have to try and upstage Gary with those fancy threads and designer shoes."

"And whose idea was that? Yours. I had to look like more than what I made, you said."

"Well, you went a wee bit overboard. But I'm working on it."

"You told me that last month."

"And now I'm tellin' you again. First, I already spoke to your lieutenant. Next, I'm gonna speak to mine. I know Theo's here because I saw him on the way in. As my great-great-grandmother on my father's Italian side of the family used to say, 'Rome wasn't built in a day.' Got it?"

"What I got, Mick, is that Sheila is the only family you actually have, and that everyone at this party is your extended family. Got it?" Vic handed Mick his cheeseburger.

"Wise-ass college kid," Mick snapped. "Can't even fuckin' count. There's only one piece of cheese on here, putz."

"Yeah, but it's American, Mick," Vic responded. "And thick, like you."

Mick looked from Vic to Walter. "I want this smart-ass kid off the grill and on scullery duty, Walt."

Walter Weber shook his head and smiled. "First, you steal our case and—"

"We didn't steal your case, Walt. But you sure as hell stole Vic from us."

"We didn't steal him, Mick. We just borrowed him for a bit. It's you guys who wanted him far enough away from Yaphank, sending him to West Babylon for safekeeping and to babysit your boy Jeff before he bailed. Besides, Vic here never really left Suffolk County."

"But now you have him working a Nassau case."

"Talk to Theo. It's only for another month, Mick. We pool our talents, we accomplish a lot more."

Mick gave Vic the evil eye and changed the subject. "You know, I think it was Redler who anonymously called in the tip on where Beth Tracy and others were buried out there in Orient Point. Interesting, also, that he was in Columbia at the time that authorities believe Jeff was murdered, though they haven't made a positive ID yet."

"If that's the case, I'd leave it alone. I'd say he did everyone a favor."

"Got that right."

"Who'll wind up with the estate?"

"From what I'm hearing, it would go to Ronald Mills, Jeff's younger brother."

"Sounds like poetic justice to me."

"The best kind of justice, Walt."

"What's Redler up to these days?"

"Writing a book about the case from what I hear."

"Fact or fiction?"

"Don't know."

"Be interesting to see."

"That it would, Walt. That it would." Mick looked over Walter's shoulder. "Ah, here comes trouble."

With beer in hand, Dan Fowler walked up to the trio and ordered. "Double cheeseburger, three slices, medium rare, please, Vic."

"That would be with one slice on top, one in the middle, and one on the bottom," Vic offered quite pleasantly.

"See Mick, *that's* how you get extra slices of cheese with your order," Walter chaffed.

Mick sneered. "Why don't you ask him if he wants his buns toasted?"

"Dan, would you like the buns toasted?"

"That would be terrific, Vic."

Mick looked up at the dog handler. "Where's Max?"

"Back there at a table with the wife and kids."

"Why not here with you? You two go everywhere together."

Dan looked around. "Not sure where the cats are. Not a good mix."

"Cats? Walt doesn't have any cats," Mick said.

Peter Danowski stepped forward. "Speaking of cats, Walt, may I see you for just a moment?"

"Pretty busy as you can see, Pete."

"That's okay," Vic interrupted. "Mick can help me out here.

Right, Mick?"

"I'm eating my fucking burger. I can't flip burgers and eat."

"Sure you can, Mick," Peter said encouragingly. "You shoveled for bodies with one hand out at Orient Point, while holding your ear with the other. Remember?"

Suffolk County's forensic hair and fiber expert removed the spatula from Walter's hand and placed the tool in Mick's free mitt. "We'll be just a minute, Mick. Promise."

When the two forensic scientists were out of earshot, Mick looked up at Vic and spoke quietly. "Vic, I want you to know two things. I never told you that you did a great job along with John and Frank. We had those fuckers fooled. Double whammy. Politics, not the police, fucked it up for us real good."

"What's the second thing that you want me to know, Mick?"

"I hate fucking cats."

W**alter** and Peter found a quiet corner. Betty, Arlene and three other women paraded by, carrying large bowls of salads and serving utensils, making room on one of the tables.

"Salads and fixings are over here, everyone," Betty announced. "Sauerkraut and baked beans with bacon are coming right out. But don't fill up, we've got ribs and chicken for later. Vic, please don't use your finger to turn the franks. Micky, hand Vic the tongs to your left."

"Yes, ma'am." With a cheeseburger in one hand and a spatula in the other, Mick reached for the tongs and handed them to Vic.

Betty turned to her husband. "Walter, why aren't you on the grill, dear?"

"Will be in a minute, oh, love of my life." Walt turned back to Peter. "What's up?"

"Remember our deal at Roselyn James' residence?"

"Sure do, Pete."

"Well, I don't see any cat. Specifically, I don't see Tabitha."

Walt Weber smiled broadly. "Come, Pete. Follow me."

Peter followed Walter down off the deck and around the side of the home. Walt led his Suffolk County colleague through a side entrance leading to the basement. Inside the finished, furnished room, Peter found Tabitha curled up next to another cat.

Pete was pleased. "I don't remember you having a cat last year."

"I didn't. I wanted Tabitha, here, to have a companion."

Pete went up to the pair. "What's its name?"

"Orbit."

Pete nodded his head approvingly. "Named after Jeffrey Mills' cat."

"No."

"No?"

"That *is* Jeffrey Mills' cat."

Pete shook his head in astonishment. "I knew you were a pushover, pussycat."

"I guess."

Pete took Walt's hand firmly into his and shook it solidly.

"Come," Walt said. "Let me buy you a cold draft. We'll let Mick stew a bit. Tell you the latest we got cooking over at the crime lab. Might need Suffolk's help."

"You can absolutely count on it, good buddy."

Back outside, a long line was forming in front of Mick Connolly. Vic and Gary were walking alongside a brightly colored flower bed of petunias and marigolds. The two were discussing a new case. Standing before the potting table, Mick watched Walt and Peter pouring themselves a beer from the sizable aluminum keg.

"Hey, Peter," Mick called out, "I thought you guys said you'd just be a minute."

Smoke rose from the grill; burgers and hot dogs sizzled. Dan Fowler stepped up to the grill.

"You back again?" Mick bellyached.

"Smells great, Mick. Need two more cheeseburgers like Vic made, and four franks. Two regular and two a bit burnt, the way my kids like them. Got a hungry family back there to feed."

"Make that four more," Frank Masselli ordered. "Two for me, and two for John. John, you want your buns toasted?" he called over to Mick's partner.

John Bailey nodded. "Sure, why not?"

"Hey, Vic. Get the hell over here and give me a hand," Mick griped.

"One minute, Mick. Be right there."

On the way back to his family, an arm loaded with the food order supported against his chest, Dan Fowler gave Walter a twenty for the Posteraro clothing collection. Peter Danowski had already done the same downstairs.

"How long you going to keep Mick on the grill?" Pete asked.

"Till the last customer on this line places his order," Walt answered straightaway.

"How much we collect toward Vic's ruined outfit so far?"

"About three hundred. The two lieutenants promise to split the balance."

"Mick got any idea as to what's going on?"

"Not a clue."

"Think he'll figure it out before the grand finale?"

"We'll soon see."

Thirty minutes later, after the smoke finally cleared, Dan Fowler once again stood before Mick.

"Got a customer here who wants four franks to go. Raw. No rolls. Should be a pretty easy order to fill, Mick." Dan held out an empty bowl.

Mick looked down at Max. "Is that hot dog handler you're with gonna cut them up for you, or are you just gonna wolf them down whole?"

"Woof," was the answer Mick received.

Mick took and placed four frankfurters in the bowl that Dan held.

"Say, *vielen dank,*" Dan insisted.

"Woof, woof," Max replied on command.

"Max says, 'Many thanks,' Mick."

Many faces watched as an exhausted, sweaty Michael Connolly lifted Max's front paws most affectionately, planting a big kiss on the German shepherd's nose. Max responded in kind before turning his full attention to the links of meat.

"Paybacks can be a bitch. Can't they, Mick?" Dan Fowler said with a straight face.

"They can, Dan. They certainly can, indeed."

Both men stared smiling at one another with certain mischief on their minds.

TO THE READER

Getting exposure, even for this award-winning author who was previously published by a traditional house before the economy took its toll, is a challenge. Small presses are competing with the 'publishing big boys' in the marketplace. You, as a reader, can help us enormously with this challenge by spreading the word.

So, if you have enjoyed this book, please help us to promote Robert Banfelder and Broadwater Books, as well as other small presses' books.

There is a variety of ways you can do so, including:

- Recommending the book to your friends;
- Posting a review on Amazon and/or other book websites;
- Reviewing the book on your blog;
- Tweeting about it and giving a link to the author's website;
- Posting a link to the author's website on your Facebook page;
- Liking the author's Facebook page;
- Following the author on Twitter;
- Pinning the book on Pinterest; or
- Anything else you can think of!

Thanking you in advance for your help—it's much appreciated.

~ The Broadwater Books Team